THE
PANDORA PRESCRIPTION

THE
PANDORA PRESCRIPTION

By James Sheridan

CAMBRIDGE HOUSE PRESS
NEW YORK § TORONTO

Published by Cambridge House Press
New York, NY 10001
www.CamHousePress.com

Library of Congress Cataloging-in-Publication Data

Sheridan, James, 1970-
  The Pandora prescription / by James Sheridan.
    p. cm.
  ISBN 978-0-9814536-3-7 (paperback edition); 978-0-9787213-5-0 (hardcover)
  1. Authors--Fiction. 2. Pharmaceutical industry--Fiction. 3. Political fiction. I. Title.

PS3619.H4634P36 2007
813'.6--dc22

2007033939

Cover design by Nicola Lengua.
Composition/typography by Rachel Trusheim.

The events and characters in this book are fictitious. Certain real locations and public figures are mentioned, but all other characters and events described in the book are totally imaginary.

Paperback edition.

10 9 8 7 6 5 4 3 2 1

Printed in the United States of America.

For Luke.

Acknowledgments

I have many people to thank for helping me with this work: the valiant physicians of the Second Opinion Underground (names confidential), Ellis Island Park Police (for escorting me off the island so gently), Grand Central Terminal, the Watergate Hotel, Mike the intrepid Miami boat captain, Port of Miami U.S. Coastguard, Dallas Police Department, Ursula, Drew Nederpelt, my editors: Rachel Trusheim and Erich Erving for their insight, Nicola Lengua and everyone at Cambridge House, Lord Toby Unwin for the use of his highly subversive library and Geraldine Roberts.

"Disobedience, in the eyes of anyone who has read history, is man's original virtue. It is through disobedience and rebellion that progress has been made."

— Oscar Wilde

FACT:

In the late seventies, a splinter group of physicians secretly established a 'fifth column' deep in the heart of the medical establishment. They called themselves *The Second Opinion Underground*.

PROLOGUE

The Queen Bee Club, Tokyo, 1957

IT WAS PAYBACK for Hiroshima.

Topless, straddling the wooden chair, Hoshi's quest for retribution was about to send a shockwave through the world. Her physical perfection concealed a wound that would never heal; the cut was too deep.

It was an affliction she wanted to share.

Uniformed conquerors threw dollars in the air as she twirled, wrapped a silky thigh around the chair and flicked back her trailing ebony hair. Her pearly smile was born from the pathetic predictability of men, yelling as if on cue.

Hoshi's distant gaze went unnoticed: the audience, mesmerized by her golden body, didn't realize she wasn't really there. She answered to a higher calling that swept her above the cigar smoke, overpriced champagne and western music.

The humiliation of this gig bore holes in her soul until 'they' showed up. They had given her life purpose. And they paid much more for her services than the Queen Bee Club. What they did with her prey once she served them up on a plate, she could only imagine. Hoshi just knew this brutal sideline soothed her pain like ice water on burnt skin. However sinister her masters were and whatever their sordid ambition, better the devil you know.

The hazel in Hoshi's eyes glazed to black. It was time.

Karma needs a catalyst.

Kneeling down, gliding a red-painted talon along the edge of her panties, Hoshi scanned the room; her gaze met the clienteles' saucer-eyes for the first time. Lowering herself to their level was disgusting, but necessary. The stench of their decadence assaulted her nostrils; even so, a hypnotic smile hid her disgust.

Shutting out the howls, Hoshi noticed an out-of-place head from the corner of her eye in the crowd. She turned to face him. His dark eyes were piercing.

He was much younger than the usual guests: a chalky-faced boy with dark hair, probably no more than eighteen or nineteen and, judging by the uniform, American military. Air Force. *Good.*

Rolling on her hands and knees, pushing her hips into the air, she crawled toward a bottle of warm sake to perform her signature move.

Clutching the bottle, Hoshi sprang to her feet. She sauntered over to the young soldier, her eyes locked on his. He knew not to touch when she moved to the edge of the stage. Her petite form towered over him as she filled her mouth with sake.

She pouted as if begging a kiss, and aimed her lips at her target. He pushed his chin underneath her and opened his mouth for the wet, hot treat.

Hoshi opened her mouth releasing a stream of liquid into the awaiting mouth of her soon-to-be victim. He gulped what he could, smiling. The crowd erupted, whistling and cheering, working up to a fever pitch at her siren-esque performance.

Once the sake was spent, she discarded the bottle and concentrated her dance on the young American, watching him melt. He was the only man in the room at that moment. It was more than he could handle and she knew it.

He was hers.

As the music faded and the cries for "more" burst out from the floor, Hoshi deftly stepped down from the stage to complete her deadly assignment. She met the pale teenager's eyes and swaggered toward him, relishing the look of disbelief that she'd singled him out.

Posing in front of him, Hoshi's sweet accent made her words all the more seductive:

"So, what's your name, handsome?"

"Oswald, ma'am…Lee Harvey Oswald."

Some wounds never heal; the cut is too deep.

MONDAY

CHAPTER 1

CLINTON LEBLANC FELT A FEVER, though he knew he was healthy. As the Potomac Plaza Apartments elevator lurched up to the third floor, the envelope in his breast pocket weighed him down, though its contents weighed next to nothing.

A tiny envelope was about to change the world forever. Pacing, alone in the metal cube, he recalled how he'd dreamed of taking these next few steps on this particular day; just these few steps out of the elevator toward his apartment.

Home.

The deed was done.

The chime of his third-floor arrival came, but the fever stayed. Coming home wasn't as comforting as he'd hoped. He didn't feel safe after all. The treacherous act he'd committed that day left grinding pangs of doubt in his stomach.

It seemed the right thing to do when the doctor had contacted him: for his father's memory, to wreak vengeance on the demons that destroyed him.

But to betray everything his father believed in…

When you make a plan, there are no shades of gray. After the plan's executed, there's no black and white.

The door of apartment 309 loomed in front of Leblanc as he reached for the key. He knew the first thing he'd see as he stepped into the hallway would be his late father standing next to President Kennedy; his mother had sent him the picture sixteen years ago, before her death of a broken heart.

His father's soul had gone long before his body. He was Kennedy's guardian angel, but when JFK needed him most he couldn't do a thing. He became a 'fallen' angel: a victim of demons.

Clinton Leblanc had fought his way into the Service and onto protection duty, just like his dad; an unconscious quest to purge the shame from his family's soul and make up for the past. But the bullet never came. No one wanted to shoot the vice president, it seemed. The Secret Service wasn't the agency his father romantically idealized.

When you look in the mirror and can't see a reflection, like your existence is meaningless, that's when something cracks deep inside.

Leblanc's front door swung open, but he didn't see the photograph of his father with President Kennedy as he usually did. All he saw was red.

Doubt gave way to all-consuming anger.

They are the traitors, not me.

It didn't matter if it was anger born from fear; it was justified. *Dad died when he didn't have to.* Leblanc would have given anything for just one more game of chess, even just one more argument. Wasted wishes were a prelude to retribution and the timing of this opportunity was like divine intervention.

The deed was done.

He patted his breast pocket for the seventeenth time since he'd put the envelope there earlier today. It burned into his chest. Revenge beckoned.

Leblanc would have slammed the door behind him but something stopped him; the sixth sense instilled in him from years at the Service. *Something was wrong.* He didn't know what it was, a smell, a sound, a sight, but something was *not* right. The fever seemed real now; beads of sweat formed on his furrowed brow. A rush of blood throbbed up his chest to his face.

Were they here?

How could they have known he broke the code? How did they know his secret?

It wasn't a surprise exactly, but then again it was. *Who the hell do they think they…*

The screeching tires of a car pulling away outside broke his concentration. Leblanc refocused on the immediate situation. *Has someone just left or are they still here?*

He felt his gut twist and his chest bulge as he withdrew his standard issue Sig Sauer from its holster and took the safety off all in one motion. His Service training kicked in; he divided the environment into a grid in his mind and scanned each section, hoping it was just paranoia.

The hallway light was on, as always, clearly illuminating the kitchen and sitting room. Nothing obvious there. He glanced down the hallway to the remaining rooms: the two bedrooms and the…

An involuntary gulp choked his breath.

The door to the study was open. He always left it closed. The lights in the study were off and there was silence, but that didn't mean anything.

Backing against the wall, Leblanc carefully avoided the creaky floorboard as he glided toward the door and darkened room beyond.

Crouching down, he stared into the blackness of the study from behind the barrel of his gun.

No movement, no sound.

He took a deep breath for composure. That was when the

faint remains of an unfamiliar odor confirmed his suspicion.

Someone's here.

Standing up, back to the wall and gun in one hand, he put his free hand through the gap ready to switch on the light. All at once, Leblanc flicked on the light and spun into the room, arriving with his shoulder blades to the wall, crouching back down. He swung his pistol in sharp jolts, scanning the room for assailants.

Nobody here.

His heart still kicking his chest, he stood up and drew another breath. So much training, so little action. He'd never fired his weapon in anger.

Leblanc's relief was interrupted with an alarming thought. *Somebody must have been there and left.* The study door couldn't have opened by itself. Whoever it was must have been looking for the envelope's precious contents.

What now? Think.

Shit. He lunged for the light switch and sent the room back into darkness.

Leblanc realized the intruder hadn't found what they were looking for and would be waiting for him to get home.

He moved to the study window where he could see the entrance to the building. His eyes flickered over the street in front of the building. Nothing but the usual array of parked cars.

Wait.

Leblanc felt his body prickle as he caught sight of a standard maneuver he was all too familiar with.

A raid was imminent.

Damn! Turning on the study light must have alerted them he was home—that was what they were waiting for.

They'd just lost the crucial element of surprise though.

Okay, okay. Do something! The door hadn't been broken

down yet so he knew they were still coordinating their raid; waiting for everyone to get in position, covering all exits. Windows would be watched through a sniper's scope.

Stay low and get out—fast.

The room spun.

But what if he was captured? There was far more at stake here than his own life. The world would change forever once he unleashed the contents of the envelope he'd kept in his breast pocket all day.

The conspiracy of conspiracies, blown. Millions of lives, saved.

Whatever transpired in the next few critical minutes, the truth must somehow get out.

How do you get the truth out when everyone's a conspirator? Even the guy in the street!

CHAPTER 2

New York City

DAN TRAVIS WINCED as he felt the light hit his face and prepared for the inevitable torture once again. He was trapped, cornered with nowhere to run. He felt his existence hanging in the balance as he squirmed in his seat.

Resistance was futile.

His eyes adjusted as he watched the eerie, shadowy figures behind the light move menacingly into position. This was it—he was about to face what people fear most, like it or not. He felt his heart race and tried to control his breathing, though it felt like he was suffocating already. His throat was parched and his head throbbed.

Then those accursed words came out of the darkness: "We're on in five, four…" The last three words "three, two, one…" were mouthed silently and accompanied by a pointing finger.

It didn't matter how many times he did this, TV appearances still scared the hell out of him. It was a world where nothing was what it seemed.

Staying focused on this book tour was a challenge. Travis's mind was with his mother who was going into the hospital today. Her diagnosis of cancer shook him to the core. He was terrified of losing her to the same disease that had claimed his father.

He was awaiting the verdict as to whether or not the cervical cancer had spread to her lymph nodes yet. Travis felt his chin quiver.

We'll know soon enough. Breathe.

Travis's interviewer today, Suzy Spencer, sat next to him and spoke in a ditzy but condescending manner. It was like fingernails on a blackboard. "Hi, everyone, and welcome back to the show! Okay. Now are you ready for a trip to another planet?"

After a short pause to bat her eyelashes at Camera 1, Suzy continued with her rhetoric. "Do you have mysterious questions you want answered? Want to go through the looking glass and unravel all those famous riddles? Me, too! Well, I'm delighted to welcome back Dr. Daniel Travis this morning, better known to his fans as the 'Man of Mystery.'"

Travis saw the red light on Camera 2 turn on as Suzy faced him, sporting the most insincere grin he'd ever seen—even for her. Her blonde 'power-bob' barely moved as she spun around. A cardboard cut-out. He marveled at how much older she looked in the flesh, despite her heavy stage makeup. He smiled nervously and let her finish. There was no way he would dare interrupt after her tantrum the last time he appeared on the show.

"Welcome, Dan!"

"Hello again, Suzy." Never had a smile been so forced. *Must try harder.*

"Now I—"

"Great to be here!" *Shit. Calm down, Dan.*

"Uh-huh. And…it's great to have you. Now I believe your new book is out and I must say, as a New Yorker myself, I'm totally intrigued…" She held the book up for the camera. *"The Great Unsolved Mysteries of New York."*

Travis made certain to pause before he spoke, to make sure she had finished. "Yes, Suzy, it's a highly specialized piece this time. This is an amazing city with secrets buried so deep one can only imagine. Until you read the book, that is."

"I'm sure. In just a moment we're going to have some callers on the line for you. But first, can I ask you a question?"

"Please do," Travis said, clapping his hands together to feign enthusiasm.

"You're best known for being an authority on more famous mysteries like Atlantis, the paranormal and the Great Pyramids, so to have the Big Apple join those ranks is quite something. Why so?"

Travis shuffled his six-foot-one frame in the seat and tugged on his jacket. Suzy looked down at her clipboard to memorize the next question. She wasn't even paying attention to the answer Travis was giving to her last question.

Nothing's what it seems.

"Well, Suzy, those more famous mysteries will always remain of great interest to me, and as new evidence is unearthed I'll be presenting it. Meanwhile, I wanted to branch out with something perhaps more accessible to the average person…kind of a reminder that riddles and mysteries lurk often where you least expect them, maybe under the very concrete you walk on." *It gets easier to remember this line as my tour drags on.*

Suzy smiled, looked up from her clipboard and stared into Travis's blue eyes. *She's scary.* The camera was back on her. "I love it. Wow. It really is a fascinating world you live in and you've achieved so much at the age of forty-two. You've had several books published and speak on this subject across the world…"

Travis nodded with a smile. *C'mon Dan, you love the attention, really.*

"Now for viewers who didn't catch your last appearance, how did you get started in all of this?"

"Well, I was quite young actually, Suzy," She looked down again, but Travis was too caught up with memories of his late father to let it bother him. "My father took me on a fishing trip off the coast of Miami and to our amazement, we saw a large ship on the horizon burn and sink right before our eyes. All we could do was watch and listen on the emergency frequency as the coastguard ferried survivors from the wreck…"

"That must have had a profound effect on you as a child. I know you've also done a lot of work on the mystery of the sinking of the Titanic, which has always fascinated me as I thought hitting an iceberg wasn't much of a mystery!"

Suzy glanced at the camera and grinned, goading a cheap laugh from the studio audience.

Travis set aside diplomacy. "That's another story, but actually, it is still a mystery as to why that iceberg did enough damage to sink the Titanic so quickly. There are various theories, some rather conspiratorial, which I won't go into now."

Travis believed conspiracies were real, case in point the Watergate scandal, but he felt discussions of such theories invited cranks. An association with such a crowd would devalue the importance of his work and thorough investigations of the truth, so he deliberately steered clear of such topics publicly.

He pressed ahead with the story about his father. "But anyway, later that day, my father told me that the ship we watched sink had gone down in an area called the Bermuda Triangle, which, as we all know, it's a place notorious for unexplained disappearances of ships and aircraft. And that was it. I was hooked from that day on."

"Alright, now I'm told we have a selection of lucky viewers who are eager to speak to you. Are you all set for a few questions, Mystery Man?"

"Of course, Suzy." *She's driving me crazy—how much longer?* It was no wonder she went through a new personal assistant every month. He'd begun to fidget with his hands.

Suzy Spencer beamed squarely at the active camera and chirped to her audience, bathing in their unconditional love for her. "First caller then! We have Mike from Iowa. Go ahead, Mike!"

"Hello? Hello, Dr. Travis?" came the elderly voice from Iowa.

"Hello, Mike."

"Dr. Travis…now I know you'll have an explanation for this. My wife claims she saw Elvis in the Wal-Mart parking lot last Tuesday and I of course told her that couldn't have happened, right?"

Travis felt a wave of relief; for a moment there he thought Mike from Iowa was serious. He chuckled heartily and replied, "Nooo…of course not, Mike. Now what's your question?"

Mike continued, "Yes, that's what I told her, too. Nonsense. She couldn't have possibly seen him last week because Elvis was abducted by aliens back in the seventies. That's my question, can you explain a little more about that? Where might they have taken him exactly?"

Travis froze and looked at Suzy who was smiling through her disgust at the telephone operators' inability to screen calls. She had no choice now but to deal with it.

"Okay, Dan? Any thoughts on that one then?" she said with a wince off-camera.

Travis was a straight shooter today. "Sorry, Mike, but you're delusional on this one—"

Suzy interrupted with a nervous laugh. "Alrighty-then, Dan, you may have a different view than Mike on this one, so let's move right along then." The light on Camera 2 went on. With the camera focused on Travis for his response, Suzy gave him a cold glare. "Okay then," he replied.

"Next caller, please. We have Zachary from Kansas. Welcome, Zach. What's your question for world-renowned 'Man of Mystery,' Dr. Dan Travis?"

Travis stifled a yawn, but his eyes confessed last night's sleepless hours he spent worrying about his mother.

Zach from Kansas crackled down the line. "Hi, Dan. Yes, about Roswell…I think it's a disgrace that our government covered the alien crash-landing up. We have a right to know, don't you think?"

Unbelievable. It's always the damn same; all people want to ask me about is little green men!

Still indignant from the previous Elvis call, Travis answered without restraint. They had it coming. "Well, firstly, let's just say that aliens had crash-landed at Roswell and there was a cover-up. The government probably did the right thing."

"Why's that?" Suzy asked, relieved, as the show seemed to have taken a turn toward sensibility at last.

"Because there would have been mass hysteria. Quite frankly, people would have died in the panic. Also, it would have offended so many religions that too many people would have been upset and, at the very least, shot the messenger: the president. As a matter of fact, an innocent radio broadcast of H.G. Wells's *War of the Worlds* not long before Roswell caused widespread panic."

Suzy Spencer rifled through papers on her clipboard then stepped in with a smirk. "But, Dan, a 1997 CNN/*TIME* poll found that 80 percent of Americans think the government is hiding knowledge of the existence of alien life forms. Are you saying all those people—most of our viewers—are wrong?"

Curve ball.

Travis wasn't rattled. "I'm aware of that poll. People want

to believe in other phenomena too, most of which there is no proof of. Look, there's no question that the events surrounding Roswell are a little weird, but we can't jump to conclusions on that basis. That's all I'm saying."

"Okay, but to answer Mike's question then, what's your take on Roswell?"

"I work with facts and here they are: Modern-day UFO visits have really only been reported in the last fifty years—a small blip in the time we've been on the planet. Space is vast. Beings in other galaxies would only be made aware of us because we emit high-frequency radio signals, and we've only been doing this for the past seventy years. Even if the aliens immediately wanted to contact us upon receiving the first signal and assuming they could travel at light speed, there would only be four star-systems close enough to have been able to reach Earth by 1947. Considering it's widely agreed now that life on Earth is the result of a freak chain of events, life in those four star-systems seems like a slim chance. At best, all we have is some anecdotal evidence regarding UFOs, which can't easily be explained."

Suzy's TV face was tugged by a frown. Travis wondered if her makeup would crack. "But to what do you attribute what people clearly described at Roswell as a flying saucer?" she said.

Travis had anticipated the question. "At the end of World War II, our government launched a top secret mission called 'Operation Paperclip' to track down and evacuate the top Nazi scientists to be put to work for us; these same scientists were the ones who took us to the moon in '69. Believe it or not, Hitler already had flying saucer-looking aircraft in production in the final days of the war. Actually the BMW factory in Prague made these advanced weapons, which were named the *Haunebu*. U.S. patent numbers even exist for these weapons, which are referred to as 'rotating jet aircraft.'" As he spoke, Travis flipped through a large file and read from it. "Yes…patent numbers 213529, 2801058—"

"So your point?" interrupted Suzy.

She was grinding Travis's nerves. "My point, Suzy, is that the Nazis we put to work probably continued these projects, and what crashed at Roswell was most likely a *Haunebu*. It's noteworthy that UFO sightings have really only become prevalent since Roswell. The public perception of extraterrestrial activity at Roswell was very convenient for the military. It distracted attention away from the real secret of the incident. Who knows? Maybe the 'leaks' from the military were orchestrated for that very reason."

Travis was on his soapbox, but he didn't care. "In the absence of valid facts from their leaders, modern society now instinctively thinks the worst. The grade-school conditioning of America holding the shining torch up to the world has worn thin. Every debacle, whether it's Vietnam or Watergate, Monica Lewinsky or the Florida Ballot recount, has made people feel they've been lied to, the cumulative effect of which we're now seeing in this conspiracy theory frenzy."

"But, Dan…"

"Suzy, the bottom line is that people will believe what they want to. When a government hushes something up and makes it mysterious, it becomes a big deal. The child in us becomes active; people's imaginations run riot and conspiracy theories are born. At Roswell, heavily armed troops swiftly showed up with shoot-to-kill orders. When people stop behaving like children, maybe that's when governments will stop treating us as such. If there were indeed advanced alien life forms watching us, my guess is they'd see us as an immature, violent and paranoid culture that they would do well to stay away from."

Suzy Spencer intently listened to the production room on her earpiece telling her to go to commercial. Travis countered the silence: "Now shall we move on?"

Less than an hour later, the ordeal was over, though Travis wondered if he'd be invited back. "I'm sorry about that, Tracy. I'm very tired and have a lot on my mind," he said to the floor director.

Tracy's oval glasses couldn't hide the glare behind them. "Look, I know you're all about the truth et cetera, but…"

"But?" Travis said with a raised eyebrow.

"It's just that sometimes the truth isn't so good for the ratings. Anyway, thanks." She smiled one of those fake smiles then hurried along to get to work on the next segment.

Travis took a long breath and was soothed with the thought of one last appearance tomorrow before heading back home to Baltimore and his mother's bedside.

There was no way for Travis to know that he would never make it to that appearance.

CHAPTER 3

DWIGHT GREEN HAD BEEN STARING at his phone for eight minutes. He knew that because he'd timed it. He looked to either side of the phone and to its rear to ensure it was placed perfectly on the desk: one inch from the edge.

Must be an inch.

His corner office was spare and orderly. But of course it was—this was the control room from where he sat as head of the family.

My Agency is family and always will be.

This was a family he could choose—not be lumbered with. No dead wood here! Dead wood, simply, was cut away. Everything had to be kept in order.

Jesus! Who the hell is this Leblanc bastard anyway?!

Green felt his teeth on his bottom lip and his nose crinkle up like a shark about to bite.

It's okay, it's okay. The dark cloud has a silver lining. He rubbed his right hand across the black glass surface of his desk and calmed himself.

It was just a simple matter of bringing Leblanc in and taking back what was not his.

How could Leblanc possibly have hoped to get away with this treachery?

Green was a volcano: one minute dormant, the next exploding. He never understood the reason for the eruptions before therapy. They were just dark clouds that came over him. Tonight, however, his explosion was justified. His world sat on a knife's edge tonight, all because of some renegade little shit named Clinton Leblanc. How could one man put so many at risk?

My family. My country.

He glared at the phone. He scowled at it. He wanted to throw it against the wall and rip...

It's okay, it's okay. The dark cloud has a silver lining.

Therapy had helped.

He forced a smile, slicked back his dark gray hair and looked away from the phone. He always had a second wash and shave at 2:45 PM and it was 2:51 PM! He wanted to have his second clean up. His wash kit had a mirror and a bottle of Just for Men in it. He kept it locked in his bottom drawer. But he couldn't leave his desk now.

What's Croghan doing all this time...

The phone rang, at last.

Green snatched up the receiver. "This is Green, talk to me."

"Sir, it's Croghan. There's no sign of Leblanc in his apartment...although his car's still parked outside. We're currently combing the rest of the building and the surrounding area," wavered the voice on the other end of the line.

Green rolled his jaw. "Do not leave that vehicle unmanned. Monitor all other vehicles in the area. He's either still in the building or very close. Set up a perimeter. He's on foot so he couldn't have gone far."

Green paused, closing his eyes. Pressing his fingers into his temple he waited for the detail leader's response. "Yes, sir. Done, sir."

Wait," Green snapped back. "Tear that apartment to pieces, and check for any calls made recently."

"Yes, sir. Sir, I already took the liberty of checking phone calls made from the premises today."

Green lunged forward in his chair. "Anything?"

"Yes, sir. It was a fax sent less than two minutes before we breached the front door. It was sent to a Baltimore number…a private residence it seems."

This was encouraging. Not only did this mean Leblanc couldn't be far away, but they had a lead: an accomplice. Green knew that the fax could not have been the misappropriated item, so there was no immediate danger.

"Whose residence was it sent to?"

Green drummed his fingers on the desk as the detail leader questioned his subordinate.

Finally, he responded. "Sir, yes, it was sent to a Dr. Travis, Dr. Daniel Travis."

"Very good. Continue the operation and get Leblanc. It's a matter of national security—keep me informed of any further developments," said Green, slamming down the receiver. Frantically, he hit speed-dial. The second it picked up, Green started barking orders.

"Norman, I want a complete file on a Dr. Daniel Travis of Baltimore City immediately and a detail at his home ASAP. Tell the detail leader to contact me when they're inside and have Travis in custody. Check all necessary records to find his whereabouts in the event of him not being home. No restrictions." Green hung up the phone with full confidence that his orders would be carried out without question.

With a sigh, Dwight Green threw himself back into his plush leather recliner, swiveling around to look at the view of Washington, D.C. from his office windows. It was going to be a long day, but Leblanc and his accomplice, Travis, would be history before dusk.

CHAPTER 4

TRAVIS SIPPED HIS SOUR APPLE MARTINI at the hotel bar. He always stayed at the Sheraton Hotel and Towers on 7th Avenue because that's where he had stayed to sign his first book deal: fond memories of less stressful times.

Since he'd found out about his mother's battle with cervical cancer, the strangest memories had been flooding Travis's mind. How she used to sing Beatles songs to get him to sleep after he'd had nightmares. That time he was bathing Chester and the little mutt went crazy and knocked her over. And that other time…

Stop. Tears were welling up in his eyes.

Travis felt helpless. He knew she'd want him to focus on his work and not worry. His mom was so proud. At times like these, Travis wished he had a sibling: someone to go through it all with.

Okay, one more TV appearance tomorrow and then home. Focus, he thought to himself. He sniffled and gulped his drink.

Earlier in his room, the bustle of the streets eleven stories below had reminded him that he needed to get more of a life. Life at ground level had beckoned, so here he was, at the bar, instead of quietly reading in his room.

Well, it was a distraction too. Why does sitting in a hotel room seem to magnify all of your thoughts?

He'd have asked for something much higher in the building, where he couldn't hear the sirens and car horns, if only he
didn't suffer from a minor case of vertigo. Vertigo is the fear
of falling and the desire to fall, so the self-help CD had said.
What kind of weird duality is that?

After lecturing in Phoenix, Arizona over the weekend,
last night's flight to JFK Airport had been smooth enough,
but maybe that was just the motion sickness pill doing its job.
Travis couldn't fly without his medication.

The most arduous part of his arrival had been fighting
the traffic. The city had practically ground to a halt due to the
threat of a transit strike. He realized the traffic situation was
dire as he watched the news on the bar's TV. At least from
this hotel he could walk to the TV station if the situation
didn't improve by tomorrow.

His throat welcomed the chilled vodka. *I actually needed
that. Could I be a borderline alcoholic? It's always the vodka I can
taste, not the mixer.*

Snapping himself out his tendency to work himself up
over trivial things, Travis turned to the window and gazed at
the people frantically trying to get somewhere in rush hour
traffic. With the strike now in full swing, crisis was rapidly
deteriorating into chaotic pandemonium as people's panic
exacerbated the situation.

It wasn't until a time like this that one realizes how pre-
carious New York City's geography is: Manhattan was an in-
credibly overpopulated island relying on free-flowing traffic
from a series of bridges, tunnels and ferries to keep it alive.
With a transit strike New York's arteries were blocked and
the city was having a coronary.

The local news reported that the talks between the city
and the transit workers' union had broken down again, both
sides unwilling to compromise. The impasse was over health-

care coverage and its ever-rising cost.

The only way on or off of Manhattan Island was now by car or boat. But the roads were choked and boats like the Staten Island ferry, judging by recent TV coverage, looked as if they were ready to sink with the number of people crowded on them. Water taxis had preposterous lines of people waiting. The TV showed the Brooklyn Bridge being trampled by hoards of commuters on foot; heads bobbing up and down officiously, it looked like a walking marathon after the starting gun.

Watching the chaos outside, the great cab fight of 7th Avenue, his thoughts were interrupted by the bartender calling out his name. "Is there a Daniel Travis here?"

"Over here," said Travis with his right hand in the air.

"Call for you, sir." The bartender pointed to the house phone at the end of the bar.

Nuts. They found me. Travis had switched his cell phone off to escape life for an hour or two.

As he placed the receiver to his ear with apprehension, he was surprised to hear an unknown woman's voice.

"Dr. Travis, hello." Her voice was soft but infused with urgency.

"Hello, ma'am, this is Dr. Travis. How can I help?"

"Yes, my name's Sonia Leblanc, a reporter for the *New York Times*. I learned you were in town for this evening only and would consider it a great favor if I could have a brief interview with you to get your input on an article I need to finish tonight. Would that be possible? I could be there within the hour." There seemed to be a lot of background noise, nonetheless, her voice was clear.

"Well, what's the article about?" He was always careful to make sure reporters weren't wasting his time with a subject he didn't specialize in.

"The Bermuda Triangle, Doctor. What time should I meet you in the bar?"

Travis found her pushiness a little irritating but that was only normal for reporters and besides, the Bermuda Triangle had a special place in his heart, even if it was a tired subject and a 'mystery' with a satisfactory explanation.

"Very well. May I call you Sonia? I'm in the bar now, so I'll see you when you get here. I take it you know what I look like?"

"Of course, Doctor. I'm just a few blocks away," she said.

"Just as well," Travis said.

"What do you mean?"

Doesn't this woman watch the news? "The transit strike!"

"Oh…yeah. See you shortly." Then she was gone.

Travis placed the receiver down and marveled at how resourceful and persistent reporters could be. He weaved his way back to his drink and thanked the bartender.

This would be a good way for him to get in the right mindset for tomorrow—a welcome distraction.

No more than forty minutes later, while making the compulsory scan around the bar to check out the new arrivals, Travis noticed a woman standing in the lobby looking into a compact mirror, preparing for her entrance into the bar. She smiled like she knew how stunning she was, and how it let her get her own way. She had black hair and flawless white skin that made him think of Snow White.

She was tall and curvaceous. Late twenties?

Just my type, Travis thought with the confident half-smile born from a second apple-tini. He wondered if it was wrong to find a girl attractive when his mother lay in bed with cancer.

She looked up and began conducting her own scan of the bar. Travis looked away, pretending to be watching TV, playing the silly but necessary game of not looking too desperate. The possibility of her as a date for the night was appealing, comforting.

Then he heard the voice from the phone. It was calling his name, "Dr. Travis?"

He looked in the direction it came from. It was Snow White. Sonia had obviously arrived. She sauntered toward him with a Cheshire cat smile and a look in her eye like she'd known him for years. It was surreal.

"Hello," he said, studying her. "Sonia?"

"Yes," she said. She clearly recognized him. Her beauty was far more intense than he had first thought now that she was closer and staring right at him. It was overwhelming. As she took the last few steps to join him at the bar, he desperately tried not to undress her with his eyes and keep his gaze fixed on hers. Clearly an attractive body lay beneath the navy suit and white lace blouse.

The clash of professionalism and animal attraction muddled Travis's thoughts. *Leave it, Dan, she's a reporter.*

Her deep green eyes searching his, Sonia slid onto the bar stool next to him.

CHAPTER 5

CLINTON LEBLANC'S NEIGHBOR, Mrs. Perkins, beamed at the prospect of company.

Leblanc had used his head start well. He snatched the page of research from his study, scribbled a cryptic note at the bottom, and faxed it to the man he intended to ask for help with getting the truth out—Dan Travis. Leblanc had gotten Travis's home fax number from the Secret Service database. A violation of protocol, yes, but he was way beyond that now.

After he was sure the fax went through, Leblanc leapt across the corridor to his neighbor's apartment, hoping to buy some time.

Mrs. Perkins was a silver-haired woman living on her own and always looking for company. Her apartment, just across the hall, was the perfect choice. On any other occasion, Leblanc dreaded bumping into her, but on this evening she would unknowingly save his life.

"Good evening, Mr. Leblanc. What can I do for you, dear?" she asked with surprise as she answered the knock. The painful monotony of her isolation had been interrupted by none other than that dashing, blond-haired man from apartment 309. He looked to be in his late forties and always wore a curious American flag pin overlaid with a gold star in the buttonhole of his tailored suits. Mrs. Perkins was always reminded of Robert Redford whenever she ran into him in the lobby, by the mailbox, or when they met in the hallway taking out the trash. She loved Robert Redford.

"Hey, Mrs. Perkins, can I borrow a stamp?" Leblanc asked with a calm veneer. The thing he needed most at that moment was, conveniently, the best thing to justify his unexpected visit.

She invited him in, just as he'd hoped, and began rummaging through one of her kitchen drawers for the stamp. The thud of intruders bursting into Leblanc's apartment across the corridor seemed to have gone unnoticed by Mrs. Perkins.

A drop of Leblanc's sweat fell to the kitchen counter.

"Are you feeling okay, Mr. Leblanc? You look a little off-color…let me get you a cup of coffee and a slice of pie, perhaps?"

"I'm fine." *If only a piece of pie would get my ass out of this mess!* "Just finished a little workout." He then realized he was standing there in a suit and tie and hoped she wouldn't dig any further. Mrs. Perkins just smiled and continued her search for a stamp.

Distracted and constantly glancing at the front door, Leblanc still noticed her apartment was an atrocious mess. It smelled of cat urine, though he couldn't see a cat anywhere.

"What a beautiful home you have. That picture on the wall, is that…"

"Was, dear. Yes, Art Perkins, my late husband. Parkinson's took him six years back now. He was a fine-looking man, wasn't he?" Bless her heart.

Much to Leblanc's satisfaction, Mrs. Perkins rambled on with her reminiscence. The longer he could stay the better.

As Leblanc nodded his head, half-listening to the late Art Perkins's obituary, he considered his next move without pressure for the first time.

Will this work?

The breathing space was short-lived.

Leblanc could hear his pursuers pounding on neighbor's doors forcing him into action. *How come she can't hear all the noise?*

The chosen gambit was his best bet, however ludicrous it sounded. Sitting it out in his neighbor's apartment was no longer an option—that much was certain.

Time to go.

Leblanc summed up his most sympathetic voice and interrupted the misty-eyed Mrs. Perkins. "Could we pick this up another time? I have a flight tonight and I really need to mail something before I leave…do you have that stamp?"

"Yes, dear, just looking," she said, dropping her head.

Leblanc snatched a pen from his breast pocket along with the envelope, the precious envelope that was the cause of tonight's fracas and the invasion of his home. He began to write on it.

This has to work.

But before he'd finished writing, an authoritative rap shook Mrs. Perkins's front door.

Out of time!

Mrs. Perkins set off toward the door with renewed enthusiasm for the uncanny stream of guests she was attracting tonight.

"Mrs. Perkins, wait!"

"I'll be just a minute."

I need to leave—now!

As the old dear shuffled out of the kitchen, Leblanc lunged for the drawer she'd been looking in. He scoured its bizarre contents, trying to remain calm enough to see a simple postage stamp.

There was another rap at the door, much louder and more

aggressive this time. Leblanc knew he was seconds away from capture and losing everything. If he was caught, the most heinous deception in modern times would be washed away and the perpetrators would walk free. His only hope would be in a certain Dr. Travis getting a fax and, most importantly, being able and *willing* to do something with it.

In that moment, Leblanc realized the futility of relying on a man he'd never met. *No, it's down to me…and only me.*

Mrs. Perkins calling out, "Be right there," sounded like a funeral drum. Leblanc realized there were no stamps in the drawer, and slammed it shut in frustration, spinning his head toward the front door. "No!"

But in that glance, his prayers were answered. Next to the grimy toaster oven on the Formica counter was a stack of mail to be posted. Resting on top was a priority mail envelope paid for and ready to go. Leblanc snatched the envelope.

There was only one way out: the third-floor balcony window. The only option, whatever it cost.

Two tall men dressed in black combat uniforms filled Mrs. Perkins's doorway. "Good evening, ma'am. We need to check your premises as a matter of national security. We're looking for a Mr. Leblanc from apartment 309. May we come in?" the leader asked. As if she had a choice.

"Why yes, he's in my kitchen right now as it happens. He came around asking for a stamp and…"

She never had a chance to finish. The two men pushed their way into her apartment, one of them producing a pistol and lunging toward the kitchen while the other frantically called on his radio alerting the rest of the team. Mrs. Perkins looked on in amazement as her home was conquered with skilled precision.

The two agents stalked through the apartment with their backs to the walls, checking corners, cupboards and crevasses with weapons drawn, yelling out "Clear!" to each other. As they blew into the kitchen, they realized their search was in vain.

Angered, the senior agent marched back to Mrs. Perkins and barked at her.

"Ma'am, you said he was in the kitchen? There's no one here, ma'am. When did you see Leblanc?"

Mrs. Perkins had tears in her eyes, shaking. "But he was right here. He asked me for a stamp. Then I went to get the door and when I came back..."

The agents looked at each other. "So you're saying he was here until we knocked at the door? This is very important and may I remind you it's a federal offense to..."

"That's right. Yes. Right up until you knocked!" she said, cowering.

The two agents looked at each other knowingly, then dashed toward the sliding glass door in the kitchen.

They yanked open the glass door with such force that it jumped off its track, and then leapt out.

Leblanc climbed down to the balcony below and heard a helicopter swoop by. He jumped from the second-floor balcony and rolled across the grass to break his fall. From there he looked up at the third-floor balcony of Mrs. Perkins's apartment. Two armed men in black fatigues were climbing out in close pursuit. Panic threw his body back on its feet.

Death was closing in.

Leblanc sprinted toward the opposite side of the building, clinging to the tree line for cover. Fitness gained from years of running alongside motorcades was of little use now.

The dash continued down New Hampshire Avenue toward the Potomac River.

Sounds of helicopters and shouting seemed to fade, but Leblanc continued his sprint, adjusting his breathing to match his pace like a professional athlete. *Now what?*

Priority one: mail the envelope.

All he needed was a lousy mailbox. But the closest mailbox was the one in his apartment building. Out of the question.

Think. Think and run.

Leblanc blasted southwest, desperately trying to recall where he could find the nearest mailbox. He heard helicopters closing in again.

Then it came to him. The Watergate.

There was a post office at the Watergate building in front of the stores next to the infamous hotel. He stepped up the pace with a fresh adrenaline surge.

Seconds later, Leblanc saw the large, dreary Watergate building come into view. As he approached Virginia Avenue, he knew he was about to expose himself to aerial surveillance. The mature oak trees had protected him well this far, but that advantage was about to be lost. Regardless, Leblanc vaulted across Virginia, dodging cars as he made a final dash. Reaching the other side of the street, he sprung over the hedges to the mailboxes and pulled out the envelope containing its explosive secret along with the priority mail envelope from Mrs. Perkins. *God bless Mrs. Perkins.*

Leblanc, panting, ripped out his pen and wrote, using the mailbox as a desk. A drop of sweat from his chin hit the envelope as he checked the address one last time. Leblanc reluctantly eased the envelope inside the priority carrier envelope, sealed it and put it in the mailbox. It was like giving someone a gift he wanted for himself. *The file is safe for now at least.*

But at what price?

Low-flying helicopters are daily life in Washington, D.C., but few people had seen one get as close as the black Augusta 109 that hovered below the roofline of the Watergate.

It hovered there eerily, seeming to stare at Leblanc.

Leblanc took a sharp breath and broke into another dash. He quickly decided that skirting the perimeter of the Watergate was his best bet. If he could just stay under cover and bide more time, he could slip into a safe place and make his way to retrieving the file. The precious file…

It's over.

As Leblanc turned the corner continuing down New Hampshire Avenue, he saw two men in black bolting at him on an intercept heading with guns drawn. He was cornered between them and the Potomac River. Leblanc heard his pursuers' shouts commanding him to stop.

His heart pumped all the adrenaline it could but, even so, he felt his throat constrict at the hopelessness of his situation. As he blew past a coffee shop and turned onto F Street, he hunted for options.

There were none.

Pushing toward the river, he saw the palatial John F. Kennedy Center for Performing Arts out the corner of his left eye and the Watergate Hotel out of his right. The poignant reminder of what his father died for on the left and the reality of government conspiracies on the right, all in one place, in one moment of time, reaffirmed his commitment and justified his actions, allowing him to dispense with 'the code' and answer to a higher calling.

But these were his last rites.

As Leblanc took his first bounding step across the Potomac Parkway, he felt a powerful thud in his right shoulder blade, quickly followed by a searing pain. The shock brought his gallop down to a canter.

He'd been struck by a high-velocity bullet.

Staggering across the road, onto the riverbank, Leblanc heard the shouts grow closer. He staggered toward an oak tree on the riverbank and clung to the river fence to stabilize himself. He turned to his attackers and drew his gun.

No sooner was the pistol out of its holster, another powerful thud and searing pain, this time in his chest. Leblanc raised his gun toward his attackers—his vision getting blurrier—and let off a hopeless shot.

Their response was instant.

This time the power of the bullet in his chest threw him over the fence and into the dark Potomac.

The water quickly engulfed Leblanc's pounded body.

Darkness. A cold chill saturated his bones.

He saw vivid images of his father—a guardian angel. He felt he could reach out and touch him.

Bright light replaced the pain.

I did it for you, Dad...the truth will come out...

CHAPTER 6

ROSEMARY JACKSON WAS A DEVOTED and loyal housekeeper who enjoyed taking care of the colonial-style home of Dr. Travis in Ruxton Village on the outskirts of Baltimore, Maryland.

But as she sat staring down the barrel of an automatic pistol, his dirty shirts were the least of her worries.

Just minutes earlier, as the motherly African-American was finishing her day's chores, the door crashed open and the house was quickly besieged by what looked to her like some sort of SWAT team; dressed in black combat fatigues and bulletproof vests, they had to be government agents of some sort, she thought, and therefore this must be a terrible mistake.

Tears in her eyes, she watched helplessly as the intruders marauded through the house, causing damage and mayhem in the residence she so meticulously cared for. She dared not speak, fearing the man behind the gun aimed at her who threatened that he *would* shoot her without hesitation if she so much as moved. Keeping still wasn't difficult for Rosemary. She was frozen out of shock and fear.

Rosemary batted a volley of thoughts and possible explanations for the whirlwind that was the last few minutes. She wondered about her fate and how her disabled husband would cope if this were the end.

With that thought, she felt her fear suddenly transform into anger.

As she saw the man who'd directed the raid walk into the kitchen toward her, she instinctively knew her waiting was over one way or the other.

Detail Leader Hicks stood before her. His face was barely visible behind his headgear. "Where's Dr. Travis?" he said, waving off the gun being pointed at her.

Rosemary's anger intensified.

This was a mistake.

"What's this about? Who are you? Dr. Travis is a good man…"

Hicks bent down to meet her face. "Listen very carefully," he said, gritting his teeth. "We are federal agents and you will cooperate or you'll be arrested. Daniel Travis is wanted for questioning as a matter of national security."

She glared back at the commander with her coal black eyes.

"Young man, arrest me on what charge? What do you want with Dr. Travis? And what in the Lord's name are your men looking for?! I'm not doing anything, son, until you tell me what's going on!"

Rosemary watched Hicks stand back up, take a deep breath, and gather his thoughts. She'd seen enough of life to recognize the frustration in his eyes. He seemed to be under a lot of pressure. More than normal, she guessed. *He's hiding something.*

Hicks took a more relaxed stance. "Ma'am, we seem to have got off on the wrong foot and I understand you must be confused."

"Son, you're the one who's confused!" Rosemary snapped back.

Her sass flew right over Hicks as he proceeded with

forced sympathy. "I assume you're the housekeeper?"

Rosemary nodded.

"Look, I'm sorry for the intrusion. Now, your employer, Dr. Travis, is needed urgently to help us with something—we're afraid his life's in danger, which is why we couldn't take any chances here. Apologies for the weapons and any damage we caused." Hicks eased his weapon into its holster.

Rosemary's expression mellowed. Anger became concern for her employer.

"So, ma'am, the sooner you tell us where he is, the sooner we can…"

Hicks was interrupted by a skinny, young man holding a satellite telephone. A patch with his name, Dekins, was sewn on his shirt. "Sir, I have Director Green on the phone. He's requested to speak to you immediately."

Hicks snatched the phone from him. "Excuse me, ma'am. I need to take this call."

Rosemary nodded as Hicks spoke into the strange phone; it looked like a cell phone from the eighties.

"Hicks here, sir. There's no sign of Travis in his home, I have my men searching the premises now and I'm currently questioning…"

Green's voice burst through the receiver. "I've just traced Travis to New York, so he won't be at home—I have a New York detail about to apprehend him, but I want the fax that was sent there tonight…have you found it?"

Hicks bit his lip. "Sir, we're looking for that fax now." Hicks had placed priority on finding Travis, who, judging by the pressure from Green, must have been armed and dangerous. Hicks put his hand over the receiver and whispered to Dekins. "Go check the fax machine and see if anything's there."

Dekins scurried off like a child.

"Very good, I'll wait while you find it. Now who did you say you were questioning?" asked Green.

Hicks glanced down at Rosemary. "The housekeeper, sir. She was here when we entered the premises."

Dekins shouted from the hallway. "Sir, we have it. We have the fax!" Hicks gestured him into the kitchen, taking a moment to give a gloating smirk to Rosemary.

"Sir, we have the fax," Hicks said into the phone.

Rosemary realized Hicks was not sincere in his earlier apologies to her, but she played along to get a handle on all this for her boss. She could clearly hear the conversation going on at both ends of the phone.

"What does it say on the fax?" asked Green.

"Sir, you better have a look at this yourself. It seems to be a jumble of handwritten notes, which don't mean much to me. It says 'Lancer's Nemesis' at the top of the page."

Green was confused by the words "Lancer's Nemesis" at the top of the fax but took solace in the retrieval of it all the same. His cryptologist could be on it very shortly if it was some sort of cipher between Leblanc and Travis.

For the first time that day, Green's smile spread across his clean-shaven face. It was one of those smiles that actually changed the shape of a person's face—his cheeks shot outwards like a caricature. And there the manic smile stayed for five seconds, glued to his face with unchanging precision as he stared straight ahead at nothing. It scared the crap out of his personal aides. Not least of all because they knew an eruption could be just around the corner despite the mask of happiness.

Green dropped the smile and, still holding the phone to

his ear, he stood up, looking down at his desk. He exhaled as events finally started going his way. Leblanc was history and Travis was a sitting duck. It was unfortunate Leblanc couldn't have been taken alive, but Green understood his men had no choice. Finding the stolen property on his body would only be a matter of time. Travis shouldn't present much of a problem, being a civilian.

"Send me the fax right away, Hicks!" Green shouted through the phone. Without giving Hicks a chance to respond, he continued barking out new orders.

"I need to get my pills," said Rosemary, heading for the door. "I have a heart problem and I need them now. I keep some in the study, so if you'll just let me through…"

Hicks, distracted by listening to Green on the phone, nodded to Dekins to let her pass. His work was done here. He had the fax and Travis was now a problem for the New York detail.

Rosemary ambled into the pine-clad study followed by Dekins. She opened the drawer where Travis kept the aspirin, as Dekins watched from the doorway, paying more attention to the strange artifacts 'this Travis guy' had on display. Dekins was reading the plaque under a silverware set salvaged from the Titanic when Rosemary spoke.

"Could you get me a glass of water please, young man?" she said, breathing heavily and supporting herself on the desk. Rosemary had always seen herself as an actress.

Dekins looked at her with pity. "Yeah, sure," he said, turning and meandering off toward the kitchen.

Rosemary had her chance.

Within two seconds she'd made her move. It was all she

could do under the circumstances, and the least she could do for kind Dr. Travis who always asked about her family, inquiring how her son's scholarship was shaping up.

Hicks finished his call. As he looked up, his jaw dropped at the sight of Dekins fetching a glass of water. He was supposed to be guarding the goddamn housekeeper!

"What the hell are you doing leaving her unattended?!" he hollered, marching back into the study with Dekins, as if dragging him by the ear.

Rosemary stood in the middle of the room, holding the pills with an arm extended to receive the glass. "Thank you, son." She swallowed the pills with a smile.

Dekins glanced sideways at Hicks as if to say, "What were you worried about, sir?"

"Alright, just don't leave her unattended again, Dekins. And delete the memory from that fax machine. I have new orders."

With the fax in his possession, it was time for Green to calculate the next move.

Purposefully, Green took four steps to the windowsill where he opened the newly created file on Dr. Travis and picked up where he'd left off. Trying to connect the dots, he thought to himself: *Leblanc and Travis, Travis and Leblanc, what would a Secret Service agent want with a historian?*

Green flipped through the pages of 'confidential' information concerning the life and habits of Daniel Travis, scouring them for a link to Leblanc's treachery. In an age of 'Homeland Security,' an individual's privacy was irrelevant.

Green took four carefully measured steps back to his chair and sat down at his black glass desk. Without looking, he placed the file dead center on the desk's clean surface. He trained his eyes on the pages as he blindly reached out for his third cup of coffee and picked it up. As he brought the hot cup of coffee toward himself while he read, it suddenly fell out of his hand. He lurched for his phone and bellowed into the receiver. "Get me to New York now!"

Green ignored the mess—hard though it was—and donned his jacket as he headed for the door.

CHAPTER 7

"SO I THINK YOU'LL AGREE, the Bermuda Triangle isn't the witches' cauldron folklore has propagated it as," Travis said with a smirk.

Sonia silently mirrored Travis's smile.

He was bothered by this girl. All through the interview she hadn't taken notes or recorded anything...

Heck, she didn't even look that interested!

"Is everything okay?" asked Travis.

Sonia took him by the shoulder and whispered in his ear, "Time is short, so I'll get straight to the point. I'm not really a reporter."

She kissed Travis on his cheek before he had a chance to reply, and whispered in his ear again.

"Act like you know me because we're probably being watched."

Sitting back, she browsed the cocktail menu pretending that she'd simply commented on Travis's suit or something equally mundane.

Travis was bemused and aroused all at once. His outrage with her having lied about being a reporter and then acting like somebody who'd watched too many spy movies was tempered by the alluring smell of her alabaster skin, her silky black hair brushing against his cheeks and the sweet vibration of her husky voice in his ear. Sonia oozed feminine appeal and when his eyes met hers, he was compelled to listen to her, regardless of what he thought of her sanity.

"So if you're not a reporter, who are you?" Travis asked while leaning over to study the cocktail menu with her. "And what do you mean we're being watched?"

Sonia smiled at him, and ordered a dirty martini from the bartender. "I work for the Secret Service, as does my brother Clinton Leblanc…" She paused to look into his eyes, as if she expected a reaction at the mention of Clinton Leblanc's name. "But I'm not here in an official capacity. You don't realize this, but my brother seems to have unwittingly drawn you into a heap of trouble."

Say what?!

Either this girl was psychotic or he really was in some kind of trouble, and she didn't appear psychotic.

"Go on," Travis said, downing the remains of his appletini.

Sonia took a small handful of chips from a dish on the bar. "All I know is that my older brother was very quiet over the last few weeks until just a few days ago. He called me to ask if I could use my New York connections to contact your publisher and set up a meeting between the two of you. He didn't want to go through the usual channels to get to you. He said he was worried about secrecy. He wouldn't tell me any more. He said he didn't want me getting involved—protective older brother bullshit, probably."

Travis nodded for her to continue, trying hard to resist the temptation of looking over his shoulder. Sonia obliged. "My brother was supposed to call me today for an update and he never did. We'd agreed upon a set time. Frankly, he's as anal as can be, so when he didn't call, I called his apartment thinking something must be wrong."

This is ridiculous—crank conspiracy callers at the TV studio, now people are following me everywhere I go! "I'm sorry to hear about that, but what does that have to do with me?"

Sonia's piercing gaze met his eyes. "When I called my brother's apartment, a policeman answered. He demanded to know if I knew where Clinton Leblanc was and if I knew of a Dr. D. Travis."

"So what does this mean exactly?" Travis asked, rubbing the back of his neck.

Sonia grabbed his arm tightly. "Listen, Dr. Travis, I'm Secret Service. I know there's no way the man who answered that call was a policeman. My brother's also an agent, on protection duty. He was secretly working on something, something big, and he wanted to speak to you in private. He's probably a fugitive now, if he hasn't been caught or killed already. He's probably dead. His computer, e-mails, phone calls, I'm sure they've all been traced and you can bet your ass whoever that 'policeman' was knows my brother planned on getting in touch with you."

Travis exhaled, his expression softened. "Well, whatever government agency wants to speak to me, they can. I've nothing to hide. I've never even met your brother. Listen, I know my area of specialty leads some to believe I'm a resource for conspiracy theories, but that's a common mistake," he said, waving a dismissive hand.

Even so, Travis couldn't help but be intrigued by what Sonia was saying. He knew he should probably walk away.

"You're so damn naïve!" Sonia interrupted, glaring down at the bar.

Travis's interest was both piqued and annoyed. *Enough is enough. She's cute, but not that cute.* "Excuse me? Okay, I think I've had just about enough of this charade for one evening…"

Sonia planted her hand on Travis's shoulder and laughed,

feigning delight, then whispered in his ear again. "Call your home and see who answers. You'll see. Whoever answers, he or she most likely killed my brother for what he uncovered. And you're linked to him now."

It seemed overly dramatic.

Travis noticed she was fighting back tears. He picked up his empty martini glass and shook it to beckon the bartender, his unsettled mind too busy to say anything more than, "Same again."

He definitely needed another drink.

What Sonia was saying seemed coherent and her warnings seemed legitimate. And what would she have to gain by hacking her way here through terrible traffic to make up a story like that?

CHAPTER 8

TRAVIS SNATCHED HIS CELL PHONE from his suit pocket and flipped it open to turn it back on.

"Who are you calling?" Sonia said.

"My housekeeper, Mrs. Jackson, to ask if she could go check on the house," Travis said, speed-dialing Rosemary. His wide eyes fixed on Sonia, Travis heard Rosemary's cell phone ring for an unusually long time before there was an answer.

What he heard drained the blood from his face.

Rosemary screamed into the phone, "Dr. Travis, they're after you! They came to get a fax sent to you about 'Lancer's Nemesis.' They have guns and they're coming for you—"

The line went dead.

Travis flipped the phone shut, staring at Sonia. His mouth hung open. Sonia's full lips tightened into a grim smirk as if to say, "Told you!"

Trying to make sense of the situation, Travis's thoughts were spinning. *Jesus. Sonia's not joking. And what's Rosemary talking about? Something about a fax with "Lancer's Nemesis" on it? Shit, shit, this is for real.* Travis felt like he'd just swallowed a brick.

Travis slid off the bar stool. "I'm gonna get some things from my room and I'll be right down. I have to get home to find out what's going on and clear all this up…oh, and you're coming with me."

Sonia's face glowed. "I'll get the check."

Travis marched across the lobby with shifting eyes, senses alert, fists clenched. A bell captain guarding the elevators gave Travis a stare he hadn't noticed him give before. Travis forced a nod and a smile for confirmation of his passage to the elevator. The bell captain nodded back.

Pushing the elevator call button, Travis joined the other half a dozen people waiting. He felt a wave of heat sear his body.

"Stay calm," he muttered to himself.

The doors opened and Travis dived through. He gathered his thoughts in the elevator, strangely envying the other six people and their normal lives.

The facts were clear though and however bizarre this turn of events was, he needed to take action. To find out what had gone wrong and put it right. *That call to Rosemary was real.*

The elevator doors parted on the eleventh floor. He didn't want to leave the other passengers behind, as if in some way their carefree existence could protect him. Travis stepped out into the corridor and turned right toward his room, just fifty feet away. As he moved further down the corridor, he heard voices emanating from his room.

Housekeeping?

Travis slowed.

Arriving a few feet from his door, to his horror, he heard the static of a radio transmitter and a voice ordering someone: "He's not here—check the drawers—we need to be ready when he comes back. Dead or alive, remember? I'm not taking any chances, you understand me?"

Oh my God. This can't be happening...yes, it is happening. Do something now!

Suddenly he turned on his heels, getting the balance between stealth and haste just right. A tip-toe became a brisk walk.

Travis bit into his top lip on what suddenly felt like an epic fifty-foot journey to the safety of the elevator.

He pushed the call button three times in succession, not knowing where to look.

Rumbling and clanking behind the closed doors signified the elevator was on its way. But the welcome noise was soon consumed by the one sound Travis hoped not to hear: the voices from his room making their way into the corridor.

Travis watched helplessly as the door to his room opened and two men dressed in suits emerged. He turned his head away and did his best to await the elevator calmly, trying to look normal. *What does normal look like?*

Travis's toes drove into the soles of his black leather shoes. He clenched his wavy, brunette hair on the side the men were coming from to hide his face.

Footsteps on the carpet.

Jesus, they're coming.

Travis wondered at what point he'd be expected to look at the approaching men. *What would an innocent person do? I am innocent!*

Travis's stomach lurched into his chest as he heard one of them call out.

"Excuse me, sir…"

No, no! Just pretend you didn't hear them.

Travis pushed the call button again. He knew he couldn't respond but that felt just plain stupid. He heard the footsteps quicken and the call repeated, only louder this time.

"Excuse me, *sir!*"

Then Travis heard the chime of the elevator arrival and the doors parted. He slid through the doors barely giving them chance to open and pushed the 'lobby' and 'close doors' buttons frantically. The walking footsteps turned into a sprint and the voice called out again, "Wait!"

Travis breathed out as he watched the elevator doors closing. But his momentary relief dissipated. As the doors closed, he saw the two men arrive with guns drawn to catch a glimpse of him.

Travis flung himself back against the wall of the descending elevator.

CHAPTER 9

AT 2650 WISCONSIN AVENUE, Washington, D.C., an elegant reception was in full swing. It featured the city's 'A-list,' all enjoying the finest caviar canapés, and all blissfully unaware that the United States Postal Service now carried a secret powerful enough to change all their lives beyond recognition, thanks to a rogue Secret Service agent.

Alex Adka was far less ignorant than the other guests. But that was his job. The gambit had paid off, but with unexpected ramifications that needed to be rectified. That's what he'd told his superiors. He could still, however, feel their heat on his shoulder. To dangle the prize in front of them only to have to snatch it away again was a mistake. He wished he hadn't mentioned anything at all until the file was safely in his possession.

Standing six-foot-three with light brown hair, olive skin and a face unnaturally gaunt, Adka declined a glass every time the tray of champagne floated by. The ambassador's receptions were noted in Washington society for their exquisiteness and he had enjoyed many, but tonight, serious work was ahead. Despite his employ in the host's service, the ambassador could not be allowed in the loop, so secret and critical was this mission.

Failure would not be tolerated.

The conversation about the unusually warm weather for

this time of year seemed ridiculously benign, but schmooz-
ing with VIPs was too important to let his disdain for them
show.

Even so, Adka felt his foot tapping in anticipation.

He couldn't help but let his eyes wander slightly as he
continued with the small talk expected over cocktails when
one of his aides approached him from across the reception
room.

"Call for you, sir," said the aide.

Adka smiled at his guests. "Please excuse me," he said
bowing, trying to hide his relief.

Adka entered his wood-paneled office and picked up
the receiver, pushing the illuminated button of a secure line.
"Adka."

A voice of cold precision replied, "Target acquired. Out."

Adka placed the receiver down and looked up with a faint
grin. He knew the acquisition of the file was only a matter of
time now; this particular agent hadn't failed him yet. Daniel
Travis was now his helpless prey.

CHAPTER 10

IN THE SPACE OF LESS THAN AN HOUR, Dan Travis's life had been turned upside down. As the elevator rumbled down to the lobby way too fast for Travis to have a chance to think, he paced violently trying to process what had just happened. He repeated over and over again: "This is for real." His thoughts bounced about his brain, first recalling what Rosemary had said to him, then to a plan of escape: from this hotel and out of New York.

Then he remembered the transit strike.

A hurricane of fear and confusion took the wind out of his chest.

Slow down and prioritize.

The flashing of the floor numbers above the elevator door felt like a countdown to doomsday: eight, seven, six.

Getting out of the hotel was the first priority. Sonia would undoubtedly be an important and valuable resource. The plan: get to her as quickly as possible and leave the building into the crowded chaos of Manhattan. Without doubt, the two men chasing him were in another elevator close behind.

Time slipped away in a blur.

The elevator bounced to a halt and with a chime, the doors parted. Travis exited out into the busy lobby and bolted for the bar. Dodging past a large party of guests who'd just arrived, he made it to the barstool where he'd left Sonia only to discover she'd gone.

Deflated, he turned toward the elevator to look for his pursuers. Nothing yet. He began a dash toward the revolving door when she suddenly appeared.

"Where have you been?!" Sonia demanded. She was poised at the exit.

Travis grabbed her arm and jerked her into the revolving door. His head whirled around just in time to see the two men appear at the elevators, scanning for him.

"No time to discuss it, we have to get out *now!*" Travis snapped.

"Okay!" Sonia saw them and didn't argue. They both spun through the door onto a Manhattan sidewalk still overcrowded with people trying to make their way home during a transit strike.

The ever-present smell of street food wafted, as usual, through the Manhattan air, but the noise level alarmed Travis. The growing line of frantic travelers outside the entrance to the hotel trying to get a cab provided them with cover. They melded into the crowd, much to Travis's relief.

Sonia grabbed Travis's arm, turning south down 7th Avenue.

Travis faced the disaster of the transit strike head on. It hadn't seemed that real until he'd entered the pandemonium. The noise from car horns and bursts of police sirens penetrated his body. The roads were completely gridlocked and more noticeably, the sidewalks were thick with pedestrian traffic. The smell of desperation filled the cool fall air as darkness descended. All this comforted Travis, as they seemed to have lost their pursuers in a blur of a thousand faces.

Keep moving.

"What happened back there?" asked Sonia.

Travis looked back at the hotel.

"Look straight ahead!" Sonia ordered. "*What happened?*"

Travis snapped his head forward like a scolded child. "They were in my room…you were right…and who the hell are *they* anyhow?!"

"Stay calm and we'll get out of this. I didn't think they'd catch us so fast. Right now I don't know much more than you."

As they marched along with the rest of the foot traffic down 7th Avenue toward Times Square, Sonia put her arm through Travis's and pulled herself close. Travis didn't pull away but turned to her, puzzled.

Sonia nodded once. "They're looking for one man, not a couple."

"Whoa there a minute," Travis said and waved a hand in front of her face. "I don't even know who these guys after me are. I just need to get to the police and tell them…"

"Forget it! Didn't you hear anything I said back at the bar? The people after you *are* the government. Police are just going to turn us in to whatever agency wants us. They've probably already got the police on alert."

"But they can't kill me! Jesus! This is outrageous…"

"Wake up, Travis! They can and they will. What happened back at your room was real. They don't hunt down a Secret Service agent for nothing—an agent who broke the code on protection duty. Right now you're affiliated with a clear and present danger to the state. Now if you wanna take your chances, go right ahead. Or you can trust me. What's it to be?" Sonia's tone didn't do her condemning words justice; it was like an innocent chat any couple strolling through Manhattan might have. It was a dinner party voice. She was good at this.

Travis bit his lip as he shuffled through the desperate crowds with her. Every fiber in his body said no, but the situation demanded that he say yes to what she was saying. *She's right… Yes, she's right. Those bastards wanted me dead back there!*

"Shouldn't we be running then?" Travis asked, looking back over his shoulder.

Sonia pulled his arm as if to bring him to heel. "No! And look straight ahead. We have to blend in as much as possible. The crowds provide excellent cover, so just walk, and turn off your cell phone."

Travis took the phone from his pocket and pushed the button.

"Why?"

"I'll explain shortly. We're going to Grand Central. It's just a few blocks over. We need to get these guys off our tail before anything. I take it you've got your wallet with you?"

"Yes, I've got it with me."

Had Travis not been face to face with two gunmen who had clear orders to take his life just minutes earlier, all of this would have seemed unreal. Instead, he found himself operating with a surreal level of awareness, his juices flowing with determination to solve this riddle, to survive the whole affair. He'd always understood different people reacted differently under pressure, the well-documented 'fight or flight' response, and he was clearly in the former category. His ability to think clearly and logically couldn't be compromised tonight, as that was the one thing that would get him out of this mess. His first task was the same as millions of others: trying to escape from New York in the middle of a transit strike. The only difference being all these other people weren't being hunted down like deer in open season!

Travis felt a moment of gratitude for the news having been on the TV in the bar just before Sonia arrived. He could now take stock of the strike. The intensity of the situation tore at his mind and he wanted to think this through for himself rather than consult this strange girl, even if she had just saved his life.

Time slipped by. Travis could feel his hunters closing in and simply sitting it out until the strike was over wasn't an option. Neither was simply walking over one of the bridges; that would make capture even easier for them. Cabs were being fought over and the roads were gridlocked. The Staten Island Ferry as well as all water taxis were mobbed with lines of hopeful passengers. Sonia was leading him to Grand Central Terminal, which seemed pointless. *Unless…*

Staying with the hoards of pedestrians pounding Broadway, Travis spoke up. "Why are we going to Grand Central? It looked pretty hopeless on the TV earlier…as every other option."

Sonia didn't answer; she was homing in on an ATM she'd just caught sight of. She clearly had a plan and knew what she was doing, but he pressed her all the same. "Sonia?"

"Grand Central's about the best place we could be from a counter-surveillance point of view. It has the highest concentration of commuter trains to get out of here. Right now you need to get as much cash out as you can. We don't have much further to go." Sonia gestured toward the ATM and they both weaved through the heaving crowds on the sidewalk to get to it.

A few buttons later, he yanked the cash from the ATM.

"Don't worry," Travis said, "I'll get us downtown from Grand Central."

Putting a second card in the slot, his smug expression melted away with a horrific realization. Travis's confidence in Sonia had just shattered. If his pursuers were from a government agency, he'd just told them where he was by the simple act of taking cash out of an ATM.

CHAPTER 11

THE PART TRAVIS WAS TO PLAY in this treason was clear to Green: his TV appearance tomorrow morning—after receiving a cryptic faxed instruction from his accomplice Leblanc—was to be the outlet for the state secret the duo had criminally acquired.

The executive jet taxied into the private hangar and command center the field office had established at New York's JFK Airport. The whine of the engines faded and the stairs lowered. Green strutted out to be met by the New York detail leader, Murphy. Murphy was a burly man of Irish stock with a potbelly and a shock of black hair.

Greetings had no place. Murphy led Green through to the offices at the rear of the hangar.

"Have you had confirmation from the TV network that the Travis interview tomorrow is cancelled?" Green said, looking at his watch.

"Yes, sir. Agents are in pursuit." Murphy winced.

"In pursuit?" Green stared at Murphy.

"Yes, sir. Travis wasn't in his hotel room and escaped the building. We're in pursuit…" Anticipating Green's explosion, Murphy immediately spluttered out what he thought was the good news. "But Manhattan's a giant rat-trap right now. The tran—"

"Transit strike?" Green interrupted. "Yes, I know all about that."

Green's cell phone rang.

"Hold on, Murphy," Green said, flipping open the phone and checking his watch again.

"What is it, Norman?" Green said, frowning.

"Sir, you called me?"

"Yes…yes. That fax Leblanc sent Travis. Send it to crypto. It didn't make much sense to me."

"Yes, sir, but just so you know…"

Green snapped the phone shut and looked at Murphy again. Murphy had led him into the offices where four other agents sat in cubicles.

"So?" said Green. "Where's Travis?"

"Sir, Travis's cell phone isn't showing up on GPS. It's possible it's not turned on or it could be an older model. But he just used an ATM near Broadway on 42nd, narrowing down his location, but it's chaos on those streets."

"I couldn't give a shit about how busy the streets are, Murphy. Find him! You have a fix on his position; now get him. Travis is a civilian who has no clue. I want to see where he leads us…hopefully to the stolen package. Simply keep his location pinpointed and stay on him. He won't be getting off Manhattan quickly tonight."

"Yes, sir," Murphy said, nodding the command to one of his men to execute the order.

Green's eyes darted in all directions over this command post. "Set up checkpoints on all remaining available exit points from Manhattan Island by road, rail, air and water—also the pedestrian walkways on the bridges just in case—you'll have all the manpower you need. I also want alerts on any unusual activity from NYPD, Air Traffic Control and the Coastguard. Now get your men on Travis's position!"

"Yes, sir, they're moving in but…"

One of the men in the cubicles shouted at Murphy, "Sir,

we have Travis! He just switched on his cell phone outside Grand Central Station. Agents are looking for him now." Green and Murphy hustled over to the cubicle.

Green tried to shut out the asymmetry and untidiness of the rushed-together office. He watched the large computer screen on the coffee-stained desk showing Travis on the move and allowed himself some satisfaction knowing he was once again in control. Travis was in no way a worthy adversary.

Travis's blip on the screen moved east along 42nd Street and then seemed to stop.

"Why's he stopped?" Green demanded.

Murphy relayed the question to the ground surveillance team leader through a headset, pushing a button to put the reply on speakerphone.

"Do you have a visual yet?"

After a two-second pause a voice relayed back. "No, sir, not yet…but in that location he's right outside Grand Central. Awaiting instructions."

Murphy and Green looked at each other.

"Shit!" Green hissed. Murphy was glad it wasn't his decision now. A busy train station was about the worst possible place a surveillance target could go; the signal would be lost underground and the possible directions of escape were many.

"Very well," Green began. "Apprehend the target, alive if possible, right now."

"Understood, sir."

Green spun around facing the map of Manhattan on the wall behind the desk and pondered the development. Soon Travis would be in detention and, under the Patriot Act, he could be held indefinitely without legal counsel. There would be plenty of time to extract the truth from him. Right this second, agents were pinpointing his exact position following the signal from his cell phone and were about to bring him in.

Green studied the commuter rail lines emanating from Grand Central on the map, tapping his foot while he waited for the surveillance detail to confirm the arrest. *Events today should never have been allowed to get this far,* he thought to himself, indignant for having to clean up after someone else.

The agent's voice finally came through the speakerphone. Green lurched to the desk, hovered over it, beckoning the expected confirmation from his subordinate. "Go ahead."

The reply sounded ominous. "Sir, it seems Travis planted the phone on someone else. Right now, we're covering all exits and dispersing agents down to all active platforms, of which there aren't many. It's crazy busy here. He shouldn't get too far. Apologies, sir, there's just so many people on foot because of the strike, it's chaos over here!"

"You idiot! I'm sending more agents. You'd better re-establish contact or you're history. Do you understand?" Green cut off the call without waiting for a reply from the imbecile and glared at Murphy, inviting an explanation.

"Sir, he really can't get too far," Murphy said and clicked a series of buttons on the computer. Seconds later, the security cameras at Grand Central showed the platforms heaving with people.

"Sir, all possible exits from Grand Central are being covered, only the Metro-North commuter lines are running and no one can get on the trains; they're too full. Even if Travis does manage to get on a train, we'll have agents waiting at all the New York and Connecticut stations and we'll board the trains ourselves at 125th Street, the last stop before it gets off the island. I've computed all his options and don't see how he can escape."

A cynical shadow came over Green's face. "Murphy, I

hope you're confident in your 'computations,' because I'm sure they have more options and I'll think of them."

Green turned around to study the map of Grand Central that showed all the commuter lines as well as the inactive subway lines. *You're going nowhere, buddy.*

CHAPTER 12

DEEP IN THE RECESSES of Grand Central Terminal, the entrance to the seven train was swarming with passengers, shouting like frustrated baseball fans. Managers from the Metropolitan Transit Authority were in the process of securing the platform and taking complaints from frustrated commuters. They were far too stressed and angry to notice a man and a woman pass by them to the end of the platform and disappear into darkness of the tunnel.

Unsolved mysteries attracted Dan Travis like metal to a magnet and this place was no exception. When he conducted research for the chapter "The Mysteries of Grand Central" in his book, he had no idea it would save his life. That's why he had gone along with Sonia's plan to come here.

Once they'd arrived, the crowds had masked their escape onto the abandoned platform and into the dark tunnel, through a maintenance door to a little known stairway. It only seemed like yesterday he was down here with a hardhat and two escorts, the damp electrical smell familiar to his senses. Even the longest-serving employees of the MTA were fearful of the notorious and mysterious labyrinth of tunnels beneath the Grand Central Terminal's landmark building. No one really knew how deep or far they went.

"The ATM was nothing to worry about. We're going to need cash, so it may as well have been now, before they had a chance to terminate your cards. They were tracking your cell phone anyway," said Sonia, shuffling down the fifth flight of stairs with her small keychain flashlight leading the way.

"Yeah, I see. And that's why you wanted to get a train at Grand Central?"

"Multiple directions to go from. Who knows where that guy I planted the phone on is heading. Hopefully far away from us."

"Okay, very good," said Travis. "Keep going. Once we get to the door at the bottom of these stairs, make a right and then we'll be on an abandoned line headed downtown."

"Okay. Aren't these tunnels manned anymore?" Sonia asked, noticing that the staircase was lit a lot brighter further down.

"Not generally, and I imagine this strike will make it even less likely we run into any transit workers."

They reached the bottom of the stairs and found a metal door with a large, scuffed sign next to it, which read: *Warning: Look Out for Rats.* Unperturbed, Sonia swung open the door and stepped into the dimly lit tunnel. "What is this place?" she asked, turning right onto the abandoned tracks.

"It's a ghost station—an abandoned one. That's it, keep moving." Travis broke into a jog. Sonia effortlessly matched the pace.

The strange sensations Travis felt while doing research for his book came back to him. He thought the eeriness of these tunnels was that they were still lit up, though completely abandoned. It made him believe that someone really was down here, perhaps the people who'd sprayed all this graffiti. But all he could hear was his and Sonia's footsteps echoing down the empty cavern. While chaos reigned on the surface, this subterranean sanctuary provided a dusty beeline to downtown.

Travis felt strangely at peace.

A vision of his mom flashed through his mind. He saw her eyes. Not the sparkling blue he knew though, more like dark deep holes.

I have to get through this!

"What exactly did your brother do in the Secret Service?" asked Travis, trying to get his breathing under control for what would easily be a thirty-minute run, the length of his daily workout on the elliptical.

"Like I said, he was on protection detail, guarding the vice president last I heard. My gut tells me he must have broken the code."

"The code?" Travis asked, dodging a low hanging wire.

Sonia explained with condescending empathy, appreciating that Travis was a civilian. "The code is like the unwritten mantra of the Secret Service. Agents should never talk about what they see or hear in the course of their protection duties. Like I said, he'd been acting very out of character lately, so I wouldn't put anything past him. Who knows, maybe he even made a recording of something he shouldn't have."

Travis's feet suddenly became wet and cold all at once. They were running through groundwater now. Travis tried to put his problem-solving brain to work while he kept up his adrenaline-fueled pace.

He thought back to what Rosemary had managed to say before she was cut off: something about "Lancer's Nemesis." *Obviously, a nemesis is a kind of ultimate adversary,* Travis thought, *but who or what was "Lancer"?*

The name nagged at him, as it had since Rosemary screamed it on the phone, but its significance eluded him. Travis knew it was best to move on and come back to this puzzle later, much like the solution to writer's block.

Travis felt the increasing pressure in his ears as the tunnel went further underground. Breathing heavily, he said, "If your brother had actually made a recording of something highly sensitive, it follows that they want it back and think we know where it is. I need to get home so we can somehow get a copy of this fax they wanted."

Sonia stumbled upon something but recovered herself and continued splashing through what had now become a steady stream of groundwater running with them. "Once we get off the island, we'll need to get back to Baltimore," she said.

"How did you know I lived in Baltimore?"

Sonia took a couple of seconds to reply. "I did my home-work. You're a famous guy in case you hadn't noticed. It says where you live on the inside cover of everything you write. Anyone could have known that, never mind a Secret Service agent!"

"Does the word 'Lancer' mean anything to you?"

Sonia slowed down to a brisk walk. Travis was relieved to follow her lead.

"Yeah, I know who 'Lancer' was. Why do you ask?"

"Because my housekeeper told me someone had sent me a fax about something called 'Lancer's Nemesis.' Now, if that was your brother, how did he get my personal fax number?" In that same moment, Travis remembered Leblanc was a Secret Service agent and would therefore have access to just about any personal information on any citizen he cared to call up. "He's Secret Service. Of course he'd know the fax number," Travis said, quickly correcting himself.

"That fax is why you're on the run…you're linked to my brother breaking the code."

Travis nodded his head in agreement. "We have to get a copy of that fax somehow. My fax machine will have a copy stored in its memory. If we get to my house, can you access the memory?"

"Absolutely."

"So who was 'Lancer' then? You used past tense, Sonia. Who was 'Lancer'?"

Sonia carried on looking straight ahead through the darkened tunnel as she answered with a sarcastic tone, "Really, Doctor, I'm surprised at you. 'Lancer' was a Secret Service codeword used in one of the most famous unsolved mysteries of modern times."

Travis played along in her satisfaction with filling a hole in a knowledge category he was supposedly a world expert on. "Go on…please enlighten me."

"Every president has a codename used by Secret Service protection detail agents for security reasons. 'Lancer' was the most well known of them all. It was the name the Secret Service gave to the late President John F. Kennedy."

Travis kicked himself for forgetting. Stress, he knew. He'd of course been unable to resist investigating the JFK enigma privately, but steered away from it publicly, the whole affair being the definitive conspiracy theory. The Kennedy White House was endearingly nicknamed 'Camelot' by the media. 'Lancer' was a reference to 'Lancelot.'

Travis thought about the fax but Sonia got there first. "So, 'Lancer's Nemesis' must be referring to Kennedy's killer—Lee Harvey Oswald—and my brother most likely broke the code over something he heard having to do with that."

Travis declined to reply. The hairs on the back of his neck stood up.

This revelation didn't sit well with him.

I know one thing. There's more to all this than a long-dead president's assassins.

CHAPTER 13

DWIGHT SAT STRAIGHT UP at his desk in a private glass cubicle, arranging pencils, files and legal pads. No matter that this was a temporary office. He found it hard to concentrate until he'd made his mark.

There. A cocoon of perfect order and symmetry.

Back to business. Murphy's failure to apprehend Travis at Grand Central had forced a dilemma upon Green: to rely solely on Murphy's men or to employ his most powerful weapon in his arsenal.

The chaotic situation in Manhattan was a window of opportunity.

Events thus far hadn't exactly inspired confidence in his agents, but as effective as his last resort would be, it wouldn't come without some explanation.

Something nagged.

Green closed his eyes tightly and pushed both forefingers against his temples as he sat forward against his desk.

What would I do if I were Travis?

Wait.

How did Travis know to ditch the cell phone? He's just a civilian. Or maybe not.

Guilty as hell!

The sound of a nearby clock ticking was deafening. Travis could soon be off the island if he could evade the checkpoints.

Decision time.

Green picked up his phone and dialed. If New Yorkers had been inconvenienced by the transit strike, they were about to get a lot more inconvenienced; an official terror alert was about to grip Manhattan.

Time to close the net.

CHAPTER 14

TRAVIS AND SONIA EMERGED from the chapel-like structure of Bowling Green station into the early darkness. The dry leaves of Battery Park crunched beneath their feet. Travis was panting, holding his side.

They shot out of the station peeping out of the ground. It was the tip of the subterranean maze under New York City. Sonia hadn't even broken a sweat. She grabbed Travis's arm like a relay baton and headed for the harbor. Travis believed if he could see beneath the surface of Manhattan, he would see a labyrinth of chasms and canyons just as historic as the landmarks on the surface.

Arriving at the water's edge, Sonia said, "Wait here." Travis looked across the harbor from the lower edge of Battery Park. He desired the illuminated New Jersey shoreline like never before.

While Travis waited, Sonia bought tickets for the only ferry people *weren't* fighting to get on: the Circle Line. Only used by tourists, it was a sightseeing boat that left from various locations in Manhattan, but the final destination was always where it started: Manhattan. Travis was confused, but right now, Sonia felt like the only person he could trust.

He was badly shaken. She was capable.

Travis was tugged from behind. It was Sonia, clutching tickets. She ushered him toward the security entrance for the

Liberty and Ellis Island ferry.

"Move. The last ferry of the day's about to leave!" she urged.

The line through security was small. Most tourists, defeated by lack of available transportation, had resorted to retail therapy. Travis and Sonia filed through security and into the boarding tent. As they emerged from the tent, Travis itched to get on board the white-and-blue, two-level vessel bobbing around in the choppy waters of the estuary.

Passengers disembarked from the previous trip. The rope preventing them from boarding lowered, then Travis and Sonia leapt on board and found a seat in a dark corner.

The cold air blew in off the water, but it was a welcome relief to Travis's overheated, anxious body.

The engines wound up and the vessel thrust away from the dock.

Sonia strutted to the onboard snack bar as the ferry rumbled toward Liberty Island, gathering speed.

Travis tried to break the catatonic state he was in. *Breathe.* He glanced back at the imposing after-dark Manhattan skyline. Downtown stood proud with towers of light. Apart from it, the horribly evident hole where the World Trade Center once was, like a deep wound on the magnificent metropolis. Some wounds never heal.

Sonia returned with two hot dogs and several bottles of water under her arm. Travis admired her beauty in more detail, despite the terror and total confusion of this last hour. Her form was muscular, toned. A compelling aroma trailed her, even after the long run she'd made. But for all her sexual appeal, it was her face that stood out; it was hypnotic. Her wide eyes seemed to suck Travis in to her cause.

The moment was broken by water from the tunnel, squelching in his shoes as he moved his feet.

Back to the horrific reality.

He bent down to take off his shoes and ring out his socks. Sonia gave up a brief smile and then turned her attention toward Ellis Island looming closer on the right of their course for Liberty Island. The ferry goes to Liberty Island, then Ellis Island, before returning to Manhattan.

"So why don't you tell me more about 'Lancer's Nemesis' on the ride?" she said with her eyes still fixated on Ellis Island, rather than the far more imposing Statue of Liberty growing bigger as they approached.

"I take it you don't think it was simply Lee Harvey Oswald who did it?" she persisted.

Travis sighed. "Something tells me there's more to all this than JFK's killers, intriguing though that is."

Sonia stayed focused on Ellis Island as she spoke. "Well, bring me up to speed anyway. Until we get that fax, it's all we have to go on. My brother didn't write 'Lancer's Nemesis' on the page and send it to you for no reason."

Travis put his head down between his knees. "Look, this is ridiculous…"

"It was a conspiracy, wasn't it?"

Travis's head shot up. He looked like he was about to tear a chunk of his hair out, his eyes confessing deep stress. "I'm in the middle of my worst nightmare and you want a fucking history lecture?! Your goddamn brother…look, I'm sorry." Travis closed his eyes, taking more deep breaths.

"Try to stay calm. We need to figure this out to make it go away and this seems like a good place to start, doesn't it? Are you doing anything else for the next ten minutes? Going somewhere?!" she questioned with her hand on his back.

Travis capitulated and started to give the most bizarre lecture of his career. He made no attempt to hide his duress. "More than 80 percent of Americans think it was a conspiracy, yes…and they're right, but they're missing virtually all the facts and evidence and completely misunderstanding the events surrounding it. Unfortunately, all the movies and nearly all the books on the subject missed it too. And that's exactly how the conspirators engineered it—we all bought it and played right into their hands."Travis realized he'd opened a can of worms and would now have to explain more.

Sonia settled into her seat, her look inviting more information from Travis.

What the hell. This ferry was chugging away slowly and there was nothing else to do. *Who knows? Maybe a distraction would be a good thing for now.* And she was right—why did Sonia's brother fax him a paper with "Lancer's Nemesis" written on it?

He adopted a keener tone. "To understand what really happened to JFK and why, I need to take you back to the little known secrets of World War II and the dubious history of the CIA."

Sonia couldn't help but interject. "You sound like you know for sure who did it," she said.

She's strangely defensive, Travis thought as he continued, "Well I don't exactly have a signed confession from the killers if that's what you mean, but when you piece together all the evidence, much of which has been deliberately suppressed, you'd have to be pretty naïve not to know who did it."

In that same moment, a tantalizing thought crossed his mystery-hungry mind. *What if Sonia's brother actually did steal a recording of some sort of conspiracy?* This would be the difference between evidence and proof. The point where conspiracy theory becomes conspiracy fact. Despite the inevitable overlap with Travis's acclaimed domain of famous unsolved mysteries, conspiracy theories were in an arena he stayed out of, in public anyway, not just because of over-imaginative clowns wildly discrediting the topic, but because rarely did anything come of conspiracy theories. Two reasons: firstly, all that was usually available was evidence rather than proof and therefore open to debate. Secondly, even when proof *did* exist, the public was largely disinterested. The Watergate conspiracy was about as close to proof as you could get to 'conspiracy *fact*,' but the American public didn't care. It didn't affect their lives enough. Politicians lie and cheat and will do anything to stay in power. So what else is new? That was the reaction to Watergate.

But despite the prospect of conspiracy theory becoming conspiracy fact due to whatever it was Sonia's brother had done, Travis's gut still didn't sit right.

I can't believe my life is in danger simply over new proof about who committed JFK's assassination.

No government today would be targeting civilians over something that happened over forty years ago and would now be unlikely to impact their interests.

Must get more information.

His attention flitted back to Sonia, who looked bemused after his previous comment about people being naïve not to realize who shot JFK.

"Didn't take you for a cynic, Dan," she said, strands of ebony blowing across her face.

"I'm not—I'm just a realist. If you don't accept the fact people will always pursue their own interests, you're in denial. It's precisely that basic instinct for survival that has kept the species alive. Now, do you want me to explain the facts or would you rather live in the ignorant bliss of the sheep pen with everyone else?" He smiled to temper any signs of stress.

Incensed by Travis's remarks and sensing his exasperation, she gestured for him to continue. Travis proceeded, trying to be more patient.

"So, during World War II, the Russians woke up one day to a big problem. One of their most respected generals—Vlasov—defected to Germany, taking his army with him. Of course, the German army welcomed the defection and had Vlasov and his men specially organized in preparation to turn on Russia under an SS general named Reinhard Gehlen. Needless to say, this sort of thing doesn't make its way into most history books."

Travis's mind flashed back to the arguments he'd had with historians who didn't want any new evidence to upset their theses—new evidence he was perpetually uncovering in the course of his research. Well, they didn't want to have their books made obsolete, did they?

"To counter this disastrous defection, the Russians employed an espionage technique, Chekist tactics, they'd used since the early days of the Russian Revolution almost thirty years earlier."

Travis couldn't help but give a smile of macabre admiration as he recalled how Russian intelligence ran circles around American and British counterparts with their skill and finesse during the Cold War.

"The Russians parachuted a fiercely loyal agent named Igor Orlov behind enemy lines. He claimed to be a Russian defector who wanted to join Vlasov's army of defectors, supervised by the German SS. The SS weren't stupid though, and they took some convincing."

"So did they see through it?" Sonia asked, her mind seeming to wander.

"No, because of these Chekist tactics I mentioned. Igor Orlov betrayed real Russian agents already in Vlasov's army in order to gain credibility and respect with the Germans. Needless to say, it worked and before long, Orlov was given a list of all the Russian defectors and access to all of the plans for this turncoat army."

"A double agent?" Sonia questioned.

"Yes, a double agent. The Germans thought Orlov was working for their intelligence as a defector, when in fact he was still working for Russia."

Travis continued, "Orlov was the reason Vlasov's defector army was never used in any significant theater of war. Orlov succeeded in convincing the Germans that the army was far too infested with Russian spies to be of any use."

The ferry drifted into Liberty Island. Travis and Sonia were momentarily distracted by the Statue of Liberty staring out to sea. She was like a beacon to the world, shining with the principles that America was founded upon.

"Doesn't matter how many times I see her," Sonia said, as if repeating a line from a movie, "she always takes my breath away."

Travis nodded. Looking up at the statue, he felt his resolve strengthen for the task at hand. In some strange way, Lady Liberty was watching over him. Imploring him.

"Carry on," said Sonia, watching several tourists board the ferry. She was listening to this story just as she had back at the hotel:disinterestedly.

Travis went on. He was enjoying the distraction even if she wasn't.

"As World War II came to a close, we found ourselves faced with a brand new enemy—the Soviet Union. In a desperate attempt to make a deal with the more forgiving Americans on the Western Front, German SS generals gathered all the documents they had on Soviets who had defected from Russia—Soviets like Orlov who of course hadn't defected at all—and offered them to the American Office of Strategic Services—the OSS, the predecessor to the CIA. Seeing an opportunity to recruit those who were clearly perceived as the ultimate anti-Communist agents, the OSS gladly accepted the surrender of the defector army and their 'loyal' Orlov: a ready-made spy network to fight the Soviets. Or so we thought."

The ferry chugged away for the short hop to Ellis Island as Travis continued.

"It's a little-known fact that the OSS's 'Operation Paperclip,' the race to recruit Nazi scientists, ever took place. But, what's even less known was an OSS operation called 'Operation National Interest.' Through this operation, thousands of the most heinous Nazi war criminals were tracked down and recruited to work for the OSS all with American taxpayers' money. Even the head of the Gestapo, Heinrich Mueller, was brought in. Many of these monsters were actively recruited in Nuremburg during the war crimes trials in direct violation of U.S. law and several international treaties. The main point is that the bulk of American intelligence services against the new Soviet threat were infected with Communist agents right from the start, thanks to one Igor Orlov. This set the stage for the Cold War. The OSS successor, the CIA, would inherit all these Soviet spies."

"But America won the Cold War," Sonia replied, unaffected by his revelation.

"By default," Travis argued. "The Communist system was flawed, which is ultimately what lost the Cold War. The USSR was bankrupt."

Sonia stood up to stretch her legs and leaned over the guard rail to try and get a clear view of the approach to Ellis Island before replying.

"Okay, but where does Kennedy's death fit in?"

Travis became agitated by her child-like impatience. "I'll explain later. Right now I want to know more about the next step."

Sonia studied the rear of the Ellis Island historical building as they began to dock.

"How fast can you run two hundred meters?" Sonia asked, her green eyes sparkling in the darkness.

"What!?"

"Okay, listen up. Do exactly as I say."

CHAPTER 15

"How the hell can he just *vanish* from Grand Central? He's not David fucking Copperfield!" Green bellowed.

Still nothing. All Green could do was pace around while his people worked on Leblanc's strange fax and try to locate Travis.

Something was missing.

Green took pride in always being business-like, but tonight was stretching his tolerance. He'd never felt such pressure in all his time at the agency. Even crises involving heads of state paled in comparison to the importance of bringing back the stolen information and ensuring its destruction. Worse still, never had he had such limited tools to work with; secrecy was just as important as the capture of the information. His hands were tied when it came to issuing a nationwide All Persons Bulletin to apprehend Travis.

That's what he would have liked to have done.

Green thought of himself as the law and an agent of the Almighty. Any adversaries were bad guys. Never once did he question why the bad guys were the bad guys. Such ferocious loyalty had carved a path for him into the upper echelons of this enigmatic agency with great speed. He never once stopped to look down at the pathetic wimps he'd trounced along the way.

And there's no way a simple manhunt was going to spoil the ride now!

Green flicked a speck of dirt from his desk and tried to think of something else, hoping for a moment of inspiration.

He recalled the words of his mentor when, much younger, Green had questioned suppressing evidence in the Congressional inquiry into Oliver North and the Iran-Contras arms scandal threatening President Reagan. Tonight, that memory had significance:

"Yeah, this is a democracy, Green, but the people need protecting from themselves and, yes, I would lie if it meant doing that."

Sensing young Green's confusion, his mentor went on in his Texas drawl, "Listen, buddy, if the boys on the hill knew half of what went on, nothing would get done! We're guarding the fence between us and the goddamn Commies, meanwhile the masses out there talk about the weather, eat cheeseburgers and play the lottery! They have the audacity to question those responsible for guarding them while they sleep in their cozy beds at night. They don't want the truth, son; they want stability. Never show folks any weakness, Dwight, or they'll turn around and bite you in the ass."

That day Green chose the path of no return. Divorced many years, he lived the saying, 'He who travels lightest travels fastest.'

Compassion was weakness.

His agency—*his family*—and country needed protecting,

regardless of all the bullshit sound-bites politicians blurted while they kissed and coddled their constituents.

I am the sword and shield—under God—and I do not take any prisoners.

Murphy ambled in with the latest activity report on New York City—the third to cross Green's desk this evening. Not holding much hope, Green thanked and dismissed Murphy.

Green sighed as he glanced through, combing his fingers down the entries, trying to get this chore out of the way so he could follow up on the photo match of Travis at Grand Central.

But something made his finger stop and question one of the entries. He pushed his intercom button summoning Murphy.

"Murphy, this entry here from Ellis Island Park Police. How old would this be?"

Murphy checked the file he held under his arm and rushed out a reply, eager to redeem himself: "Twenty-two minutes ago, sir. It's just a minor…"

"Somebody deliberately set off and threw a fire extinguisher in the Ellis Island museum! How do you get to Ellis Island from Manhattan, Murphy?"

Murphy plodded toward the large map of New York City behind Green's desk and pointed. "By ferry, sir. The sightseeing boat, the Circle Line. It leaves from Battery Park and stops at Liberty Island on the way…"

Green glared at the map, homing in on Ellis Island. Then he saw it. He tapped his finger on it and snapped his head back to Murphy.

Murphy confirmed the hole in their net. "Do you think…"

Murphy didn't get a chance to finish. Green jumped up from behind his desk and dashed to the door. Murphy didn't need to be told to warm up the chopper.

Sprinting through the hangar offices, Green felt his body tighten. *I am the sword and shield, and Travis is about to feel both come down on him hard.*

Green's gut had rarely failed him.

CHAPTER 16

NEARLY HALF OF ALL AMERICANS can trace their family history to at least one person who passed through Ellis Island between 1892 and 1924 when it was a processing center for immigrants. In its day, it represented the last gateway to the freedom of America for immigrants fleeing oppression and poverty. Now a museum and popular tourist attraction shadowed by its neighbor, the Statue of Liberty, this small island represented a gateway to freedom for Travis and Sonia.

Twenty-two minutes before Green read the latest New York City incident report, the marine police and K-9 division encamped on the island responded to an unusual incident in the main museum.

Sonia and Travis treaded down the gangway onto Ellis Island, straight ahead into the museum before them, just as Sonia had instructed.

But then came the tricky part.

Travis's stomach felt like a helium balloon, churning away and threatening to regurgitate the questionable hot dog he'd eaten on the ferry. He was forced to break the law for the first time in his life. But as Sonia had said: "It's either that or lose your life. Your choice!"

Sonia was the epitome of calm.

As they entered the museum, Sonia peeled off to the right while Travis continued straight through to the exit that led to the memorial garden on the opposite side of the building.

He waited. It wouldn't be long. Sonia would appear and join him for the next phase.

Back inside, Sonia worked her way through the milling tourists and found the nearest fire extinguisher. It was in the quietest part of the room. Tourists were gathering in the main entrance lobby, preparing to depart.

Sonia unhooked the fire extinguisher and moved back toward the busy lobby, concealing it as best she could as she positioned herself behind the façade of a display near the back exit where Travis had gone.

Then she set off the extinguisher and hurled it at the main entrance.

Before the cries of shock and alarm went up from the crowd, Sonia was deftly moving to the back exit.

Once outside in the darkness, she sprinted toward Travis, pulled him away toward the back of the building, veered left at the water's edge through an open gate into an abandoned part of the island away from the tourists.

They waited quietly behind the trees and eyed their goal, heavily guarded: Liberty State Park, New Jersey. There before them was their escape to the mainland, an iron service bridge used by Ellis Island employees, but guarded at either end by police. The security at the New Jersey side was more of a gesture with one officer sitting in a car to check vehicles entering the island.

Right on cue, Sonia and Travis watched as the police units stormed the museum, leaving the entrance to the bridge unguarded.

Sonia's diversion had worked perfectly.

She wasn't going to give them any time to reconsider their reaction.

"Now!" she shouted and they bolted for the entrance to the bridge.

Travis felt the adrenaline surge through his body and his jaws clench as he finished the short dash to the bridge, apparently going unnoticed by the police. He jumped up onto the bridge and continued his sprint to freedom.

"There's gonna be a guard at the end of the bridge, he'll be on high alert now. When we get to the other side, *if* he becomes a factor, I want you to break off to the right and leave him to me. You got that?" Sonia shouted to Travis ahead of her.

"Got it!" Travis said, his pounding heart fueling him for the fastest sprint of his life, as his shoes banged loudly on the unlit metal bridge.

Liberty State Park loomed ever closer as they approached the other side of the bridge. Travis's nervousness had dissipated during the run. *Is this exhilaration?*

Travis began to make out the taillights of a vehicle parked in front of what looked like a two-foot high, retractable metal barrier that stopped cars from getting in without clearance. He winced and prepared to break to the right as Sonia had instructed, now facing the reality that the officer in the car would have a gun and would probably no hesitation using it.

With no more than fifty meters to go, Travis watched as two headlights pierced through the darkness, and stopped in front of the police vehicle.

"Follow me now!" Sonia said. She continued her sprint, keeping her body down and moving to the right. As the police officer got out of his vehicle to inspect the car coming the other way, she leaped over the small barrier and turned right into the darkness of the park. Travis followed close behind.

They'd made it to New Jersey—the mainland—and Sonia was leading Travis toward Jersey City, towering directly ahead of them.

The rotor blades of Green's chopper were still spinning as he heard the news from the Ellis Island Park Police Superintendent. Just minutes after the fire extinguisher incident, the police officer on the New Jersey side of the service bridge reported seeing two people—a man and a woman—run from the island and into the trees. He'd been busy checking a car, but noticed them as they slipped by.

Two people.

Green's hunch about Ellis Island was right it seemed, but who was this woman?

He ordered his men to conduct searches in Liberty State Park and Jersey City, but Green knew it was time for the next step.

It was obvious where Travis and this woman were headed.

CHAPTER 17

THE SECOND HE COULD TEAR himself away, Alex Adka retired to his office, the monotonous and superficial droning of the D.C. elite resounding in his ears. With a sigh, he relieved his aching knees by sitting at his desk. He began wondering when he would hear more news from his loyal agent. Minutes were crawling by.

He decided to pass the time productively, with a smirk that could only be born from sheer admiration for a subject. Adka flicked his mouse, bringing his computer out of hibernation and attached a small cable to a discreetly hidden outlet on his wristwatch, connecting it to his computer. He accessed an encrypted file saved in the flash drive embedded in the timepiece.

Adka knew better than to be online even with all the firewall security available, but everything he needed was right here. With so much at stake tonight, Adka felt the need to reassure himself, so a review of his agent's more than adequate qualifications was in order.

The file started as early back as 1979. Even in childhood, it was clear this agent was destined for brilliance. Adka read with interest and visualized the incident as it had played out. This child had reported its own parents to the authorities for their treachery.

Such a demonstration of loyalty to the State did not go

unnoticed.

Adka's thoughts were jolted back to the present by a light flashing on his phone: the secure line. Finally. His agent was checking in with an update. Even though the line was secure, he knew this conversation would be short and cryptic. He picked up the receiver and spoke his customary welcome.

"Adka."

"Fax located. Target's intentions are 90 percent as suspected, interception of package imminent. Target is not alone. Elimination of target a possible necessity. Out."

CHAPTER 18

TRAVIS SAT SHELL-SHOCKED in the passenger seat of the Toyota Camry Sonia had stolen in Jersey City. How much more bizarre could the day become?

He stared at I-95 as it was swallowed up by the beam from the car's headlights. Sonia gunned the vehicle southward toward Travis's home in Baltimore.

Somebody slap me and say it's all a bad dream.

There are people who want to kill me over a fax I've never seen, sent to me by a Secret Service agent I've never met. I've now committed two crimes. Meanwhile, my mom's on her deathbed. Possibly. He reached for his cell phone to call the hospital then realized the phone was gone.

A casualty of this ridiculous fiasco! Travis punched the door handle. *Not that using the phone would have been a wise idea anyway. God, I'm living out some sort of movie. This is the kind of shit that only happens to other people!*

I don't deserve this.

Nonetheless, whoever these people were, whatever they wanted with him and why, this was reality.

They do really want me dead.

Travis's thoughts snaked back to the reason he wasn't dead already: Sonia. A resourceful New York Secret Service field agent who'd compromised her career and freedom to find her missing brother. He suddenly felt deeply in her debt. The mixture of emotions now fueled his resolve to find the truth, for both their sakes: sympathy and gratitude for Sonia and anger over the gross injustice and endangerment of his life.

Travis felt a fire stoking inside of him and felt strong, in control. Sonia had gotten him to safety. Now it was time to step up and do what he did best: solve mysteries. Travis knew his life literally depended on it.

He removed his unforgiving leather shoes to relieve the pain from the blisters he'd begun to feel now that the adrenaline in his system had ebbed. He stretched his feet into the warm air circulating in the passenger seat foot well. Considering a two-hour journey lay before them, he thought a welcome rest was now in order, leaving his analytical mind completely unabated.

He turned toward Sonia, breaking the silence.

"Thank you."

Sonia's cold expression thawed begrudgingly as she gave Travis a forced smile, silently staring out into the darkness.

"I know you're worried about your brother, but we'll figure out what this is all about. For both our sakes," Travis said.

Sonia's face turned cold again. Colder than before.

"He's dead. I just feel it. And these bastards are going to pay. Whatever it is they're after, we're going to find it first and finish what he started. Do you have any more thoughts about what the hell this is about?"

Travis fell silent. Sonia's training seemed to have kicked in. Perhaps how she's dealing with the trauma.

No looking back—let's just get on with this.

"These people will be waiting for us at my house. It's an obvious move we're making," Travis said.

"I know that. And they probably know that we know that too. But leave it to me."

"What about this car? Sooner or later someone's going to report it stolen and…"

"My countermeasure will serve us well for long enough."

Travis nodded with raised eyebrows, his confidence in her boosted by the ingenious escape from Ellis Island. Back in Jersey City, Sonia had told Travis to look out for a popular car with a common color, nothing that would stand out to any pursuer. The white Toyota Camry they spotted was perfect. The hard part was finding another car of the same model. Sonia still hadn't explained why.

"All we know this far is the fax your brother sent me was titled 'Lancer's Nemesis'—a clear reference to JFK's assassins. Your brother was protecting the vice president and possibly discovered something incriminating." Travis paused as this recap of events only served to remind him he was missing major parts of the puzzle. *Keep an open mind.*

Travis knew this was the best course of action when seeking a 'Eureka moment,' as his late father called them. Travis's dad, Pete, would watch old black-and-white Sherlock Holmes movies with his son and explain how Sherlock's signature method of solving the crime was the best way to solve any problem. Holmes and his long-suffering assistant, Dr. Watson, would find nothing but dead ends and it would seem like their investigation was going nowhere.

Holmes would make it his first task to fill his head with as much data as possible relating to the crime and suspects. Then he'd let his subconscious do the rest. The thing about the subconscious mind was that it didn't work on demand—it worked its creative magic when at rest. From the frustration of getting nowhere, Holmes would decide to go to the theater (to relax), much to Watson's outrage and bewilderment. Then sure enough, during this period of relaxation, the lightning bolt came to him. Pete Travis reminded his son that the scientist famous for saying 'Eureka' was Archimedes, whose discovery of displacement theory came to him while relaxing in the bath.

"Until I get more data, I think I should finish explaining who really killed JFK and why," Travis said.

Sonia pushed back into her seat. "So the OSS, who would later become the CIA, inherited Soviet double agents who were already in that Russian turncoat army?" she said.

"That's right. And this is extremely relevant to JFK's murder because it epitomizes Soviet intelligence tactics at the time of his death and to this very day," Travis said.

"To this day?"

"Sure. Governments may come and go but intelligence services remain. The current Soviet intelligence agency—the SVR—was merely a name change for its sinister predecessor, the KGB, and before them was the NKVD. Threats may heighten and lessen, enemies may come and go, but the people, tactics and motives remain."

Travis proceeded with the story: "In 1947, the CIA was born as an autonomous agency with absolute power to conduct covert operations of its own accord. National Security Council Directives allowed Dulles—the founder—to operate clandestinely through businesses and charities, thus keeping the power of this agency under wraps. The newly born CIA picked up where the OSS left off, Soviet double agents and all."

"And what was this Orlov guy doing throughout all of this?"

"Igor Orlov? He, and other Soviet double agents, were prospering and up to their same old tricks by wheedling their way into the newly formed American intelligence agency. He would blackmail Russians into joining the Americans and becoming double agents for the KGB. Then turn them in to the Americans as spies, thus increasing his credibility greatly."

Their stolen Toyota passed a rest area. Travis noticed a parked state trooper vehicle and turned his head toward the speedometer.

"Don't worry," Sonia assured looking in her mirror, "I'm under the speed limit."

Travis calmed himself and went on with the story, trying to steer things back toward his objective: explaining who killed Kennedy and why.

"Anyway, in 1959, the CIA launched what was their most covert and daring mission to date. In the creation of a new unit—codenamed ZR/RIFLE—the seeds of Kennedy's murder were planted."

"What was ZR/RIFLE?"

"ZR/RIFLE was designed for the sole purpose of 'wet operations.'"

"Wet operations. You mean…"

"Wet ops, Sonia, are best known as *assassinations*. Through the CIA, ZR/RIFLE put America in the murder business."

Travis was puzzled. Why hadn't Sonia reacted to this revelation? He turned to face her. She was looking in the rear view mirror.

"Shit. That cop's behind us."

Travis felt his gut tighten.

CHAPTER 19

GREEN STARED AT THE LIGHTS of downtown Philadelphia as his jet darted back to D.C., pounding his clenched fist on the white leather armrest at precisely two-second intervals.

The satellite phone ringing snapped him out of his fixation.

"What is it, Norm?" Green questioned, his eyes shiftless.

"Sir, none of the car rental companies in Jersey City report anything."

"As expected, they stole a car then?"

"No stolen cars reported yet, sir, but that would seem a likely scenario, yes."

"And highway patrols have been advised?"

"Yes, sir. Nothing reported yet. Nothing from Newark airport either."

"There won't be. They stole a car and they're headed for Travis's home. This girl he's with knows what she's doing. Any ID on her yet?"

"No, sir. The Liberty Park officer's description was just too vague. Sir, I have the cryptologist here on the line for..."

"Put him on and thank you, Norman," Green beamed. He was charming to those who encountered him briefly.

After a second pause, a much younger voice came on the line.

"Hello?"

"You come up with anything on that fax?" asked Green.

"Still working on it, but it's obvious Travis doesn't have the Apollo File."

Apollo File: the codename Green had given to the information Leblanc had stolen.

"Agreed. Okay. On my way back to Washington, so we'll speak then."

Green hung up and nodded to himself. Travis and the girl were headed for certain elimination now.

Casualties of war.

The satellite phone rang again.

"Green."

"Sir, it's Croghan." The voice was hesitant, nervous.

"What is it, Croghan?" Green spoke as if Croghan was his long-lost son: warm, concerned. Manic.

"Sir, I have some information I think you might...something I didn't enter in the report...and I apologize in advance..."

"Spit it out, goddamn it!" Green shouted, accompanied by a fine spray. The volcanic change had come.

"The apartment Leblanc escaped from—the one belonging to a Cathy Perkins?"

"Yes, I read the report. I know who she is."

"Sir, one of my men has since told me that during the debriefing of Perkins she said Leblanc had come around asking for a stamp."

The line fell silent. *Why's this little prick telling me something so triv...*

What did Leblanc want a stamp for? Unless...

"Croghan, you'd better thank God you told me this when you did. If I'd have found this out too late, you'd be hanging by your balls from the Washington Monument!"

"Yes, sir."

"I'm coming back to Washington to handle this myself. Give me Perkins's address and get your guys away from there, do you understand?"

"Yes, sir. And once again my humblest…"

"Don't you *fucking* screw up again, Croghan!"

Green wiped his ear with a white silk handkerchief then dialed his personal assistant, Norman. Travis and his little girlfriend could do whatever the hell they liked, although they'd die doing it.

I'll get the Apollo File before they do.

CHAPTER 20

TRAVIS FELT HIS TOES burrow into the Toyota's carpet.

The New Jersey state trooper's black Dodge Stratus closed in the rear view mirror, the officer probably running a check on the license plate this very minute.

"What are we gonna do if he pulls us over?" Travis shrieked.

"Don't worry, I doubt he will," Sonia said.

Doubt?

The state trooper pulled out and drove alongside them.

Shit. This is it.

Sonia looked ahead with her left arm on top of the door, driving like it was a Saturday night cruise. Travis watched the trooper out the corner of his eye, expecting the flashing blue lights to burst out any moment.

The police vehicle paralleled them for a few seconds, and then accelerated away. Travis exhaled and looked at Sonia, her face unruffled, nonchalant.

"I guess this car hasn't been reported stolen yet?"

"Wouldn't matter if it was," Sonia said, shrugging.

Travis had seen that expression before—back on Ellis Island. "Alright wise-ass, what did you do this time?"

"Switched the license plates with that other Camry we found. Even if this was reported stolen already—which I doubt—they'd be looking for a different license number."

"Right…but now there's some guy with the wrong license plate and when he realizes…"

"Yeah, right. And how often do you check the rear of your car to make sure your license plate is the correct one? Even so, we'll need to switch this car soon."

Travis couldn't resist touching her: just a platonic pat on the shoulder to congratulate her. She was beautiful and brilliant. Watching her drive had been a distraction the whole ride.

It felt good to touch her. She barely noticed.

Not long after entering Delaware, Travis noticed a highway sign. This section of the interstate was the John F. Kennedy Highway. It made Travis wonder how the death of one man had such a lasting impact on a country.

He knew there had to be some kind of link between JFK and this mystery, and continuing a review of the story might serve him well.

The signpost gave Sonia the same idea. "So, let me just go back and make sure I have this straight," she said. "The CIA, formerly the OSS, was deeply penetrated by Soviet agents from its inception after the war, due to the OSS recruiting Nazis on the run or Nazi sympathizers, several of whom were actually double agents already working for Soviet intelligence, the most prominent of which was Igor Orlov?"

"Yep, that pretty much sums it up," Travis nodded.

"And they formed a special operations unit within the CIA codenamed ZR/RIFLE, which carried out assassinations. That's the story so far, right?"

"Yes."

"So, ZR/RIFLE couldn't have been much of a secret with all the Soviet infiltration," Sonia said.

"No, it certainly wasn't, and that's highly significant for the purposes of this story, as you'll see."

Travis smiled to himself. At times like this he missed his old teaching job. His students would devour this sort of unorthodox lecture, much to the disdain of the History department faculty. It was Travis's regular delivery of strange but true history that kept his students spellbound. He once told them about the British claim to California: Sir Francis Drake's original claim to California in 1579 in the name of the Queen had never been challenged and the British never ceded California. The kids were hooked. Travis's open mind, unique investigative skills, and obsessive dedication to finding the truth meant his views often clashed with accepted history. He had had more than the odd tussle with historians in his investigations, particularly on archaeological matters such as the Pyramids—supposedly tombs for pharaohs and yet no human remains had been found in them. The mummies were not in the Pyramids. On many occasions, the established and accepted view made little sense, but because 'the experts' on the subject had spoken, it was 'case closed.'

Sensing Sonia's impatience with his pause for reflection, Travis continued his story. "And even worse was that we had virtually no intelligence coming our way of any use. The double agents in the 'Agency' were feeding us nonsense from Russia. The Berlin Wall went up as a complete surprise and one would have hoped that with a CIA base in Berlin at the time, we would have had at least an inkling of what was going on. In the late fifties, over one hundred CIA agents were either arrested or shot by the KGB and no one could figure out what was going on or why."

Travis noticed the green hills of Maryland in the darkness and felt a surge of relief, whatever ordeal lay ahead of them. He paused for breath and carried on.

"In fact, Berlin was seen as such a failure, the CIA effectively pulled out of there, the secret war in Europe lost. They had to retreat to a battlefront much closer to home—Cuba. In 1959, Fidel Castro and Che Guevara overthrew the corrupt Batista government. Only after the coup were American suspicions confirmed; Castro was a Marxist who'd allied himself closely with the Soviet Union. Ninety miles south of Florida the Communists we all feared were right on our doorstep."

Travis caught Sonia staring at him.

He continued.

"After the Berlin defeat, the CIA was determined not to lose this battle. They began recruiting anti-Castro Cuban refugees from Miami University and set up a base there—code-named JM/WAVE. The plan was to invade Cuba in 1961 at the Bay of Pigs using these anti-Castro Cubans—supported, trained and equipped by JM/WAVE. Out of this recruitment, brutal right-wing groups emerged, such as the Alpha 66 Commandoes."

"Okay, I've heard of that incident. The Bay of Pigs was a defeat too, wasn't it?" Sonia asked.

"Totally, and for the same reasons as always."

"What do you mean?"

"Castro's intelligence service—the DGI—was trained by the KGB and worked closely with them. Due to the Soviet double agents penetrating the CIA, the DGI knew all about JM/WAVE. The DGI used the same Chekist tactics taught to them by the KGB to infiltrate the CIA Miami base. Several of these recruited Cuban refugees calling themselves 'anti-Castro activists' were actually DGI agents."

"Jesus!"

"Yes, quite. The Bay of Pigs defeat was attributed to Kennedy not providing enough air support, but the reality is that it failed before it even started due to Soviet and Cuban double agents infiltrating the CIA."

"Wasn't Kennedy the president then?"

"Yes. Because of the Bay of Pigs debacle, he and his brother Bobby decided to take firm control over the CIA."

"So did the Kennedys put a stop to all the covert activity?"

"On the contrary," Travis said. "There were *more* covert operations under the Kennedys than any other government before or since. In fact, the Kennedys found a new mission for ZR/RIFLE. It was renamed 'Operation Mongoose' under the Kennedys."

Sonia thought she understood the game now. Travis would pause, relishing the suspense, and she would have to beg for more.

The reality was that Travis was simply in shock and not exactly firing on all cylinders.

"The purpose of that operation being?" she asked.

"To assassinate Castro. The order was given that no U.S. citizens should be used as assassins so it could not be directly linked back to the White House. But of course, Cuban and Soviet intelligence knew all about 'Mongoose' right from the start because of their penetration into the CIA. Needless to say, all attempts to kill Castro 'mysteriously' failed."

"So how did they try to kill him?"

Travis shook his head in disbelief and scoffed under his breath. "They contracted the Mafia. The mob had been losing revenue from their Cuban casinos ever since Cuba was taken over, so they seemed like a good choice," Travis said sarcastically. "Anyway, things came to a head over Cuba in 1962 when Khrushchev, now the Soviet leader, decided to ship several nuclear missiles to Cuba."

"The Cuban Missile Crisis," Sonia deduced.

"That's right," Travis paused, recalling his father telling him how people across the country dug bomb shelters in their backyards during the crisis. "An extremely aggressive move which brought us to the brink of World War III. The missiles were no doubt shipped in at Castro's request to defend him from American aggression evidenced by the Bay of Pigs and Operation Mongoose. Thankfully, JFK played the situation calmly and made a good call using diplomacy. It's probably this event that gained Kennedy a reputation as a man of peace. Kennedy and Khrushchev made a secret agreement to resolve the crisis—Kennedy agreed to cease attempts to assassinate Castro, and the Soviets would remove the missiles from Cuba. JFK ordered a cessation of Operation Mongoose. But a lot of people had a lot to lose by a cessation of hostilities between the superpowers. Peace wasn't in everyone's best interests, especially the CIA. Not long after relations warmed between Kennedy and Khrushchev, on November 22, 1963, Kennedy was shot dead in Dallas and there were several shots, not one."

"I know. I've seen the Zapruder Film plenty," Sonia said.

It was then that Travis remembered he was talking to a Secret Service agent whose training would have included watching the assassination of JFK home movie by Abraham Zapruder. Zapruder happened to be filming Kennedy's motorcade that fateful day in Dallas. The Zapruder Film, as it came to be known, showed several shots. Travis always contended that that's how any sane, unbiased individual would see it.

"And there was a massive cover-up afterwards by the CIA and FBI, right?" Sonia said.

"Yeah. Course there was, and the Secret Service was involved too—at least two agents lied to the Warren Commission. The Warren Commission was set up to investigate the murder of JFK and its final report was riddled with inaccuracies and inconsistencies."

"Most people realize that now," Sonia said.

"But not for the reasons most people think," Travis said, craning his head toward her.

"What do you mean?"

"There were two reasons for the cover-up. The first was the incompetence and string of negligent mistakes made by the FBI, CIA and Secret Service, none of which wanted to look bad and lose funding or, worse, have their top people fired. The FBI and CIA had extensive files on Lee Harvey Oswald before the shooting. Everything was interlinked and the CIA certainly didn't want its involvement with the mafia and Operation Mongoose getting out! The FBI knew that the Alpha 66 Commandoes—who'd directly threatened Kennedy—were in Dallas and they didn't alert the Secret Service. The motorcycle formation escorting the motorcade was wrong and the Secret Service agents didn't even notice. And those protection agents were too slow to react after the first shot, of course, you'd know that already, Sonia."

"Yes, but go on," Sonia said, seeming to brace herself, her hands both at the six o'clock position of the steering wheel.

"It was a security screw-up in every way imaginable. The route was widely publicized in advance and should never have included that sharp turn: slowing the motorcade down almost to a standstill. The forward team neglected the grassy knoll and book depository as possible sniper's perches and, as a result, spectators were wandering around freely. The night before the assassination, nine of the Secret Service agents on Kennedy's watch were out drinking late and..."

"I know! My father was one of them, okay!" Sonia blurted.

Jesus, what did she say?

"I'm so sorry… I had no idea," he replied. "Your *father* was one of those agents?" *She may be able to help solve this puzzle better than I thought.*

Sonia's eyes glistened with tears. Then she composed herself, sniffing. "It's okay," she said. "Carry on. You said there were *two* reasons for the cover-up. What was the second?"

"Okay. The second reason the government covered up what happened was to protect the identity of the assassins from the American public."

"Why?"

"Because there would have been mass hysteria if the public had known who really did it."

Still a few hundred yards from Travis's house, Sonia tugged the steering wheel right, into a dark, tree-lined dirt track. Ruxton Village is quiet even in the day, but by night, you can hear the critters rustle in the bushes.

They're in my house.

Travis gazed out in every direction like this place was all new to him: a stranger in his hometown. The glaring injustice was never more apparent.

"I'm on foot from here. Draw me a layout of your house and where the fax machine is. And tell me the name of your neighbor. You stay put," Sonia said, handing Travis a paper and pen from inside her navy suit jacket.

Almost frozen from the surrealism of the moment, Travis nervously penned a layout for her. "How are you gonna get to the fax memory?" he asked.

"No time to explain. You done?" She had one shapely leg already out of the car.

Even at a time like this, Travis found her distracting. *What is it with guys?*

"Here." Travis handed the map to Sonia. Then she swung the other tantalizing leg out and dashed into the darkness. *We have to get a copy of that fax.*

"Change of clothes would be nice while you're there," Travis muttered to himself.

CHAPTER 21

TRAVIS CLUNG TO THE STEERING wheel with clammy palms, rolling his jaw. The warmth from the car heater clashed with the cold Maryland night air outside, steaming the windows.

Nothing would have felt better than to walk into his home. The whole journey there, Travis imagined that was exactly what he would do when he got here. Stupid, of course.

He sat in the driver's seat staring at the RPM gauge hovering at idle, doors locked and lights off. Without a key, if the engine stopped they'd have no transportation.

And what about poor Rosemary!? Is she still in there or in some damp cell somewhere? This is all too horrible.

How dare these people do this! I'm innocent, my home has been invaded and my life endangered by...my own government.

Travis jerked his sleeve back to check the time. Eightfourteen. His eyes locked on to the gold Seiko watch his father gave him. His mom was only a short drive south of there—Harbor Hospital, downtown. *So near. If she dies, does that make me an orphan?*

Travis blew out like he was trying to extinguish birthday candles. To hold back the tears forming in his eyes.

Hard to believe that only several hours ago he was telling the story of himself and his father in the Bermuda Triangle on national television. An involuntary flashback of a sultry evening on a Miami vacation came into view. It seemed indulgent, but comforting.

"Alright, Danny Boy, let's do it—let's solve this mystery together. But let's do it properly or not at all. Look at the facts and keep an open mind." Pete Travis had once said to his son. As an Army Intelligence Corps veteran, he always did things properly and honestly.

Young Daniel and his father read about all the strange occurrences in the Bermuda Triangle and their possible explanations, but Daniel still had questions.

A trait time would not erode.

"Dad, there's really no mystery is there?"

Daniel felt let down by all the sensational writings about some kind of mysterious force in the Bermuda Triangle scuttling ships and downing aircraft, when the truth lay in a number of geographic anomalies in the area. Natural phenomena such as 'blue holes'—a hole in the ocean bed producing fresh water—had caused several ships to lose buoyancy. The Bahamian Islands from the air all look very similar and the lack of navigational aids there meant many, usually amateur, pilots had gotten lost. Trouble being that if you went too far east and missed the islands altogether (perhaps after getting into a cloud), there was nothing but water and only a question of time before the fuel burned up. Throw into the mix how prone the area was to violent and sudden electrical storms and you had a recipe for disaster.

"It appears, based on the evidence, there's no mystery, son." What started out as a little father-son bonding had taken a darker turn. Pete Travis saw himself in his son's probing eyes, recognizing the path the young man had ahead of him.

"So why do some people make it appear that way then on TV and newspapers?" Daniel said with a perturbed frown.

Pete Travis understood he was about to chip away a little of his son's innocence. "That's why it's important to look at the facts and keep an open mind, son. Look, newspapers and TV shows are a business and therefore need to make money. They do that by giving people what they want to hear."

"And people want to hear that there's a mystery? Don't they want the truth?!"

Pete sighed mightily. "Well, not always, no. People sometimes want to believe there's something out there that's bigger than they are, somehow controlling everything. It's like a replacement for having a mom and dad when you're an adult. I guess people find comfort in that thought. They want stability and comfort most of all."

Travis began drawing star shapes on the steamed-up window of the stolen car. "Get the facts, son. Then eliminate the impossible. Whatever's left after that has to be the answer, however improbable or inconclusive that may be." Whether his dad got that from a Sherlock Holmes movie or the Intelligence Corps, Travis didn't know or care. Dad was Danny Boy's hero regardless.

He then remembered his dad say something profound and chilling, the expression on his father's face cold, as if he had personal experience of it: "Remember, Daniel, when human beings are involved in solving any mystery, you have to ask: 'Who would perpetrate this and, most importantly, what was their motive? Who stands to gain the most from this?' Answer that question and you're on the right path." In retrospect, Travis appreciated his dad's advice for the future, possibly sensing his son's newly devoted passion for uncovering the truth behind a mystery.

A rap on the window jolted Travis out of childhood reminiscence, making his heart miss a beat.

Sonia.

She was waving a piece of paper.

CHAPTER 22

As THE LANDING GEAR of Green's jet clunked down on final approach to Washington Dulles Airport, his satellite phone rang for the third time.

"Yes, Norman."

"Everything's ready for you, sir."

"I'll come by on the way."

"Yes, sir. I have the file on Perkins waiting for you. Leblanc's apartment building mailbox was checked as you asked and nothing was found."

"Okay. Are Croghan and his men out of Perkins's apartment now?"

"Yes, sir."

"I'll see you in my office shortly then."

Click.

Christ. Leblanc's old man would be turning in his grave if he knew what his son had done, Green thought. *To think of the things his old man must have had to keep his mouth shut about, only for his kid to do the exact opposite.*

Green recalled how agents on JFK's watch had to turn a blind eye to the parade of call girls and actresses being snuck into the White House. Agent Seymour Hersh later admitted how on several occasions, JFK visited the Mickelson Gallery in Washington to have professional photos taken in various positions with naked women. All this as well as his ongoing affair with actress Judith Campbell, a mistress who was also having an affair with Sam Giancana—the very same mafia boss the CIA had hired to kill Castro.

What a mess.

But Leblanc's father kept his pie-hole zipped. A man of honor.

He'd be turning in his grave!

Green thought of his own father. Green had had little tolerance for his parents, even as a child.

CHAPTER 23

SONIA TORE OUT of Baltimore in a southerly direction at Travis's instruction, while he studied the fax under the dim interior light of the stolen Camry, one hand on the handle above the window as Sonia pushed the car to its limit. How Sonia had retrieved a copy of the fax had gone unnoticed in light of the anticlimax Travis held in his lap. *This is the reason for all the trouble?!* The piece of paper had little on it, but its link to Travis was painfully obvious:

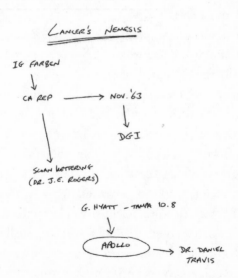

Just as Rosemary had said, there was a fax and "Lancer's Nemesis" was written as the heading, indicating all this really was about Kennedy's killers, assuming there was no other interpretation of "Lancer."

Travis's analytic mind went into overdrive in the mobile study of the stolen Camry.

Leblanc and Sonia were siblings and their father was on Kennedy's protection team. And the date on the fax, Nov. '63, the month and year Kennedy was killed. And the reference to the DGI—the Cuban Intelligence service that thwarted Operation Mongoose.

Did Leblanc uncover something about JFK's assassination while on protection duty of the vice president and somehow record it? While a record of something incriminating seemed likely, Travis still found it hard to envisage a JFK cover-up being discussed by modern politicians—politicians who didn't even know the truth about the assassination themselves or even give a damn about it.

Travis glanced up at the downtown Baltimore skyline now looming (*Mom's close*) while Sonia squinted against the interior light. She was silent.

C'mon, think. He rapped his knuckles against his forehead.

Travis knew incorrect conclusions in any analysis were usually the result of an unsound base theory. All too often people make their mind up about something based on a hunch or a whim and only look for facts that fit that theory. Many academic works were written that way. Travis knew all too well; a historian or a scientist would refute or discredit a piece of evidence conflicting their work, especially if it meant ripping up their data and starting again. It was more about gaining credit and Nobel prizes than truth.

Build a theory on a faulty premise, faulty foundations, and it's a house of cards.

Travis's determination not to fall into that trap, especially when his life depended on a sound conclusion, was almost debilitating. Believing this was about JFK's killers felt all too easy, but thankfully, some words seemed out of place on the page, giving some doubt.

"Sonia, do any of these words and phrases mean anything to you: 'CA Rep., IG Farben, Sloan Kettering, APOLLO, Dr. J.E. Rogers and G. Hyatt Tampa 10.8.'?"

"No, can't say they do. Isn't 'CA' is an abbreviation for California? And 'Rep.' an abbreviation for Republican? 'Apollo' was the space program that Kennedy started, and the last part sounds like a person named Hyatt who lives in Tampa. Maybe someone who met my brother on October the eighth, '10/8,' which is today's date. Where are we headed?"

Travis pretty much concurred with Sonia's first impression against his own. *Need more information.*

"Washington. Get back on I-95 South," Travis said.

"Okay, but why?"

"I've a friend there, someone we can trust," Travis said. "George Kramer taught me most of what I know about the Kennedy assassination. Maybe he knows of a link here. At least it'll be a safe place for us to figure out our next move."

"How come this George Kramer guy knows so much?" Sonia stopped squinting at the road as Travis switched off the interior car light.

"Remember I told you about the OSS?" Travis said.

Sonia nodded. "Mm-hmm."

"George Kramer used to work for them and then with the CIA where he was once head of Counter Intelligence. A spy catcher. Long retired—here, take a left here."

"And he's still alive?" Sonia questioned, spinning the wheel.

"Last I heard."

Shit. I hope so.

CHAPTER 24

"I SAW THE MOVIE," Sonia said as she snaked the car out of Baltimore and back onto the highway. "The JFK assassination, according to that New Orleans District Attorney..."

"Jim Garrison," Travis interjected.

"Yeah, him. According to him, in that film, it was a coup d'etat. Kennedy was ousted from power by his own men because he was against the Vietnam War."

The fax tortured a distracted Travis.

"That's the general consensus, in conspiracy theory circles anyway, and probably so with the 80 percent of Americans who think it was a conspiracy. Even the U.S. government admitted in 1977 that there was a 'probable conspiracy.' And yes, there *was* a coup d'etat behind the assassination."

"But you said the CIA, FBI and Secret Service covered up the truth to protect the American public from the true identity of the assassins so they didn't freak out. In other words, the CIA, FBI and Secret Service didn't do it?"

"JFK was killed because of a coup d'etat, but not an American coup d'etat."

"Go on," Sonia said, her jade eyes fixed on the illuminated asphalt ahead.

Travis reclined his seat a couple of notches for the hourlong journey to George Kramer's home in D.C., and capitulated to Sonia's incessant questions.

"Remember I told you about the assassination division of the CIA codenamed ZR/RIFLE?"

Sonia nodded. He continued, "Well, the Soviets were doing the same thing themselves. In 1954 Khrushchev became Secretary General of the Communist Party and created the KGB—the Russian intelligence service most people recognize, with its infamous 'sword and shield' emblem you see on the cover of so many spy novels. Anyway, Khrushchev wanted fast results from the KGB and gave them authority to kill anywhere in the world as long as the assassin and the weapon couldn't be traced back to the Kremlin. They used non-nationals to carry out wet operations."

Sonia looked uneasy, but Travis was used to it. Everyone to whom he told the story became defensive and unsettled.

"The key issue is what was going on in Moscow in the early sixties because that's where the coup d'etat was taking shape. In 1959 Khrushchev gained power of the Communist Party. Before and during the Cuban Missile Crisis, Khrushchev was extremely belligerent toward America. In one famous speech he actually said, 'We will bury you.' But after going to the brink of war with Kennedy during the Cuban Missile Crisis, things started changing drastically. Kennedy and Khrushchev began negotiating secret treaties to reduce tensions; one of these was Kennedy's promise to cease Operation Mongoose."

Sonia recapped: "Mongoose: the CIA plot to assassinate Castro."

"Yes. In return, Khrushchev took the missiles out of Cuba. The two of them even set up a hotline to speak to each other. Back in Russia, Khrushchev set about making internal reforms to the Soviet Union, one of those reforms being to slash the benefits provided to upper echelons of the Communist Party. The Kremlin hardliners didn't take kindly to Khrushchev selling out Russia by going soft to the West, and removal of their privileges was the final blow. They wanted to oust him and so a plot was hatched between Leonid Brezhnev and a very powerful woman named Yekaterina Furtseva—she effectively held power over the KGB. In the wake of the Cuban Missile Crisis, Khrushchev had gained a reputation as a statesman and his relationship with Kennedy is what gave him his power, so the conspirators believed. This relationship and reputation had to be destroyed if their coup was going to be successful. Little did they know that they were about to be handed an opportunity on a plate to do just that."

"So where does Lee Harvey Oswald fit into all this?" Sonia asked, snatching a glance at Travis while she drove.

"Good point. Okay, so I've now set the stage for Oswald who was nothing more than a pawn in the big game. People yammer on about whether Oswald worked alone or not, but that's a convenient diversion from the real issue: who Oswald was working for and *why*?" Travis paused to let the importance of what he just said sink in.

"Let me tell you the facts about Oswald. In 1959, Oswald walks into the U.S. embassy in Moscow to formally announce his defection to Russia. Unbeknown to him, he was speaking to a CIA agent. Oswald repeatedly insisted that his defection be formally noted and that he would divulge all his secrets to Russia. His exact words were, 'I served in Japan. I was a radar technician.' The CIA agent reported that he felt the whole thing was extremely rehearsed and contrived and he filed a report stating as much."

"Didn't that report alert the CIA?"

"Unfortunately not. This is an example of why there was a cover-up: to hide government incompetence when JFK was shot. Had the report been followed up on, alarm bells would have rang because Oswald's file would have shown he was formerly serving for Marine Squadron One at Atsugi Air Base near Tokyo. This very fact lies at the heart of the JFK riddle."

"Why was that so important?"

"Atsugi Air Base was where the U2 spy planes were based. As a radar technician, Oswald would have known everything the enemy needed to know to shoot one down. Trajectories, runway lengths, the whole nine yards."

"Yeah, I read about one being shot down before JFK was killed?"

"That's right. The U2 spy plane was a major headache for the Soviets and a major success for the CIA who ran it. Operating at around 50,000 feet and out of missile range at that time, the Russians had no idea how to stop them, so they freely flew over Russia and wherever else they pleased taking pictures. That's how the missiles in Cuba were discovered. Khrushchev told the KGB to end the U2's reign of superiority by shooting one down. As we now know, they succeeded."

"How?"

"Oswald's friends on the base reported that he often went on leave in Tokyo. He confided to one friend that he'd met a hostess from a high-class strip joint called the Queen Bee Club and had fallen in love with her. Oswald brought her back to the base one day to prove to his buddies she was real. They reported being knocked out with how beautiful she was. Oswald's salary could in no way have paid for this girl's company."

"So he meets a hooker in a bar? So what?"

"What I'm about to tell you is a little known, yet verifiable fact: five of the girls who worked at the Queen Bee were on the KGB payroll with a mission to recruit any personnel from Atsugi who would be able to divulge information about the U2. Actually, the Queen Bee Club was one of the KGB's most intensive recruiting stations. The CIA later learned that several CIA officers, and even U2 pilots, had struck up relationships with girls from that bar. Little coincidence that a U2 was finally shot down in 1960."

"So Oswald was recruited by the Soviets?"

"Hard to believe that he wasn't when you know about his relationship with the girl in the Queen Bee Club. His 'defection' to Russia came two years later and despite popular folklore, he was quite the marksman. The standard line we've been fed is that Oswald was this disillusioned young man, an idealist, trying to make a name for himself. Oswald said after his arrest, 'I'm a patsy.' Does that sound like the words of an idealist who wanted to make his mark on the world? The official line from the Soviets about what happened to Oswald in Russia was that they sent him to Minsk to work in a radio factory, as they failed to see any value in his defection. Yet he enjoyed a luxurious apartment and the same pay as a senior Soviet officer, with perks only enjoyed by senior party members. Needless to say, Oswald being useless to them was a well-constructed cover story."

"So what *did* the Soviets have in store for Oswald?"

"In…1961, yes 1961, Oswald went back to the U.S. embassy in Moscow and claimed he wanted to re-defect back to America, now with his new Russian wife, Marina. None of this adds up, does it?"

"Well, no. Not really."

"Do you recall our friend Igor Orlov and his adventures? Remember Chekist tactics of confusion and deception?" Sonia nodded. "And doesn't all this sound like those same tactics?" Sonia nodded again.

Travis smiled and continued. "Once the Oswalds were in the U.S., the FBI intercepted a letter sent by Marina Oswald to an undercover KGB officer in Washington. More letters followed. Oswald's mother asked him why he had come back, to which Lee replied, 'Not even Marina knows why I returned.' In the summer of 1963, Oswald got on a bus to New Orleans and established himself as a Castro sympathizer, whilst becoming involved with an *anti*-Castro movement in New Orleans—again, classic Chekist tactics of misdirection and deception used by Russian agents. The important thing this: why did Oswald start associating himself with Cubans at all?"

Sonia drove on with a blank look on her face.

"Remember I told you how Khrushchev and Kennedy made a secret deal after the Cuban Missile Crisis? And how part of that agreement included Kennedy agreeing to stop trying to assassinate Castro through the CIA's Operation Mongoose?"

Sonia nodded.

"Well, the CIA *didn't* pull the plug on Operation Mongoose."

"So the CIA broke the agreement?"

"Yep. And, of course, the Soviets would've known this because the CIA was so heavily infiltrated with Russian double agents. *That's* why you have to go back to the end of World War II to understand who the designers of JFK's assassination were."

"I see the relationship. The CIA inherited Soviet spies from the OSS, which meant that the CIA breaking the agreement to stop Operation Mongoose was known to the Russians. But how does that relate to Kennedy's death?"

"Good point. The Soviets then told Castro that the CIA was still trying to kill him despite Kennedy's guarantee that they would stop. In fact, Brezhnev and Furtzeva took great pleasure in delivering the news to Castro."

"Right. Like you said, Cuba and Russia were Communist allies."

"Yep. And how do you think Castro reacted when he heard the news?"

Sonia didn't get a chance to answer.

"Slow down!" Travis shouted.

"What?! What is it?" Sonia said, jamming her foot on the brake. The car behind them swerved around, sounding their horn.

"Asshole! Not you, that guy," Sonia said. "What is it?"

Travis's eyes locked on a road sign pointing to various hotels as they entered the outskirts of D.C.

Sonia tracked Travis's stare.

"Hyatt!" Travis said. "'G. Hyatt' from the fax. It's not a person. It's a hotel…Grand Hyatt. The Grand Hyatt in Tampa. Something happened there today involving your brother and we need to know what. Your brother's apartment is in D.C., right?"

"Yes. Potomac Plaza."

"Great. We'll go there before Kramer's house. We have to find out what happened in that hotel."

CHAPTER 25

"LET THE CRYPTO GUY IN, Norm, then I'm going to Perkins's and Leblanc's apartments," Green said over the speakerphone.

The cryptologist swaggered in with a file under his arm. Young and casually dressed, he seemed out of place. He had black hair, round glasses and freckled skin. He was like a fully-grown Harry Potter.

"Good evening," he said, scuffing a chair across the carpet before slouching into it.

"But…where's Magglio?" Green demanded.

"He's sick. I'm his assistant…"

"Sit down. What have you got?" Green wasn't interested in knowing his name. *Magglio had better be dead or dying.*

"Well, this fax isn't so much a matter for crypto."

"Why not?" said Green, frowning. This kid was treading a thin line.

"There're no codes or anything on it. Just looks like a lot of research notes and a message from one person to another—Leblanc to Travis in this case."

"Right, like you said before. Travis probably doesn't have this Apollo File…"

"It's likely that Travis will return home to try and get a copy of this fax and then go looking for the file. But you surely know that anyway."

Did this kid just interrupt me?

"Yes! I know that. And don't interrupt me." Green's big smile softened the blow, as he straightened the blank legal pad in front of him.

"Assuming your trap succeeded, and Travis and the female did in fact go to his house to retrieve a copy of the fax, I imagine they'd be heading to this Dr. Rogers mentioned on the fax. It's very possible they didn't get a copy though."

I don't like him. But I need him. Fucking Magglio.

Green bit his lip, but the darkening anger showed in his eyes. "Explain these other references on the fax, and you'll address me as 'sir.'"

Green's mood change and laser-beam glare made the crypto's head jerk back. "Sorry...*sir.*"

CHAPTER 26

Alex Adka suddenly felt nauseous, not sure if it was the forsaken dinner or the agent biography before his eyes.

He unfastened the top button on his white silk shirt and plodded to the small refrigerator in his elegant study. It tastefully blended into the environment with a wood-paneled door. He pulled out an ice-cold bottle of vodka and a jar of pickled herring. He poured himself a glassful, straight, and returned to the file to read more.

After becoming an operative in the intelligence and espionage division, Adka's agent had been put to work immediately; the talent demonstrated during training accelerated his agent to the spearhead position of the mission. The agent became a double agent, penetrating foreign intelligence.

Adka had to stop reading when he got to the part about torture.

His private phone rang, catching him mid-sip.

"Adka."

"Progress continues slowly. Confirm all objectives remain."

"Confirmed."

CHAPTER 27

SONIA SWUNG BACK into the car, after stopping for water and snacks at a gas station on the way to Potomac Plaza—Leblanc's apartment building.

Travis clutched the public phone cable like it was a lifeline.

"Good evening, Grand Hyatt Tampa."

"Yes, I'd like to speak to a guest…Clinton Leblanc," Travis said.

There was a pause on the line while the operator looked in the room directory. "No one here by that name, sir."

"Oh, my…Clinton said he would definitely be there. Did he check out already?"

"Hold, please."

The mention of this hotel with today's date, in the position it was located on the fax, was an obvious key to the puzzle.

A new, officious voice came on the line—a different person—clearly the operator's supervisor by her tone.

"Sir, that information is confidential."

Travis had to think on his toes. After a pause he put on a deeper voice. Travis was mid-sentence when he realized how dumb he sounded.

"Good job, ma'am. I work for the Secret Service and I'm pleased to see you're sticking to security protocol." He swung the mouthpiece away, wincing at the blatant lie he'd just fed her, hoping she'd swallowed it.

The voice came back singing like a bird. "Thank you. Yes, the conference has been quite a success so far. I've never seen anything quite like the security here, but we all totally understand. You can be assured of more of the same tomorrow for the last day. We do hope you choose us next year also. May I assist you further, sir?"

"No, thank you, and you have a good night. Carry on," Travis said, trying to curtail exhilaration in his voice.

He hung up the phone and redialed the same number. His heart banged away, a cocktail of fear and anticipation. No need to feign a 'Secret Service voice' on this call. Just as well. Travis was a lousy impersonator.

"Good evening, Grand Hyatt Tampa."

"Reservations, please."

'On hold' music played, its mind-numbing indifference insulting the critical nature of the situation, while Travis drummed his pointer finger on the earpiece.

"Reservations, good evening."

"Yes, I'd like to book a room for tonight please."

"I'm sorry, sir, the hotel is completely closed to the public today and tomorrow for a private function."

"What about the bar and restaurant? And fitness club?" Travis said, the banging in his chest increasing.

"I don't think you understand, sir. The hotel, its facilities and grounds are all very much out of bounds to you and any members of the public."

Bull's eye.

Travis slammed the phone down, staring at it.

A car engine revved. He looked around. Sonia gestured to get back in the car.

Travis swung in. Sonia squealed away, then veered into

a parking space a few hundred yards along the street, hiding from the glare of the gas station lights. The Washington Monument stood above them judgmentally, as they sat, drank and ate.

"Any luck?"

"Possibly," Travis said. "I need to get the number of an acquaintance, but I'm sure the Grand Hyatt Tampa is the location of the Bilderberg Conference this year." Travis winced to even say the word "Bilderberg," but events today had conspiracy written all over them.

"What's a Bilderberg conference?" Sonia said. "And who's the guy you need to call about it?"

A mouthful of Doritos garbled Travis's voice. "Each year a select group of politicians and industry leaders get together; they're the most powerful people in the world. The first meeting was about fifty years ago at the Bilderberg Hotel in Holland. That's how these meetings got their name."

"So what's the big deal about these conferences? Sounds pretty dull," Sonia said.

"Of course, you're not a protection agent—you're a field agent—but I imagine your brother knew all about them."

"No doubt."

"The strange thing about these Bilderberg conferences is their secrecy. Armed guards are everywhere and a luxury resort, usually in a small town, is completely off limits to the public."

Travis found it hard to conceal his outrage at the most ominous fact about Bilderberg conferences. "The media know about these secret conferences—the collection of people who attend quite literally control the world and its economy—and yet it's never reported. Officials from news networks have attended before but abide by strict rules of a confidentiality agreement. The guy I need to call is Wally Pritchard. He's a conspiracy theory buff who manages to find out where these conferences are being held each year and sometimes even smuggles himself in by posing as an attendee. It shouldn't be difficult to find his number. Right now let's get to your brother's apartment and see what we can find there. If my suspicion is right, I'll bet your brother was on protection duty at a Bilderberg conference today and 'broke the code,' as you guys say. He blew the whistle on something he overheard. But why?"

"Alright. Let's see what we can find at his place then."

The car sped down Constitution Avenue, west toward Potomac Plaza.

"You still haven't concluded the JFK story," said Sonia.

"Relax. We'll go to George Kramer's house after your brother's and you can hear the rest from the man who explained it to me," Travis said, his head awhirl with possibilities of what the Bilderbergers could have said today. And how much of it Leblanc recorded.

CHAPTER 28

Mrs. PERKINS OPENED THE LATCH with a quivering hand to see a gentleman with slicked-back gray hair and deep black eyes dressed in a crisp, black suit. He had a broad smile across his face: like a crocodile.

"Yes?" she answered.

"Good evening, Mrs. Perkins. I believe you were expecting me? My name's Dwight Green."

"Oh, yes, dear. Please come in," she said, easing the door back. "Come through to the kitchen. Can I get you a coffee or something?"

"No, thank you, Mrs. Perkins—you've had enough to do tonight already, haven't you?"

Green set the charm control to maximum as he practically danced her into the kitchen. He averted his eyes from the junk that clogged this shabby apartment.

Let it go—I'll be out of this little shit-hole soon enough.

Mrs. Perkins smiled, though weary, and welcomed the bit of gossip tonight's events would create. A re-run of *Murder She Wrote* was competing with their conversation, but she didn't seem to notice.

"Well, yes, I have had a lot going on tonight. It's all been quite confusing. Is Mr. Leblanc in some kind of trouble? Your men wouldn't tell me. I find it hard to believe, dear…although they do say it's always the quiet…"

"Don't you worry about poor Mr. Leblanc. I just need to ask you a few questions to wrap all this up and then you can get some rest. Would that be okay?" Green eased into the seat next to her at the shaky breakfast table, stroking her arm with his manicured hand.

"That would be fine, dear, yes."

"Excellent," Green said. "You said Mr. Leblanc asked for a stamp when he knocked at your door?"

"Yes, that's right. He seemed to be in quite a hurry."

"I'm sure he was, Mrs. Perkins. Did he say what he wanted it for exactly?"

"No. But he was very insistent that he needed one."

"And did you find one for him?"

Mrs. Perkins paused for thought, rubbing a tired eye with her wrinkled fingers. "Well no. I was looking in the drawer where I usually keep the stamps but couldn't find one and... then your men knocked at the door. You know, that Croghan person really could improve his manners," she said, wagging her pointer finger.

"I quite agree, Mrs. Perkins, and I apologize for his conduct, but he had your safety in mind at that time. Could you show me the drawer you were looking in?"

Mrs. Perkins pushed herself up and shuffled toward the middle drawer underneath the counter top. Green trailed her.

"This one."

"May I?" said Green, gesturing at the drawer.

"Please do."

Green scoured the drawer but couldn't find any stamps. He recoiled at the disorganization. *Doddering old coot.*

"Mrs. Perkins, are you sure you keep stamps in this drawer?"

"Well, usually, yes. As it happens I have a stack of mail I

need to send over there and...oh!" Mrs. Perkins's gaze froze at the letters ready to be mailed next to the toaster on the counter.

"What is it?" Green said, his eyes panning.

"I had a priority mail envelope right there."

Green's hairline moved back from his crinkled forehead, his worst fear confirmed: *Leblanc mailed the Apollo File to someone.*

Little asshole's parting shot. Damn!

Green fought the urge to slap her. "Why did you have a priority envelope here?"

"Oh, silly me! I went to the post office today to mail some important investment forms by priority mail, but I forgot the forms. They would be closed soon, so they said to buy the postage on the envelope and post it in the box outside later on. I hadn't got round to it when Mr. Leblanc came. He took it, didn't he? How rude."

"Mrs. Perkins, this is important: what else did Mr. Leblanc say? Did he give you any indication at all about where he might be sending whatever it was he wanted a stamp for?"

She truly wanted to help this charming man. "We talked about my husband, Art, who died of Parkinson's a while back and that's really it, I think. I'm sorry I can't be of more help."

Green's eyes searched hers.

"Are you sure I can't make you anything, dear?"

It was time to go across the hall to Leblanc's apartment.

"Mrs. Perkins, thank you. You've been a big help."

CHAPTER 29

TRAVIS AND SONIA EDGED OUT of the elevator on the third floor of the Potomac Plaza, heading for Leblanc's empty apartment. *Sonia, Leblanc's sister, shouldn't attract too much attention,* Travis thought.

It seemed like a comfortable place to live. There was a homey quality about the corridor and the faint smell of cooking accentuated it. The whole sensation provided hollow comfort.

"So, we're looking for 309, right?"

"Number 309," Sonia said, looking unsettled.

Her brother may well have been killed here, Travis considered.

"Are you okay?" Travis said, patting her back.

"I'm fine."

The entrance to apartment 309 looked as foreboding as death's door. Sonia raised a slender finger to push the buzzer, but then paused and spun around to Travis, her eyes meeting his. A misty sea of green confessed nothing.

"Listen," she said. "Something doesn't feel right. Go and wait by the elevator."

"Why?"

"The front door's in perfect condition."

"And it shouldn't be?"

"I doubt the people who raided this place would've knocked and there's no evidence of a forced entry. I'm going to ring the buzzer and then break in. I'm still unknown to anyone who answers. If anyone answers."

"Okay. I see," Travis said, turning to retreat back to the elevator.

Halfway there, he looked back and caught her watching him. Sonia looked back at the door and pushed the buzzer.

As Travis approached the elevator he heard the door open to 309. He spun on his heels to watch and eased himself against the wall.

Someone's in? Sonia looked just as shocked.

Travis could hear the conversation clearly.

"Hello?" came the irritated voice from behind the door.

Sonia looked at the pudgy man standing at the threshold holding the door. He wore khaki pants and a white T-shirt with a napkin stuffed in the neckline, very much at home.

This wasn't Leblanc.

She glanced at the number on the door, bemused and alarmed. "This is 309 right? Apartment 309 Potomac Plaza?"

"Yes. Can I help you?" the man said, clearly annoyed by the unannounced guest.

Travis watched Sonia take a step back. She looked spooked.

"This is Clinton Leblanc's apartment. He lives here and has for the last two years," Sonia stammered.

"What are you talking about? I'm not Clinton Leblanc— my name's Beckshaw—I don't even know a Clinton Leblanc. I've lived here for three months. Who are you? What's this about?"

Sonia caught a glance of some mail inside, on the table next to the door. Sure enough, it was addressed to a Mr. G. Beckshaw. She stepped away, her face matching the color of her eyes. Beckshaw closed the door, still confused.

Travis and Sonia stared at each other with open mouths

from opposite ends of the hall, telepathically sharing the confusion and horror.

Across the hall, inside Mrs. Perkins's apartment, Green tried to politely refuse the last ditch hospitality, which had suddenly erupted from his host.

"No, thank you, Mrs. Perkins, really...I'm not hungry."

"Well, okay. Have a nice evening, Mr. Green."

"I will. You too. And thanks again...we'll be in touch." *Jesus, shut the hell up already.* Green backed into the corridor, brushing himself down and wringing his hands.

He waited for the door to close behind him, then turned and walked down toward Leblanc's apartment.

Outside 309, he saw a beautiful, black-haired girl. She turned and her eyes met his.

CHAPTER 30

TRAVIS PUSHED AWAY from the wall to make himself look less suspicious. The smartly-dressed man walking down the corridor hadn't noticed him, anyway—he'd walked out of his apartment facing away from Travis, then looked straight at Sonia and froze. *Why was he walking away from the elevator?*

The guy was in his late fifties with slicked-back gray hair, tall build. He was dressed in a tailored black suit, with a distinct air of authority about him.

Sonia's eyes didn't once dart over to Travis. *To avoid drawing attention to him,* he thought.

Time seemed to grind to a halt.

Sonia composed herself and politely said, "Good evening," as she started walking back to the elevator.

The man replied, "Good evening," still studying her, standing perfectly still.

As Sonia passed the man, he continued. He seemed friendly enough.

"Were you here to see the gentleman in 309?" the man inquired. "I've been wondering what's been going on over there tonight. Do you know anything?" The man seemed genuinely concerned.

"What did you hear?" Sonia asked.

Travis watched as Sonia stopped next to the man, clearly

seeing him as a way of gathering more information rather than a threat. Travis stood at ease now, relaxed and hopeful Sonia would get something out of him.

"Well, there was quite a bit of commotion," said the man, hesitating as he felt for something inside his jacket. "I heard a lot of shouting. How do you know the man in 309?"

Sonia's face didn't flinch.

"It's all very strange," she begun. "The guy in 309 says he's been living there for months, but he's not the person I came to see."

"Well, maybe you got the apartment number wrong," said the man.

"Let's go and see the doorman together. I'll ask if he knows anything."

The man then gestured toward the elevator and Sonia followed, thanking him. Travis stepped forward in preparation for the inevitable introduction from Sonia as the man looked in his direction.

In that instant, as the man eyed Travis, his face paled but quickly recovered. The look didn't last more than a second, but it seemed odd. *He probably wasn't aware I was standing there all this time*, Travis thought.

"Good evening, sir," Travis said.

"My friend," Sonia interjected.

"Good evening to you, sir," said the man. "Pleased to meet you." He looked genuinely pleased, sporting the widest smile Travis had ever seen.

He pushed the call button for the elevator and stood in silence, smiling at Sonia and Travis. He scanned Sonia intently. They smiled back and looked away. His presence sucked the energy from the air.

"I hope you can find out what happened here tonight," said the man. "I was just saying to your...girlfriend?"

Travis and Sonia looked at each other uncomfortably and didn't reply.

"Sorry, your friend, that we'll go and ask the doorman if he knows anything."

"You're most kind, sir," said Travis. "Sorry, I didn't catch your name?"

"Croghan. Dwight Croghan. And it's no problem, really."

The elevator chimed open and the three entered. The man pushed the button for the lobby nodding at Travis and Sonia, respectfully.

The doors began to close when a cragged hand appeared between them. The doors bounced back open.

Mrs. Perkins.

"Mr. Green! So pleased I managed to catch you."

The man's face dropped, visibly shocked and agitated. "Could this wait, Mrs. Perkins? I have an urgent matter to attend to right now. As I said, I will call you, now good night." He then took her by the arm and moved her out of the elevator, holding the doors open with the other hand.

She looked shocked.

The odd change of character didn't go unnoticed by Sonia. Travis saw a cynical twinkle in her eyes and watched her surreptitiously study the torso of the man. She gave Travis a glance.

The man spoke to them through that ridiculously large smile. "Poor old dear. I'm doing her will for her and she really won't stop worrying about it. She hassles the crap out of me about it and she's hopeless with names!"

Travis forced a chuckle.

The man's smile shot into a tight pout.

As the doors closed again, Sonia pushed the button for the next floor down—number two.

"I know someone on the second floor," she said, raising her eyebrows. "I'll see if they heard anything and meet you in the lobby...Mr. Croghan, was it?"

Now Travis knew something was wrong. Sonia didn't know anyone on the second floor, unless she hadn't told him.

"Sure," said the man.

The mechanical hum of the elevator was the only sound. The atmosphere turned cold and the journey to the second floor lasted forever.

The doors opened with a chime and Travis and Sonia exited. "See you in the lobby then. Really appreciate your help, sir," said Sonia.

"Oh, you're welcome. See you in a second," the man replied.

As Travis and Sonia crossed the threshold to the second floor, Travis watched in slow motion as the handle of large pistol came down on the back of Sonia's head.

She went down.

Travis looked back at the man, to then stare down the barrel of the very same gun, just inches from his face.

CHAPTER 31

TRAVIS FROZE. His breathing was an uncontrollable flurry. He squeezed his eyes shut.

I'm dead. I'm dead.

But no shot rang out.

His eyelids sprang open. The man's black eyes were locked on Travis's. Sonia lay on the carpet groaning and immobile. Barely conscious.

Green handcuffed her with his gun still locked on Travis.

"You stupid asshole," Green hissed at Travis through gritted teeth. "Where the fuck is it? You wanna die, you little prick?!" He shoved his gun further into Travis's face.

"Sir...there's...there's been a huge mist—" Travis stammered, eyes wide with submission.

"What? You think I'm stupid? You treacherous little bastard! Where is it?"

"I don't know anymore than..."

"Last chance before you have a little accident. You heard of the Patriot Act? I can do what I want with you. No lawyers. *You little shit!* Where did Leblanc send the goddamn file!?" Green screamed, rubbing his thumb over the handgrip of the gun.

Travis held his hands in the air, silently. Fear melded with bewilderment as the horrifying realty cut deeper into his mind. *This guy's above the law.*

Green persisted. "Listen, Travis, I know your buddy Leblanc sent a priority envelope somewhere today, okay? It's over. I'll find the file. Now, you can cooperate and tell me where he sent it and maybe just do some jail time. Or let me find it the hard way and…like I said…I don't want to have to shoot you in self-defense. Understand?"

"I don't know! I've never even met this Leblanc! That girl's his sister and she asked for my help." Travis knew he shouldn't feel guilty for telling the truth, but felt conflicted for risking the woman who had helped him escape from Manhattan.

A manic smile transformed Green's face. He tilted his head, toying with Travis: a madman with a gun.

"Dead or alive." That's what they said back at the hotel. Maybe this Green guy won't shoot here, in a public place, but there's no way out. That much is certain—the glare in this creature's eyes—this is personal.

I am not going to die!

Green slithered a hand inside his jacket and flipped open a cell phone, fixating on Travis's head through the sight of the weapon.

"This is Green. Send a car."

Now's the time. He's probably going to want you dead anyway. Travis's trepidation was stilted with his lack of expertise and experience. This was the first time in his life that he'd looked down the barrel of a gun, never mind having such a maniac behind it.

Travis watched Green cry out in pain and surprise. He stumbled back against the closed elevator door then steadied himself.

Life lapsed into slow motion again.

Must have been Sonia. She was still on the floor, trying to get back on her feet, but she still looked out of it. *She must have lashed out, semi-conscious.*

Green dropped his phone and instantly turned his weapon on her.

Something snapped inside Travis. *He's gonna shoot her!*

Travis dived at Green like a school kid in a playground brawl, slamming him back against the elevator doors with a metallic clang.

Green dropped the gun. Travis could smell Green's cologne as he landed on top of him.

Then he felt Green ram a fist into his gut and snarl in his ear, "You fucking little bastard!"

The blow forced Travis down on all fours. He struggled to recover.

Green leapt for his gun. "I'll shoot you both!"

"No!" Travis jerked a leg into Green's path. It intertwined with Green's, tripping him. Green growled with anger as he stumbled, now crawling for the gun.

Survival instinct took over. With a burst of primal rage, Travis jumped to his feet and thrust his heel at Green's back.

It's either me or him.

But Green thwarted the kick, catching Travis's swinging shin and twisting it. Travis's high school tactics were no match. Off balance, Travis went down like a rag doll.

Travis knew he couldn't let Green get to the gun. Sonia had relapsed, groaning on the floor, barely moving, still handcuffed.

Travis rolled over toward Green a few inches away from his gun. Travis wrapped his arms around Green's middle like a tired boxer.

"Get the fuck off me!"

Travis tugged Green away to the side, tightening his bear hug with no clue about what his next step would be. Green's blows were ineffective in this position. Both men gasped and strained.

Once more though, Green's training made up for any strength he'd lost in age.

Green slammed the back of his head into Travis's. The blow hit Travis in the forehead. It was enough to daze him and loosen his grip. Green fell onto his back. Travis dived on him in a last ditch effort, to re-establish the grip on his torso.

But Green's answer was final this time.

He lifted his knee in between their bodies and pried Travis off by a few inches, just enough, then with the other leg, kneed him in the groin and threw him off into the open stairwell.

Travis landed at the edge of the stairs with a painful thud, cracking his head on the concrete step. From the force of his attack, Green fell into the doorway slightly behind Travis, leaving his gun behind.

Everything went dark.

Travis found himself blinking down at the first step with drips of blood quickly forming into a pool of crimson. *His* blood. His head throbbed like a just-rung bell.

Hurried footsteps approached. It was Green, lunging at Travis's battered body, preparing to kick him down the stairs.

This is it—he's going to kill me.

The footsteps stopped. Travis heard a familiar voice.

"Freeze, asshole!" Sonia stood behind Green with his gun trained on his head. "Move away!" Somehow, Sonia had gotten out of the handcuffs. Training? Special equipment? However she did it, Travis felt he could breathe again.

Green shuffled to the side of the stairway with his hands in the air. His expression of shock quickly melted into the reptilian smile. "Don't do anything stupid, sweetheart—you're already in enough trouble and my men'll be here any second."

"I heard him call them," Travis croaked, dragging himself to his feet, holding his bleeding head. Sonia deftly moved into the stairway, the gun on Green.

Green studied Sonia with a glow of realization. It was no longer a secret. She was a highly trained professional. That explained everything.

Sonia yanked Travis to his feet, still staring defiantly at Green. She guided Travis down the remaining flight of stairs as if he was a blind man without saying another word, weapon locked on target.

Green's mad smile broke as he helplessly watched them disappear down the fire escape. "You can run but you two are as good as fucking dead."

"Follow us, you die," Sonia shouted up at him, glaring as they maneuvered away.

Out of sight, Sonia bustled Travis down the remaining staircase and out of the building, all the while hearing the chilling rant of Green echoing down the concrete stairway: "Fucking dead!"

They dashed to the car, as Travis struggled to see through just one eye—the other eye he closed to keep the blood from running into it. Sonia threw him into the passenger seat and climbed through the driver's door, looking back at the exit for Green. He didn't come.

She pounded the gas pedal, speeding the car away from the building, into the night.

Travis slumped back in the seat, holding his head, wondering what sort of injury he'd sustained. He'd never been in a fight. It was an out-of-body experience, like playing a part based on someone else's life.

"You'll be fine," Sonia said, handing him the used napkins from their gas station meal. "Press this against the wound. Which way to Kramer's house?"

Shock gripped Travis's larynx. His pain was overshadowed by disbelief. He couldn't speak.

"Which way?" Sonia persisted. "C'mon, Dan!"

"Second left!" Travis spat out the directions to Kramer's house in a panicking jumble of words. She seemed familiar with D.C.

As his breathing slowed, the questions came. "What made you suspicious of that guy in the elevator?" Travis asked, cupping his eye.

"I saw the bulge of a shoulder holster under his jacket and then he gave us an explanation of what he did for that old woman when we never asked for one. His real name's clearly Green, not Croghan."

"Impressive. How's your head?" Travis muttered. He remembered he wasn't the only one injured.

"I'll live. Just have a headache," Sonia said, rubbing the back of her head. She looked at the blood on her hand and casually wiped it on the side of the seat.

"That son of a bitch tried to kill us back there!" Travis said.

"No shit."

Travis felt violated, as though in some way life from this point on would be irreparably different, even if it all ended well. And that was a big *if.*

"Get us to Kramer's as fast as you can. This thing has to end."

"I'm on it. But if he'd have wanted us dead, we'd already be dead," Sonia said, speeding the car through a blur of lights in central D.C. "We'll need to dump this car far from Kramer's in case Green managed to get a look at the license plate... Left here?"

"Yes," replied Travis, his mind recovering from panic, refocusing. Something Sonia had said just a second ago struck a chord.

"Kennedy's killers did the same, by the way," Travis said to the window, jealously eyeing regular people enjoying regular lives in a downtown tapas bar. It was like seeing the world from behind bars, this stolen car his prison.

"Kennedy's killers did what?" Sonia said.

Travis turned to Sonia. "Kept giving explanations and insisting on their innocence when no one asked." Travis looked out the window again.

"Kramer can finish the story while I make a few calls. I just hope he's in."

God, my head hurts. If Travis had been in any doubt about all this being for real, he now had a physical injury as confirmation. The pain jerked Travis's memory back to something Green had said. *Where did Leblanc send the file? Why did he ask me th…*

Travis turned to face Sonia, his glittering blue eyes full of revelation.

"Your brother sent the file somewhere! That's what…son of a…"

"What?!" Sonia said, glancing at him as she screeched around a corner.

"Green asked me where Leblanc had sent the file…he thinks we're in league with Leblanc and so we must know where it was sent. Green doesn't know where it went. He said Leblanc sent it by priority mail, so it'll arrive a day or two after it was sent, if I'm not mistaken. But where would he send it?"

Eleven minutes later, after abandoning the stolen Toyota about a mile from their destination, Travis and Sonia speed-walked along the row of terraced Victorian-style homes on the northeast side of D.C.

"That's it," Travis said. "Number 8432, Kramer's house."

They marched up the steps to the black front door, hoping the darkened windows only meant Kramer was in bed.

They huddled into the doorway as Travis rang the bell.

Nothing. He waited ten seconds. It felt like ten hours. It would just be a question of time before Green found them.

Still nothing. They were exposed. Green was probably locking down the city this very second.

"What now?" Sonia asked, as if to blame Travis for Kramer not being home.

Travis was out of ideas. "I don't know. We need somewhere safe to..."

The door creaked open and bounced against a heavy chain. From behind the chain, in the darkness, a gruff, elderly voice barked at them.

"Who the hell is that?!"

"Uncle George?"

Sonia gave Travis a puzzled glance.

"Is that you, Danny Boy?" The voice mellowed from delight and surprise.

"Sure is!" Travis burst out.

A fumbling, wrinkled hand yanked at the chain and the door opened. There in the doorway stood a silver-haired man, dressed in a 'Hugh Hefner' red smoking jacket.

"So are you gonna let us in, old timer?" Travis said, trying to mask his urgency to get off the doorstep.

George Kramer grabbed Travis by the ear and pulled him toward his frail form, beaming. "You're not too old for a good kick in the pants, son... I was fighting Nazis when your daddy was in diapers!"

Sonia stared at Travis for an explanation, a thin black eyebrow raised.

Travis glimpsed back at her with a battered and bloody eye as he staggered into the house. "He's an old friend of my father's. Come in."

Sonia followed Travis over the threshold, patting Green's gun concealed in the back of her pants.

CHAPTER 32

FOR THE SECOND TIME TONIGHT, Potomac Plaza Apartments were electrified with Green's men swarming around like ants. One group was taking fingerprints from the elevator as it sat frozen on the ground floor. Puzzled, frightened residents were being questioned in corridors and stairways. Flickering red beams from the Chevy Suburbans parked outside invaded the brown Formica-clad lobby. The murmuring of residents filled the air, impressed with the resources employed to protect the good citizens of Washington, D.C.

Center stage: Green was condescendingly ordering Detail Leader Croghan. "I want those fingerprints analyzed as a top priority. I need to identify that girl. When'll Sanchez get here?" Green said, stowing his new gun in his shoulder holster and snapping the securing strap over it. He looked like an armed businessman.

"Twenty minutes from now, sir."

"Good. Did any of the residents get the license plate of the stolen vehicle?"

"Yes, sir. Washington P.D. are on it now."

"Excellent. And both Dulles and Baltimore airports are alerted?"

"Yes, sir. They're not going anywhere."

"Alright. Carry on. I'm going for a walk. And don't you

ever hold any details back on me again or I'll end you. Do you understand me, Croghan? Perkins and that stamp information were crucial!"

Green marched out of the building, waving off the agents guarding the lobby. They were practically bowing as he brushed past them. No doubt these grunts were wondering what he was doing here, but Green knew his presence would ensure a thorough job. Grunts were there on a need-to-know basis.

Green turned left toward the Potomac River, retracing the route Leblanc had taken earlier that day. But all he could see was Travis and the girl. *That fucking girl.*

Damn!

They'd already be dead if he hadn't tried to get info out of Travis. In hindsight, he should have shot them both dead. Upon reflection, Travis and the girl couldn't know where the file was—or what were they doing there at Leblanc's apartment.

The rules had changed.

Leblanc sent the file to someone by priority mail. As long as I get the file before Travis...or take it from him...I don't care whether they live or die.

Green gazed at the heavens, scouring gray clouds for divine inspiration. God was on his side. There was still hope. The file could arrive at its destination tomorrow—Tuesday— or most likely Wednesday. *There was still time...*

Green's cell phone chirped.

"Green."

"Sir, it's Norman. No luck with the USPS. Priority mail goes into the system too quickly to recall and there're just too many priority envelopes leaving D.C. at any given time to narrow it down enough."

"Okay. Can they narrow it down to all priority mail dispatched from a single post office if we give it to them?"

"They seem pretty vague on that. It's late and the senior personnel aren't in. I can try again tomorrow, sir."

"Alright, Norman, stay on it."

Click.

Tracking Leblanc's final footsteps, Green came face to face with the Watergate. Foreboding to most, its dark history was meaningless to Green. He'd seen enough of politicians' power-hungry antics firsthand to know that the episode with Nixon was nothing. The only difference was that Nixon was dumb enough to get caught.

Green broke into a jog as he weaved through Virginia Avenue traffic, replaying Leblanc's final moments.

Then he saw it.

Fluorescent tubes beamed down: it might as well have been the Lord's light shining on the only mailbox between Potomac Plaza and the river. Green stopped short and sat on the shrubbery wall opposite the box, never taking his eyes off it.

It was a waiting game.

Right now his cryptographer was working on a shortlist of destinations for the file, taking into account all of Leblanc's contacts and the content of the fax sent to Travis. His assistant Norman was trying to negotiate a shortlist of destinations from the USPS. And soon he would have an ID on the girl.

But Green wasn't very good at waiting, particularly when he knew his own existence swung in the balance.

Jerking up onto his feet, Green began to pace in an exact square on the sidewalk next to the mailbox, his cleft chin pointing down at the chalky paving stones.

Must be an exact *square.*

After the third lap, the ritual halted and his glazed eyes

locked on to the full moon as it burst out from behind a wispy layer of cloud.

Fuck. Let's do it.

Green snatched out his cell phone and opened the battery pack, revealing a prepaid and untraceable SIM card hidden on top of the one regularly plugged into the phone.

He switched them over, making the next call untraceable—a trick he'd learned not from Agency training, but from his adulterous bitch of an ex-wife. The Agency was his family now. That's why he made this call. To protect his family.

A deep, Eastern-European accent picked up on the first ring: "Yes?"

"I need to meet up…at the usual place," Green said.

CHAPTER 33

THE RICH ODOR OF PIPE TOBACCO and expensive brandy permeated every nook of Kramer's house. The walls were clogged with sepia photos of a much younger George Kramer. Four glass display cases lined the hallway, each one bursting with curious weapons and emblems. One case sported a large metal Nazi eagle captured from a stronghold in World War II, as the inscription on its stand noted. Another case boasted an old KGB badge.

Kramer was a hunter and these were his trophies.

The last glass cabinet housed an array of devices, which could only be described as antiquated spy gadgets. A small Minolta camera and a cigar lighter with a magazine of two bullets protruding from its base were among the best.

With his cane in one hand and Travis's arm in the other, Kramer ushered them into a room with a wall-to-wall bookcase groaning with piles of good cloth and leather-bound books and a blazing fire.

"I'll get you two a brandy and then you can tell me how you got that bump on your noggin," Kramer said to Travis, totally calm about what was clearly an emergency. "Take a seat."

Travis forced a smile, picking up on a joke from his childhood. "Why, don't you…"

"…like them?!" Kramer and Travis said in unison. Kramer was jovial, but Travis just the opposite. Kramer poured the brandy into three tumblers.

The old guy's attempt to settle Travis's nerves had failed badly.

Sonia grimaced to emphasize feeling like a third wheel.

"This is Sonia," Travis said.

Planting himself in the soft leather sofa, Travis felt the presence of the framed photo on the mahogany side table burn into the left side of his face. He wasn't looking at it, but he knew it was there.

Pangs of guilt flooded through his gut as he craned his neck around and absorbed the picture of himself standing next to Kramer at his graduation. He'd been gone too long from this welcoming museum.

As Travis watched Kramer stagger along, steadying his beverage, guilt faded to sadness. *We're getting older.*

Despite his age, Kramer's faculties fired on all cylinders. His worldly experience and appreciation for cutting to the chase meant the customary exchange of greetings, introductions to Sonia and the obligatory 'catch-up' were forsaken. Travis's injury, coupled with the unannounced arrival late at night, wasn't lost on this canny old relic of wars gone by.

Travis welcomed the Hennessy XO into his throat: a warming elixir. He lowered the glass and felt the weight of tonight's burden ease with a long exhale.

Sonia downed hers in a single gulp and placed the glass on the side table.

With one corner of his mouth screwed up, Kramer stared at Travis like he still saw him as a little boy hiding something.

"Alright, Danny, what's going on? Sonia, dear, there's a first aid box in the kitchen if you'd like to dress this poor guy's wounds."

Travis nodded at Sonia and gestured to the kitchen.

When she'd left the room, Kramer winked at Travis and

slapped him on the knee.

"Cute broad, Danny. Where'd you find her?"

Travis sniffed a laugh at Kramer's jibe, then relayed the strange events of the last twenty-four hours to his old 'uncle' while Sonia treated his beaten brow. As the words poured out, Travis could barely believe he was talking about himself.

"Danny, you're a goddamn trouble-magnet. You always were ever since you were a kid. Jes—" A deep, chesty cough tamed Kramer's jesting rant.

Travis flashed a gaze at Sonia, feeling chastised and hoping Kramer wasn't going to dredge up any embarrassing childhood memories. Thankfully he proceeded.

"Alright, so let me get this straight. Some guy called Clinton Leblanc—this young lady's brother and a Secret Service agent protecting the vice president—sends you a fax making references to Kennedy's assassins even though you don't know him. And this guy Green has been chasing your ass ever since, because Leblanc may have overheard and or recorded something he shouldn't have and seems to have sent a copy of that to somewhere unknown. And this Green thinks you're in on the whole thing."

"That just about sums it up, sir, yes," Travis said. Kramer's simplistic recapping made the whole thing seem fictional, but the throbbing above Travis's eye was real enough. Despair ground through him. It felt like they were getting nowhere and the walls were closing in.

Somehow, tonight, he'd become a fugitive.

"Let me see this fax then," Kramer said, holding out jagged, arthritic fingers.

Sonia handed Kramer the fax. They both watched in silence while Kramer produced his half-moon reading glasses. He read through it, emotionless, apart from a furrowed brow.

"Would you pour us some coffee, dear? It's in the kitchen ready to go," Kramer said without looking up but obviously talking to Sonia.

With raised eyebrows, Sonia stood up and swaggered back into the kitchen. Somehow, Kramer's misogynistic tendencies could be forgiven—a privilege that comes with age. Travis tried to hide his smirk with his hand.

She strutted in a minute later and handed some hot black coffee to Kramer. He accepted it without a word, still eyeing the fax:

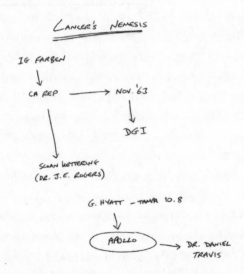

Kramer's eyes stuck to the page. "And this reference to G. Hyatt and Tampa, you say this was the place and date where this incriminating conversation was probably overheard?"

"Yes…I believe so. I need to make some calls to be sure," Travis said.

"You can help yourself in just a second, Danno… You also, I take it, intend to contact this Dr. Rogers guy?"

"Of course," Travis replied, gulping the last of his brandy.

Kramer's eyes hadn't looked up once. He began muttering under his breath. "IG Farben…IG Farben…IG Farben…son of a bitch!"

Kramer's sharp gray eyes met Travis's, his face confused. Sonia and Travis sat forward, hoping he'd put some light in their darkness.

"I'll tell you what I know," Kramer began. "Tell you all I can about what's on this page, but I gotta tell you, not everything stacks up. This here: 'Lancer's Nemesis' rather dramatically refers to Kennedy's killers, as does the reference to 'November '63'—the month and date JFK was shot. And the 'DGI'—the Cuban Intelligence Service fits the bill. But 'CA Rep.' and 'Dr. J.E. Rogers' mean nothing to me with regard to JFK's shooting—and that tells me we're missing something."

Travis nodded, delighted with Kramer's corroborating his suspicions even if it was bad news.

"Apollo?" Kramer continued with his detective voice. "The position and context of this word suggests it's merely the name of the objective—perhaps simply a codeword for an operation. Maybe even the name of the incriminating recording of Leblanc's. As the lovely Sonia could tell you, those Secret Service guys would have a codeword for taking a dump if they could."

Sonia giggled at the truth behind Kramer's joke. Even though the Secret Service obviously didn't have a codeword for using the bathroom, there was a codeword for just about everything else.

"Apollo. First thought is the Apollo Space Program. Kennedy started that of course..." Sonia began.

"What?! You think all those dumb conspiracies about the moon landings being faked might be true? No, it's not about the space program and I'll tell you why in a minute," Kramer said, peeling the half-moons from his eyes.

"Apollo: the Greek God of Truth," Travis said.

"Broaden your scope, Danny! Greek Gods often had *multiple* things they were the Gods of. Apollo was also the Greek God of medicine and healing. Doctors take the Hippocratic oath to always act in the best interests of their patients, and that used to mean swearing by Apollo."

Confusion ruffled Travis's face. "So what's the relevance of medicine and healing?"

"Exactly my point," Kramer said, waving a crooked finger like some decrepit lawyer in a courtroom. "This fax doesn't make *any* sense. It's talking about two different things altogether."

"Not if you take it as meaning Apollo the God of Truth. This was Leblanc's simple reference to the truth coming out about JFK or most likely something related to the assassination," said Travis.

A wicked grin tightened Kramer's jowls. "You think that way because you don't know about *IG Farben* and *Sloan Kettering*."

The back of Travis's neck prickled. He felt Sonia jerk forward on the couch. "And you do?" he said.

"Yes. Firstly, Memorial Sloan Kettering is a very old and famous hospital in New York City. A friend of mine who had cancer ended up there. So, that's the second medical reference if you count Apollo."

Travis began to appreciate Kramer's confusion over this fax. "So what about IG Farben?"

Kramer frowned as he pushed a feeble breath out. Suddenly this friendly old guy's face had morphed into that of a cold and hardened warrior about to relay something he'd tried to put behind him. An old war wound had just been re-opened.

"IG Farben was originally an extremely powerful German pharmaceutical cartel. Which is the *third* medical reference here. IG Farben was around before and during World War II and based in Frankfurt. They manufactured Zyklon B gas…"

"The gas the Nazis used to exterminate Jews," Travis blurted out. Travis knew there had been a powerful pharmaceutical cartel that supported Hitler's rise to power, but the name of it had only just become apparent. "That was IG Farben?" he asked Kramer. "The one who helped sponsor Hitler?"

"It was. And here's how I know about them: near the end of the war, American bombers were leveling German cities and infrastructure as a prelude to invasion. The famous one thousand bomber raids—many made by daylight."

Both Travis and Sonia nodded like schoolchildren in their favorite class.

"Frankfurt was no exception. I mean that place was smashed because it was an industrial powerhouse. Well guess what? American bombardiers had strict orders from us OSS guys *not* to hit the IG Farben building."

"What's the reason that building was spared then?" asked Travis.

Kramer leaned forward and tapped Travis on the knee. "Remember, Danny, how I told you about Operation Paperclip and Operation National Interest?"

Sonia interjected. "Yes, he told me. The OSS operations to recruit Nazi scientists and spies, even the really evil ones."

Kramer's eyes pierced Travis's. Travis knew that look—he'd seen it as a child when Uncle George read him the occasional ghost story at bedtime. Kramer was about to tell him something new.

Something dark.

"Paperclip and National Interest were both conceived by the OSS from their post-war headquarters: the IG Farben building in Frankfurt, on the thirteenth floor. But officially, there was no thirteenth floor in that building."

CHAPTER 34

"WE'VE FOUND THE STOLEN TOYOTA, sir!" Croghan cried out across the lobby of Potomac Plaza.

Green shot to his feet from a scuffed mock-leather couch he was resting on after his walk. Sanchez had finally showed up with the facial recognition software and Green was describing the girl with Travis.

"D.C. police just radioed in," Croghan said with hope for redemption after the whole Perkins stamp incident.

"Good. Start sweeping the area. Conduct discreet inquiries. They won't be far from the vehicle. And I want updates on all stolen vehicles in the city as they come in just in case they switched cars!"

Green sat down hard on the couch to see Sanchez's computer simulation of the girl protecting Travis.

"No...the nose was thinner at the bridge," Green said.

Sanchez made some adjustments. Green was being careful only to select characteristics that were 'nodal points,' so the computer could create a 'face-print.' The software needed fourteen to twenty-two nodal points; nodal points included distance between eyes, width of nose and depth of eye sockets.

"That's better...and a shade darker on the hair...and slightly shorter."

More adjustments.

The process continued tirelessly until Green found himself staring at a photo-like image of the girl. Green slapped Sanchez on the back like they'd just made a business deal and gave him the smile.

"That's it! That's her. Send that off along with the prints from the elevator to biometrics and see what comes back."

Sanchez scurried off, cradling his laptop.

Croghan approached Green, this time much more quietly. "Sir, I have your car outside and Meyer is waiting in it as requested."

"Thank you," said Green, turning to the exit. "Call me the second anything comes back on the photo and the prints."

"Yes, sir. And should I get her face and Travis's on the D.C. police wires with an order to apprehend?"

Green stopped in his tracks, frustrated by Croghan's request. Despite it being the obvious choice, the delicacy of the situation tied his hands once more. "No, Croghan, and don't question me, just do it!"

"Sir."

Green's driver swept open the black sedan's rear door and Green stepped in to find Meyer, a dark-haired, dark-skinned man dressed in a tailored suit. Green clunked the door shut and handed the driver a scrap of paper with an address on it. The car screeched away.

"Meyer, thank you for joining me." Under these disconcerting circumstances Green knew he had to play this carefully, at least to begin with.

"No problem, really. I would have come sooner only I didn't have cover after Leblanc went missing earlier."

"I understand. Thank you. Now, you were Agent Leblanc's junior partner on protection duty for Vice President Cooke down in Tampa?"

"Yes, sir." Meyer nodded once.

"So now we have more time, why don't you tell me your side of the story again, and what alerted you to tell me about the security breach? What exactly happened at that meeting?" said Green.

CHAPTER 35

"WAIT A MINUTE," said Sonia, perched on the edge of the leather couch. "So you're saying the OSS—the predecessor to the CIA—had links with IG Farben, the pharmaceutical cartel that sponsored Hitler and gassed the Jews? That's why Farben's headquarters in Frankfurt was one of the few still standing after Allied bombings and why that became the OSS headquarters for rescuing Nazis after the war?"

Kramer patted the book he'd brought down from his personal library. "Unless several Senate and House Committee reports from 1928 to 1946 are total falsehoods, yes." He offered the book to Sonia and Travis at an open page with a photograph of the Nuremberg Trials, demonstrating IG Farben's management of Auschwitz.

Kramer continued, "People yammer on at dinner parties about how terrible the Holocaust was without even knowing what was really behind it. Few realize that in the twenties and thirties, eugenics, a pseudo-science that inferior races should be segregated so as not to infect the gene pool of the more intelligent, was actually sponsored by the U.S. government and taught in American universities. So no surprise that American interests got behind IG Farben."

Kramer took the book back and explained his previously highlighted sections. "IG Farben was formed in 1926 by a Swiss banker and a German industrialist. By World War II it had become the most powerful cartel in history with interlocking agreements with over two thousand companies worldwide, including many American companies such as Alcoa, Dupont, Proctor and Gamble, Ford Motor Company, the list goes on. It actually outright owned Bayer, Bristol-Meyers and Squibb pharmaceutical, all the big pharmaceutical giants and this is why I say IG Farben on that paper is probably another medical reference. You know, people think all these companies actually compete against each other in the consumer's interest but nothing could be further from the truth."

Sonia and Travis acknowledged him with slow nods, drinking it all in.

Kramer flipped through a few pages. "The largest of these marriages between IG Farben was with Standard Oil, owned by the Rockefeller Empire."

Kramer fluttered through some more pages.

"Ah, now this is interesting and indicative of Farben's power: before and during World War II, if an American newspaper was unfriendly to Hitler, IG Farben's partners and subsidiaries had a contract to withdraw advertising from the offending paper. Is it any wonder it took so long to convince the American public to join the fight against Hitler?!"

Travis shook his head. "And that's how media was, and is, controlled by big business. No network or newspaper is going to run a story which adversely affects one of their commercial sponsors."

"That's just the reality of the world," said Kramer. "Anyway, what else have we here? Mmmm…okay, the story continues…before and during World War II, millions of

American investors' dollars went to IG Farben via investment banks like Goldman Sachs. Ford Motor Company in Germany supplied Hitler throughout the war effort. Before the war, IG Farben sold all its foreign holdings to a newly formed company under the same ownership called IG Chemie, but it was based in Switzerland so to appear neutral and avoid any confiscation of assets. Then that company changed it's name again, this time it was called Interhandel. Six months after the war, IG Farben's factories were operating at full capacity once again and the officers of the cartel walked away from Nuremberg either free or with very light sentences."

Kramer took a slurp of coffee and flicked through a few more pages. "After the war, in 1953, IG Farben's assets were transferred to Hoechst, Bayer and others and in 1962 the Rockefeller empire took back control of the IG Farben linked assets it had before the war. The Rockefeller Empire, through IG Farben, became the dominant player in the American pharmaceutical industry with a variety of lucrative patents."

Kramer closed the book, tapped a middle finger on it and gave Travis a mischievous look. "And I'll tell you something else which just came to me—something not in this book. As you know, Danny, Allen Dulles was leading the OSS and then founded the CIA. Well, his brother John Dulles became a voting trustee of the Farben-controlled American companies."

Sonia spoke up. "So is that the link to JFK then: the CIA involvement with IG Farben? This doesn't make any sense...unless you're saying the CIA killed Kennedy."

"No, it doesn't make any sense," said Kramer. "And the CIA didn't kill Kennedy, contrary to popular conspiracy theorists, though they did a pretty good job of covering it up all the same."

Travis interjected now. "So these pharmaceutical giants we all know today have a skeleton in their closet. So what?"

"Drugs are to America what oil is to the Middle East, Danno: a bargaining chip for world trade and sanctions. It's a big deal."

"Okay, but what's the connection with JFK's assassins?"

Kramer grabbed the fax from where he'd left it on the mahogany side table and studied it closely again. Then he slapped the back of his hand on it, thrusting it at Travis and Sonia:

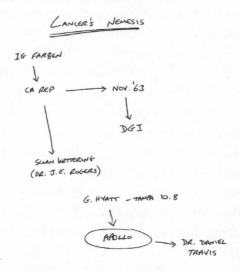

"Okay, so we now know what each of these things on the page are, apart from 'CA Rep,' but there's no obvious connection between them all. It's like the left side of the fax is speaking about medical or pharmaceutical references and the right side about JFK's murder."

"Agreed," said Travis.

Kramer went on. "But the penultimate reference is *Apollo*, which could be a reference to the Greek god of medicine or truth, so that goes either way—JFK cover up or pharma…"

"Wait," said Travis. "What you're saying about the page being divided in two makes sense, and if a link between the two exists, it has to do with this 'CA Rep' because that's where the arrow joins the left and right sides of the page."

"Makes sense," said Kramer with one eyebrow raised.

Travis pushed out his hands and closed his eyes. Kramer and Sonia instinctively knew to be silent and still.

"George, how might Blake have discovered all this information about IG Farben?" Travis asked.

"Well, it's matter of public record, but, if I'm not mistaken, the Secret Service is under the Treasury Department, is it not?"

"Yes, it is," Sonia replied.

Kramer went on. "At the end of the war, all captured files on IG Farben were handed over to the Treasury Department as well as the Department of Justice, so all this lays in Secret Service archives, I imagine."

"Okay. Excellent," said Travis.

The two men beamed at each other in a congratulatory fashion.

Sonia raised her hand like a schoolgirl, complete with the petulant tone as she spoke. "Excuse me, all this is very interesting, but how is any of it going to lead us to the file and get this Dwight guy off our backs?"

"Good point," conceded Travis, pounding his fist on his thigh. "All we can do is keep going. There's more information we need, starting with this Doctor Rogers and finding out what the hell *CA Rep* means. Once we find the link between JFK's killers and these medical references, we might have a better idea."

"He's right," said Kramer. "Daniel, go make some phone calls."

"Yes, sir. You're not on the Internet are you?"

"Internet schminternet. Scoot."

Travis snorted and left.

"Meanwhile, would you finish the story Travis started about JFK's killers?" Sonia begged.

"I'd be delighted to, dear," said Kramer, reaching for his pipe. "If you'll make us all some ham sandwiches. You must be hungry. Hold the mustard on mine."

"Okay," Sonia said. "But let me just quickly use your phone to check my messages before Dan uses it."

"Help yourself. I'll make the sandwiches," said Travis from the other room.

Travis felt comforted and secure by the setting.

At least for now.

TUESDAY

CHAPTER 36

AT MIDNIGHT, the black sedan drove drove east down Constitution Avenue past the glowing White House. Green stared out the window at it and continued debriefing Meyer.

"I assume you haven't violated the law by telling anyone else anything about this."

"No, sir. I have not," replied Meyer robotically.

"Good, very good. Relax. You've done good." Green patted Meyer's shoulder.

"Where are we headed, sir?"

"I have a meeting on the other side of town, so forgive me for conducting this interview in the car. Tight schedule."

Meyer nodded uneasily. Green's power wasn't lost on this young agent in his early thirties. And he didn't have to be this pleasant to him.

"So, you said Leblanc was acting strangely in Tampa and when you walked into the room unannounced, you found him standing on the conference table, closing a ceiling tile? And he said he was doing the routine sweep for bugs again?" said Green, brushing the lint off of his right leg.

"Yes, sir."

"So what made you suspicious?" Green smiled, trying to make this feel like a conversation between friends over a couple of beers. He slapped Meyer's knee.

"Apart from the fact we'd already swept the room for

bugs? Just the way he was acting. The way he was when I walked in… He explained what he was doing when it should have been obvious to me what he was doing. His face went red. He just seemed nervous."

"And that's why you swept the room on your own later on and found the device. You did well, Meyer."

Green clasped his hands together like he was about to pray, thankful for Meyer's instinct. Secret Service agents on protection detail were notoriously good at following their gut. It was all they had to detect a shooter before he could act; once an assassin pulled the trigger, it was too late. And conversely, agents were pretty bad liars, probably a legacy of the fierce and unquestioning loyalty to their government, which was both inherent and drummed into them. This paradox had worked against Leblanc and in favor of his partner, Meyer.

Green's cell phone rang.

"Sir, it's Croghan. We just got something back on the girl with Travis… You're not gonna believe this…"

CHAPTER 37

TRAVIS SAT AT GEORGE KRAMER'S DESK in the study, preparing to make some important calls. The pain from the wound above his right eye actually felt good; a reminder that he was alive. He'd never looked death in the eye until Green had put that gun in his face. He felt like a changed man, like nothing would feel the same again. He was hardened, brutalized.

Ready to fight back.

First call was to check his voicemail messages in case anything had happened since he disposed of the cell phone back in New York.

The first message was Travis's agent. "Dan, it's Drew. What the hell's going on?! I just got a call from the network to cancel tomorrow. Call me."

"Dr. Travis, hi, it's Martin Koslowski. Just to thank you for your brilliant talk in Phoenix this last weekend. We'll be asking you back next year for sure. Thanks again. Awesome."

"Mr. Travis, just letting you know that the books you ordered are in."

"Hi…whoever this is, we just found your cell phone. Call me at (212) 555-4934 and I'll send it to you."

Whoever said New Yorkers had no time for anyone?

"Dan, it's Drew. Keep your cell on, dude. You need to call me. Tonight."

"Hey, Danny, it's Candice." Travis been dating Candice—a girl who thought a fancy restaurant was one that served wine. She ended every sentence like she was asking a question by adding an irritating inquisitive high note at the end. That life seemed so far away from the nightmare he was living.

"Mr. Travis, it's Maggie from next door. There's been a lot of shouting and activity coming from your house. I know you're away so I went over to check it out and they seemed to be policemen. Said they were responding to an alarm, but I didn't hear anything. Oh, and your grass is a good few inches too long, so if you wouldn't mind?" You could count on Travis's only neighbor to know every little event in the village. She was a member of the Ruxton Village Homeowners Association.

"Drew again. Shit, I'm worried now. What's going on?"

"End of messages."

No updates on poor Mom yet, but nothing is expected until Wednesday anyway.

Please be okay. I'll be by her bedside soon enough.

Let's end this.

Travis found the number for Wally Pritchard, the conspiracy freak, and dialed. He heard the muffled voices of Kramer and Sonia in the next room as he waited for Wally to pick up.

Kramer lounged back on his leather couch, smoking his pipe with the remains of a sandwich on the table next to him. He was in his element, entertaining a beautiful and enchanting girl with black hair and the greenest eyes he'd ever seen. He hadn't lost his touch, it seemed. Sonia sat listening to someone who wasn't just regurgitating stuff from books; this was someone who lived through what he was talking about.

"You see, my dear, it's hard to appreciate today just how things were back then in the fifties and sixties without being there. It was the height of the Cold War—I mean, people were *really* frightened of the Soviets. It was total hysteria, and for good reason, in my opinion." He paused and slid out a twenty-dollar bill from a pewter money-clip on the side table, then handed it to Sonia.

"Flip it over and look at the back."

Sonia looked at the reverse of the bill.

"You see what it says under 'The United States of America'?"

"You mean 'In God We Trust'?" she asked.

"Yes. Now, most people think that's always been there, but actually it was *added* in 1955 to reassure the American people that they had nothing to fear from Communism. We also added the reference of God to the Pledge of Allegiance among other things at that time for the same reason."

Sonia saw the point. "And the KGB recruited Oswald in Tokyo, so if the American public would have discovered that…"

Sonia froze.

Kramer finished the thought for her. "Mass hysteria and cries for war—*World War III*—so honey, you bet your sweet ass the CIA, the FBI, your very own Secret Service and the Warren Commission covered the whole thing up. Hell, who cared if that meant conspiracy theories started about Kennedy's own government killing him—anything was better than people thinking the Soviets did it! They were also trying to cover up their own incompetence, so needless to say, they… we…were highly motivated."

Sonia smiled and handed the twenty-dollar bill back

to Kramer. "Yeah, Travis explained the paranoia that set in around the time of Kennedy's death. But wasn't that whole 'Reds Under the Bed' thing and the CIA witch hunts considered baloney just a few years later?"

"That was a convenient cover for the truth: truth was the CIA was riddled with KGB spies," said Kramer, folding his arms.

Kramer continued with unquestioning authority. "All that convenient skepticism of Soviet infiltration changed in 1994 with the arrest of Aldrich Ames—a counterintelligence officer in the CIA of all things—who'd worked for nine years as a KGB mole and betrayed many of our men in Russia." Kramer's head dropped as if in mourning. He contemplated how those CIA agents apprehended by the KGB would have died: the Stalinist tradition of *vyshaya mera*. They would have been taken to a room, made to kneel, then shot in the back of their heads with a large caliber pistol so their faces would be unrecognizable. Then their bodies buried in a secret, unmarked grave to further punish their loved ones. After the moment's silence, Kramer continued.

"Then in 1999, with the capture of the *Mitrokhin Archive*, the game was really up for the CIA and their efforts to 'cover up' just how infested they were with Soviet agents—as well as a lot of the truth about Lee Harvey Oswald and our friend Igor Orlov too—the guy Danny already told you about. A major embarrassment for the CIA-sponsored historians who tried to play down the roles Orlov and Oswald played."

"The *Mitrokhin Archive*?" Sonia said.

"A fascinating story. Vasiliy Mitrokhin was the KGB's head librarian. He actually copied just about every key KGB file for ten years prior to 1985. He meticulously squirreled away the whole thing waiting for the right time to defect, which he did, handing the whole thing to British Intelligence.

The British MI6 put him through many tests to authenticate his background all of which he passed without question, plus we know he was for real because his files filled in the many gaps we had. And it matched our own agent reports and electronic intercepts. The KGB's successor, the SVR, to this day is very touchy about the whole affair. In fact, everyone assumes that the secret war between us and the Russians ended with the Cold War, when it actually intensified."

Sonia rocked on her seat. "Okay. So what's the rest of the story about 'Lancer's Nemesis'?"

"Alright, let's get to it, but I wanted you to understand the background behind the whole thing so what I'm about to tell you makes sense."

In the study, Travis listened to Wally Prichard's phone ring and ring, but no reply. He called again.

Come on, answer!

Travis's wish was granted with the sound of coughing on the line. He heard a woman's British accent.

"Who the bloody hell is this calling at this time of night?!"

"Sorry, ma'am. I'm looking for Wally Pritchard?"

"At midnight? He's not here anyway—he's in Tampa for another sodding Bilderberg thingy. Waste of time if you ask me, but as long as he's out of my way..."

Bingo.

"Thanks. Would you happen to know which hotel he's staying at?"

"Hilton, I think. Look, who is this anyway?"

"I'm an old friend—thank you." Travis hung up. He didn't want to draw any attention to his inquiry from anyone other than Wally. After getting the number for the Hilton Tampa, he dialed.

"Good evening, Hilton Tampa. How may I direct your call?"

"Wally Pritchard—he's a guest."

"One moment please."

Ringing, then finally another British voice, this time a man's.

"Hello?"

"Wally, it's Dr. Travis. Dan Travis. I met you last year at…"

"Good Lord! How the devil are you? Blimey, it's late! To what do I owe this pleasure? How did you know where to find me?"

"Your wife told me… Anyway sorry to call so late, but are you down there for this year's Bilderberg?"

"Yes I am. It's over at the Grand Hyatt. They're usually held in spring but they changed it to fall this year—but that didn't fool me. Did you know those bastards bugged my hotel room again?"

"Really? Unbelievable. Listen, Wally was there anything different about this year's conference? Did you manage to get inside?"

"Nah, bloody security. All the bodyguards were alerted to the possibility of my presence. It seemed a lot tighter than normal this year. Still, after sniffing around hotel staff and watching who arrived, it was plain to see it was the usual crowd of fascists hell-bent on world domination each and every one of them—bastards!"

Travis had to interrupt otherwise he'd have been on the phone all night. "Was Vice President Cooke there?"

"Yes, yes he was. That's what I've been trying to say. Sorry I was waffling there. He was there alright, with his Secret

Service stooges in tow. Most unusual for a VP to attend one of these, I must say."

"It is? What do you think a VP attending means?"

"Buggered if I know exactly, but the president could never go to one of these—he'd send his deputy if it was a critical matter. What better opportunity for a meeting than when all the world's biggest players in finance, industry and media are all under one roof? Bloody scandalous! It really is. We have a right to know what these bastards talk about each year—they're playing games with our lives!"

"Why could the president himself never go to a Bilderberg meeting?"

"Too high profile. Remember, these things are deliberately kept low key. The president has to account for every minute of his day. He couldn't simply vanish for two days unnoticed without drawing attention to the existence of Bilderbergers—but a vice president, no problem."

As Wally ranted, Travis recalled how the seeds of Bilderberg were planted as far back as 1908 on Jekyll Island. That meeting spawned the Federal Reserve, a title Travis always found ironic; the Federal Reserve wasn't federal—it was a private entity owned by banks. And it had no reserves either. Never did.

"Okay thanks, Wally. I really appreciate it and sorry again for disturbing you."

"Oh. Right-o then. Glad I could help. Cheers."

Travis hung up with wide eyes staring at the charred Nazi flag in the glass frame in front of the desk.

So it was true then.

Travis summarized the events as he understood them: *Leblanc was protecting Vice President Cooke at an unusual appearance at a Bilderberg conference. He most likely obtained something highly sensitive, clearly because he knew in advance the rea-*

son for the meeting, and then mailed a copy of that file somewhere before his demise. What could be so sensitive that a loyal Secret Service agent would break the code of confidentiality?

Travis rubbed a sweaty palm upward on his face. It was getting late and he was fighting exhaustion after the events of the previous day, but questions still stormed his mind.

What would make Leblanc do that? It must have been something personal to him. Something so emotional it allowed him to override the value of his own life. Travis recalled Sonia saying their father was one of the agents protecting Kennedy. *Did Leblanc hear something about JFK's death that would have absolved his father? But what about the clear references to medicine Kramer identified? Would a vice president really be discussing "Lancer's Nemesis" at a Bilderberg conference decades after the event?*

Need more facts. It was time to call a Dr. Rogers at Memorial Sloan Kettering Hospital, New York City.

Please don't say I have to go back to New York.

CHAPTER 38

ALEX ADKA DESPERATELY TRIED to have as little of his cashmere suit touch the back seat of a D.C. taxi as possible. Normally he'd be sitting in the back of a pristine limousine with diplomatic plates, but this unexpected meeting called for complete anonymity. He leered at the upholstery and wondered how on Earth people traveled in such filth.

But the risk of grime and dust finding its way onto his pressed pants was of little significance. There were greater problems to deal with. Why hadn't the file been recovered yet? It was almost one o'clock on Tuesday morning and here he was, in a taxi, going to meet up on the other side of town at his agent's request. *Too many bugs back at the office for this conversation.*

The taxi driver spouting small talk to merit a tip interrupted his thoughts. "So, where you visiting from?" He'd clearly picked up on Adka's accent. The driver was a thickset man with a jovial way about him.

Though there was no way he would divulge any information to the driver, Adka found the intrusion oddly relieving, thinking he'd get insight into the mind of someone who would do this for a living. Someone who would drive around in squalor, listening to the masses in the back seat engage in banal conversations. The driver's blatant cheeriness in light of that fact was curious to Adka, who was never exposed to such people.

"Born and raised here," the driver said proudly. "I've just about seen it all right here from the front seat. People sure do live complicated lives in this town!"

"Yes, they do," said Adka, glancing out the window at the White House. "And how about you..." Adka looked at the driver's ID card on the dashboard and engaged his skills of diplomacy: using a person's name and taking an interest in them. People love the sound of their own name. "...how about you, Clarence? Is your *life* complicated?"

"No, sir. The Lord takes care of me." Clarence squeezed out a contented chuckle.

"Fascinating," said Adka.

CHAPTER 39

UNLIKE TRAVIS, Kramer showed no signs of sleepiness as he swilled another glass of Hennessy XO. "Does that bring us up to speed?"

Sonia marveled at the intellectual energy such an old guy possessed. "Yes, that's about it so far."

Kramer settled back, gazing at the ceiling, deep in past memories. A past he'd lived through on the front lines. "I'll never forget what CIA deputy Justin O'Donnell said at the inception of ZR/RIFLE: 'If the U.S. engages in assassination as foreign policy, then we had better expect our targets to respond in the same way.' Even Vice President Johnson warned that someone would try to get even. And get even they did. What goes around, comes around, Sonia. It's called the 'Cycle of Hate' and the desire for revenge is what fuels it."

Kramer leaned forward. His eyes sparkled at Sonia, relishing what he was about to say: a war story he'd obviously entertained others with before. "Alright, let's put the pieces together. You know, ever since Kennedy was shot, people have argued and argued about the wrong things."

"What do you mean?"

"All types of experts and wannabe experts have been trying to figure out the number of shots, exit and entry wounds, autopsies being tampered with, where the shots were fired from, was it the infamous grassy knoll? How many shooters there were, yada, yada, yada. All that's a bull-crap sideshow and that's the way it was intended to be—a distraction from the key issue."

"Which is?"

"That Kennedy was shot, plain and simple," Kramer snapped back with a crooked pointer finger soaring into the air. "The question is: *who shot him and why?* That's the question our government didn't, and probably still doesn't, want answered. The best way to keep people distracted from the truth is to encourage open debate, but to limit the spectrum of the debate. News networks do it all the time these days—if there's a debate people assume the issues are being addressed, but not if the voice of criticism isn't even in the debate. Go ahead and argue all you want about how many shooters there were, just don't say it was those Russians—*that's* what the government wanted and that's what they got."

"I guess that makes sense."

"Listen, here's why I say this whole sideshow is a bunch of crap. For some inexplicable reason, the majority of Kennedy assassination analysis has fixated on a totally nonsensical thesis: that if it was a single shooter, it wasn't a conspiracy and if it was more than one shooter, it was a conspiracy. Many books have been written, all arguing over the number of shooters and slopping out 'definitive' conclusions on that basis. You start out with a faulty premise and the whole thing is a house of cards. In the intelligence business, people get killed that way."

Kramer shook his head and chewed his lip. "A *lone* KGB or CIA assassin, acting alone—as they often do I might add—eliminates a target on government orders. And that's *not* a conspiracy!?"

Sonia's eyes widened. Kramer went on impassioned. "Do you see? You can watch the Zapruder Film 'til you're blue in the face. It won't tell you who did it and why. *And that's the issue.*"

"So it was a conspiracy?"

"'Course it was. And don't look so surprised—for as long as humans have walked the planet they've instinctively looked after their own interest, that's how we've survived. So to think conspiracies don't go on is childish."

Sonia shuffled. "But how do you keep something like that quiet in this country? There are too many people involved."

"Ah, well it *is* difficult. That's why so many people have come out to speak about it—and conveniently disappeared I might add. But, it isn't difficult, by any means, to keep things a secret in a dictatorship: a closed society where people are frightened of saying anything against their government."

"Go on."

Kramer smiled and produced pieces of typed paper from a book he'd taken off the shelf. "This is a timeline of some of the notable events of 1963, the year JFK was shot. These things all happened in the build up to his assassination."

```
Feb 22: Moscow warned the U.S. that an
attack on Cuba would mean war.

Feb 27: The USSR said that 10,000 troops
would remain in Cuba.

Mar 19: In Costa Rica, President John F.
Kennedy and six Latin American presidents
pledged to fight Communism.

Apr 27: Cuban premier Fidel Castro arrived
in Moscow.

Jul 8: U.S. banned all monetary transactions
with Cuba.
```

Sonia studied it. "Okay. So no surprises there. It was during the Cold War and just after the Cuban Missile Crisis so tensions would be high…although I thought you said relations improved between Kennedy and Khrushchev after that?"

Kramer winked and handed her the second piece of paper. "Now compare it to this one. This too is a timeline of events in 1963."

```
Feb 19: The Soviet Union informed President
Kennedy   it   would   withdraw   "several
thousand" of an estimated 17,000 Soviet
troops in Cuba.

Feb 20: Moscow offered to allow on-site
inspection of nuclear testing.

Jul 25: The United States, the Soviet
Union and Britain initialed a treaty in
Moscow prohibiting the testing of nuclear
weapons in the atmosphere, in space or
underwater.

Sep 20: In a speech to the U.N. General
Assembly, President Kennedy proposed a
joint U.S.-Soviet expedition to the moon.
```

Sonia read then compared the two pieces of typed paper. "Weird. It's like a totally mixed message. This page suggests the Soviets were being militant and the other just the opposite."

Kramer helped her thoughts along. "Like the Kremlin was in conflict with its own objectives?"

"Yes. And this is the conflict over Khrushchev with his

desire to reform and the hard-liners putting pressure on him to do the opposite?"

"Yep. Sounds like fertile ground for a coup d'etat, wouldn't you say? And notice how Cuba's in the middle of all the aggressive events?"

Sonia nodded as Kramer continued. "And here's one last 1963 timeline for you."

```
Sep 26: Lee Harvey Oswald traveled on a
Continental Trailways bus to Mexico.


Sep 27: Lee Harvey Oswald visited the
Cuban consulate in Mexico.
```

"So, my dear, as Daniel told you, it was indeed a coup d'etat in Russia that sowed the seeds of the plot to kill JFK. Now let's get right to it and look at what actually happened. Don't be so shocked that one country would try to assassinate another country's leader; the British tried to assassinate the Russian premier Stalin before World War II."

In the study, Travis was on the phone with Sloan Kettering Memorial Hospital.

"What do you mean Doctor Rogers isn't there? You mean he's not on shift right now?"

"No, sir, he doesn't work here anymore."

Damn. "Could you put me through to his old department?"

"Hold, please."

After a long couple of minutes, a weary voice came on

the phone. "Hello."

"Good evening. I'm trying to find a Doctor J.E. Rogers," Travis said.

"Yeah. He doesn't work here now though. Would you like to speak to another doctor?"

"No thanks. Do you happen to know where he went?"

"Yeah, he went to a children's hospital in uh…Florida somewhere. He left just recently."

"Tampa…?"

"No…Miami. That's it. Miami Children's Hospital."

"Thank you." Travis hung up and pounded *411*.

CHAPTER 40

"WHAT DID YOU FIND on the girl, Croghan?!" Green shouted, lurching forward in the back seat.

"It's good news and bad news, sir."

"Don't play fucking games with me, spit it out!"

"Yes, sir. Sorry, sir. The good news is a man walking his dog in the area of the abandoned Toyota said he saw a couple matching the description of Travis and the girl walking away from the area of the car. We're questioning him now. Hopefully he'll tell us where they went or at least give us a shortlist of possible locations."

"Alright. Good. And do we have any news yet on the girl's fingerprints and photo-match?"

"That's the bad news, sir. They won't let us have that information. Something about security procedure and protocol."

"What do you mean? Incorrect paperwork or something?"

"No, sir. They had a match on the girl but they won't tell us who she is."

"That's a bunch of inter-agency bullshit, Croghan! Jesus, I thought after 9/11 we were supposed to be working together!"

"Yes, sir. Maybe tomorrow we'll get through to someone more senior?"

"Leave it to me... The second you get an address from

that poop-scooper you go round there and get Travis and the girl, you understand? Keep me up to date, got it?"

"Yes, sir."

"And Croghan, when you get the address, don't knock on the door, break it down. This is a matter of national security," Green said slowly and clearly, as though he was explaining it to an infant.

Green slapped his phone shut and beamed at Agent Meyer still sitting next to him. "Meyer, you've been most helpful. Now stay in contact and remember, this is highly classified. This meeting never took place. You understand?"

"Of course, sir. What meeting?"

"Very good. Now get out. This is the last stop."

CHAPTER 41

"THERE'S NO LISTING for a Doctor J. E. Rogers, sir, but I can give you the number of Miami Children's Hospital. If he's just moved to Miami he probably won't show up yet," said the operator.

"Okay, thank you. Just the hospital number then please," Travis said, raking his fingers through his hair.

Travis scrawled the number down. Eleven digits later, another voice came on the line.

"Miami Children's Hospital."

"Good evening, Dr. J.E. Rogers, please."

"Dr. Rogers isn't here right now, would you like his voice-mail?"

"No thanks. When will he come on shift again?"

"Let me see now…one second."

A low-flying helicopter buzzed the house. Travis flinched.

"Okay, ready. Sir?"

"I'm here."

"Dr. Rogers will be on tomorrow evening at six o'clock."

"And there's no other way to contact him?"

"No, his other contact details are confidential."

"Okay. Good night."

Travis dropped the receiver down and slumped over the antique desk, staring at the fax.

IG Farben. The cartel.

A memory crashed into his head: a lecture to a history class about Hitler's rise to power.

Travis couldn't resist the temptation to offer the class an alternative and realistic cause of the rise in response to a particularly naïve question from a student who should have known better. "Hitler needed financial backers from somewhere to get to power, backers who had a motive," Travis had said.

A bright-eyed blond girl in the front row regurgitated a textbook answer. "But Hitler rose to power out of the discontent and poverty of the German people—he manipulated them by playing on that. Do you have a different view?"

Travis paused as he realized he was about to take this class through the looking glass. He knew them well enough by now to know this was probably a class set up, but to his mind history was about the quest for truth, so he continued.

"Hitler still needed heavy financial backing from somewhere, and he got it in a big way. You guys are old and wise enough by now to appreciate that money influences politics—the person with the biggest war chest and the most influential backers wins, right?"

He watched the class sit back, contented that they were about to embark on one of old 'wildcard' Travis's thought-provoking, and often chilling, digressions from the syllabus. "So my friends, if you agree that money is the key to taking control of government, it stands to reason that the most powerful businesses are in the best position to select candidates to suit their own ends."

Travis gazed out the window on to the University of

Maryland campus as he asked the loaded question, "So what sort of entity would support a dictatorship?"

The class went silent for a few seconds. Then a young African-American man with round glasses answered, "One who stands to gain the most by a dictatorship…but in a totalitarian government there is *no* free enterprise, so why would *any* business owner back Hitler?"

A mischievous smile beamed across Travis's face. "Exactly. A totalitarian government—a complete dictatorship—controls all businesses. In fact, all manufacturing and retailing is entirely centralized. In other words, my esteemed colleagues, healthy competition is eliminated."

The class sat expectantly as their favorite lecturer proceeded. "What sort of business entity seeks the elimination of healthy competition in a free market?"

This time the silence was a little longer, until the same young man came back with an answer. "Cartels!"

"Precisely, Mr. Williams. *Cartels.* The reality of fascism is that monopolies control the government, who in turn control the monopolies, but in a way that favors the monopolies, of course. This is the essence of how the Nazis seized power—they got financial backing from very powerful cartels who appreciated that a dictatorship eliminated free enterprise, thus eliminating competition."

The class was awed by this revelation, even though they knew it had no place in any exam. Travis went on. "You see, monopolies and cartels don't represent free enterprise—capitalism—the spirit of America. No! What they represent is an *eradication* of capitalism. In that sense, their goals are similar to communists'. Fascism and communism are remarkably similar as you well know—they both require monopoly of industry, control of the media, secret police and an enemy of the state—a boogeyman—to survive. Any reader of George

Orwell's *1984* would have difficulty in saying whether 'Big Brother' was communist or fascist—all you can see is that 'Big Brother' is a dictator...or a totalitarian government, if you will."

Realizing he was running out of time to teach these kids what they actually needed to know to pass their exam, Travis began to wrap it up. "So, what sort of cartel would sponsor someone like Hitler?"

Blank faces urged Travis to answer the question himself, "As well as various banks and the Roman Catholic Church, it was *healthcare cartels*. Bismarck was the first modern leader to introduce socialized healthcare, which allowed him to take government in Germany long before World War II. This was a vote-winner with medical care being so expensive—ironically due to the cartels price-fixing. Learning from this, it was the *pharmaceutical* cartels that predominantly financed Hitler. Totalitarianism offered them a system that would eliminate competition. And let's not forget that in war, demand for medicine goes up!"

Glancing at his watch, Travis delivered the usual mind-bending question he liked to leave them with. "So, ladies and gents—as we should learn from history's mistakes, let's turn to our country *today* and ask the question: 'Is our republic working according to the Constitution?' To think so is like saying politicians don't make policies to protect the cartels and conglomerates that put them there and funded their campaigns. Big government is essentially controlled by big business. Also, consider this: the American flag you see at a presidential address, in a courtroom or post office has gold trim around the edge. Does that look like the American flag we all know and love?"

"But isn't that just a way of making the flag look nicer and more official?" said the blond girl in the front row.

"No. The flag you see with gold trim around the edge in official government settings is not the flag of the United States of America."

Travis looked around at the students and reveled in their reaction to this bombshell. He was starting to realize revealing strange and little-known truths to people was his calling. He went silent waiting for the inevitable question. The young girl down front obliged him. "So *whose* flag is that then, Professor?"

"That flag, Miss Foster, is the flag of the Corporation of the United States of America."

Travis enjoyed his position as he continued to enlighten them, "In 1933 the American government essentially went bankrupt—Roosevelt declared as much with Executive Orders EO6073, EO6102 and EO6111. Powerful cartels stepped in and bought the debt, creating the Corporation of the United States of America, which replaced the United States of America as an entity and remains to this day."

Just then, a stocky, blond-haired young man with an angry and confused expression spoke out. "Dr. Travis, I love my country, though, don't you?"

The rest of the class turned to the outspoken student with disdain. Travis simply smiled inwardly and turned to the window again. He answered the young man sensitively. "Mr. Harris, is it not possible that an individual can love their country but dislike their government? Is that not how this great country was founded? Where would we be if the settlers of the New World had not loved their country and despised their government—the British government? The Boston Tea Party was fueled by this exact sentiment. It's precisely *because* a person loves his or her country he or she should carefully watch and judge that same government entrusted with the care of its citizens, and no one would agree with me more than the ultimate patriot, George Washington himself."

Travis now addressed the whole class, competing with the end-of-period bell. "You're a new generation and you must learn from the past. A people should not be afraid of their government, the government should be afraid of its people—or who knows from where the next Hitler might spring."

Those were the days; days when Travis's audiences were open-minded students hoping to change the world into a better place. He'd traded them in for confused TV viewers who didn't want the truth if it was inconvenient or scary. People today were frightened by their own shadows, let alone their own government.

Travis heard Kramer's voice become raised in the next room and blinked back to reality: a reality where *he* was very much afraid of his own government.

"Put yourself in Castro's shoes, Sonia. It's 1962, you're the leader of a small country in full knowledge of an American plot to assassinate you. America then tells you it will abandon the plot but secretly continues. And then, the country watching over you and protecting you comes along and gives you a green light to assassinate the leader of the United States in order to send a message. What would *you* do?"

"I see where you're heading. Castro's intelligence service—the DGI—killed Kennedy. Sounds like a plausible explanation, but that's not proof he did it, or that the Soviets sanctioned it," said Sonia.

Kramer stared at her silently before answering.

"Of course, you're right. I don't have any proof. But there's so much evidence pointing to this conclusion, you'd have to be crazy not to agree, either crazy or very naïve. People would prefer not to believe such things—it's far more comforting to think Oswald was just some nut-job, an angry young man trying to prove a point. It's called *denial* and people are pretty good at that."

Sonia changed her tone suddenly as she realized how skeptical she had begun to sound. "Sorry, I see. I guess that makes sense."

"More to the point dear, your lives have been endangered tonight because of something to do with Kennedy's assassins, 'Lancer's Nemesis,' so no, I don't have a signed confession from the killer, but we need to establish who the *most likely* suspect is."

"And that's Castro?"

"Yep. Castro. The Soviets had to sanction it though and the coup d'etat leaders manipulated Castro to serve their own end."

Sonia's face hardened again. "Wait. People have looked at Castro as a possible suspect and time and time again they've come to the conclusion he didn't do it."

Kramer expected this objection and his answer came before Sonia could go any further. "Yes, that's right. And you know how they came to that conclusion?"

Sonia shook her head. "No."

"Because Castro publicly said it would have been insane for him to have killed Kennedy. Oh well then, that's it, case closed. Castro said he didn't do it, so that's that!" Kramer threw his hands in the air theatrically. "Some reporter flies over there and says he looked Castro in the eye and asked him outright if he killed Kennedy and he said no. They say that Castro wouldn't have dared do it for fear of retaliation. Of course, an American retaliatory invasion of Cuba was never going to happen after the Soviets openly stated that it would mean war with Russia. That's why us guys at the

Agency recruited anti-Castro Cubans in Miami and trained them to invade at the Bay of Pigs—so we could invade and say it had nothing to do with us. What a joke that was."

Sonia was silent.

Kramer calmed himself down. "Sonia, look, this is a sound piece of advice for life in general: 'Always look at the source of your information and ask what their agenda is.' Is the information I'm being given tainted because someone has something to gain by giving that information? Me? I have no agenda. I just want the truth. Hell, I couldn't give a damn if you said Marilyn Monroe's ghost killed Kennedy as long as you show me convincing evidence!"

"Alright, so sum it up then. Who do you think killed Kennedy and why?"

"Well, here's what I believe. Some of this is fact and some of it is my conclusion based upon evidence. Following on from what Danny has already told you that is," Kramer said, looking around the room as if to enlist support from his books and antiquities.

Sonia nodded, her arms folded. "Okay."

"Khrushchev wanted reform in Moscow and was edging toward peace with Kennedy. Brezhnev and Furtseva conspired to oust him, something the hard liners in the Kremlin would gladly go along with if the CIA continued with Operation Mongoose despite agreement to cease and Soviet spies relayed this back to Moscow. Brezhnev and Furtseva saw this as the perfect opportunity—if they could make it appear as though Khrushchev had lost control of Castro and simultaneously halt the thawing of relations between Moscow and Washington, the coup against Khrushchev would take place."

"Right," said Sonia.

Kramer went to get up and Sonia moved to assist him,

but he waved her off with his cane. "Oswald was originally recruited by the KGB and most likely gave the critical information about the U2. But Furtseva sent him back to America on a mission. It would have been in her best interest at that point to make it appear as though Oswald did not work for the KGB, of course. Naïvely, people use this as evidence for him being a lone gunman. He then hangs around with Cubans, both pro-Castro and anti-Castro, the latter were CIA sponsored, so no doubt he mixed with them to make it appear as though the CIA killed Kennedy in order to cause confusion in good old-fashioned Russian agent style. He visits the Cuban consulate in Mexico (a well known pass-through for Soviet and Cuban intelligence). His mission was to work with the DGI and help them assassinate Kennedy. Also Oswald was sent in as a gesture from the KGB to say 'we're behind you.'"

"Help them?" Sonia asked, tilting her head and frowning.

"Yes," affirmed Kramer, turning to face her. "I believe Oswald really was the 'patsy' he claimed he was. He was working in the Texas School Book Depository—Kennedy was shot from the sixth floor of that building—and it would have been easy to plant a rifle there with his prints on it. The real assassins were two DGI agents named Policarpo and Casas and their escape is public record."

Kramer ambled toward his decanter of brandy. "After Kennedy was shot, U.S. Border Patrol closed all borders. However, the borders weren't closed to light aircraft. In Mexico City, an Air Cubana flight destined for Havana was delayed five hours and didn't leave until Casas arrived on a light, twin-engine plane from Dallas. He then boarded the airliner without going through customs. Later that year, our agents in Cuba heard from Casas's aunt confirming he was in Dallas on the day of the shooting. Those agents also reported that

Casas was suddenly flush with money. Policarpo followed a few days later."

"And what were the Soviets doing?"

"Well, my dear, they were the ones who engineered this, and rather masterfully, but they didn't pull the trigger. It was as much in their interest as it was in certain American politicians interests to ensure that the truth about Oswald didn't come out. The Soviets leaked stories to the world press that Oswald was the shooter before the shooting even happened—as a result he was picked up approximately an hour after the shooting which has to be one of the fastest arrests in history—and they picked him up in a movie theater. Now why would he go to a movie theater? By mistake, probably because of the time difference, a New Zealand newspaper reported Oswald had shot Kennedy even before the shooting had taken place!" He'd have been on a bus, train or whatever to get the hell out of Dallas, not sitting in a movie theater—unless he was there to meet someone—like his Soviet handler."

"And what about Oswald himself getting shot?"

"You mean by Jack Ruby? Well, that one remains a bit of a mystery, but needless to say, both Russia and America wanted Oswald dead. At that stage and when you're in that position, your life expectancy's pretty short. Whether Ruby worked for the KGB, DGI or CIA, we'll probably never know. Oswald telling the world he was just a 'patsy' probably wasn't a smart thing to do—it would have indicated that he was going to talk. Ruby wrote notes and spoke to several people saying that Kennedy was killed as part of a conspiracy. Ruby said that he'd been maneuvered into killing Oswald who was just a patsy. He died of lung cancer, we're told, just before he was due to testify in front of Congress. He said he'd been 'injected' with cancer cells."

"Alright, so 'Lancer's Nemesis' was Castro—the Cubans.

Or the Soviets?"

"Good question. I guess it depends on your point of view. But if the Cubans pulled the trigger, the Soviets engineered it and did a great job at covering their own tracks, but I saw through it all along."

"Go on."

"Sonia, have you ever heard the quotation from Shakespeare, 'The lady doth protest too much'?"

"Yes. From *Hamlet*, isn't it?"

Kramer smiled approvingly. "You're a smart cookie. Yes, it is. Have you noticed how when someone is guilty of something he or she becomes overly defensive? Noticed how if someone talks about some aspect of him or herself too much, it probably isn't true? Like they've got something to prove?"

"Yeah, sure. Kind of like why low-income people are attracted to ostentatious jewelry?"

"I guess," Kramer said through a chuckle. "Starting just weeks after the JFK assassination, the Soviets sent us a series of defectors with a common message: 'We didn't do it.' They threw explanations at us when none was asked for. In short, Kennedy was killed by Castro after the assassination was sanctioned by the KGB. Brezhnev and Furtseva had their coup d'etat and ousted Khrushchev blaming him for losing control of Castro. Operation Mongoose finally ended and everyone on the Russian side of the fence lived happily ever after. If this were a court case, I think my case would stand 'beyond a reasonable doubt.' The Soviets had motive; they had the most to gain and the evidence certainly points that way if you have an open mind..."

Travis came through the door with a cup of coffee, weary-eyed and with slouched shoulders.

"We have to make a decision," he said, and slumped into an armchair.

CHAPTER 42

DETAIL LEADER CROGHAN WAS LODGED in the passenger seat of a black Chevy Suburban with his team of four and a WASP: one-man battering ram. A couple matching the description of Travis and the girl had been seen entering one of the houses not too far from the abandoned Toyota. Croghan and his men were on their way to take down Travis and the girl once and for all.

There's no way Croghan was going to screw up this time. Still having a job at daybreak was top priority for him.

As the Suburban careened north through the quiet dark of Washington, D.C., he worked through the game plan in his mind. Due to Green's curious but strict instructions to keep everything low key, he had no search warrant. Strictly speaking, this meant he would have to knock and then wait twenty seconds before smashing the door down.

But hey, Travis's hearing couldn't be too great because Croghan would just say that he did knock. As long as the paperwork was straight, it was his word over some scumbag's.

That door was going to be smashed in without warning.

Croghan glanced back at the three guys in the back seat and then the driver, McPherson. "Still no word from Green?" Croghan asked him.

"Nope. Tried him four times to let him know we're on

our way. Do our orders stand?"

"Well, he's gonna be pissed if I wait around and let them get away, isn't he?"

"Green's always pissed. Crazy son of a bitch. Why's he getting his hands dirty all of a sudden? And what's all the secrecy about?"

"Yeah, well you thought he had a bug up his ass before today... Jesus. Hey, you know Norm? His assistant?"

"Yeah."

"Norm talks to me. Not even he knows what all this Travis crap is about—said the whole thing's even above his security clearance."

"Yeah, well, whatever. I say we just nail this Travis son of a bitch and get home. Make all this bullshit dead and buried."

"I hear ya."

Croghan turned in his seat to face the guys in the back. "Let's make this a clean dispatch and cover all possible exits. The girl is particularly slippery and she's known to be armed. We want them alive preferably, but you're authorized to kill if need be."

"Yes, sir," they all said in unison, their faces a study in uncompromising loyalty.

Croghan checked his weapon, then held it up before looking at them all again. His face was stern. "You screw up and I'll shoot you myself, got it?"

"Yes, sir," they said again in unison, only smiling this time. They knew he was kidding. But one of the men in the back, a rookie named Wilson, wasn't so sure.

"What's going on tonight, sir? What's all this about?" came the innocent voice of inexperience.

"Our job is not to ask why, kiddo, it is not to ask why,"

Croghan replied, gazing forward. *Why should he care anyway?*

The Chevy slowed as they approached their destination.

Wilson took a sharp breath and gulped.

CHAPTER 43

KRAMER PROPPED HIMSELF UP against the fireplace while Sonia and Travis sat in adjacent chairs. It was past one o'clock in the morning and everyone except Kramer was exhausted.

The only sound came from the embers cracking on the hearth as they each silently worked through the dilemma.

Kramer spoke first, pointing his cane at Travis. "Well, you can bet Green intends to visit this Dr. Rogers too. If he hasn't done so already, that is, and the doctor's an essential part of this puzzle if you ask me."

Travis nodded. "Agreed. The question is this: do we wait until the doctor comes on shift and try to call him, or do we drive as fast as we can to Miami…" Travis paused remembering they had no means of transportation and continued, "to try to get to him before Green does?"

Kramer threw another wrench in the works. "Green has you at a disadvantage, Danno. He has the means to find the doctor's home address down there."

"Possibly not," Sonia said. "If he's just moved down there, like Travis said, he's possibly off the grid. Maybe in a hotel or short-term rented accommodation."

"Possibly," said Kramer, still looking at Travis as though the decision fell on his shoulders. "But it's a risk either way. If you drive down to Miami you'll perhaps intercept the doctor before Green, *but*...you may have positioned yourself poorly once you figure out the location of the file." Kramer studied the fax again. "Jesus, Sonia, if your brother was trying to tell us where he sent this 'Apollo' thing, he sure did a lousy job."

Sonia ignored the comment. "I have a friend in the Service. Someone we can trust. It's too risky for me to go to headquarters but he could use our database to find Dr. Rogers's home address...if he has one yet."

"Sounds like a plan. That is, if you don't say too much and you're sure you can trust him," Kramer said.

"What would you do, George?" asked Travis, once Sonia was gone.

Kramer turned toward the fire in silence, tapping his cane against the hearth while he thought.

After a minute he turned to Travis with a glimmer of trepidation in his gray eyes. "Into the breach, Dan Dare! I'd go to Miami. You can take my car—it's only an old Crown Victoria but it'll get you there."

"Thanks, but I don't want to drag you into this. If it gets traced back to you..."

"Nonsense! I'll report it stolen after giving you ample time to get down to Miami. If your old man was around he'd do the same for you."

Travis's spirit grew, as if his father was with him, speaking to him through his old friend. "Alright, that's the plan. Miami it is."

Travis turned his head toward the study to call Sonia just as she materialized in the doorway. "Sonia, we're moving out."

"Where to?"

Kramer answered for him. "Pack your sunglasses, sweetie, you're off to the sunshine state."

"Miami?"

"Yep," said Travis, throwing himself to his feet. "George is lending us his car. We'll take it in shifts and drive through the night, and day, I guess." It suddenly dawned on Travis the long drive that lay ahead of them. Miami was over a thousand miles away.

"Okay," said Sonia. "And we're meeting my friend from the Service at a gas station on the other side of town. We'll see him and then drive down. He'll have something for us on Rogers."

Kramer strutted into the middle of the room and began directing the operation, relishing the adventure. "Alright then. Go upstairs and get some blankets and pillows, Sonia, along with all the supplies you can carry from the kitchen. Plenty of coffee!"

"Yes, sir," Sonia said with a salute.

Kramer put his hand on Travis's shoulder. "And when you get to Miami, I want you to look someone up."

CHAPTER 44

CROGHAN STOOD BEHIND MCPHERSON who was clenching the battering ram. They were waiting for the team to assemble in their positions before smashing the door in. The rookie, Wilson, had his back to Croghan.

Croghan heard voices inside and felt his heart pounding. It'd been one hell of a night, with the earlier raid on Leblanc's apartment.

Croghan hand-signaled to McPherson for the second time, holding up a clenched fist facing outward to confirm his order to hold position. McPherson acknowledged him by making the shape of a circle with his index finger and thumb, only this time more emphatically as if to tell his commander, "I know already!"

The signal came from the rear of the house. They were in position. Croghan gave the order: "Go! Go! Go!"

McPherson smashed open the door and ran into the house shouting with Croghan and Wilson trailing, their guns pointing out in all directions, hunting for a target, covering all possible threat locations.

Croghan heard a scream from the rear of the house. *The second team had reached the target.* He bounded in the direction of the scream. Now there were shouts from his men: "Freeze! On your knees, hands on your heads!" Wilson and McPherson covered Croghan as he moved.

Croghan burst into the room to see a couple kneeling down with their backs to him.

She had black hair; he had brown. He was naked. The girl was wearing a black garter-belt and fishnet stockings. The second team men were pointing their guns in the couples' faces, as the two suspects helplessly sobbed.

Pathetic.

Croghan strutted to face the couple, stowing his pistol, satisfied and completely in control of the situation. As he looked at them, his triumphant gloat collapsed. This was the wrong couple.

The room fell silent apart from the couples' sobs.

Croghan punched a hole in the dry wall. "Jesus!" His team stared at him, bewildered.

Sonia packed Kramer's old Ford with blankets and provisions at the rear of the house, completely oblivious to the unsuspecting couple just one block away being terrorized by a paramilitary force.

Travis leaned back against the side of the car, facing Kramer.

"Love the color. Didn't know these Crown Vics came in corrosion blue," Travis said.

"It's four more wheels than you had ten minutes ago. Still, at least you got your sense of humor back, Daniella."

"Right. Someone trying to shoot me is funny. I forgot. Anyway, you said you wanted me to look up someone in Miami?"

Kramer spoke loud enough for Sonia to hear as well. "If things get dicey down there you'll need more than that pea-shooter Sonia's carrying."

Sonia glanced up at Kramer in surprise, and flashed him a half-smile.

Kramer rocked back and forth in his velvet slippers, his eyes flitting about. The look was lost on Sonia, but Travis knew from a legacy of spending many summer days with Uncle George.

Something's wrong. Is he frightened for me?

"Danny, try to find Ramón Martinez when you're there. He's a good man…or used to be anyway. He was a Cuban contract agent for us way back during the Bay of Pigs. He really owes me one. Tell him I sent you."

"He was one of *those* guys?" Travis said, wincing.

"Yes, yes. Stop stressing. He was recruited at JM/WAVE and ran black ops in Cuba for us, but you can trust him. He knows his way around town and is good in a pinch—and he knows a lot more stuff about what was going on in Cuba back then. He might be able to shed some more light on this 'Lancer's Nemesis' conundrum."

Great. More guns.

Kramer sensed Travis's apprehension and moved in close to Travis. He whispered, "Look, I'm not gonna lie to you, son, this is gonna be tough, but you can do it. I know you can. Just do what you do best and don't be scared. Now, I lost contact with Ramón a while back, but he used to own this café. He was always there."

Kramer handed Travis a piece of paper with the name and address of the café on it.

"El Hoyo?" said Travis, reading from the paper.

"Yep. It's downtown, but don't worry. Driving that old crap-heap, you'll fit right in there!" Kramer said, slapping Travis's shoulder.

Travis smirked but failed to see the funny side, suddenly feeling fearful again.

"We're ready. Saddle up," Sonia said. She hugged and kissed Kramer.

As she swaggered to the driver's door, Kramer patted his heart. "You're too much for my old ticker, dear. Safe journey."

Travis didn't need to say a farewell—his expression said it all. *Crazy old stiff. I love ya.*

But as Travis turned to the passenger door, Kramer grabbed his arm and spun him around, sneaking a glance to make sure Sonia was in the car before he spoke. His pupils dilated and his face looked sharper than it had the whole night. "Be careful, Danny. I love you, son."

Travis hugged Kramer, ripped opened the door and swung in before his emotions got the better of him.

"Now get outta here!" Kramer shouted, slapping the hood as if the car were a horse.

Fan belt squealing, the shabby Ford trundled off down the dark drive toward the street. Kramer stood on the sidewalk, waving with his cane.

When the car was out of sight, Kramer's expression turned cold and serious. Something had disturbed him about tonight's encounter. He had to take action. He hobbled back into the house to make a phone call. *It was a mistake to come here*, he thought, tightening his lips.

Some things are more important than family.

Kramer had an old friend in the Agency to call. And just to be sure, Ramón Martinez would take care of Danny Boy too.

CHAPTER 45

GREEN FURIOUSLY PACED a square into the darkened sidewalk on the industrial outskirts of D.C. The rendezvous was off schedule and he had to remain out of contact for security purposes.

Green hated tardiness—*hated* it—but this meeting was necessary. Green's biggest struggle was the necessity of dealing with people he didn't—no he *couldn't*—respect, because of their sloppy behavior. Dwight Green wove a web of protocols even his closest comrades could never understand. Most people offended his senses.

But desperate times called for desperate measures.

My family. My country. Under God. Green looked at the heavens for comfort, but all he felt was the bitter, empty chill of an October night.

The squealing brakes of a taxi broke the silence as it lurched to a halt on the other side of the street. A tall man with brown hair and a chiseled face eased out of the cab. He was immaculately dressed.

Finally.

Green bit his lip, took a breath and sauntered to the agreed meeting point at the side of the warehouse.

Seconds later, a tall, angular man joined him. The man spoke with a foreign, possibly Eastern-European accent, though his English was excellent. "So what do I owe this un-scheduled pleasure?" He didn't look at Green as he spoke nor did Green look at him.

Green couldn't help himself. "Late. You're late, Phoenix. I've got a lot of fucking things going on tonight, you know?"

"What, you think I would just sit around and wait for you?"

Impertinent shit. Green slapped his chest three times. Ignore the insolence and get what you want. "In the dead drop are the details needed. It's in the usual place. Once you have that I may need you further. Keep your schedule free."

"No problem. I'll call you when I have something."

CHAPTER 46

AFTER MEETING WITH HER FRIEND from the Service, Sonia jogged out of the gas station store and swung back into the car. "You still awake?"

"Yeah," Travis said. "I'll sleep first shift. Wake me up in a few hours for my turn and don't fall asleep on me."

"You bet," said Sonia waving a large cup of coffee. She started the engine and screeched away in the direction of I-95 south for the second time that night.

"How was your Service friend? Do you think he'll find anything on Rogers?"

"Not sure. I'll check in with him later tonight. And don't worry—I was discreet and we can trust him."

Travis padded the rear with blankets and pillows, trying to block out the strong smell of George's pipe tobacco lingering in the padding. The flat, wide bench seat of this old jalopy was a welcome consolation for its age. "They don't make 'em like they used to," he said, nestling into his quarters. "This old battleship has its advantages…"

A rattling noise shot out of the hood accompanied by a brief vibration, then suddenly stopped.

"Yeah," said Sonia. "Let's just hope this thing gets us there in one piece. Get some sleep—it'll be your turn soon."

"Yes, Mom," Travis said. His strange affinity for this girl

had grown exponentially as the night had worn on. No matter how bad things had gotten, her presence soothed him.

He rested on his side with legs curled up and closed his eyes. He opened them again, deep in thought. "Sonia?"

"What?"

"Let's say we manage to find the file and get the word out. Do you think people will be happy or sad when they find out?"

"Not sure what you mean." She was concentrating on pulling onto I-95 behind a fast-moving truck.

"Well, let's say there's something deeply incriminating in it, and people learn their government lied to them. No argument, they lied to protect their own interests. No more debating, conspiracy theory becomes conspiracy fact. Will they be happy or sad?"

"I...don't know," she said.

It seemed to Travis that Sonia hadn't contemplated the repercussions of their adventure beyond figuring out what had happened to her brother. "What's on your mind?" she asked.

"People and how they are. They'll deny the existence of anything they care to, just because it suits them. They want to be able to trust and to believe their leaders regardless of what they do, but this file could change all that. It will be right before their eyes. Jesus, no wonder they want it so badly."

"Go to sleep. It's too late and you're getting too deep. Miami is fifteen hours away at best."

Travis closed his eyes again.

Cramped though he was, his weary mind and body gave way to the monotonous drone of tires on asphalt and the toasty warmth of the heater. He felt himself drift into a deep sleep, blissfully unaware of the multiple enemies rallying against him.

CHAPTER 47

ADKA CAREFULLY SLID BACK into the taxi. "Thank you for waiting, Clarence, you're a gentleman."

"Oh, no problem, sir."

By now, Adka had Clarence, the taxi driver, eating from the palm of his hand. Adka always marveled at how far being nice to the 'little people' got him in his political career. Clarence served no political value, but the act was too embedded in his soul to stop when in public.

"Where to now, sir?"

"Do you know this place?" Adka handed him a piece of paper with an address on it.

"Sure—we're on our way. How did your meeting go?" Clarence asked, ogling his debonair passenger in the rearview mirror.

"Fine, thank you. Clarence, could you put some music on, please? I need to think."

Clarence fiddled with the radio and found an easy listening station, while Adka gathered his thoughts. His agent had requested identification and tracking on certain targets and it was now his task to ensure the threat they presented to the operation was neutralized.

CHAPTER 48

GREEN'S DRIVER WAS TAKING him home. Green flipped open his phone and checked his messages.

"Sir, it's Croghan. Negative contact: the lead we were given turned out to be spurious."

Shit.

Next message: "Dwight, Jack Rehnquist. Returning your call. You can get me at home: (202) 555-9873."

Green dialed Rehnquist: his counterpart at another secretive government agency.

A sleepy voice croaked over the phone. "Rehnquist."

"Jack, it's Dwight returning your call. Sorry to wake you, but it's urgent."

Coughing on the line. "I got your message earlier, Dwight. Something about a check you got us to run on a girl. Her file's classified. Nothing I can do I'm afraid on this one—my hands are tied."

"Oh c'mon, Jack, that's party-line BS and you know it. Help me out here," said Green, fighting to remove any sign of desperation in his voice. But it was lost on this experienced politician who, just like Green, had clawed his way to a premier position of power.

"What's going on, Dwight? What have you got yourself into?" Rehnquist's croaky voice morphed into a conspiratorial whisper. "Yours isn't the only call I've had tonight about this.

My phone hasn't stopped ringing, for crying out loud."

There's no way I'm telling him what this is about, no matter how far we go back. Wait. Did he just say someone else had called? It must've been Norman.

"Look, Jack, I just need a favor from an old buddy. I'm getting real pressure on a few things here. C'mon, whaddya say?"

"The answer's no. Not on this one. Like I said, it's out of my hands now. What are you worried about anyway? The appropriate department will take care of her."

Click. Rehnquist hung up in his Georgetown mansion and went back to sleep.

Green snapped his phone shut and kicked the car door hard. *We'll have to take a less subtle approach.*

On the other side of town, Phoenix arrived at the grave and found the dead drop. He opened it to see the faces of his targets—a man and a woman. One was marked 'Dan Travis,' the other 'Unknown.'

CHAPTER 49

"I'M SCARED, DAD," said a tearful, seventeen-year-old Daniel Travis.

"Don't be scared, son. Ever."

"But, Dad..."

"Daniel, I want to tell you something. The most important thing I've ever told you."

Daniel handed him a glass of water as his father gathered the thoughts of his fading mind.

Dan's mind wandered. *I can't believe he'll be gone soon.*

"Daniel, your fear will take you to the one place you're afraid of."

"What do you mean?"

"Your focus determines your future: your reality. If you focus on the worst things happening, by worrying about it and putting it in your mind constantly, somehow those things have a funny way of coming true. It's like prayers being answered, in a way."

What I would give for just one more week, just one more fishing trip. Please.

"I love you." Daniel couldn't hold back the tears any longer. It was hard for a teenage boy to try to be a man in front of his paternal tower of strength, his role model.

"Love you too, son, now be strong," he said, handing his son a tissue. "Don't ever be afraid and focus on good things—

things you want to have happen and your noggin will do the rest. Trust me…"

"Wake up, sleeping beauty!" Sonia slammed the door as she climbed into the back seat. "It's your shift!"

Travis shook and opened his eyes. It was still dark outside and the skin was stiffening above his eye surrounding his wound. He should have felt terrible to be woken from a deep sleep, but didn't. Sonia was here. She had brought coffee for him.

"Where are we?" Travis mumbled, propping himself up. It appeared to be some kind of rest area.

"Somewhere in North Carolina. You feel okay? I can carry on if you want."

"No, I'm good," said Travis, reaching for the coffee and rubbing his eyes, the rich aroma tantalizing his nostrils. "So now you know how I look in the morning," he said.

"Hmm, I guess."

Something clicked inside Travis. Trepidation. Fear. Primal instinct. Who knows?

He reached over to Sonia and kissed her on the mouth. He expected her to kiss him back with closed, pursed lips, but when his mouth touched hers, she opened them slightly. Soft, warm, inviting.

It was the opening he needed. He exploited it.

At the same second, her tongue was deep inside his mouth. Their breathing quickened. He felt her gentle breath from her nose on his cheek. Her aroma was scintillating. His arms moved to her waist, his hands were a perfect fit between her breasts and hips, the narrowing of her hourglass shape.

His grip tightened.

She held his face, as he held her around the waist, both of them clinging to life itself.

CHAPTER 50

IT WAS 7:12 AM ON TUESDAY MORNING when Norman approached Green with freshly brewed Kona coffee in Green's special cup and a cherry Danish with the almonds painstakingly removed. Green glanced up for inspection and waved the breakfast to his desk approvingly.

Norman looked too old to be an assistant. He was in his late fifties with gray hair and a lived-in face with tired and jaded blue eyes. He was always immaculately dressed and well groomed (Green would settle for nothing less).

Norm had prospered in his post because Green didn't see him as a threat, and he was, after all, remarkably efficient and resourceful. Most of all, though, he put up with Green's eccentric crap.

Green took a long slurp of his Hawaiian coffee as he surveyed his assistant. Norman had been in this post for three and a half years and knew not to speak until spoken to. Norm sometimes felt Green deliberately created long silences to test his patience with that protocol. Most of Green's protocols were designed to catch people out so he could exert his power over them.

"What news, Norman?" came the inevitable question.

Norman handed Green a piece of paper. "Sir, no word from United States Postal Service yet, I'm still pushing them, but frankly, it's like hitting your head against a brick wall. I've also been chasing up an ID on the girl from the biometrics we sent and I'm still getting stonewalled there too…"

Green interrupted as he cut his pastry into equal bite-sized pieces with the pre-wrapped plastic knife and fork. "Leave that one for now."

"Very good, sir. And cryptology is still working on the fax, but nothing yet. There are just too many variables to pinpoint an address the envelope could have been sent to."

"Goddamn it," Green spat through a mouthful of pastry. "What about Leblanc's hard drive and contacts made from phone records?"

"Yes, sir. Based on the assumption that Leblanc sent the file to an acquaintance from his contact records, there are a total of seventy-eight home addresses in addition to the workplace addresses of those people."

"So then we need to post agents at those locations pronto. That seems like the best we can do until we figure out that fax," Green said.

"Sir, priority mail will take one to two days to reach its destination, so we're looking at an arrival of the Apollo File today or tomorrow at the latest. We can, of course, post field agents at each of those locations for that duration, but it will stretch the resources of the field offices involved. Agents may have to be taken off other cases to achieve that…"

"Norm, this takes priority over everything else, do you understand? So whatever it takes, and I couldn't give a damn how much bitching you hear about it. They can look for another job if they like."

"Understood, sir. I'll make it happen right away."

"And Norman?"

"Sir?"

"I take it we still have agents posted at Miami Children's Hospital?"

Norman was on the way out of the office to relay Green's orders to the field offices but took his seat again as he knew he should. He was like a dog on a leash: a slave to Green.

"Yes, sir. Unable to trace Dr. Roger's home address in the Miami-Dade area and surrounding districts. He's off the grid for now, but we're ready at the hospital as soon as he arrives on shift today."

"Good, but keep this low-key. Travis and the girl will be on their way to meet this Dr. Rogers and I want them taken *quietly*."

"I'll remind them, sir."

"You do that. And get cryptology to draw up a shortlist of the most likely to receive the file. Tell them to come see me when they're done."

"Yes, sir." Norman got up and headed for the door once again but was stopped a second time by Green speaking. More power games.

"And Norman?"

"Sir?"

"Fire Croghan."

"Yes, sir." Norman finally left and hurriedly began making phone calls.

When he was left alone, Green reached for his phone and dialed the man he'd met in secret last night.

CHAPTER 51

SPECIAL AGENT GARY REESE BLEW through security in the huge J. Edgar Hoover building at 935 Pennsylvania Avenue with the same pride he'd felt throughout his twenty-eight-year career with the Federal Bureau of Investigation. The famous headquarters was seven blocks long and eleven stories high—the imposing overhang of the top floors created the impression that people below were being watched from above, which was no coincidence.

There was more enthusiasm than usual in Reese's stride as he sprung into the elevator going to the fifth floor: the Strategic Information Operations Center (SIOC). That morning a vague voicemail had told him to report for briefing at once. Not since the morning of September 11, 2001 had he sensed such urgency, but the difference *this* morning was that no one else in the building shared his feeling.

In his mid-forties, Reese wore an off-the-rack black suit and blue tie. The color of a tie was the only indication of any individuality in this place. He was of stocky build, five-foot-eleven, auburn hair and blue eyes with a twice-broken nose: a constant reminder to those around him that he had taken down some hard criminals in his time. Tough and unquestioningly loyal, he epitomized everything the media-embattled Bureau wanted to stand for today.

He marched into the expanse of the SIOC's series of

low-ceilinged rooms, each looking like the news room at a television station with video monitors, digital clocks, desks and green chairs. He proceeded to Operations Room B as per his instructions.

When he walked into the room, he experienced the first of several surprises to come in the hours ahead.

One person occupied the vast, sterile room: the head of the FBI, David Jensen. Reese closed the door behind him and stood facing Jensen, sitting at the head of a large conference table reading a file.

"Sit down, Special Agent Reese," he said without looking up.

Reese obliged and observed the silence that followed as Jensen caught up on what was going on. This was an unusual matter. To have only one agent in on the briefing with Jensen was most strange.

Finally, Jensen spoke. "Reese, you have an impressive record. And that's why I've especially selected you for this case."

"Thank you, sir. What's the case?"

Jensen looked up at Reese with emotionless black eyes set deep into his pocked face, underneath a completely bald head. The media dubbed him "Spock" for his emotionless press conferences and obsession with cold analysis, but Reese was happy with the direction this recently-appointed Jensen was taking the Bureau. After a catalogue of debacles under the previous directors, Jensen was desperately trying to clean up the Bureau's image and remove old skeletons from the closet. His methods were criticized internally as ruthless, but Reese liked that. *Whatever it takes to get the job done.*

Reese knew the truth. Despite the poor image portrayed by the major newspapers—who could smell blood—the Bureau had quietly been doing an excellent job away from the spotlight of the 9/11 aftermath and buck-passing. Reese's department was cleaning up a lot of the mess from its rival agency, the CIA.

"Right now, you're wondering firstly why *I'm* here in this room, and secondly, why other agents aren't assembled here with you," Jensen deadpanned.

"The thought had crossed my mind, sir, yes."

"This is a *highly* sensitive matter, Reese. I'm sure I don't need to remind you that none of this can leave this room."

"Of course, sir."

Reese was all too aware of the leaks the Bureau was currently suffering from; the media and less well-known foreign governments had been buying secrets from FBI insiders.

"The Bureau just can't suffer another embarrassment— our reputation's on the line here. This one needs to be watertight: executed with discretion and precision. The people under you are on a need-to-know basis. You'll have full cooperation from any SAC you want, anywhere in the country, but they're not to know the nature of your mission." To give Reese automatic power over any SAC (Special Agent in Charge) was a big deal.

"I understand, sir." *What the hell's happened?*

Jensen sprung up and strutted toward Reese. Perching himself on the table in front of Reese, he handed him enlarged photos of two individuals and a case file.

Reese studied them. He vaguely recognized the man, but the girl was unknown to him.

"You need to find these two people ASAP and bring them in, but you need to do it right. I don't want any lawyer letting them walk because of poor procedure on our part. Reese, do you recognize that man?"

Jensen was deliberately not saying the names of the people in the photos or any other details, and neither was Reese, as everything was clearly marked *For Eyes Only*.

"Yes, sir."

"Good. Now you know why this is sensitive and the media needs to be kept out. This guy's well known. I need an agent I can trust. And here's the file on the girl." Jensen slapped a dossier on the table over the photos. Reese opened it.

His freckled forehead crinkled upwards as he read whom the girl worked for. "You've gotta be kidding!"

"I don't have a sense of humor, Reese. Now you're wondering what the link is between these two people. Truth is, I don't have that answer right now, but they cannot be allowed to complete their objective!"

A second dossier fluttered onto the table. Jensen commentated while Reese read. "Both the man and the woman were brought to our attention last night through two trusted independent sources."

"Hell of a night, sir."

"I think that's a logical response, Reese, yes."

CHAPTER 52

INSTEAD OF FEELING RELIEVED by the alluring skyline of downtown Miami, all Travis felt was nauseous. It was after three o'clock in the afternoon on Tuesday and he found it hard to believe he'd been on the run for almost twenty-four hours. That realization ushered in an overwhelming feeling of fatigue like payback for the adrenaline binge of last night. He'd managed to get a total of five hours sleep in the back seat, but it had been broken by bumps in the road and cramped conditions. The sort of sleep one gets on a long overnight flight. It was sleep, but somehow it didn't count.

When it was his his turn to drive he'd had no trouble staying awake. His mind had gone into overdrive, trying to find the missing pieces of the puzzle threatening his life and, like it or not, Sonia's. His memory of their passion had numbed the pain, exhaustion and despair. The rich scent of her skin was on him and it gave him strength. That feeling, combined with the dull ache from the wound above his eye, had drawn out something primal within him. He felt like a warrior and realized he was a changed man.

Who was tired as hell.

He stole a glance at Sonia sleeping on the back seat. Curled into a ball, her long black hair strewn around two pillows, she looked beautiful even in this situation. He had been waiting for an opportunity to wake her. Arriving in Miami seemed reasonable. They were almost there and he needed something to keep him sharp. *Lame excuse.*

"Sonia?"

She stirred. "We there?"

"Yep, look." Travis gestured at the approaching skyscrapers of Miami, poised on the edge of the Atlantic, basking in the late afternoon sun.

"Kramer's old wreck did the job then," she continued as she climbed into the front seat. "When it wouldn't start again after that gas stop in Georgia, I thought we were screwed. So you have that address for Ramón's café?"

"Yep. Feels like we're driving into the jaws of a dragon going after this Dr. Rogers though," he said.

"That's why we're gonna hook up with Ramón first. We'll need some muscle to get to that doctor. Stop at a strip mall when you see one—we need a few things."

Sonia adopted a professional tone as if nothing had happened between them. Travis fought to conceal his disappointment. *Just as well, we have a job to do.* He tuned to the reality of what possible dangers lurked at the foot of the shiny towers on the horizon.

"And, yes, you were great last night," Sonia said as she checked the magazine of the gun she'd stolen from Green.

CHAPTER 53

IT HAD BEEN A LONG and frustrating day for Green, and his staff had felt the brunt of his frustration. He'd harangued them with extraordinary vigor. Norman was sitting in front of him for the seventh time that day.

"Norman, what's happening?"

"Sir, at your request all possible names and addresses from Leblanc's contact list and phone records were covered by agents today, but no priority envelope has shown up yet."

"So it's likely the file will arrive tomorrow?"

"Yes, unless…" Norman hesitated. He should have known better than to think aloud.

"Unless what?!"

What the hell. "Unless, sir, Leblanc sent it to someone whose address is not in his contact list or phone records."

Green sprung up, shoving his chair back against the wall. Norman felt himself flinch in fear of having the stapler, which lay on the desk, thrown at him, but Green silently walked to the window.

Finally he spoke.

"Alright. Keep those men posted there until I say, in case the file arrives tomorrow. We have to plan for the possibility of Leblanc sending it to someone who wasn't in his contact list or phone records, which means figuring out that fax."

"Yes, sir. That sounds like a good move." Norman knew

how to play the game; he'd throw an idea out and then let Green think it had been his idea all along.

"Tell me again what time Dr. Rogers goes on shift?" Green said, still staring out the window.

Sure, for the hundredth time today. "Six o'clock, sir, and the agents are standing by."

Green paused for thought, rubbing a finger through his hair. "Okay. If we assume the file wasn't sent to one of Leblanc's contacts, then we have to rely on a combination of the United States Postal Service, this Dr. Rogers and that snot-nosed cryptologist. Plus we need to keep Travis and the girl out of the way."

"Yes, sir," said Norman, covertly doodling a picture of a log cabin on his clipboard. "That all seems logical."

"Okay, so then you know what to do and whose ass to kick, Norm."

"Yes, sir." Norman knew that was his cue to exit.

Green reclined back into his chair and made a call. While it was ringing, Norman entered the office again. Green covered the receiver and silently mouthed at Norman: what?

Norman whispered, "I've got a Special Agent Reese wanting to ask a few questions?"

"Not now," Green whispered back, waving a hand.

The phone picked up finally. "Yes?" came the foreign accent. It was Phoenix.

"It's me, what do you have?"

"An ID on the female. I've left the details in the usual location." Phoenix hung up.

Excellent.

Green blew out of his office, passing Norman. "Norman, I'm on the road again. You know where to call me."

"Yes, sir."

"And when I get back that cryptologist had better have

something for me. And keep chasing those postal service morons—they must at least be able to narrow it down."

In the garage, Green's new driver was waiting, holding the door open for him.

Green leapt in. "You know this intersection? That's where you're going."

"Yes, sir."

The driver screeched the car out of the parking lot and past the armed sentry into Washington.

The black sedan hacked its way through heavy afternoon traffic in the Capitol. The Apollo File was going to show up somewhere, probably tomorrow, but where? *In any case,* Green thought, *Travis and the girl can't be allowed to make it there first.*

CHAPTER 54

THEY ABANDONED THE CAR and started off on foot. George Kramer would soon have to report his car stolen. The south Florida heat and humidity hit Travis immediately, in stark contrast to the chilly night air of the northern states they'd driven through.

They could only be in inner city Miami. Most of the signs were in Spanish; salsa, merengue and hip-hop seemed to be the soundtrack.

Travis recalled stories of tourists who'd taken the wrong exit from the freeway and had been shot. *How anyone would be dumb enough to roll down a window and ask for directions in this place is amazing,* he thought. Everything matched the stereotypical image of a downtown ghetto, except for the sound of police sirens in the background—unlike in the movies, they weren't there. Evidently, the police weren't stupid enough to hang around here.

Travis had been to Miami for vacations and conferences but only to the glamorous South Beach area. White sands, palm trees and beautiful people. The difference between those memories and what he saw now was enough to make him wonder if he was in the same city.

Or living the same life for that matter. He wondered if *anything* in his life would look the same again.

On the corner of the street was a trash can with flames

billowing out of it and, under the shelter of a doorway, lay old mattresses. Standing in the middle of the sidewalk was an elderly Hispanic man holding up a sealed jar containing a clear liquid of some sort, as if it was for sale. Whether he was simply crazy or not was a question Travis didn't even ponder; he was looking across the street at El Hoyo—the café where they were supposed to find Ramón Martinez.

"Come on," Sonia said, looking at her watch. "We only have an hour and fifty-two minutes before Dr. Rogers comes on shift. Let's find this Ramón guy."

Sonia and Travis eased across the street toward the café. It didn't look very busy from the outside though the windows were dirty and mostly covered with advertisements: beer, Cuban sandwiches and empanadas were prominent features.

They emerged through a curtain of hanging beads into the café. Immediately, the occupants—eight Cubans of varying ages and sizes—looked up and stopped talking. Travis had hoped their disheveled appearance would allow them to blend in here.

Apparently not.

The café was nothing more than a hole in the wall and offered little shelter from the oppression of the sultry Miami air. A ceiling fan was as good as it got, but all that seemed to do was swirl around the stench of cigar smoke. The walls, once white, were now discolored yellow with grime.

The short, chubby man behind the counter with arms hairier than Travis's head gestured at them to sit down. "Si?" English translation: "Get out of my café."

The regular patrons went back to what they were doing: playing dominoes, eating sandwiches and conversing in Spanish. Sonia sat down and Travis approached the counter to ask where he could find Ramón. His Spanish was only '101,' but he gave it his best shot.

"Señor, dónde está Ramón Martinez?"

"Ramón who? I neber hear o' heem. You wan' eat?" The guy behind the counter could speak English. Kinda.

Travis wasn't hungry but hoped buying a sandwich might buy some time. "Two Cuban sandwiches please. I was told Ramón Martinez owned and ran this café and spent most of his time here?"

"Look like someone tell you wrong."

"Is there another café El Hoyo? Is this the wrong address? Maybe I'm at the wrong place?" Travis showed the man the piece of paper with the address of the café that Kramer had given him.

Smoking a large cigar, the man spoke while he slapped butter on some bread. "Señor," he said, dropping ash into the sandwich as he spoke, "Only one café wi dees name an dees dee only address in Miami like dee one on da' paper. Eere." He slid two plates across the counter, each with a slimy looking sandwich. Travis paid him and walked back to Sonia with the sandwiches.

"I wouldn't eat those," he said, slumping into a plastic seat opposite her.

"Screw it then—we'll go and get Rogers ourselves—but I don't know what the hell Kramer was thinking sending us here." Sonia pushed the plate away in disgust.

They were starting to attract attention. One of the younger men was giving them an uneasy stare.

Travis whispered, "It just doesn't make any sense."

"What doesn't?"

"Kramer wouldn't have just come up with this address. We'll need this guy Ramón's help, something tells me. We've got no car now and we're in a strange town. That guy who tried to kill us is probably expecting us; if and when we do figure out where this Apollo File is, we'll need some way of getting to it quickly and in one piece. Shit!" Travis slammed a hand down on the table and hung his head.

"Okay, okay. Take it easy, Dan. You're right. Listen, why don't you get over to the hospital and check things out and I'll stay around here and see if I can't find out where Ramón is? You'll need to make contact with the doctor in person, since it was your name on the fax. We have to get him to trust us. I can call you when I find Ramón."

"How? I need a car."

"Kramer won't have called it in just yet, so you'll be fine. It's only twenty minutes away from here anyway," she said, placing a hand on his arm.

"Okay. Let's get outta here now—I don't feel too comfortable talking about any of this here. We'll call Kramer from that payphone across the street and verify the address."

"Let's go." Sonia shot up and marched out, Travis trailing.

CHAPTER 55

PEOPLE VISITING CEMETERIES generally walk slowly, as if in some way rushing around would bother the dead. Such was Green's frustration as he bustled along the main walkway into the cemetery where the dead drop had been left by Phoenix. Cemeteries made excellent dead drops. You could come and go at any hour of the day and not look suspicious.

The identity of the girl who was stupid enough to point Green's own gun at him was about to be known. The last twenty-four hours had seemed like an eternity and here at last was something concrete to go on. Knowing the identity of the girl would make it easier to get her and Travis out of the picture and might even give him a clue as to where Leblanc had sent the Apollo File.

C'mon, c'mon…outta the goddamn way!

Green wended through mourners scattered along the path to the grave. *There it is.*

Green knelt beside the grave and hung his head as if to pray, but he was actually looking at the grass about six inches above the bottom right corner of the grave border.

The dead drop was there as promised. A hollow metal spike stuck in the dirt.

He casually reached over and plucked it from the ground. He made the sign of the cross, waited five seconds and left the grave.

Green popped open the top of the hollow spike. There was a portable USB storage device, presumably holding the data he needed.

CHAPTER 56

As TRAVIS STOOD in the phone booth across the street from El Hoyo, all he could hear was endless ringing. He loosened the collar of his thick, green shirt; it felt heavy and sticky in this climate. *Pick up, George!*

Nothing.

A cricket's rapid chirp sounded like laughter. Travis turned from the booth to find Sonia waiting for him. Hopefully she'd had more luck with her call in the adjacent phone booth.

"What did he say?" she asked.

"Nothing. He wasn't in. How about your Service friend?"

"Nothing happening there either. Let's just proceed as planned."

Sonia handed Travis the second of the two 'pay as you go' cell phones she'd bought from the strip mall as they'd entered Miami. She'd been setting them up while Travis used the payphone.

"You remember everything I told you?"

"Yeah, I do. Thanks."

"Don't forget the balloons," she said, pointing to the six helium balloons of various colors she'd also bought from the mall. "Let's go. Be careful," she added.

Travis stared at Sonia intently. Something in his gut told

him he wouldn't see her again, but he dared not let on how he was feeling.

"I'll let you know just as soon as I find anything on Ramón. You be careful at that hospital. This doctor probably hasn't got a clue what's going on and there'll be men expecting you."

Travis was walking back toward Kramer's old Ford as she spoke. He gave her a friendly salute, got in and drove off. He watched her march along the sidewalk as he veered out into the street. She looked vulnerable, but he knew Sonia could take care of herself.

As Travis made his way to Miami Children's Hospital, he worked through how he was going to tackle the situation in his mind.

Travis was a strong believer in the power of visualization. To vividly picture an event happening—an event playing out the way you wanted it to—programmed the subconscious accordingly and made one react in the right way. Travis had often argued this point to explain events others were quick to label as 'supernatural.' Astrology, divine intervention and premonition being the most common examples—if we program our minds to believe something will happen, good or bad, it's likely to happen, and when it does, the belief in the 'supernatural' event is reinforced. Travis's conclusion was that the whole thing was a self-fulfilling prophecy.

The key part of the plan he and Sonia had devised was to get to the hospital as early as possible to figure out how and where to intercept the doctor before Green's agents, and get him to a remote and public place. Travis nearly ran a red light as he fumbled with the road map. He thought it best to visualize getting there quickly and in one piece, first and foremost.

After tearing through palm tree-lined blocks of colorful single-story buildings in West Miami, Travis edged the car into the hospital parking lot. Unusually positioned for a hospital, it was hidden away in the middle of a residential area. He found the entrance ironic as he drove by.

The exterior of Miami Children's Hospital was like something a child might have built. Walls and pillars of merry colors resembled a patchwork quilt, which had been constructed from nursery bricks. Travis found it hard to comprehend that this innocent place was to be the setting of a conflict that threatened his very existence.

His heart began pounding at the thought of people all too willing to shoot him dead, possibly already in his vicinity. The fact that this was a public place gave him no recourse from the imminent terror; Green had government approval to orchestrate his assassination.

Deep breaths. Time to get to work.

Travis tuned out the voice of fear nagging at him and found the warrior within. He puffed out his chest and tapped into the outrage and anger that had brought him this far. He replayed Sonia's rushed briefing in his head and almost immediately, the focus he required arrived, unchecked and powerful. He suddenly felt like a loaded gun.

Travis parked the car, clenched his jaw and put on the sunglasses Sonia had bought. He made sure he didn't forget the helium balloons from the backseat, though they detracted from the *Scarface* persona he was desperately trying to conjure. Sonia had argued that, in any other location, he'd have stood out but approaching a children's hospital, just the opposite. Plus the balloons obscured a clear view of him.

Travis stared at his watch. Over an hour to go until the doctor came on shift.

Just as Sonia had told him to, Travis began to study the battlefield. They agreed the mostly likely point the agents would try to pick up the doctor would be as he got out of his car in the physician's garage. Possibly one would be waiting in the hospital too. *There's only one way to be sure.*

Despite his casual saunter, perspiration accumulated on Travis's battered brow as he watched the entrance to the physicians' garage. Whether it was caused through his nervousness or the moist evening air, he couldn't be sure. Probably both.

Two groups of people converged on the hospital entrance, one carrying a large furry bear. A wave of relief swept through Travis's gut. He fit in.

The physician's annex of the garage was small, under cover and right next to the hospital reception. Travis boldly strode into the parking garage, the dim light and the balloons providing welcome cover. He made a beeline for the reception area while surreptitiously looking at the parked cars for anyone sitting in them. Sonia had told him the agents' car would be parked facing nose-out, to allow an expeditious departure, whereas most people park nose-*in*, out of laziness.

Nothing seemed to fit the bill. *They probably aren't here yet. Good.* Now he could watch the physician's parking lot for the arrival of both Green's agents and the doctor.

Travis edged into the hospital reception area, looking for a photo of Rogers to be able to identify him. It wasn't until Sonia explained this part of the plan that Travis realized he'd overlooked that 'small' detail. The next consideration was calculating an alternative exit if the agents blocked the main doors.

The young woman at the reception desk was on the

phone, flipping through pages of a celebrity gossip magazine. She smiled at Travis who, to her eyes, was just another visitor.

Travis held back a few feet from the desk and scanned for a physician directory.

Unsuccessful, he caught the receptionist's dark eyes. She was a beautiful Hispanic woman with a pleasant manner.

"I'm looking for a physician directory?" It was surreal. He was making an innocent inquiry in a little children's hospital, but he felt like he was a drug smuggler trying to get through customs.

"Sure," she said. "In the pharmacy down the hall is a computer terminal. It'll be available there."

"Thank you, ma'am." It occurred to Travis just then he hadn't had access to the Internet since this whole drama began. *No time to check emails now.*

"Oh, you're welcome," she began, "but you'll need to wear a pass. Do you have ID?"

Travis froze. Sure he had ID, but it could alert someone. He was even *thinking* like a fugitive now! His mind raced. What choice did he have? There was no other way to identify the doctor.

"Sir…do you have *ID*?"

What the hell. They probably know anyway. "Sure. Here you go."

"Thanks. Please look into the camera."

After Travis handed her his driving license and gingerly posed for the webcam, she printed off a sticker, showing his name and picture. He thanked her, barely stuck it to his shirt and hurried past the security guard into the pharmacy to use the terminal. He peeled off the name sticker and shoved it into his pocket.

Travis dived into the wooden chair facing the screen and

followed the directions. A physician directory soon materialized. He scrolled down. The title appeared: "J.E. Rogers, M.D., Oncology." Next to the name was a picture of a man who looked to be in his late fifties wearing square bifocal glasses, gray hair with a side part, blue eyes and a chubby face with a sober expression. Travis stared at the picture, burning the image into his mind. *This guy is the key and soon he'll be here.*

The word "oncology" made an image of his mom flash before his eyes. Rogers was a cancer doctor.

Travis jumped up and hustled down the corridor in search of an alternative exit. He didn't have to walk far. Just to the left was the emergency arrivals entrance. Travis walked through it, back into the humid Florida evening. He found Kramer's car and, just as Sonia had instructed, re-parked it as close as possible to his backup exit, then went back to the physician's parking lot to wait.

Everything's going swimmingly.

Now all he had to do was wait for Rogers, convince him to urgently leave, with a stranger, all the while avoiding Green's men.

It had all sounded so easy when Sonia had explained it earlier.

CHAPTER 57

SONIA CURSED UNDER her breath again. "Ramón Martinez is a fucking ghost!" *No one's heard of the son of a bitch. Senile old coot Kramer probably got the town wrong.* And it wasn't helping that her Spanish wasn't that great in a town where it was the primary language.

She thought about calling Travis on her cell phone to see how he was doing but thought better of it. She wondered if she should have gone with him. Maybe she overestimated his capability to pull the operation off successfully.

Without drawing much attention to herself, she made her way down the shabby street—it was littered with multi-colored store fronts, all of which had seen better times, some boarded up. Her long black hair and bedraggled appearance were serving her well in this environment. *It is Travis who stands out here*, she thought. In that moment, she realized it was better that she'd taken this assignment after all.

Her gut twitching interrupted her wandering train of thought.

Something wasn't right.

Her training kicked in, though her demeanor didn't change. She carried on walking exactly the same way in the same direction as before, but her senses were on high alert.

As she approached the intersection, she knew she had to use this opportunity to cross the street. She made a right turn, being careful to only look straight across the street to her destination—not behind her—but still used her peripheral vision to look back. She waited for an opening in the traffic and edged across the street, fixing her vision on the glass storefront dead ahead.

As she came within range of the glass, she stared at the reflection. Her eyes confirmed her previous feeling.

She was being followed.

CHAPTER 58

DISCREETLY POISED ON THE WALKWAY between the reception and the physician's garage, Travis felt the circulation cut off from his hand that held the balloons. As he changed hands, he noticed he'd been clenching them so tightly he practically had to pry open his fingers. The nauseating sound of cracking knuckles served as a reminder of the fragility of life—*his life*—right now in this place.

So far he'd seen three cars enter so far: each BMW transported a physician in teal scrubs. From this vantage point he could also see any cars coming from the street in front of the hospital. Still, there was thirty-four minutes to go until six o'clock. Travis desperately hoped Rogers would get there early.

Travis eyed another car purposely darting from the street toward the physician's parking lot. It was a lone man in a Mercedes. *Must be another physician.*

The Mercedes entered, headlights blazing, and parked, nose-in against the wall furthest away from Travis.

A middle-aged man got out wearing glasses. He had gray hair with a side part and a gray suit. Travis was hopeful, but this was all he could see from the back. The man turned, clicked his key, making the cars lights flash with a double-beep. The man's face instantly registered.

Dr. Rogers was early for work!

There's no sign of Green's men, Travis thought, gazing back at the street for confirmation…

Travis's relief snapped into panic. A black sedan drove through the hospital entrance as the doctor was plodding toward reception.

Okay, Travis, you're on. Do something! Fast!

The sedan was slowing, as if the occupants were unsure where to go. *Bad sign.* It was close enough now for Travis to see two men in the car. *Not good.*

Travis's gut clenched. These were probably Green's men arriving. He wanted to deny it was happening but knew that was futile. The time to act was now.

Travis held back as a speed-of-light debate played out in his head. The parking lot wasn't the place to persuade the doctor. Following that thought, he realized he already had a security pass from earlier—as would the doctor—but Green's agents wouldn't. One agent would stay in the car and another would obviously enter the hospital to check. He might have some sort of a badge he could flash at the security guard, but hopefully there would still be a delay. *Wouldn't there be?*

Okay, approach the doctor inside.

The doctor blew past Travis. Travis reassured himself this was the guy and followed him, glancing back to see the black sedan approach the entrance to the parking lot.

Travis and the doctor almost entered reception together. But instead of sweeping past the security guard, Rogers stopped to talk to him. *Come on!* As Travis heard them exchange pleasantries, he turned his head to see the black sedan park in the distance, next to the entrance to the parking lot, and a single man in a suit get out.

It parked rear-end in. *Definitely not good. Come on, Rogers. Move!*

After thirty seconds of banality, which seemed like thirty

minutes, Dr. Rogers ambled on up the hallway. Travis followed with his balloons. He stared at the back of the doctor's head almost in a trance. He resisted the thought creeping into his mind: *How did I get into this position?* Instead he recalled the rest of Sonia's advice: "You'll have to get his attention fast, then get him out of there to a public place. Be succinct."

Alright, let's do it. "Dr. Rogers!"

The doctor stopped and craned his head back to see Travis.

"Yes?"

Rogers had an intimidating presence, but Travis stuck to his guns.

"Doctor, were you recently contacted by a Clinton Leblanc?"

The doctor didn't respond. Travis held out the fax Leblanc had sent. "Leblanc's dead, but he sent me this fax with your name on it and I believe you're in grave danger this very minute. Please come with me now." *Wow—did I just say that?*

"Who are you?"

Rogers hadn't called security or simply walked away, so that was encouraging to Travis.

"My name's Dan Travis and I assure you that I'm deadly serious. I mean you no harm. I have a car outside. We should leave right away. People who want both you and me are right behind us. Please, this way." Travis gestured toward his backup exit. He felt a drip of sweat meander down from his temple and hoped the doctor hadn't noticed.

The doctor froze his eyes, seeming to scan Travis like an MRI. Travis gestured again to move to the exit.

Rogers knows exactly what I'm talking about.

"Alright," said Rogers, and he walked with Travis.

Yes! Travis kept a pace behind.

As he turned, Travis caught sight of the man in the

suit—the one who'd got out of the black sedan. He was at reception talking to the security guard. Just as Travis looked away, nearly out of view, he saw the security guard point in their direction.

He didn't wait to see what would happen next.

"Run!" Travis ordered, breaking into a sprint. "They're here!"

The doctor didn't say a word. His face turned white and he started to run.

Travis grabbed the doctor's arm and bustled him out the ER entrance. "Move! That's my car," he said, pointing at the Ford.

Travis swung into the driver's seat, rammed the key in the ignition and turned it.

Nothing.

No!

He tried again. The doctor fell into the passenger seat, gasping for breath. Nothing. The doctor eyed Travis with his mouth open.

Travis slammed both hands on the burning hot steering wheel. "Piece of shit!"

The man in the suit burst out of the ER doors and panned his head around.

C'mon! Travis tried again. The engine turned but sounded reluctant.

Come on, come on.

Then, as if Kramer's car suddenly knew the stakes, the tired engine shuddered to life with a tinny rattle.

"Okay!" Travis rammed the transmission into gear and stamped on the accelerator.

The man in the suit was running at the car.

"Look!" Rogers screamed.

"Shit, shit!" Travis sputtered, trying to push the gas pedal through the floor. The small street offered no maneuvering space.

Thunk! Realizing he'd missed them, the man in the suit banged his fist on the trunk as they sped away.

"We have to get some distance. Right now he's running back to his car and his partner!" Travis cried out, but he was really thinking aloud about what Sonia would do.

The doctor spun his head around to look out the rear window, then sat forward and corrected Travis. "No! His partner's picking him up!"

"Shit!" Travis glanced in the rear-view mirror.

"Take a left here and keep making turns. This neighborhood is a maze. We should be able to lose them no problem—they're still a block or two behind us," said Rogers.

Travis followed the doctor's directions with little regard for stop signs. They turned and turned, weaving their way out of the residential area with no sign of their pursuer.

Travis's breathing slowly recovered, but he kept looking into the rear-view mirror more than out the windshield.

Minutes later, they arrived at a strip mall.

Rogers continued his instruction. "There's a small café over there. You'd better park this some place else."

Travis found it hard to believe the men following them would find the car now, but he obliged. The car rocked to a halt and Travis shut off the engine, which had started hissing. It might not start again, but he could always call Sonia and get a cab or whatever from here.

Travis's shoulders relaxed while he stared out the windshield. He'd done it.

"You coming?" Rogers called.

In silence they walked to the café, each not knowing what to say to the other or where to start but both knowing why they were here. Travis wanted to be inside, somewhere safe and out of view—the questions burned inside his head. Finally, some answers.

Once inside the small café, they ordered two café con leches and sat at one of the small tables in the corner.

Travis burst through the silence by presenting Rogers with the fax and telling him about the events that had torn his life apart in the last twenty-four hours. His trust in the doctor was unconditional. Travis left no detail out.

When Travis had finished his story, Rogers sat staring out the window at a thunderstorm creeping in on the landscape. The torrential rain began to hammer down on the cars outside.

Cleaning his glasses with a napkin, Dr. Rogers finally spoke with pragmatic precision, accompanied by an ominous crack of thunder. "Travis, there's a silent war going on in this country. And like it or not, you've just walked right into it."

CHAPTER 59

NORMAN KNEW TO CHOOSE his words well when speaking to Green. "Sir, you've had another call from Special Agent Reese and the cryptologist…"

"Not now, Norm. I don't want to be disturbed," snapped Green as he hurried into his office, slamming the door behind him.

Green pushed the USB storage key into his computer as he dropped into his chair, and peered into the monitor.

He studied the information from Phoenix. The information his supposed friend Rehnquist had denied him.

The blood drained from Green's face as he scrolled down the screen. He froze, his mouth half open, wincing. *No wonder Rehnquist was forced to turn the matter over to another department!*

The eyes of this no-longer-mysterious girl stared out of the screen at him defiantly. *Evil, godless little bitch.*

Green gulped involuntarily. Worst of all, he felt out of control.

Slapping a hand on the desk, Green recalled how she'd helped Travis get away right from the start. Everything became clear as to why she had been involved and why she was so capable. He ripped out the USB device and pushed it into his pocket.

The dark cloud came.

Green knew that picking up the monitor and throwing it out the window—or even smashing it over Norman's head—would do no good, but he wanted to do it all the same.

Breathe, breathe. He felt like he was choking.

It's okay, it's okay. The therapist had told him that even the darkest cloud has a silver lining—you just have to look for it. He gazed out his window and actually looked for it.

After a minute or so, he swept around to the door and called for Norman.

Norman sat down before speaking, as if he were a well-programmed robot. "Sir?"

"Who's this special agent who's been calling me?"

"Reese, sir, Special Agent Reese from the Bureau. The cryptologist is also waiting to see you."

"Good, send him in and get Reese on the line while I'm waiting."

CHAPTER 60

TRAVIS FELT LIKE one of the violent thunderbolts from the raging storm outside had hit him between the eyes. He was cowering in some forsaken café, next to a man he'd never met who could possibly save his life. After hour upon hour of confusion and despair, it finally seemed as though the mystery was about to be unraveled, at least a little.

"Doctor, do you know where Leblanc might have sent this Apollo File? Can you see a relationship to the Cubans, Soviets or Kennedy's assassination with anything you know about this?"

"No to both. Sorry." Rogers shook his head. "Barely knew Leblanc."

Travis knew there was a reason Rogers was mentioned on Leblanc's fax.

"What war, Doctor? You said there's a silent war. What happened at Sloan Kettering?"

"Alright. You told me your story, now I'll tell you mine. But let me first tell you what 'CA Rep.' means on that fax. Leblanc was in touch with me recently—when you said his name, I knew you were for real. I can only tell you what I told him. You rightly deduce that CA is an abbreviation for California, but Rep. is short for Report."

"California Report?"

"Yes. It's a medical report made public record in November 1963."

"November 1963?" Travis looked at the fax again:

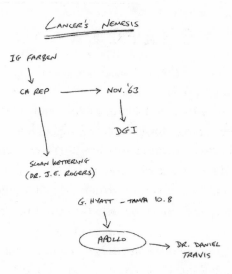

The California Report was linked to the side of the fax that he and Kramer had agreed referred to Kennedy—November 1963 being when Kennedy was shot—so this was a curious revelation. In fact, it now seemed everything on the fax was medical apart from the title, "Lancer's Nemesis," and the "DGI"—the Cuban Intelligence Service. Was the fact that this California Report came out the same year and month that Kennedy was shot the link? If so, how could that possibly tell him where the file was?

"Yes," Rogers continued. "The California Report was released on November 1st, 1963 and it essentially outlawed a substance called Laetrile. The report was first published ten years before, but *that* date is when the law to ban Laetrile was finally brought into effect."

Travis knew there was no apparent link to Kennedy's killers in all this, but he had to listen regardless. Experience had taught him to keep digging as one clue often lead to another. Eventually you'd get there, if you kept an open mind.

Rogers went on. "The Report was commissioned by the pharmaceutical cartel, obviously referenced in this fax by their historical name of IG Farben. To understand what happened at Sloan Kettering and why the California Report was even commissioned, I need to explain the background behind all this. Make no mistake, what I'm about to tell you is factual and constitutes the biggest medical cover-up in history."

The mention of a cover-up instantly heightened Travis's interest. He was convinced that a cover-up was exactly what he'd been entangled in, regardless of any links to JFK.

"Travis, there is a cure for cancer and always has been."

What?! No surely, n...

Dad.

Mom!

On any other day, if any other person had told Travis this, he'd have shrugged it off. But this was no other day and this was no ordinary person.

Travis screwed up his eyes to remain attentive to the story, however much he may not have wished to hear it.

"It all started in 1952 with a doctor from San Francisco named Ernst Krebs. Krebs advanced the theory that cancer was not so much caused *by* something as a *lack* of something. That something was a vitamin called B17, found most concentrated in the kernels of apricots."

This sounded just too alien to Travis. "What? You're saying a vitamin found in apricots—in any supermarket—cures cancer? How so? Why hasn't it been used then?"

Rogers sighed, clearly accustomed to the knee-jerk reaction. "Look, I'll answer all your questions, but if you don't like the answers, that's your problem."

Rogers eased Travis into the revelation with a well-rehearsed speech. "They once thought it crazy that vitamin C could cure scurvy. In 1747 a young surgeon in the British Navy discovered that citrus fruit provided relief. But because of scientific arrogance, it took another fifty years for the Royal Navy to carry limes on board their vessels. Once they did, they were able to surpass all other sea-faring nations. To this day we call the British 'limey' for that very reason."

Travis felt as though he was a student sitting in one of his old lectures; the kind of alternate histories his students would love to hear. Rogers had plucked interest out of skepticism. Travis's heart raced for his mother as well as the location of the Apollo File now.

"You see, scientists are trained to look for *complex* solutions to problems. This validates their training. Simple explanations for anything invalidate that. Doctors have become American icons—practically hailed as gods you dare not question—but they're just humans who've been fed information. They're only as good as the information they've been told. But, who's providing them with this information and what do they have to gain by doing so?"

Rogers paused as he gestured for another coffee to the waitress.

The paradox made sense. Who better to know how flawed the system was than an insider? A thousand questions raced through Travis's head, but he resisted the temptation to preempt anything or interrupt; the doctor had an awkward way about him. Although Rogers had gladly raced to the car with him, it was clear he bore little sympathy for Travis's predicament.

"Billions of dollars have been spent and decades have gone by, but cancer remains more prevalent than ever and still the same thinking goes on. There's a word for doing the same thing every day but expecting different results: *insanity*. Or perhaps, Travis, it's something darker than plain stupidity that's caused the deadlock?"

The second round of coffees arrived. Rogers calmly stirred sugar into his as he continued, staring out into the heavy rain pelting the sidewalk.

"Have you heard of a tiny kingdom in the Himalayas called Hunza?" asked Rogers.

"No. Why?"

"Because the people of Hunza were unwittingly participants in the largest clinical trial of Laetrile ever. They never have cancer and often live to one hundred and twenty years old. In this place the number of apricot trees a man owns measures his wealth. Apricots are the staple diet—they're used for everything. Cooking oil, you name it. But recently, Western foods have been creeping in and sadly the first signs of cancer have appeared there."

"Surely that's because they're not subject to all the pollution and carcinogens we are in the West?" Although the Hunza story was interesting, Travis couldn't resist playing devil's advocate.

"You have a reasonable argument. Unfortunately, it's erroneous. The compound that's behind vitamin B17, or Laetrile if you will, is called a nitriloside which is found in a great deal of fruit and vegetables. It's just that it's at exceptionally high levels in an apricot kernel. Would you say that California is polluted and therefore fairly conducive to carcinogens?"

"I would, yes," Travis said, after a thought for smog-riddled cities like Los Angeles.

"Okay then. The Seventh Day Adventist Church in California, which is by the way over 100,000 strong, has an incidence of cancer less than 50 percent of that of the rest of the state. Not cancer-free, mind you, but it's better than most. The only difference in their way of life from others is that they're vegetarian, therefore they consume more nitrilosides by default."

Travis's critical mind ground through the data it was receiving. The evidence was increasing but more was needed. Something told him Rogers was nowhere near done. Confusion set in over what Leblanc's connection to this was with the heading "Lancer's Nemesis."

"Anyway. Moving back to Dr. Ernst Krebs, he built on these clues and created Laetrile: a kind of purified form of B17, extracted from apricot kernels. He needed to test it first for non-toxicity, so he used animals and then *himself*, reason being that Laetrile contains cyanide."

"Cyanide? But that's lethal!"

"And yet apricots and apple seeds are full of cyanide and they're readily available in supermarkets," quipped Rogers. He then grabbed the saltshaker from the table and held it up. "See this stuff? Would you put it on your food?"

"Salt? Yes. It's harmless."

"Well, the chemical name for salt is sodium chloride—a composition of sodium and chlorine. Would you eat chlorine?"

"No, of course not. It's toxic."

"And the reason why is that chlorine's a substance that can only be harmful in isolation. If you separated the chlorine from this salt and ate it, it would be toxic, but combined with sodium it's just table salt."

"Yes, I see, but what's your point?"

Travis saw the doctor groan inside at having to explain this to a layman. He'd often noticed a kind of hostility when talking to medical doctors, he'd guessed because his own doctorate was not medical.

"The point, Mr. Travis, is that Laetrile is as harmless as table salt—unless you're a cancer cell. The reaction with Laetrile and a cell causes the cyanide component to be released and it thus kills *that* cell, if it's a cancer cell. However, a protecting enzyme called rhodanese is also released during this reaction that protects healthy cells from the cyanide. A cancer cell doesn't produce any rhodanese so it gets eliminated by the cyanide. But by your reaction, you can see how easy it was for the establishment to discredit Laetrile. Just say the word 'cyanide' and it's game over. Incidentally, while Laetrile is *not* toxic, all conventional methods of treating cancer are *highly* toxic, so you can hardly use the toxicity argument anyway."

"I can see that. So who do you mean by 'the establishment'?" Travis probed Rogers like a detective trying to surmise some kind of possible location of the Apollo File.

"I'll tell you in a minute, but suffice to say, it's anyone who has a lot to lose from Laetrile being hailed as a cure…or for that matter, anything being hailed as a cure."

"What do you mean?"

"Look, Laetrile is a natural substance, a vitamin. You can't patent a natural substance, so there's no money in it."

Travis felt nauseous considering where this was all heading, but he'd long ago lost his innocence and the belief that man isn't motivated by money and power, regardless of the consequences.

"And you said earlier, Laetrile was outlawed. Why would you outlaw a natural substance?" Travis said.

"Exactly," said the doctor with a grim smirk on his face. "In 1956, Krebs was introduced to a resourceful businessman called Andrew McNaughton who really got behind Laetrile. McNaughton was the son of a World War II general who was also previous president of the United Nations Security Council. Arguably, McNaughton was the single most important person behind the Laetrile movement. In the early sixties, through the McNaughton Foundation, the first Laetrile clinic opened to the public in Dallas and the results were impressive."

Travis's ears pricked up. "Dallas, Texas?"

"Yes," said the doctor, confused at why that location should cause so much excitement.

Dallas: the town where Kennedy was shot. This, along with the November 1963 California Report release date was the second link to JFK's assassination. But it was also a weak link. There had to be something more.

"Then the war began," continued Rogers. "It was McNaughton against the cancer industry, and that's why the California Report was commissioned—to end the debate once and for all by silencing the Laetrilists. But the report was riddled with lies and inconsistencies."

"Sounds a lot like the Warren Commission's investigation into Kennedy's assassination," said Travis.

CHAPTER 61

SONIA HEARD A THUNDERSTORM in the distance, closing in. The air rich with moisture, the once blue sky now dark, the light had transformed into an eerie luminescence.

She knew this would level the playing field.

Sonia wished she hadn't left the gun in the glove compartment for Travis. She was on unknown ground and unarmed. Her pursuer was most likely armed, but experience and training had taught her how to get out of most situations.

The second the pursuer knew he'd blown his cover, the stand off would break, possibly not in her favor. If this stranger had wanted her, she'd have been taken by now, but whomever it was seemed content to observe her, for now.

Sonia had walked at least seven blocks and knew this couldn't go on if she was to find Ramón. She patted the cell phone in her pocket, hoping Travis was okay and continued on her quest.

Clouds unloaded. The moment she'd been waiting for was here. One way or the other, she was going to find the Apollo File.

She saw an alleyway up ahead and kept walking until she was next to it. Turning into it, she ran. She was immediately out of sight of her pursuer but knew he'd be close behind.

The man following her was dressed in a black suit and had dark hair. He ran to the alleyway where Sonia had disappeared and cursed himself at the fact that he'd clearly blown his cover.

This was a first. *Shit, she's a pro.*

He pulled a gun from his shoulder holster and crept down the alleyway, calling on his radio for backup.

CHAPTER 62

TRAVIS SCRIBBLED NOTES onto a napkin as Dr. Rogers continued with the story of Laetrile, Krebs and McNaughton. Rogers had the presence of a modern battleship. His arguments seemed bulletproof. But incredible yet believable as the story was, any link to the whereabouts of the Apollo File was elusive.

"So as I said, on November 1st, 1963, the sale and use of Laetrile was outlawed in the Land of the Free as a direct result of the California Report. And yet, to this day, Laetrile is legal and readily available in many other countries around the word. In fact, thousands of Americans fly to countries like Germany, Switzerland and Mexico every year to exercise freedom of choice and cure themselves of cancer. But I'm getting ahead of myself."

Could this save Mom!?

Rogers took a sip of coffee before continuing. Travis marveled at his composure after having been chased away from his own hospital. Something told him there was a part of this story that would explain his reserve.

"The two cancer surgeons who directed the California Report—Garland and MacDonald—were the very same guys who once said tobacco was in no way a cause of lung cancer. MacDonald was even quoted in the press as saying, 'a pack a day keeps lung cancer away,' so their credentials are questionable, I think you'd agree," said Rogers, looking cynically at Travis over the top of his bifocals.

Travis nodded.

"And guess who sponsored those trials that determined cigarettes didn't cause lung cancer?" added Rogers, waving a pointer finger.

"The tobacco industry?" said Travis.

"The tobacco industry."

A frown from Travis stopped Rogers from continuing. "But surely a clinical trial is simply that. It either works or it doesn't. Can you manipulate results that much?"

Rogers took a deep breath and replied with a sad, frustrated tone. "Have you ever heard of the studies of scientific bias?"

"No, but it sounds ominous."

"Basically, a scientist carrying out an experiment can and often will sway the outcome to what he expects or *wants* it to be. It's been proven. A group of identical rats were sent to two different labs for testing. One lab was told the rats they were given were bred to be smart and would run through the maze quickly, while the other lab was told the rats they were given were unintelligent and would run the maze slowly. The results that came back reflected their briefing: the rats that were supposedly smarter ran the maze quicker and the rats which were not ran it slower, and yet the rats were all the same. There are many other examples too."

Travis had always found differing opinions to be an occupational hazard in his profession but never imagined it would be the case with science. In his world, if you started out on a fact-finding mission with a conclusion already in mind, all you saw was evidence to suit that conclusion. And most likely twisted evidence too—the eyes saw what they wanted to.

Rogers carried on. "But here's the thing. Even with

these two clowns Garland and MacDonald rigging the report—with tricks like not using a high enough dosage on the mice—Laetrile *still* showed positive results. But they suppressed those results, even though the report itself, under closer inspection, actually makes a positive case for Laetrile in Appendix Three and Four. They even had to admit on page four of the report that all patients had an increase in appetite, weight gain and sense of well-being. These things are *precisely* the sort of indicators scientists look for when determining the favorability of results."

"So why's this California Report so significant?"

"Because once a heavily backed report like this is published, it sets a precedent. Doctors—like lawyers citing previous case trials—use reports like this as a point of reference to regurgitate medical opinion rather than make up their own mind. Do you see? Those two surgeons practically buried Laetrile, just like their sponsors wanted."

"I see. So that was it then?"

"No. Although Laetrile was made illegal in America, it was hard to suppress the murmurings of the masses. People got wind of the Laetrile clinics having cured people of cancer before the ban. McNaughton had the money to apply to the FDA to do his own trials—trials that would *not* be rigged—so that's what he did. If he had gotten the FDA to approve its use, that would have solved everything. He applied for an IND…"

"IND?"

"Yes, Investigation of a New Drug, Phase One. And the FDA did grant it. But they quickly revoked it, claiming Laetrile was toxic. As if chemotherapy isn't. The FDA also made some lame excuse about how the doctors who had used Laetrile hadn't kept sufficient clinical records to begin IND Phase One, but Phase One studies don't require such clinical records. The FDA even banned the testing of Laetrile. Now why would you even ban *testing*?"

"And Laetrile definitely isn't toxic?"

"Well, maybe if you ate the kernels of five hundred apricots in a day, you'd get sick. If you eat an excess of *anything* you get sick. Aspirin is actually twenty times more toxic than the same amount of Laetrile. But that wasn't the end of the war by any means and that's where Sloan Kettering came into play."

Travis edged closer to the doctor as his voice had hushed into a conspiratorial whisper. That and the fact this hospital was directly referred to on Leblanc's fax.

"There were several attempts to silence the Laetrile movement, which by the early seventies had gathered some steam. In each case—just like with the California Report—the statistics were either suppressed or distorted with cleverly worded statements. But the mother of them all was the Sloan Kettering debacle. Between 1972 and 1977, Laetrile was tested by the eminent Dr. Kanematsu Sugiura—the senior researcher at Sloan Kettering with over sixty years experience. He had a worldwide reputation for being totally impartial. Other famous cancer surgeons said that they would never bother running tests after Dr. Sugiura because they knew his results would be solid."

Rogers laughed cynically, shaking his head. "Those bastards on the board at Sloan Kettering were so arrogant they actually believed the crap about Laetrile not working, which is why they allowed Sugiura to test it—knowing he'd disprove it. But it backfired on them and it turned out to be a major embarrassment—an embarrassment followed by a messy cover-up."

Rogers cleared a path through the empty cups and plates as he became more demonstrative with his hands, his emotions starting to bubble up. "At the end of Sugiura's tests, he concluded Laetrile stopped the spread of cancer, improved general health, inhibited the growth of smaller tumors, provided relief from pain and acted as cancer prevention. Sloan Kettering then made a statement to this effect: 'Dr. Sugiura has never observed complete regression of tumors in all his experience with other chemotherapeutic agents.'"

"So what could they do now? The results were there to see!"

"Yes. Trouble is, Sloan Kettering's board was made up of representatives from the pharmaceutical cartel. Sugiura's results were not what they wanted to hear. They stood to lose a great deal as a result—a large portion of the hospital's revenue came from treating cancer. Even worse, all this was now a matter of public record."

As logical as all this sounded, Travis didn't want to hear about a deception of this scale. To think his father could've been saved. And that his mother still *could* be!

"All hell broke loose. Never before had Sugiura's work been questioned, but that was about to change with the profits under threat. They set about doing the experiments again, this time with different researchers—no doubt researchers who were more concerned with furthering their career than finding the truth. Trouble was other doctors in the hospital already had run the tests again—Dr. Stockert and Dr. Schloen had even better results! So they used other researchers and little by little, the Sloan Kettering cover-up took shape. They gave it the California Report treatment, continuing to run the experiment again and again—lower dosages used on the mice, et cetera. The easiest thing to accomplish in the world is failure, Travis, and accomplish it they did. It was simply a matter of silencing Sugiura and saying that he bungled the tests. But Laetrile worked so well, they had to do several rigged experiments to discredit it. The last one was done at the hospital by a doctor who mixed up the mice. Half were treated with saline and half with Laetrile. The deliberate mix-up of the mice meant that the untreated mice did a lot better than the treated mice. And since when did saline cure cancer?!"

Travis shook his head, scowling. "I just find it hard to believe that a hospital could…would do this. How could they possibly hope to keep it quiet?"

"They didn't! Some of us took our Hippocratic oath more seriously than career advancement or research funding. A secret group of doctors in the hospital were outraged by the cover-up and published a newsletter called *Second Opinion*. They circulated it to the press anonymously. The *Second Opinion Underground* managed to get the press spotlight on the affair, probably because Sloan Kettering's Assistant Director of Public Affairs was one of the members. He was the one forced to write the press releases stating that Laetrile was ineffective, but in November 1977 he went public and told the press about the whole cover-up from start to finish."

Travis knew the next part of the story. "Let me guess what happened next. The media inexplicably moved on to the next big story and an apathetic public forgot all about it?"

"Hole in one. The media are lazy and have little concern for truth, just keep the ratings up with new sensational headlines. People find a story boring after a while and don't want to believe anything bad can happen. They'd rather die of cancer than be so unsettled as to think that the very people they believe to be protecting them can do evil. It was effectively nothing more than the systematic and deliberate murder of thousands of people. Genocide."

"And where did you fit in with all this, Doctor?"

Rogers whispered intensely without looking at Travis.

Travis couldn't help but bring his head close to hear him against the bellowing storm outside.

"I was, and still am, a member of the *Second Opinion Underground*. And the resistance isn't dead—in fact, it's re-emerging. Like I said, you've got caught up in a secret war, just like your friend, Leblanc."

CHAPTER 63

UNEASY FOOTSTEPS SPLATTERED through the rapidly rising puddles. Sonia used a discarded soda can to prop open the lid of a dumpster and hid behind it, water dripping from her nose like a leaky faucet. She felt no fear.

It was dark except for the occasional, intensely bright lightning that would blind her pursuer if she judged it right. She knew he would check inside the dumpster and then she would strike. *Over in a second.*

Footsteps approached then stopped. Sonia scoffed at the predictability of such an amateur—someone who had no idea who they were dealing with.

She felt the vibration of the dumpster being opened. She heard the empty soda can drop to the floor with a clatter, knowing this would draw his attention in the opposite direction.

It was time.

Sonia wheeled around from behind the dumpster, keeping her head almost as low as her hips, and drove her foot into the ribs of the man.

Crack!

He howled in surprise and pain.

He jerked his pistol in the direction of the assault and let off a round—just as expected, but by then she was behind him.

Sonia drove her knee into his back. She thrust his hand

holding a gun against the dumpster. He dropped the weapon, grunting helplessly. He fell to the floor writhing in pain.

Sonia deftly scooped up the pistol and kicked him in the groin as if it was a penalty kick. He shrieked on the soaking wet concrete in a shriveled ball, hands on his crotch.

She stood over him, pointing the weapon straight at his head, with one foot holding his face in the deepening puddle. "Who are you working for?" She cocked the gun.

"Fuck you, bitch!"

She kicked his head. Another cry of pain. He spat blood and laughed.

Why's he laughing? Sonia looked around but could see nothing in the darkness.

Then she heard the whistle of a bullet strike a metal pipe next to her.

Sniper.

She dropped to her knees, driving the gun barrel into the man's temple. Another bullet zipped past. This time it struck the pipe lower down at the same level as her head. He laughed again. The sniper was trying to make Sonia back away from her captive.

The sniper obviously had an infrared scope and the bullets were coming from the other end of the alleyway. Sonia was a sitting duck.

"On your feet!" she ordered.

As the man rose, she rose with him, using him as a shield.

Thunder shuddered the skies and the rain blasted down harder than before. The advantage, which had once been Sonia's, was working against her. She was the hunted.

Sonia edged backwards, away from the sniper.

She felt something strike her hard on the back of the head. Unconscious, she fell.

CHAPTER 64

"So IF YOU'RE THE RESISTANCE, who's the other side?" Travis asked.

"Think about it. There are now more people employed in the cancer industry than there are cancer patients. It's a 110-billion-dollar-a-year industry. If it ceased to exist overnight, it would damage the national economy. Hospitals have millions tied up in radiology equipment, drug companies the same in lucrative patents for toxic chemotherapy, doctors have their livelihoods to protect, non-profits have salaries to pay, the list goes on. The vast majority of these people aren't even aware they're part of the problem, they've just been denied the facts like the rest of us."

Disturbing. Sickening. "What do you mean by 'the non-profits'? Like charities?"

"Sure. The American Cancer Society and the National Cancer Institute exist because cancer exists. No more cancer, no more ACS and NCI. These organizations are vast, with cash reserves of millions of dollars, but here's the thing: for every dollar the ACS spends on research, they spend over six dollars on salaries and fringe benefits. In 1998 it spent a million bucks on political lobbying, in direct violation of its non-profit status. Instead of finding a cure after all this time and all those donations, it's spent money trying to *suppress* Laetrile with a smear campaign. Have you heard of Dr. Linus Pauling?"

"No."

Rogers pushed his fingers against his temples and closed his eyes. "Linus Pauling won the Nobel prize *twice*. His exact words about it were: 'Everyone should know that the "war on cancer" is largely a fraud, and that the NCI and the ACS are derelict in their duties to the American people who support them.' Two other Nobel prize winners, Dr. James Watson and Dr. Albert Shatz are quoted as saying similar things."

"So who's the enemy you are fighting against?" said Travis, pressing to stay on track.

"Many institutions have a lot to gain by suppressing a cure for cancer but, most of all, the pharmaceutical cartel. Drug pushing is legal for those guys. Switch on your TV and you'll be deluged with commercials telling you to ask your doctor if this drug is right for you. Jesus, I even saw one commercial that didn't even say what the drug was for—it just showed a bunch of happy people and told you to ask your doctor about it! And when they get to the doctor's and ask about it, the doctor is so frightened of a malpractice lawsuit he gives it to them—plus he gets incentives from pharmaceutical companies. Is it any wonder why healthcare costs have risen? Why can't people see the connection?"

Travis was about to temper Rogers's rant, but he continued speaking before he could butt in.

"Any doctor who's brave enough to think for themselves and administer or recommend Laetrile therapy has their license taken away. He or she will be imprisoned and branded a quack. A quack? What a joke! *We're* the quacks!"

Travis's focus was more on his mom than Leblanc's fax at that moment. "You mean conventional cancer therapy is quackery?"

"Absolutely. Look, the so-called approved cancer treatment focuses on the tumor, which is nonsense if you think about it—the tumor is the symptom not the cause—that's why a tumor only has approximately 15 percent cancer cells. We evaluate treatments based on reduction in tumor size even though there are relatively few cancer cells in it. We kid ourselves that we're treating the cancer by cutting, burning or poisoning the tumor. Jesus, why don't we just use leeches and be done with it?! But even taking that into consideration, Laetrile *still* reduces tumor size."

Rogers shuffled in his chair. "The FDA, the AMA, the NCI and the ACS are all in the pockets of the pharmaceutical cartel. The drug companies have grown so powerful, with so many fingers in so many pies—government, media, you name it— it's been a tough battle. A battle we've been losing until recently."

"How's that?"

"The public's mood is changing. Ever since scandals where approved drugs kill people, they're losing faith in the medical establishment who keep announcing hollow breakthroughs and pushing drugs that do nothing but kill people. Demand for organic food is growing exponentially—people are finally getting that you eat artificial crap and you get sick—they're finally appreciating organic food isn't some health craze. It's how food always was—free of carcinogenic chemicals! The recent development though, and most people don't know this yet, is that the First Lady has got behind Laetrile. It's an information war and the tide is turning."

Travis stared at the fax, looking for something to jump out at him.

"Have you told me everything you told Leblanc...no more, no less?"

"Yeah, I'd say that's about it. What exactly happened to Leblanc anyway? Why's this Apollo File so damned important?"

"I wish I could tell you. One more question. Does DGI mean anything to you?" asked Travis, referring to the fax.

Rogers pondered briefly. "DGI? I believe that stands for Disseminated Gonococcal Infection. Not my specialty, but it's something to do with gonorrhea, I believe. Why?"

Travis realized that probably had no bearing whatsoever on the fax but made a note all the same.

Rogers eased himself up. "Alright, I'm going now. I'll lay low until all this has blown over. Here's my email address. Don't worry, it can't be hacked," Rogers said, writing something on a napkin. "Let me know any developments. I'll call a cab."

Travis shook the doctor's hand. Rogers turned and walked out of the café into the pouring rain and vanished in the darkness.

It was time to check in with Sonia. Travis called again and again as he sat in the café finishing his coffee. *Ten minutes and no reply, I'll call her again shortly.*

Sighing, Travis left the café, hoping Kramer's car would start.

As he turned his back on the street and closed the café door behind him, a black sedan screeched up to the sidewalk out of the wet darkness.

He turned in the direction of the noise, but before he could do or say anything, two men were upon him.

One man held a cloth to Travis's mouth. He smelled chemicals, and everything went black as he felt his body go limp.

CHAPTER 65

"THANKS FOR TAKING THE TIME for my call, Mr. Green, I really appreciate it."

"Not at all, Reese, what can I do for you boys at the Bureau today?" The hierarchy had been established early on. It was in the way Reese and Green addressed each other.

Green stood up, paced the perimeter of his office, one foot from the walls. His charm oozed through his wide smile down the phone, somehow without dropping the authority and power.

There was no love lost between Green and the FBI; they'd been trying to swallow up Green's mysterious agency since its inception, albeit to no avail. It was nothing more than political games and Green was exceedingly adept at those. But Reese might be of some use. God had told him so.

"Mr. Green, I'd like to offer the Bureau's assistance in helping you track the two suspects you encountered last night." Reese's tone sounded purposeful, but Green knew he was hiding something.

"That's very generous of you, Reese. What do you propose?" Green played along, leaving the ball in Reese's court.

"Well firstly, if you let me know why and how you encountered the suspects last night—how you came to fingerprint the girl—I could get my people working on something." Reese was careful to avoid saying the names of the suspects due to recent security leaks at the Bureau. Green was aware of the leaks but knew Reese was speaking about Travis and his accomplice.

There's no way I'm letting him get to the Apollo File.

"Just a routine investigation, Reese. Of course, what would help me is if you could get an ID on the girl. Rehnquist sure won't cooperate." Green of course knew Sonia's ID anyway, but he was probing Reese, trying to figure his angle.

"Same here, I'm afraid—I'm locked out too. Whoever she is, it's triggered someone's alarm bell in this town."

Now Green knew he was lying for sure. "So how do you propose to assist? And why is the Bureau interested in such a minor investigation? The girl's really unimportant to me."

There was a short pause. "Well, as you know we have considerable resources at our disposal and we're obviously interested in this matter due to the clear sensitivity of the girl's identity, whatever that identity is. You know how us Hoover boys are." Reese forced a short laugh. "Anyway, let me know what I can do to be of assistance. You know where to find me."

"Okay, Reese. I sure appreciate it and I'll let you know if and when I find anything else out about the girl. Have a nice night." *Interfering little moron.*

Green dropped the phone down and stared at it. Thinking. Calculating. Time was running out.

Tomorrow morning the Apollo File should turn up somewhere.

Green called Norman in.

Norman entered, a thin smile wrinkling his weary face. He could barely contain his enthusiasm, which for Norman was a rarity. Green eyed him with anticipation. Norman knew he had to sit down first.

"Sir, they've got it! The post office has a shortlist of all priority mail sent from Washington, D.C. on Monday!"

"Excellent!" Green clenched a fist and pounded the desk.

"And that's not all, sir."

"Oh?"

"You remember you asked Miami-Dade P.D. to alert us of any reported stolen cars showing up with Virginia, Delaware or D.C. plates? We have one."

"Good. And what news of Dr. Rogers?"

Reese sat at headquarters, staring into a blank legal pad. Finally, Green had spoken to him. Things were clearer.

He called Director Jensen.

"Yes, Reese. How's it going?"

"He won't play along and no news on where to apprehend the fugitives."

"Alright, so what are you going to do about it?" Jensen sounded desperate; his dependence on Reese's skills was more disconcerting than flattering.

"I'll have to shadow him and, at some point, he'll take us right to it. I'll carry on with my investigation, sir."

"Please do, Reese, please do. Whatever you need."

Reese already knew what he wanted. "A jet with plenty of fuel and full mobile operations capability for starters."

"It's yours. Ready and waiting at Dulles."

"And I do have full cooperation from all SACs when I want it, right?"

"Reese, just tell me which field office you need help from and if the boss there gives you any grief, tell him to call me."

"Thanks, sir. Have a good night."

"Reese, that's not possible until you have what we need. Go get it."

WEDNESDAY

CHAPTER 66

TRAVIS AWOKE FROM A SLEEP, devoid of dreams. As consciousness returned, his most recent memory filled him with panic.

Oh, God, no.

He instinctively lunged up, but nothing happened. His hands and ankles were tied with locking nylon cable.

Who did this? How long have I been asleep? At least he wasn't dead. But why wasn't he?

Cell phone! Travis fumbled and stretched his tied hand to his pocket.

Gone, of course.

As Travis's vision restored and adjusted to the light, he surveyed his surroundings. He lay on the floor in a small brick room with no windows, like a closet, surrounded by old ropes and an empty wooden crate. He could smell water—not the sea, more like a river. He could hear the occasional car or truck, moving fast, like he was close to a freeway or interstate. There was faint noise in the distance; people shouting as if they were at work and the sound of boxes being moved.

Travis inched his body to the door and pushed his foot against it. It wouldn't budge. He felt the shadow of fear and panic but shut it out. He thought about crying for help but decided it might endanger him further.

There's a reason I'm not dead, they want me alive. What's

the time? How long had he been here? He twisted his wrist against the nylon cable to see his watch.

No!

It was twenty-three minutes past midnight. If Leblanc had sent the Apollo File priority mail, today was the day it should show up. And this was the day he'd know about his mom.

But there he lay, helpless in a cell. He had to do something. Anything.

He dragged himself across the concrete floor, then raised both legs and brought them down hard against the wooden door. The shock of the blow ran up to his knees.

He continued banging and shouting, "I'm ready to talk!" The voices outside had stopped. Perhaps they'd heard him. Travis listened with the back of his head pressed against the cold, hard concrete floor, breathing heavily.

He heard heels scuffing over the floor.

Travis stared at the moldy ceiling with wide eyes. His breath quickened with the uncertainty of who was approaching and what they might do to him. There was the sound of a key and the door unlatching. The door swung open with an ominous groan.

Travis winced in the bright, artificial light that spiked into the room. He could make out the shape of two men. One short and one tall, both with black hair and dark skin.

The taller man came over to Travis. Travis lay on the floor, expecting a weapon in the man's hand. He pulled Travis to his feet. As his eyes adjusted to the bright light, Travis could see their pistols still in their shoulder holsters.

The tall man produced a hunting knife, and put it against Travis's face. Travis flinched uncontrollably, shutting his eyes, holding his breath. The man steadied him and snickered. Travis opened his eyes to see him using the knife to cut the nylon cable from his ankles. He held the knife up again before stowing it on his belt.

"One wrong move and I'll gut you like a fish. Comprendez?"

Travis nodded, panic-stricken. The man took his arm and led him out of the room.

As Travis shuffled out of his prison, he winced at the clinical harshness of the light and allowed the two men to lead him. As his eyesight adjusted he could see where he was. It wasn't as he'd expected.

It was a large warehouse lined with offices and closets that clung to the perimeter. Travis was now in one of these closets. He could only see one exit. It was a large metal door, almost a wall in itself, clearly on rollers like an aircraft hangar door. The structure appeared to be concrete and the walls were shoddily painted in gray, white and pink.

The walls were thick with large wooden crates, bearing a label with a black logo on which was printed "Lando Transportation, Inc." There must have been half a dozen other men in there. One older man was on the phone in a glass-partitioned office by the door, two were sitting at a table playing dominoes and another three were lifting boxes. All of them were armed and all of them stopped and stared knowingly at Travis as he was dragged toward the center of the open space.

A wooden chair sat in the middle of the warehouse. Travis guessed this was his destination.

If they'd have wanted me dead, I'd be dead. I can explain all of this.

But as Travis drew closer he saw something disturbing: a car battery at the foot of the chair with cables attached. About six feet in front of the chair was a table and sitting on the table was a tool that looked like surgical pliers.

Travis felt faint. His throat tightened and his mouth went dry.

The men threw him in the chair and tied him down with more nylon cable.

Travis's heartbeat quickened. He tried not to look at what were surely instruments of torture, but it was irresistible. Beads of perspiration began to soak his shirt.

The taller man sat to one side while the short man reached down for the red and black cables attached to the car battery and rubbed the metal clamps together. Sparks flew by Travis's face. The man laughed.

"What do you want?!" Travis burst out, making no attempt to mask his terror.

The man said nothing. Instead, he walked over to the glass office and motioned at the older man sitting within. The older man acknowledged him with a dismissive wave and finished his call.

Travis watched the dirty glass door of the office open and the older man walk out. He could get a better look at him now. He had thinning black hair. Not balding, just thin, black hair. His skin was light brown and covered with pockmarks from his cheeks to his neck. The face was chubby. He was about five-foot-six, had a potbelly and wore an off-white shirt that was creased and open mid-way down his chest where thick, white chest hair poked out. Reading glasses dangled from a chord around his neck. He wore ill-fitting jeans with a belt, which struggled to keep them the right shape. He must have been in his mid-sixties.

The older man waddled over with great confidence; a combination of being overweight and being the head honcho of this sordid operation. He stood before Travis with his hands on his hips, looking at him with distinguished black eyes. After scanning Travis up and down with disdain, he spoke.

"You wanna have your fingernails removed one by one?"

The voice was foreign and the English was broken, but it spoke quickly and calmly.

Travis stared past the man, speaking at the large pliers. The words barely came out. "No...no."

"And my friend, just in case you're getting any cute ideas, forget it. Nobody knows you're here and no one can hear you. No matter how much you scream. And scream you will."

Travis squirmed in his chair. "Look, I don't know who you are or what you want. There's possibly some kind of mix-up. I have no concern what it is you do here, but you'd do well to let me go about my business. I have a partner who..."

"Who's coming for you? I don't think so," scoffed the man.

"Be assured, sir, they'll be beating a path to this door as we speak," Travis replied.

The fat man gave a triumphant smile and nodded to the tall associate on the other side of the room. Travis sat in silence and waited for whatever hideous order was about to be carried out.

Thirty seconds later, Travis's hopes were shattered as Sonia was pushed out in a wheelchair.

She was bound with cables and had duct tape across her mouth and a large bruise across her cheek. She glared daggers at the older man.

"You mean her?" the man asked.

Travis studied her for injury. In this state Sonia's presence made something snap inside him. "Who are you and what do you want?!" he screamed.

"No, no, my friend. Who are *you*? And what do *you* want?"

"What the hell do you mean? It was you who abducted us! You're saying you don't know why?!" A torrent of confusion and panic slapped Travis across the face.

The man in charge looked at the men sitting at the table and laughed in amazement. They laughed with him.

"Don't play dumb with me, you little asshole. The only reason you're not alligator bait right now is that I wanna know why you were looking for me. There's not a place downtown you didn't ask for me. Real smart. Why don't you just send a fucking telegram to Castro? That's a pretty new approach for the DEA, isn't it?"

Jesus, he thinks we're the Drug Enforcement Agency!

"DEA? No, this is a big mistake!"

The older man turned away and pointed to the short man with his thumb. "Aw, fuck it. Pull his nails out then kill him…and her!"

"No!"

The short man headed for the table with the pliers and the boss sauntered back toward his office.

Think!

Wait, why did he think we were trying to find him?

No, it can't be. It's worth a shot! Travis bellowed for his life.

"Ramón Martinez!? George Kramer sent me to find you. That's why we were looking for you. To ask for help: payment for a favor!"

Ramón Martinez, the older man in charge, stopped walking away and turned to face Travis.

CHAPTER 67

GREEN WARNED RELEVANT STAFF that Tuesday was going to be an all-nighter. When the sun rose on Wednesday, the USPS would deliver a small priority envelope to someone, the contents of which would shatter everything he worked for, stood for and was.

Green, Norman and the young cryptologist—Maynard—sat in Green's office well into the first hour of the day that would change the world.

"Norman, tell me again what happened at that hospital in Miami. How the hell was there no sign of Travis or Rogers?"

Green was too distracted by other matters—Special Agent Reese and the USPS—to have given this much thought. He looked tired and spoke with an agitated voice Norman hadn't encountered before. It was frightening to be in uncharted waters with Green. Norman could see his career teeter in front of him.

"Sir, it's very strange and I've been over this with the agents who went to the hospital three times now. The security guard said he saw Rogers enter the building, but he never showed up at his office where our guys were waiting for him. And they haven't seen him since. They don't recall seeing anyone matching the target's description either."

"You know what, Norman?"

"Sir?"

Green stood up and leaned over the desk like a praying mantis. He spoke, looking right between the two men and grabbing the phone from his desk. "I am sick and tired..." his tone was calm to begin with but then erupted like a volcano, "...of my men *fucking things up!*" He hurled the phone across the room. It smashed against the wall.

Both men cowered down into their seats.

Maynard sprang back up, but Norman winced and stayed silent. He knew the truth, though he hadn't dared mention it. Give him a few seconds.

"Sir?" Norman tested the water first. He knew what he was about to say was correct, but all he could see was his pension and healthcare going up in smoke if he screwed this up.

"What Norman?" Green's tone had tempered. He was rubbing the back of his neck and looking at the floor on the other side of the room. Norman paused to be certain of every word before letting it out.

"Sir, I can't help feeling as though you're being too hard on yourself."

"Oh? How's that?"

Excellent, he'd caught Green on the back foot and he seemed calm and receptive. Maynard could see how Norman had survived so long in this position.

"Well, sir, you've had your hands tied by the sensitivity of the operation. You've been unable to give our field agents enough information to have the freedom to investigate. They've been wondering what this is all about and they've been operating blind. To be fair to everyone, this isn't the sort of thing we usually handle." *Now for the sweetener.* "Frankly, I think the job you've done, keeping all this in mind, has been incredible."

There was a silence during which Norman could've sworn

he saw the young cryptologist shake his head. *Little bastard.*

Green slumped down at his desk. "You're right of course, Norm."

Norman tried hard to stifle the deep exhale of relief. *We're back to 'Norm' again. Good.*

"Let's work the problem with that in mind, then. First of all, get me the hospital on the phone would you, Norm?"

"Right away, sir."

Norman thumbed through the papers on his clipboard to find the number, but realized Green's phone was in pieces on the other side of the room. As if he'd planned to do so all along, Norman took out his cell phone and dialed the number. When it started ringing, he passed it to Green.

"Miami Children's Hospital."

Green's smile sprang across his face. "Yes, good evening, ma'am. My son is going to be admitted for a tonsillectomy, but I do worry about security in this day and age. Could you tell me what security is like there? Do all visitors have to give you their name?"

"Oh yes, sir. We take a copy of their driver's license for a pass that they must wear at all times. Otherwise they wouldn't get past the entrance."

"Thank you." Green hung up.

"Idiots. Norm, get those Miami morons on the line and tell them to go back to the hospital and ask security if our targets checked in. Use your desk."

"Yes, sir." Norman left the room with a spring in his step. He'd survived and gotten Green's mind back on target.

That left Green and the young cryptologist in the office—Nick Maynard. He needed this guy despite his disrespectful manner; he was all Green had.

"Well, Nick, if you want a job done properly, you have to do it yourself, I guess. What do you think?" Green knew he had to play this kid to get the best out of him. He was nothing more than a rebellious teenager in his eyes and knew exerting authority would just make him go the other way. Norman came back in the room and returned to his seat.

"I guess," said Maynard.

"Alright," said Green. "Let's have a recap. A lot of new developments have taken shape and we still have plenty of time."

Green walked over to his whiteboard where he'd marked out their actions and progress.

"Essentially," Green began, "we've won."

CHAPTER 68

IT WASN'T OVER YET. Travis and Sonia were still tied up as Ramón Martinez tottered back from his office with a chair for himself.

Kramer had told Travis that Ramón was an ex-Alpha 66 Commando. Alpha 66 was a violent faction of the anti-Castro Cubans recruited at Miami University by the CIA in the early sixties. They were trained and equipped by the Agency to invade Cuba at the disastrous Bay of Pigs campaign. Some of these men were also running black operations in and out of Cuba, including acting as double agents. Ramón used to be a CIA contract agent: a world where the lines between legal and illegal were blurred at best.

Ramón arrived in front of Travis with a scuffed wooden chair and fell back into it, looking Travis up and down as he spoke.

"Nobody finds Ramón. Ramón finds you."

Ramón spoke about himself in the third person; a dead giveaway of delusions of grandeur. Travis knew he was in no position of power. *Feed his ego.*

"I'm sure about that, sir. And I'm sorry about the way we went about this, but time is of the essence. Kramer hoped you'd be able to help us, as we were in Miami anyway. Kramer thinks a great deal of you—he told me you're the best."

Ramón reclined back on the chair legs with his hands behind his head.

"And he was right!" Ramón sat forward again, probing deeply into Travis's eyes. "And who is Kramer to you then? What's your name anyway? What do you do?" Ramón asked, as if introductions mattered all of a sudden.

"My name's Dan Travis. I'm a writer. And this is Sonia—Sonia Leblanc." Travis was just about to say what Sonia did for a living and then paused, mouth still open.

Oh and by the way, she's Secret Service. Yeah, that'll go down well.

Ramón saw the hesitation. "And what does she do…Travis?"

Shit. Think fast.

"She's a self-defense instructor. She's my friend."

"And what's Kramer to you?" Ramón shifted in his chair and waited for the response, a suspecting hand resting on his weapon.

"Kramer is a friend of my father's. They worked together during the Cold War. Kramer sends his best."

"Does he now? And how is he? Still enjoying retirement in Colorado? Is he out of a wheelchair now?" Ramón suddenly switched to a dinner party voice.

Travis saw through the ruse immediately. "Kramer's retired and living in *Washington, D.C.* and he never was in a wheelchair, but he does have a cane. We were at his house just last night."

"And if I call Kramer and tell him all this, he'll verify what you say?"

"Of course." *If you can get a reply, that is. Damn it! Where the hell is Kramer anyway?*

A frown tugged at Ramón's face as he glanced from the floor to Travis.

Then he suddenly looked up with wide, solemn eyes. "Holy shit. You're that kid Kramer told me about—wait, what did he call you? Danny Boy!"

"Yes, yes. That's me!" Travis was practically singing.

"Raúl, desátalo y sácalo de esa silla!"

The short man who'd dragged Travis from his cell ran over and cut the nylon cables. Then Ramón looked at Sonia tied to the wheelchair.

"Danny, your girlfriend over there put two of my boys in the hospital a while ago—one who was following her and another who tried to tie her up. She's a fucking doomsday machine."

"Sí, El Diablo!" exclaimed the short man who was evidently called Raúl.

Travis tried to contain his laughter at Raúl thinking Sonia was a devil. He winked at Sonia as he answered Ramón. "She'll be fine now, she knows you're going to help us and not harm us."

Sonia nodded at Ramón.

"Raúl, déjala ir a ella también," said Ramón.

Raúl looked nervous and didn't move.

"Hazlo ya. No te hará daño!" said Ramón, forcefully gesturing Raúl toward Sonia.

Raúl approached Sonia and cut her nylon cables at arm's length, like he was lighting fireworks.

The second her hands were free, she ripped the tape from her mouth and stood up defiantly. Raúl backed away with his hand on the gun, a moment she seemed to enjoy.

"Did you find Rogers?" Sonia asked Travis. She looked as though she'd been to hell and back. Her hair was matted and her face was dirty, in addition to being badly bruised.

"Yes, but still no clue as to where Apollo was sent and by now Green'll know we're in Miami. I had to show ID at the hospital reception."

Ramón stood up and interjected. "Alright, I have no clue

what you're talking about, but George Kramer once saved my life. He's a good man and I'm in his debt. However, you've caught me at a bad time, as we're in the middle of a big shipment. What exactly do you want from me?"

Sonia immediately answered, "A safe house, for one thing."

"You're here. Stay as long as you want. There's a computer in my office if you want it and you can have your cell phones back." Ramón nodded at Raúl. "Raúl, devuélveles sus teléfonos," he said. "Things are going to get a little hectic around here for a while, but as we say in Cuba, 'Mi casa es su casa.'"

"Thank you, Ramón," said Travis.

Beneath the hard exterior, Ramón seemed like a good man. More than that, Travis liked him. He had an unusual charisma that reminded him of Kramer. Not surprising, considering the life he's led. People talk about history—learn about it—but like Kramer, this guy *was* history.

"Okay, let's get to work," Sonia said, motioning Travis toward Ramón's office.

CHAPTER 69

GREEN LEANED ON THE WALL next to his white-board, tapping the marker on each item he'd previously scrawled. He'd already been over these items twice, but Norman and Nick Maynard knew it was about thinking aloud; the repetition would hopefully bring out new ideas. That, and the fact that Green lived for repetition.

"So listen up. Leblanc's contacts and phone records were useless. The data provided by the USPS has given us the names and addresses of all priority mail sent from Washington, D.C. on Monday and none of them were on Leblanc's contact list."

Norman nodded. "Yes, sir. We had all the USPS shortlist data entered and cross-checked against Leblanc's contacts and phone records and no match."

Green continued, "Okay. So somewhere here in this list of names and addresses is the destination of Apollo, which is why I say we've won." He held up a stack of paper and dropped it on the floor. "But there aren't enough agents to cover all the addresses, even if we posted agents at the post offices to intercept it before delivery. There are too many, too widely scattered across the country. Too many variables."

"Correct, sir," said Norman. "Right now, our agents are awaiting orders on which addresses to cover. We have to make a decision before dawn. The only other alternative would be to have them drive around all locations in their respective areas one by one. Of course, the risk is that whoever receives the file may have disappeared by the time we get to them."

"Whoever the file's headed for must be someone Leblanc trusted and would know what to do with it. Though once they see what's on the file, I doubt *anyone* would have any doubt about what to do with it." Green had now pissed himself off by making that statement.

Norman knew that face and tried to put the fire out. "But if our agents move fast, there's a good chance we'll get to it first. If the recipient does run before we get to them, we'll be fast on their tail. I think the main threat is Travis and this girl." Norman didn't know the name of the girl—Green had kept that to himself.

Green's hard expression mellowed. "Okay, good. So we had an abandoned car report from Miami?"

"Yes, sir. It had Washington plates and a Sig pistol in the glove compartment. It was four miles from Miami Children's Hospital."

"Shit, that has to be Travis. Who's the car registered to?"

Norman flipped though the papers on his clipboard again. "One George Arthur Kramer. He reported it stolen yesterday. It all checks out. We sent an agent round, but Kramer hasn't been home."

"Alright, so Travis and the girl are in Miami. And you've alerted all airports and airlines in Florida?"

"Yes, sir. And bus and train stations. Miami P.D. is in the loop also, though they don't know why we're looking for them. They're not going anywhere."

"That's what we said in New York and in D.C."

"Yes, sir, but the difference now is that the Apollo File could be anywhere in America and therefore easily out of driving range for them. Car would be their only means of making it after the measures we've taken."

"Well let's hope it turns up in Seattle, then," said Green.

"That would be excellent, sir, but we're also making the assumption that Travis will find out where the file is. We have the advantage."

"Unless he made contact with that Dr. Rogers."

"Yes, but our analysis shows Rogers wouldn't have been able to tell Travis anything about the destination of Apollo. The motel Rogers has been staying in down there wasn't on the USPS shortlist, and neither was his home or work address, past or present."

"Okay, good point. And they wouldn't have headed for Miami and tried to meet up with Rogers if they knew where the file was?"

"Correct, sir. Miami Children's Hospital reported that Travis did check in there with security, so he was there alright. And Miami is where we'll contain him."

"Good. Keep them contained in Miami." Dwight turned to Maynard. "Meanwhile, Nick and I have to figure out where the file was sent. Get me Leblanc's fax, Norm."

"Here you go, sir." Norman handed Green a copy of the fax. "And sir, don't forget that none of the addresses on the USPS shortlist are in South Florida."

"Yes…good. All we have to really worry about is deciphering this fax. At least narrow down those addresses a little."

CHAPTER 70

As SONIA SPED OFF to Ramón's office, Travis felt compelled to confront Ramón. There was unfinished business, however busy Ramón was. Ramón had his back to Travis and was directing the men shifting boxes.

"Ramón?"

"Yes, Señor Danny?" He turned and placed a hand on his shoulder, like they were suddenly buddies.

Travis gave an uneasy glare to Ramón.

Ramón sighed mightily. "Listen, I'm real sorry about what happened. Really I am. But this is…it's a sensitive little operation I run here. You understand?"

"I'm not used to being abducted and threatened with torture."

Ramón became sullen and tight-lipped. "Yep, I can see how that might have shaken you up," his tone insincerely apologetic. "Listen, you and me, we're from different worlds. Kramer knew me a long time ago—things have changed."

Ramón gave a single, obligatory nod and turned away.

"But will you help us?" Travis said.

Ramón stopped walking and turned back to Travis again. "Sure!"

"Thanks. We're running out of time." Travis went to reach for the fax from his pocket.

"But not just now, uh?" Ramón said.

"Ramón…"

"Danny, time's running out for me too. If I don't get Aunt Nora's transport moving right now, my clients aren't going to be happy. Not a good thing. I'm kind of a middle man, you see, and when things go sour in my line of work, the middle man gets fuckin' squashed by the people on either side of him!"

Ramón marched away, yelling in Spanish at the men moving boxes.

Travis had no clue what "Aunt Nora's transport" meant, and probably didn't want to know. He glanced over at Ramón's dusty glass office where Sonia was busy on the phone, as if she worked there. She was waving him in, but Travis motioned the time-out hand gesture.

The enormous hangar-style doors to the warehouse were cracked open. An uncontrollable urge to breathe fresh air overcame Travis. Once again, death had been dangled in front of him. He needed to swallow some of the dark, steamy Miami night air to tell himself that he was still on this Earth. Travis strode outside.

The thunderstorms had cleared and were now in the distance, emitting an occasional faint rumble, illuminating the horizon. The warehouse was on a river somewhere in Miami. The building was light pink and seemed a lot larger on the outside. As he'd guessed earlier, it was next to a freeway stretching over the river. Three boats of different sizes lay in the inlet next to the warehouse, one of them covered.

"You're on the Miami River," said Ramón from behind. "About three miles inland of downtown."

Time to go back inside. Travis sucked in one last dose of the fresh, post-storm air and hustled back in toward the office where Sonia was.

"How's it going?" Travis asked, closing the glass door behind him.

Sonia whipped her head away from the computer monitor and met Travis with a raised eyebrow. "Where were *you*? Planning a boat cruise?"

Travis snapped back. "Listen, I don't know what kind of world you and this Ramón come from, but that scared the shit out of me, okay? Just needed a little time-out." Then he withdrew as a rewarding thought came to him. "Did you really put two of Ramón's guys in the hospital?"

"Gladly. The first one would've been dead had I not wanted to question him. How did it go with Rogers?" Sonia looked at her watch as she spoke with a sense of urgency Travis hadn't seen thus far.

"Good. What are you doing there?" Travis asked.

"Cross-referencing Internet searches with our fax."

Travis knew exactly what she was doing, as he'd used the same research method himself. You'd put two seemingly unrelated terms in a search engine together and see what comes up. The results were often surprising.

"Anything?"

"Nothing of value. I'll keep going. Tell me what Rogers said. I'll cross reference that too."

Travis recounted everything from the meeting with Rogers, using the napkin notes he'd taken. Half an hour later, they had a list of references from Rogers to add to the ones on the fax. But still nothing showed up which might have indicated the destination of the Apollo File.

"It doesn't make sense!" Sonia said, rubbing the back of her neck.

"What?" Travis knew the answer but didn't want to pre-empt any analysis.

"Everything on the fax is a medical reference—apart from DGI—and the title is about Kennedy's killers. The only connections we've got are the California Report coming out the same month and year as Kennedy's assassination and the first Laetrile clinic starting in the same town he was shot."

"That's all I can see right now too," Travis said.

"In any case, how in hell does this tell us an exact address where the file was sent?"

"It doesn't. And that's because we're missing something. Your brother wanted me to find that address and somewhere in all this lies the answer."

Travis sat with his head down, hands in his hair. "You want some coffee?" He'd noticed a dirty pot of coffee on the far side of the warehouse.

"Sure. If it's drinkable," said Sonia, still frantically typing into the search engine.

Travis ambled across the warehouse to the stained and messy coffee station. The coffee was hot and black, which was promising. He poured it into two foam cups and walked back into the office. He handed Sonia her cup as she typed away, the changing colors of the monitor reflecting off her 'Snow White' skin. Hard to believe she had been just a stranger back in New York. That seemed like another lifetime; Travis's affinity for her had grown so much in such a short time.

Time to push reset.

Travis wandered back out to the riverside. He sipped his rejuvenating coffee and watched the frenzied activity on the dock continue. He studied Ramón. In some small way, he felt connected to Kramer through him and, in turn, connected to his father. He gazed up at the stars in the tropical night sky and closed his eyes, examining the recesses of his mind.

Miami.

Where it all started with a fishing trip as a small boy, watching that ship sink into the Bermuda Triangle.

His dad's words during that fateful vacation sparkled into focus:

"Get the facts. Then, when disseminating the facts in order to come to a conclusion, eliminate the completely impossible. Whatever's left after that, has to be the answer, however improbable or inconclusive that may be. Remember, Daniel, when human beings are involved in solving any mystery, you have to ask: 'Who would perpetrate this and most importantly, what was the motive? Who stands to gain the most from this?' Answer that question and you're on the right path. Son, you start out with a faulty premise and the whole thing becomes a house of cards. In my business, people die that way. Your mind has to stay open and never make assumptions about anything."

Travis sniffed a chuckle to himself and drew his gaze back down to Earth, where Ramón continued to hustle contraband into his boats.

Travis felt a tingling sensation from the crown of his head to his neck. It was something his dad had said: "Eliminate the completely impossible. Whatever's left after that, has to be the answer, however improbable or inconclusive that may be...start out with a faulty premise and the whole thing becomes a house of cards..."

He was stung in the gut by a thought.

No.

Jesus!

Travis tossed his coffee in the river, spun on his heels and sprinted back into the office.

"Sonia, listen. We've had a mental block because the title of the fax has nothing to do with anything medical, let alone cancer, right?"

"Yeah, I think so. Yes."

"So what if the title of the fax is wrong?"

"Wrong?"

"Let's just backtrack and keep an open mind for a second. Look at this with completely fresh eyes. We were only assuming the title said 'Lancer's Nemesis' because that's what my housekeeper said."

"Okay."

Travis scooped up the fax from the desk making sure Sonia could see it:

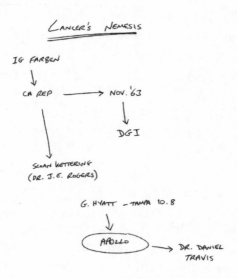

Sonia watched Travis's mouth open wide. "What? What is it?!" she asked.

"Son of a bitch!" Travis said, squinting with disbelief at the fax.

"What?!"

"Your brother's handwriting sucks," said Travis, smacking his hand against the fax, tossing it at Sonia. "It doesn't say 'Lancer's Nemesis'—it says '*Cancer's* Nemesis'!"

CHAPTER 71

IN GREEN'S OFFICE, the all-nighter dragged on with the cryptologist, Nick Maynard, in the spotlight.

"Sir, I still don't get where the reference to the DGI fits in. Everything else matches. It's possible that if a link is found it could guide us in the right direction, but I can't say for sure."

"Nick, I understand it's not an exact science and we already have a good game plan to pick up Apollo, but I'm just trying to get the best possibility," Green said, wringing his hands.

"And that's what you'll get. I'm more interested in the direct reference to Travis at the bottom of the page and that's what I'm working on right now. I'll have to get back to you."

"Alright, you do that. Don't go too far away." *Useless little snot-nose.*

Green turned his attention to Norman who was patiently awaiting either the next directive, or the next outburst.

"Norm, once we figure out where Apollo was sent, I want to be there. I just don't trust the capability of our field agents. In any case, I don't want any of them getting any cute ideas about taking a peek at the contents, or worse, making another copy. I mean, Jesus, what the hell has it come to when we can't trust our own people?!" Green threw his arms in the air.

Norman knew the answer but wasn't sure if Green wanted to hear it.

Screw it. He needs to hear it, but with a pretty bow on top.

"Sir, you're right, it's a crisis."

"Yep, it sure is."

"Record levels of burn-out, alcoholism and depression. People have no idea how thin 9/11 stretched us—and none of this is your fault, sir."

Green nodded at Norman. "I know, I know. Christ, is it any wonder we have morons like Croghan as detail leaders? There was a time when agents would stay for life, now we're losing them like no tomorrow. No one gives a shit anymore."

"It's a different generation, sir. We never used to question or ask why, we'd just do it."

"Damn straight."

"And it's the administration too," Norman continued. "Slowly one president after another's eaten away at the mission we were originally intended for. Add that to a generation of kids who ask 'why' all the time and you have a recipe for disaster—the country's populated by people whose approval of their president inversely correlates to gas prices for heaven's sake. What hope is there?" Giving Green the problem but then blaming others was Norman's ticket to survival.

Green just stared out the window and listened. He swung round in his recliner to face Norman.

"Like I said, I'm not leaving this in the hands of field agents. Their orders stand, but I want to be there to ensure there are no more screw-ups."

"What do you propose?"

"Call the pilot of my jet and have him calculate a point equidistant from all the towns on the shortlist."

"Yes, sir. What's your plan, if I may ask?"

Green stood up and walked toward the window, staring at the night sky. "Tell him to turn the plane into a flying gas can. I'm gonna have him fly me to that point and go into a holding pattern there. The cryptologist is coming with me. I need you here as an anchor."

"Okay, I'll tell Nick to prepare."

"And tell him to bring what he needs—including his teddy bear and pajamas. We're gonna solve this thing mid-air. Either that or one of our agents will let us know where Apollo shows up and we'll swoop down and get it before Travis and his little helper know what hit 'em."

CHAPTER 72

SUDDENLY, EVERTYHING DR. ROGERS said commanded new importance as Travis contemplated the fax from a different perspective—a *medical* one. Time had never seemed like such a precious commodity; minutes went by like seconds as dawn approached.

"But that still doesn't explain the reference to the DGI," Sonia said, pointing to the entry on the fax.

"I know—I'm still thinking."

"Neither does any of this tell us where the file was sent, does it?"

"No…just let me think!"

Sonia huffed and strutted back to the chair at the desk, despondent and disappointed, while Travis gathered his thoughts. "Sonia, how did your father die?"

Sonia looked shocked and then answered after a pause. "Cancer—it was lung cancer."

"Were your father and brother close?"

"I guess. Where are you going with this?" She appeared agitated. Defensive.

"We have to put ourselves inside your brother's head and think through what must have been the build up to all this."

"Okay?"

Travis began pacing like a trial lawyer as he offered his theory. "Okay, so let's say your father died of cancer and your brother became eaten up with that and made it his quest to figure out a way he might have saved his dad—maybe it just started out as a research project entitled 'Cancer's Nemesis'? Like Kramer said, you Secret Service people like an operational code word for everything."

"Go on."

"He then reads about the Sloan Kettering debacle and gets deeper involved—possibly with this *Second Opinion Underground* and Dr. Rogers. During his research he comes across two things: the California Report came out the same month and year Kennedy was shot and the first Laetrile clinic was in Dallas. His father was on protection detail that day in Dallas, so those two similarities might have struck a chord with him. Then in time, he finds out about a Bilderberg conference, possibly about a related cover-up and so he makes the Apollo File."

Sonia looked unimpressed. "That all sounds great, Professor, but it still doesn't explain the reference to the DGI, or more importantly, the location of the file."

"Correct. Which makes me wonder if the final mystery, the reference to the DGI, is the key to the location?"

The realization dawned on them at the same time. They shouted the same thing in unison: "Ramón!"

Travis leapt out of the office to find Ramón. He headed out the door but literally bumped into him.

"Aye, yi, yi—take it easy, Danny—you finished with my office now? I gotta use the phone."

"Ramón, we need your help. Can you spare a little time now?" Ramón looked at his watch while Travis waited like a hopeful child.

"What do you want?" Ramón huffed.

Travis ushered him into the office and took a seat opposite him, next to Sonia.

"We need you to think back and recall everything you can about the DGI," said Travis.

"The DGI? Cuban Intelligence? What the hell's that gotta do with you?" Ramón asked.

"Please, just let me ask the questions?" Travis said, gingerly.

"Okay."

"Alright. Ramón, did the DGI have anything at all to do with cancer, or a cure for cancer—even anything medical at all?"

Ramón looked blank. "No, nothing I can recall."

Sonia and Travis looked at each other. Sonia was decidedly despondent, but Travis persisted.

"I'd like to run some words and phrases by you. Please think about the DGI and all your experiences to do with them and even your time as an agent in Cuba and Miami—everything from that time?"

"Okay."

"And if anything I say rings a bell, let me know okay?"

"Okay."

Travis took out the notes he'd made from his meeting with Rogers and the fax. He began, leaving a pause after each word, hoping Ramón would interject.

"Here goes then. IG Farben...the California Report... Sloan Kettering...November '63..."

Ramón interrupted, but Travis knew why. "The month and year Kennedy was shot by the DGI."

"Okay, Ramón, I'll keep going though. Apollo...Dr. Rogers...G. Hyatt..." Travis then switched to the notes taken from the meeting with Rogers. "Ernst Krebs...Laetrile...B17...the Second Opinion Underground...Linus Pauling...Andrew McNaughton...Stockert... Schloen...Sugiura...apricot kernels..."

"Wait," said Ramón.

"What is it? Which thing?"

"No, it's nothing. Forget it."

"Okay. Clinton Leblanc…Green…" Travis was reaching and Ramón still looked blank.

"No, nothing rings a bell, Danny. Sorry. Is that it?"

"Yeah," said Travis, defeated for now. "Thanks, anyway." Ramón snatched a notebook from his desk and waddled out.

"Shit," said Sonia. "Why do I feel like this is going nowhere fast?"

Travis shrugged off her remark. "Let me at the computer, Sonia, I may as well check my email."

Sonia sprung from her place in front of the screen.

"Why don't you take a nap?" Travis said. "You might find you think clearer after."

"Maybe in a while. You want some more coffee?" she asked.

"Sure, why not."

"You think there might be something of use in your email?"

"I doubt it, but it'll help me regroup my thoughts. I haven't checked since Monday afternoon."

Sonia left the grubby little office and went for another caffeine fix while Travis logged on to the Internet, pounding the keyboard with veiled frustration.

His email account popped up and he realized why he checked his email three or four times a day. There were 106 new messages. Travis scanned through as quickly as he could, looking for anything unusual, muttering to himself. "Spam…Drew…Spam…University…" On it went, but nothing pertinent to this crisis. He opened each email that wasn't spam and quickly looked over it, but the content of each one was entirely innocuous.

Travis always thought a person's email inbox was a reflection upon that individual's life, and now, as he sat here reflecting on his own, it was like an out-of-body experience. There were a number of emails that on any other day would have caused him some consternation, but now those problems were laughable in their relative triviality. *What I would give right now to have this as the only thing there was to worry about. Happiness really is all about comparison.*

Sonia ambled in, handed Travis his coffee, then walked out again and headed outside the warehouse, silent.

Travis called his cell phone voicemail to see if anything had turned up there.

"Sorry, you have not entered the correct code."

He tried again, this time making sure he didn't fat-finger the keypad.

"Sorry, you have not entered the correct code."

They've blocked it! Bastards.

Each time he felt his resolve waning since all this started, something like this would happen and stoke the fire in his belly. Trying to stop Travis from doing something was like waving a red flag at a bull. *Who do these guys think they are?*

Travis thought about making more calls but thought better of it in case the call might be traced. Sonia would know for sure. He'd ask her.

There was one more thing to try.

Travis had an online fax account; he could view faxes anywhere with an Internet connection. These days he was spending so much time away from home, it seemed like a good idea. Any faxes he received at home, his housekeeper Rosemary had forwarded to his online account. All she'd have to do is push a button and the last fax to have come through would get forwarded.

He typed in the URL, though in retrospect he doubted anything would have come from his home after it was raided. Still, there may have been faxes from other sources.

The screen popped up and he logged in to his account. There were five faxes. He scanned through them. Three were junk faxes, so he deleted them. One was from his CPA: a statement.

The last one made Travis swallow a mouthful of coffee so fast he nearly choked.

It was a fax from home. And it was sent on *Monday.*

Did Rosemary manage to send the fax before the house was raided? Surely not! Good for Rosemary. That would have saved Sonia the effort, had he known. But hindsight was 20/20. They were on the run after all.

On the run. How'd that happen?

Travis opened the document. Sure enough, there it was—the very same fax Sonia had retrieved back at his house and was now sitting on the desk in front of him. Travis closed the file and logged off...

Wait.

Something wasn't right. Travis typed in the URL again and logged back in to his fax account. He opened the file Rosemary had sent once more to make sure he wasn't just seeing things. It was late. *Maybe too much caffeine.*

A gulp constricted his breathing.

He scrolled down to the bottom of the page and stared, mouth wide open. *What the hell?*

Inexplicable!

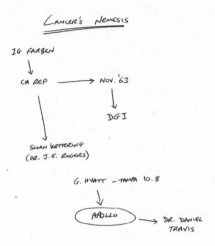

Lancer's Nemesis

IG FARBEN → CA REP → NOV. '63 → DGI

SLOAN KETTERING (DR. J.E. ROGERS)

G. HYATT — TAMPA 10.8 → APOLLO → DR. DANIEL TRAVIS

Travis: Find the common link. Apollo's at the town he started, address where cancer ended.

This fax was different from the one Sonia retrieved. There was more writing—hurried writing—at the bottom, and it matched the rest of the fax, so presumably it was written by Leblanc. It read: "Travis: find the common link. Apollo's at the town he started, address where…" Travis focused. *Was it Lancer or Cancer?* "…ended."

Travis's mind was spinning with a tempest of excitement and bemusement. "Sonia!"

CHAPTER 73

IN A REMOTE HANGAR at Washington Dulles Airport, the flight crew of Green's jet made preparations for their flight. First Officer McClellan was busy shuffling paperwork and entering computer data, while Captain Jakes half-heartedly flipped through a flight ops manual. They sat in a brightly lit glass cubicle full of charts, manuals and computer screens showing various weather charts. Outside in the pale darkness of an unlit hangar, sat the gleaming white Dassault Falcon jet, poised like a bird of prey.

"McClellan, what kind of dumbass games are we playing here? I've never heard of an instruction like this."

McClellan spoke into his computer monitor. "Boss, I have no idea, but unless I finish getting this data into this mapping software, Green's not gonna be a happy camper."

Jakes continued regardless. "I've seen a lot of crap in my time—flew some pretty freaky flights in the Gulf, hell, even saw a UFO once—but this is just plain weird."

"Yes, boss."

"At times like these the commercial airlines look a lot more appealing, don't they?"

"Yes, sir, they do."

"So how's it going there? What time's wheels up?"

McClellan hit the ENTER key like he was swatting a fly. "Done. Sorry, what was that, boss?"

"When are we headed out?"

"Oh, Green wants us to be at the waypoint by eight o'clock Eastern this morning. Then we enter a holding pattern and await further instructions."

"And what did you calculate the waypoint as?"

McClellan pointed to the monitor where a map of America was displayed with a multitude of dots marked. "See these? Each of these is one of the towns we were given by Green. We were asked to calculate a waypoint equidistant from each one, but I've had to guesstimate."

"Guesstimate?"

"Yeah, guesstimate." *If you'd have been helping me for a change instead of whining, it might have been a hell of a lot more accurate too.* "Yes, boss. The instruction was total nonsense. How can any point be equidistant from a bunch of random points on a map? We'll have to be closer to some than others. What they *meant* to tell us was to calculate a point that had the best chance of getting to any of these towns the fastest. It won't be a mid-point as much as a point closest to the highest concentration of towns in this data."

Captain Jakes hadn't considered the flaw in their orders and now felt a little embarrassed. "Of course, Number One, glad you caught that. Good job."

"Here's the waypoint I calculated." McClellan pointed to a section of the map he'd enlarged.

"Digby?" questioned Jakes.

"Yeah. It's a waypoint on that airway there. I figure if we hold at flight level 340, we'll miss this layer of icing and save gas too."

"Looks like it's somewhere over Tennessee."

"Sure does—a town near Memphis called Bolivar actually."

"So if we end up having to go to Los Angeles…"

"Then it'll take longer than if we need to go to Charlotte,

but what else can we do?"

"You're right. We have to base this on probability. I'd better call Green to make sure he understands all the same. Hey, but don't forget the time zones—we'll gain time as we go west—we'll gain an hour as we hit Tennessee alone."

"Good call, boss, I factored those in already."

"You're a good man, Charlie Brown. And what time do we need to leave to make it there by eight? I may as well let Green know that while I'm at it."

"Eleven-thirty Zulu—six-thirty as far as they're concerned."

"Alright. And we'd better make some fuel computations. I'll need to know with maximum fuel how long we can hold for from eight o'clock, and still make it to the field farthest from the holding point with minimum reserves, accounting for weather at each destination."

"Sure thing, boss."

Captain Jakes called Green.

McClellan was busy with his calculator and flight log, but caught sight of his captain's paler expression as he put the phone down.

"What's up, boss? I take it they weren't too happy about being told their instructions were a crock!" McClellan said, laughing.

"No…no, it's not that." Jakes paused and shook his head. "This gets weirder and weirder. That's it, tomorrow United is getting my resume!"

"What?" said McClellan.

"Green just told me we'd have an additional passenger."

"No problem, I'll adjust the paperwork. Is this in addition to Green and this Nick guy?"

"Yeah. This passenger has to stay out of sight the whole journey. We're not to ask his name or let anyone know of his presence on the flight," Jakes said as he threw his hands in the air, "or we're both fired."

"Really?" McClellan asked sheepishly.

"Yeah."

"Alright, but I'll need to know his details for the manifest. Does he have any bags with him?"

"As far as I'm concerned, this guy's not on the manifest. Understand?"

CHAPTER 74

SONIA DARTED INTO THE OFFICE. Travis was waiting for her with a print out of the version of the fax Rosemary had sent. She stared incredulously at the paper. "I...I can't understand..." she mumbled.

"Sonia," Travis said, "how do you explain it?"

Silence.

Travis thought aloud. "*Your* version of the fax was missing this and it's pretty crucial, but why? This fax looks like the original. Look, the handwriting matches and everything."

Still, she stared at the fax in silence.

"Sonia, how *did* you get a copy of the fax from my fax machine memory?"

"Your fax machine memory must have been screwed up. You're right though—this is definitely the original. How'd you get it?" she asked.

"My housekeeper forwarded it to my online account. We've been working blind!" Travis said with the faint beginnings of a smile.

"This is great news!" said Sonia. "Let's figure this out then." Sonia took a seat and started reading the message at the bottom of the page.

Travis began to study it with her. "Okay, what I think happened is your brother wrote this at the bottom just before he sent it."

"Damn! I knew we were missing a piece of the puzzle. I knew he wouldn't have made it so hard for us," she said, her deep green eyes widening.

"Alright, we're not through this yet. I think Leblanc started out looking for a way to beat cancer, probably sparked by something that piqued his interest, and he titled this paper 'Cancer's Nemesis.'"

"Agreed," said Sonia.

"During his research, he encountered similarities with Kennedy's death. Then he sends this fax to me, probably because he sees me as a suitable medium to either carry on the work he'd started or as a reliable recipient of what he named the Apollo File."

"Makes sense."

"Fine. But then he comes under pressure and, realizing he has to get the Apollo File out of Green's reach, he writes something on the bottom of this paper and faxes it to me. To assist me in locating Apollo."

"Okay. Yes, I can see that."

"Now we have to decide whether he said cancer or Lancer in that note at the bottom of the page. I think he'd have known I would have seen the similarity between cancer and Lancer in all this."

Sonia searched through the drawers.

"What are you looking for?" Travis said.

"Magnifying glass," Sonia said, still searching. "Ramón!" she shouted out the door.

After a few seconds of Sonia bawling, Ramón materialized. "What? What the hell's wrong, woman?"

"You got a magnifying glass somewhere in this shit hole, Ramón?" Sonia spoke like they were old friends, or old enemies. She was clearly still upset about Ramón abducting her, though Travis sensed more hurt pride than anything else.

"What the hell do you think this is? Office Depot?" Ramón said and stormed off.

"He's no goddamn help!" Sonia said, still rifling furiously through the drawers. "Goddamn coke dealer, that's all he is."

"Well, your bedside manner could use a little work," Travis said, grinning as he watched her. "We may still need him and you'll probably get a lot more out of him by being civil."

Sonia ignored Travis. "Here, try this instead," said Travis. He gave her a dirty glass abandoned on the desk.

"Alright, that'll work." She used it to magnify words and letters around the page.

Travis knew what she was up to immediately. "So," he said. "Can you see any consistency between the letter C and L?"

Sonia studied the fax for a couple of minutes and then handed the glass back to Travis. "Here," she began, "you take a look."

Good. She's deliberately not saying anything so she doesn't influence my decision. Studies of scientific bias, just like Dr. Rogers said.

Travis clutched the glass and began shifting it around the page.

"It's a tough call," he said.

"Too close to call?" Sonia said.

"I'd say so, yes. It was easier to see on the bigger letters in the title, but this new writing at the bottom is much more hurried. Plus the title made a lot more sense as 'Cancer's Nemesis,' but this one could be anything. We've already made one false assumption. I don't want to do that again."

"So what do you suggest? We're running out of time!"

"Whoa, calm down. I suggest working only with what we know it says there and hopefully that will make the rest of the sentence clearer," Travis said, placing a comforting hand on her shoulder.

"Okay. So we just focus on this: 'Travis: find the common link. Apollo's at the town he started,'" she said, sharply exhaling.

"Yep. So let's start—the text already implies that the common link is a person: a man, so that's a beginning."

"And he's a link between what two things exactly?"

"Your brother will have seen certain links and similarity between Kennedy's assassination and this business about Laetrile and the pharmaceutical cartel—it's my belief he thought I'd see it too, once I'd researched this fax."

"Okay, so..."

"So we're looking for a common link between cancer and Lancer—in the context of this fax, of course. And it's a man, so let's draw up a shortlist of all the men we can think of who might have a common link and investigate where they started. That should tell us the town where your brother sent the file and then we'll work on the address. Sound reasonable?"

"Yes—alright, let's make that list," replied Sonia.

With a blunt, chewed pencil, Travis grabbed a scrap of paper and scribbled all the relevant men's names he could think of.

"Alright, what we need to do now is enter these names into the Internet and cross reference them against each other and see what we can come up with."

"Alright."

"Now remember, the point of reference is cancer, not Lancer. Let's work on the same premise as the title of the fax. Your brother was working on something to do with cancer and found out about a link with Kennedy's assassination—something most likely to do with the DGI. So let's see if we can figure out what your brother did."

Sonia hesitated. "Yeah, but thinking about this now, there are so many different variables here and so…"

"And *so* we're wasting time talking!"

CHAPTER 75

SPECIAL AGENT REESE SWIVELED himself around in his desk chair, staring at the ceiling. The FBI needed him tonight like never before and yet he and his boss Jensen were the only people who knew why. So why was Jensen tucked up in a warm bed in Georgetown while he stared at the ceiling, trying to keep his eyes open?

Because Jensen's too high profile. And I'm expendable...

But he had never been under any illusions about how the game worked and it never made his loyalty waver throughout his entire career.

The phone rang. His eyes widened as he snatched it off the desk.

"Reese here."

"Yeah, this is Dulles Airport Clearance Delivery—you asked for a call if tail number N566SS filed a flight plan?"

"Yes, sir, I did!" Reese sprung up from his chair in anticipation, knocking over a cup of pens as he scrambled for a biro. "One second!"

Green's pilots had just filed a flight plan. "Go ahead, please."

"Okay—well it's an unusual one. They filed to a waypoint over Tennessee called Digby where they intend to hold until further notice."

"Hold? You mean a holding pattern?"

"Yeah."

"Got it, thanks. Anything else you can tell me? When are they leaving?"

"Let's see here…it was filed for six-thirty this morning, Eastern Time."

Reese hung up and pounded in the eleven digits. This was it.

"Hello, this is Special Agent Reese. I need the mobile operations jet ready to leave Dulles at six-forty this morning. Take all the fuel you can carry and file to hold at a waypoint as close to Digby as possible—it's in Tennessee somewhere. Not *at* Digby, just close by."

The FBI pilot confirmed his instructions.

Reese caught him before he could hang up. "And Captain—this is *highly confidential*. You're the only person who's aware of this order, so we'll know where the leak came from. I'll brief you further when I get there."

Reese drummed eleven more digits into the phone.

"Jensen here." The voice was surprisingly crisp for this early hour.

"Sorry to wake you, sir."

"Been awake for hours, Reese, what is it?"

"He's made a move—kind of. He's filed to hold at a waypoint over Tennessee. I'm following him."

"Alright. Be careful he doesn't get wind of us getting a piggy-back ride."

"Yes, sir, of course. I've set up a direct and confidential link to Air Traffic Control to monitor where he goes after the holding point, but I do worry about leaks—they're civilians. Can you get me…"

"AWACS? It's done. Anything else?"

"No, sir. Thank you. Will be in touch when things are clearer."

CHAPTER 76

"LISTEN, I HATE TO RAIN on your parade, but even if we do figure this out, how do we get out of Miami fast enough and undetected by Green?" asked Sonia, pacing around the small office.

She was right of course, but Travis was fixated on the immediate problem. "One step at a time. And would you stop doing that? I'm trying to work through this."

"Sorry, but we've tried everything—every single cross reference we know about. There's no link between the DGI or the Castro Regime and this whole Laetrile cancer thing," she said, hurling a pencil across the desk, continuing to pace, despite Travis's request.

"Not as far as we can see anyway," Travis said.

"What do you mean?"

"There *must* be a common link—a man—or your brother wouldn't have written it on the fax. When we know who that is we can find out where he started and we're home and dry."

"Yeah, provided we can get to wherever the thing is in time…"

Ramón burst in. "Okay, when you guys have finished playing word games, I'd like to use my office," he said, staring at Sonia from behind his reading glasses. "And when are you guys outta here anyway? This ain't no freakin' YMCA!"

Ramón's timing was off, even though what he said was in

half-jest. Travis could see Sonia was about to lose it, but his words got stuck in his throat.

"Ramón, fuck you!" she shouted, squaring up to stare into his eyes defiantly. This was a disturbing side of Sonia Travis hadn't seen.

"Get the fuck out of my office, right now—unless you wanna be back in that wheelchair! Permanently!" Ramón wasn't playing around anymore.

Sonia fired back calmly. "Yeah well, let me know which idiot I need to send to ER this time—without your stooges to protect you I'd kick your ass right back to Cuba, you fuck-ing…"

Travis wedged his body between them. "Okay, okay guys, that's enough!"

Ramón interrupted, laughing scornfully. "Listen, lady, I don't fight fair. You should be careful—you owe me your life."

Travis had his hands on each of their shoulders, but he was looking at Sonia. "Listen, this isn't helping anyone—remember what we're here for. Settle down, will you?"

Sonia barged past them both and stormed out of the office.

"Charming girl, where'd you find her?" Ramón said, taking his seat at the desk.

Travis sighed and slumped into a seat in the corner of the office, adjacent to Ramón who was now busy on the computer. He found Ramón's lack of interest in his predicament curious as well as frustrating.

A mischievous glint flickered in Travis's eyes.

"What happened, Ramón?" Travis said.

"Say what?"

"Why are you so angry at the world?"

Ramón looked into the monitor as he replied: "Aye, yi, yi,

spare me the bullshit analyst crap, would you? I'm busy."

"Yep, your services must be in big demand, Ramón—and you sure are making the world a better place in the process."

Ramón spun his chair around to face Travis with a wicked grin. Travis had succeeded in getting Ramón's attention with the remark, just as planned. He just hoped not in the kind of way where he got shot as a result.

"What did you say?" Ramón replied, like he'd just been asked for a fight in the parking lot.

"I was merely saying you're a drug dealer, and you are… aren't you?"

"And if I was?"

"Nothing…but you're breaking the law, so I just wondered what happened. You were once a great asset to this country, Kramer said."

"Listen, Kramer's a good man and the only reason I'm even having this conversation with you is because you know him, but you don't know shit, kiddo!"

"I know the law," Travis said, working Ramón further.

"Like I said, you don't know shit." Ramón turned back to his desk, but Travis wasn't letting go of the first revealing interaction he'd had with Ramón, regardless of how hostile it was.

"What do you mean? The law is the law," Travis argued.

Ramón laughed as if the argument was over before it had begun. "Law is a subjective word, my friend—and it's okay for our own government, the same government which makes those laws to break them, I suppose?"

Travis sat in silence. Ramón had a point, but he let him continue by faking an unconvinced look to keep the debate alive.

Ramón turned around to face Travis again and continued with zeal. "It's okay for our government to commit murder, like they did with ZR/RIFLE? And I don't care how bad the people the CIA targeted were, if you shoot a rapist you'll go to jail, won't you?"

"I guess I will. But this is drugs, Ramón. An addictive contraband, which kills people."

"Drugs? I just fill a need in the marketplace. It's called freedom of choice, my friend—freedom—and that's why I came to this country, because I thought it was free."

"Yeah, but not if those choices you make kill you!"

"What, and tobacco isn't an addictive substance which kills you?"

"Good point, but…" Travis tried to interject, but Ramón was now into a well-rehearsed speech.

"And what about drugs? People pick up drugs from the pharmacy all day long—the whole fucking country's addicted and the drug companies are pushers! Bunch of goddamn hypochondriacs, that's all we are! You telling me Prozac's not addictive, not a drug that makes you high and lets your problems melt away? Shit, contraband's a subjective word depending on whether our government and the fat-cats who sponsor them can make money from the substance…hell, astro-turf's legal in a lot of countries!"

"Astro-turf?"

"Marijuana."

"Oh." Travis thought about how Laetrile had been banned. *Apricot kernel extract made illegal contraband?*

"A quarter of the world's prison population resides in our jails and half of them are in the slammer for falling foul of our dumb drug laws," continued Ramón.

"I see your point…"

"So please, don't lecture me about right and wrong, my friend, when your very own government doesn't know the difference!"

"You're right, Ramón." *Now that he's awake, let's start getting deeper.* "I guess life as a CIA contract agent made those lines between right and wrong pretty unclear, didn't they?"

"You bet your ass!" Ramón said, getting back to his work.

Damn. The DGI and Cuba was the key to this whole deal and sitting in front of Travis right now was a man who'd infiltrated them. Why couldn't Ramón help?

He must know something.

"How did Kramer save your life, Ramón?"

Ramón glanced back at Travis. "It's a long story and it's very late— he gave me some information which saved me a shit load of trouble."

"What information?"

"Aw shit. You really are a pain in the ass."

"The biggest! Ever since I was a kid, according to Kramer." Travis grinned warily. *Keep him talking and reminiscing.*

"Back in the days just before Castro—the late fifties—I was already in touch with Kramer and others in Washington as a contract agent in Cuba—but I was just the son of a café owner to everyone who knew me." Ramón smiled nostalgically and jerked his head to the left. "Best mojitos on the island." Then his face hung heavy in stark contrast. "The CIA knew something was going on and that Castro would probably seize power, and that he was a commie, but they did nothing. Make no mistake, the Batista government before Castro at the time were damn corrupt—no better than Castro actually—but they weren't communists…"

"What happened?"

"Apart from those bastards stealing my country, you mean?!"

"Yes, that's what I mean," Travis said.

"You ever been to Cuba, Danny?"

"No, I haven't."

"It's beautiful…one day I'll return. Cuban families are strong—very strong." Ramón's expression of joy suddenly turned to a pained wince and his eyes welled up.

"What happened?"

"My older brother…he…"

Travis sat in silence. He felt for Ramón but this conversation wasn't very helpful. *Stay with it.* "Go on…"

"It was my fault—I should have seen the signs—my brother Ricardo became influenced by Castro's movement right under my goddamn nose! Can you believe that? But now Ricardo's dead—he was chased by the Batista police and got shot—and I was a CIA agent for Christ's sake!" Ramón stiffened his trembling lip by biting it. "Still, it made me look like a Castro sympathizer to the new regime, so I was positioned perfectly as a CIA spy."

"What sort of operations did you advise?"

"All kinds of intel… You know, there was a curious thing going on which I figured out eventually but too late," Ramón said.

"What was that?"

"The Batista government should have been able to put up a better fight than they did, but Castro was able to locate Batista's armaments pipeline and sabotage it."

"How did he do that?"

"Double agents again. The bastard KGB trained Castro's DGI and taught them all they knew—and they were too good for Batista. Can you believe one of those double agents was a Canadian?!"

"Really? What was his name?"

"Can't remember now, that was all a long time ago." A perplexed expression came over Ramón's face.

Travis tried a new tact. "So what other operations did

you…"

Ramón's face suddenly lit up.

"What is it?" Travis said, leaning forward.

"Shit, shut up, would you already?!"

Travis withdrew like a slap blew across his face. He sat in silence, watching the cogs turn in Ramón's head.

"Run those names past me again," Ramón said.

"What names?"

"Those names you were saying earlier: about the DGI and so on."

"Sure, why?" Travis sat forward in expectation. "Think something rang a bell?"

"Maybe, go ahead and hit me with them again."

"Sure. Okay…here we go…Ernst Krebs…Dr. J.E. Rogers…Sloan Kettering…" But for each word Ramón shook his head quickly and waved to go on the next one.

"…Andrew McNaughton…Sugiura…"

"Shit! That's it! Son of a bitch—holy crap—how'd you get that name?"

"Which? Sugiura?!"

"No, McNaughton!"

Travis rifled through his notes from the meeting with Dr. Rogers. "Here it is—okay. McNaughton was considered the most important person behind the Laetrile movement, formerly at the United Nations, he was introduced to Ernst Krebs in the sixties."

"Well, I don't know what all this is about, but you asked me if there was a link between McNaughton and the DGI. There is."

"What is it?" Travis tried to stay calm, not to interrupt Ramón's recollection, but the butterflies in his stomach were in top gear.

"Andrew McNaughton—and after what you told me

about him I know it's the same Andrew McNaughton—was a double agent for Castro."

"What? You're kidding?!"

"He had a lot to do with Castro getting to power. He was a Canadian, but Castro made him an honorary citizen of Cuba to thank him for everything he'd done for the revolution."

"And what was it he did for Castro?"

Ramón smiled in admiration. "He was one clever son of a bitch—he used to be a gun runner for the Batista government. He'd pretend to be on their side by selling them armaments, but then inform Castro when and where those armaments were being shipped so they could be hijacked."

"That's it! That's the DGI link! So he was a Castro sympathizer? Doesn't seem right—he was a businessman who was helping a communist regime get to power?"

"Well, it wasn't as clear cut back then as it is in your history books. The lines between right and wrong were blurry. The right-wing Batista government was evil and corrupt and Castro didn't officially say he was a Marxist until he took over. McNaughton genuinely thought he was fighting for a noble cause, just like my brother Ricardo before those Batista bastards killed him. I know for a fact that McNaughton had very good friends who'd died fighting for Castro—they detested the Batista dictatorship that much."

"I see." Travis recalled how famous writers like W. H. Auden and George Orwell had fought a similar battle for the communists in the Spanish Civil War to overthrow a fascist dictatorship in the thirties, so it seemed this Andrew Mc-Naughton was in good company. Those authors later turned on communism.

Travis took a sharp breath, then lunged up, focusing on the clock above Ramón ticking away. "Ramón, thanks!"

"No problem!" He slapped his hand on Travis's back and got back to work. "Let me know when you want another history lesson, my crazy friend."

Travis ripped open the door. "Sonia! We have it!"

CHAPTER 77

GREEN AND NICK LOUNGED in the back of the sedan as it blew its way to Dulles Airport in the early morning darkness. Green wanted to get to the hangar early to discuss the flight plan with the pilot and ensure confidentiality of the third passenger. Meanwhile he pressed Nick for answers.

"Sir, I'm doing what I can, but as I've said, this really isn't a matter of cryptology: there's no code to break here or anything." Nick slid out his copy of the fax from his black leather laptop case he had over his shoulder:

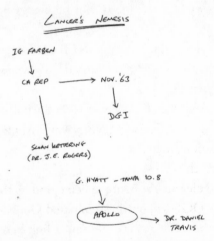

"You see, based on what you've told me, we know this whole fax refers to a cure for cancer as the title suggests."

"Right. I know," huffed Green.

"We know what all the references mean individually on the page and that the bottom two lines were added in haste to get a message to Travis."

"Go on, make your point," Green said, teeth biting down on his bottom lip.

"The only thing which doesn't fit the profile is the note about the DGI—there's something clearly missing here—it may be some code between Leblanc and Travis that only they would know how to decipher. It could be that Travis knows something we don't—that's the problem."

"If so, why's he in Miami? We know for a fact the Apollo File wasn't sent anywhere in that area."

"Again, that's not really my field, but I'd say it meant he was looking for Rogers. So yes, I see your point—he doesn't know where the file is. But he may have an advantage."

"Not anymore. He's staying in Miami. Anyway, let's not worry about Travis—let's concentrate on narrowing down this USPS shortlist."

"Okay. Well, then it clearly rests on the bottom two lines where Leblanc is effectively telling Travis where to find the file. No questions there."

"That much is obvious."

"This whole thing's about medicine, and on that basis, the reference to DGI is about Disseminated Gonococcal Infection: gonorrhea. But I don't see how a link between cancer and gonorrhea can give you an address."

"Alright. I know all this. But there must be something else we're missing."

Nick spoke to the misty window. "Of course, if you told

me what was on the Apollo File and what happened in Tampa I would…"

Green's eyes glazed over. "Look, I've told you already. That's classified. You know all you need to know. There was a meeting down there and Leblanc stole some privileged information. I told you this whole fax is about cancer which should be good enough—and I don't see where fucking gonorrhea comes in!"

Nick edged away in his seat. "Yes, sir. Neither do I, because the common link is clearly a man. Maybe the man is this Rogers guy—he started in New York, so maybe the file will turn up there?"

"I already thought of that. It's a possibility, if a little obvious."

"Sometimes the simplest answer is the best."

"Sometimes," Green said, staring into the dark sky.

CHAPTER 78

TRAVIS MET SONIA at the doorway of Ramón's office.

"We got it," he said. "Ramón said Andrew McNaughton was a double agent for Castro and the DGI. He's the common link."

"And that's the same guy Dr. Rogers told you was behind Laetrile?"

"Has to be!"

"So what are we waiting for? Where's the fax?"

Ramón was on his office phone. Travis leaned in and grabbed the fax and his notes from the desk and hurried Sonia away to the coffee-stained table and chairs on the other side of the warehouse.

Travis commanded the discussion. "Okay, so let's see how that fits with the bottom two lines on the fax.

"So here's the first part." He read it aloud: "'Travis: find the common link. Apollo's at the town he started.'"

"Okay and where did McNaughton start then?" asked Sonia.

Travis had considered this from the second he'd heard Ramón say McNaughton was linked with the DGI. "It depends in what context."

"What do you mean?"

"I mean where he started *what* exactly?"

"Jesus, this doesn't seem any easier."

"Not if you take it out of context. I think it's a fair assumption that the context is the one relevant to the fax…this fax about 'Cancer's Nemesis.' We should work on his involvement with cancer."

"Okay. And where did Rogers say McNaughton started his crusade with Laetrile?"

Travis knew the answer from memory but ruffled through his notes just to be sure.

"Here…here it is. Yes, the first Laetrile clinic opened up in Dallas, Texas."

"So working on that context, the town Apollo was sent to is Dallas?"

"Yes." Travis could hardly believe they may have just figured out where the file was sent. "So let's apply that thesis to the second half of the bottom two lines on the fax using Dallas as the probable destination."

Sonia grabbed the fax and read it: "'Travis: find the common link. Apollo's at Dallas, address where cancer ended.' Or is it: 'Travis: find the common link. Apollo's at Dallas, address where Lancer ended'?"

"Let's try the first one—where cancer ended. So that could be the address of that first Laetrile clinic, although it would no longer be a clinic, I imagine."

Sonia stood up and began pacing, her eyes aglow with possibility. "Wait a minute," she said, waving her pointer finger. "Put yourself in my brother's shoes…"

"Okay. Go on," Travis said.

"He's a Secret Service agent—like me—he'd have probably known the people after him would seize his contacts file from his computer and check his phone records. He wouldn't have been dumb enough to send it to one of those addresses, I don't think."

"He was probably under pressure though," Travis

argued.

"Maybe, but even so, he's a professional and I know how he'd have thought."

"Of course. Go on."Travis felt sympathetic about the loss of her brother, although Sonia didn't seem too upset to speculate about the moments before his death.

"So that would mean he'd have to send it to an address *not* in his address book: one that he would know from memory."

Travis lurched forward. This was an excellent piece of deduction. It made perfect sense in theory. "Yes!"

"And on that basis, would he have known the address of the first Laetrile clinic from memory?"

"No, most likely not."

"So maybe we're wrong about Dallas being the town he started? You said McNaughton was at the United Nations building before. If that's where he started, that could be an address he'd know by memory—if you just wrote 'United Nations Building, New York City' on the envelope, I'd bet it would get there!"

"Could be,"Travis said, rubbing his chin and squinting.

"You don't think so?"

"It just doesn't sit right. How could Leblanc be sure it would end up in the right hands? The United Nations is a high concentration of politicians who probably have a lot to lose. Plus, it's out of context with the fax."

"Well, do you have any better ideas?"

Travis fell silent and studied the fax. Sonia slumped down in exasperation.

Travis pointed at the word they couldn't decide on: cancer or Lancer. "Would you say the word starts with a capital L or capital C? I mean, in either case, does that mystery word start with an L or a C? And is it a capital letter?"

Sonia looked at it closely. "Yeah, I'd say that was a definite capital. Capital L or capital C. But how does that help?"

"In the middle of a sentence, would you write the word 'cancer' with a capital C?"

"Well no, but…"

"No, because 'cancer' is not a proper noun," Travis continued.

"Alright."

"And would you spell Lancer with a capital L?"

"Yeah, I guess… Yes, because it's the name of a person—so it *does* say 'Lancer'?!"

"I think so. Damn, I can't believe we were so stupid."

"Forget about it," Sonia said. "Apply it to the sentence and let's see."

Travis read from the fax again, replacing the references with the ones they theorized. "Apollo's at Dallas, address where *Lancer* ended."

They both looked at the fax. Sonia's expression was vacant, but Travis sprung out of his seat so fast it clattered across the concrete floor.

"Oh my God!"

"What?" Sonia asked.

Travis closed his eyes, holding up a hand to silence Sonia.

Travis felt his body shiver… He tested the theory in his head and came up with the same conclusion. It fit perfectly. Finally, he addressed Sonia who was poised to pounce on his words.

"Sonia, your brother wouldn't have needed his address book to send Apollo where I think he sent it."

"Alright. Carry on."

"And it's an address pretty much everyone in America alive during that era would have committed to memory."

"Where?!"

"It fits to use Dallas as a destination. It's where the common link—Andrew McNaughton—started the first Laetrile clinic. So, if Leblanc had the sense not to send the file to someone from his contacts file, he'd have had to send it to an address in Dallas he would have known by memory, and I can't see how he'd have known the address of the first clinic there, can you?"

"Probably not. No."

"So which address *do* you know in Dallas?" Travis said, with a wry grin like he was lecturing one of his old history classes.

Sonia's mouth dropped open. "But..."

"It's a museum now, so it's a legitimate address. The point where Lancer ended refers to the point Kennedy was shot, and he was shot on the street so that doesn't have an address..."

Sonia interjected, her mind working in unison with Travis's. "But the place Kennedy was shot *from* does—that's the point from which Lancer ended!"

Travis planted his palms on the table leaning forward and confirmed Sonia's suspicion with urgency. "Leblanc sent the Apollo File to the sixth floor of the Texas School Book Depository, Dallas, Texas—now known as the Sixth Floor Museum!"

CHAPTER 79

CAPTAIN JAKES AND first Officer McClellan greeted Green and Nick as they stepped out of the car. It was parked in the hangar at a time of night when even Dulles Airport was silent.

"Good evening, sir," said Captain Jakes.

"Good *morning*," snapped Green. "It worries me when my pilot doesn't know the difference between evening and morning."

Jakes chuckled nervously. "Of course, sir. I meant..."

"You understand the importance of this flight?" Green interrupted.

"Yes, sir."

"You'd goddamned better."

Jakes felt a chill as Green brushed past him, heading for the hangar office with Nick in tow. McClellan shot a frightened glance at his captain.

"What is it?" McClellan asked.

"Look, just keep your head down and do your job and let's get through this with our careers intact, okay?"

"Sure thing."

"You get those fuel figures and the load sheet ready?"

Green called to the pilots from the office. "Are you coming in or what? I didn't get here early so I could sit around this grease hole for the hell of it."

"Right there, sir." Jakes turned to McClellan. "Stay here and carry on. I want this aircraft checked and checked again."

Inside the glass-walled briefing room, Green waited with Nick, seated around a gray circular table. Captain Jakes edged into the seat opposite the men.

"Captain, I want to ask your professional opinion as an experienced pilot," Green said.

"Of course."

Green beamed at Jakes. "This is classified and you're under the Patriot Act."

"I understand—as always, sir." *This is heavy.*

"If you suddenly found yourself stuck in Miami and needed to get out by plane *undetected*, what would you do?"

Captain Jakes was relieved. At least he thought so. "Undetected? And I presume the airlines are out of the question?"

"Yep. All airline reservation and check-in desks are alerted to look out for you." Green rocked back with his arms folded, hoping to find a chink in the armor of his plan to constrain Travis.

"Well that only leaves GA—general aviation. I'd rent or charter a plane and avoid the airlines."

Green's face widened still with the smile. "Air Traffic Control's in the loop. All general aviation flight plans out of Miami come through me. As soon as I see you and where you're headed, you're history."

Jakes wasn't beaten though. Here was a legitimate opportunity to wipe that smug grin off of this asshole's face without getting canned for it.

"Not if I fly VFR and don't file a flight plan!"

"VFR?" Green asked.

"Visual Flight Rules—if I don't enter clouds I can fly

VFR and I'm not required to file a flight plan. I'd just take off, leave Miami airspace and you wouldn't know where I was going."

"You can do that?" Green threw his chair forward.

"Yes, sir," Jakes said with smug satisfaction.

Green stood up and walked toward the corner of the room, finger on his mouth. A sharp frown had wiped the smile away. It was a good call to come early and pick the pilot's brains.

Nick countered Jakes. "What about the control tower on the airport you took off from? They'd know you were leaving."

"I'd still get out no problem," Jakes said.

"How?" asked Green.

"I'd use an uncontrolled field: one that doesn't have a control tower. Pilots give themselves their own take-off clearance—there are a bunch of airports like this around Miami and most of the country."

"You can do that too?"

"Yep." But Jakes suddenly looked doubtful. He continued. "Ah, but I know how you'd get me if I did that."

"How?" Green said, leaning across the table.

"I'd show up on Miami radar, but I suppose if I turned my transponder off..."

"Your transponder: the thing that sends a code to air traffic to let them know who you are?"

"Yes, sir. But even if I switched it off, Miami would get a primary return."

"Speak goddamn English, would you?"

"Sorry, sir. I mean they'd see a dot on their screen but wouldn't know who I was."

Green spat at Nick. "Do you get that, Nick?"

Nick nodded. Green made sure he understood the order.

"I want any aircraft showing primary returns only on Miami radar to be reported along with the direction they're traveling—I want them tracked throughout their entire flight. Details sent to Norman who'll liaise with me."

Nick flipped open his cell and relayed the orders to Norman, then put his hand over the receiver. "Sir, why don't we just order Miami Air Traffic to make VFR flight plans mandatory for the next twenty-four hours?"

Jakes interjected enthusiastically. "Yeah, that'll help." He then turned to Green. "But it still won't stop me taking off from an uncontrolled airport and switching my transponder off. You'll still get that blip on the screen though. Assuming you can talk a pilot dumb enough and desperate enough to put his license on the line."

"How so?"

"It's illegal to fly in Miami airspace without a transponder and not be in radio contact—it's Class B airspace. And with the current heightened security, I wouldn't be surprised if you quickly had a couple of F-16s on your wingtips forcing you down."

"Excellent. Once we have a final destination I'll want to apply those same tracking procedures there too, Nick, just to make sure."

Jakes continued, "Yes, sir that will just about nail it—provided of course the final destination is a major city like Miami—you'll bag him, sir, you'll bag him."

CHAPTER 80

TRAVIS'S JUBILATION WAS FLEETING and hollow. Sonia knew Dallas was over thirteen hundred miles from Miami and would take more than twenty hours to get there.

"I can't find Ramón anywhere!" Travis said.

"This isn't going to work—even if we left here now by car, we'd be there late tomorrow night. The file will have come and probably gone by then. Shit!"

"Car's out of the question."

"Well, like I told you, forget any type of mass transit. You can bet Green'll have that covered."

"That's why I'm trying to find Ramón—maybe he has some contacts we could charter a plane through or something…under someone else's name or whatever."

"I don't see any other option if we want to get to Dallas before Green. Assuming he knows the file's in Dallas."

Travis slid a chair back and positioned it to face Sonia, then sat on it. "Listen, Sonia, you need to let it go with Ramón because he's about our only hope right now, like it or not."

"Shit, I know. I'll be calm. Where the hell is he, anyway?"

"He'll show up. Remember, what goes around comes around."

"*Alright*, I said. Jeez."

Ramón arrived as if on cue. He'd been in the bathroom. Travis spun out of the chair and swung open the door of the office. "Ramón!"

Ramón waddled over. "Aye, yi, yi, don't go in there for a while. What can I do for you now, my friend? You wanna do a crossword together or something?"

Travis ushered him into the office. The second he was across the threshold, Sonia made her peace. "Ramón, I—"

"No problem. I *would* have kicked your ass though." Ramón smiled and held out a hand as a truce. Probably an unwashed one, but Sonia took it anyway.

"Ramón we need transportation," said Travis.

"Transportation? Good. I was wondering when you guys would be outta my face! I'll arrange a car for you—"

"Sorry, Ramón, that won't work."

"Why not? Where do you need to go?"

"Dallas."

"So drive to fucking Dallas."

"By nine in the morning?"

"What's the rush?"

"Long story. I'd be happy to tell you when it's all over. I was hoping you might have some contacts for chartering a plane?"

"Oh, you travel in style, my friend. Something wrong with American Airlines? Oh shit, I forgot you got this government guy looking for you, don't you?"

"Yeah. He'll have airlines covered," Sonia said. Travis nodded.

"And you think chartering a plane will work?" Ramón was shaking his head.

Travis looked at Sonia. She nodded at him and confirmed Ramón's doubts. "He's right. It's a risk for sure. Green won't have missed that one."

Travis fell down into the seat, holding his head in his hands. Ramón wandered out into the dark.

"Told you," Sonia said.

"Told me what?" said Travis, stroking both hands through his ruffled hair.

"He's hopeless."

"That's really not that helpful right now."

"Sorry."

"Don't worry—this thing's done anyway." Travis looked at his watch. "It's nearly three. Get to Dallas by nine? I don't think so." His head sunk down toward his lap. "Damn!"

It was a little after three when Ramón meandered back into the warehouse with Raúl and two of the other men in tow. Travis assumed they were going about their business, but Ramón put his head around the door.

"Can you both come out here?" he asked. "There's not enough room in there."

Travis and Sonia shuffled out of the office. Travis felt exhaustion creeping in. His feet dragged and his eyes were failing him as the adrenaline rush faded.

He felt a faint glimmer of hope sweep over him. *Somehow, some way, Ramón might have worked something out.*

"Yes, Ramón?" Travis sidled next to Sonia.

Ramón looked at them both in turn as he spoke. "Ramón has the solution to your problem!" Raúl nodded and made firm eye contact with Travis.

Travis felt his heart leap. "You do? What? How?" he said with renewed excitement. He felt Sonia step forward in anticipation.

Ramón looked at Raúl briefly and turned back to them with a villainous grin. "We're going to fly you there. Now it will still take about five hours, so we need to get our asses in gear if we're going to make it there by nine for you."

"Ramón, I can't thank you enough. Will we get out undetected though?"

Sonia interrupted before Ramón could answer. "Yeah, thanks and all, but your flight plan will show up and you'll be on Miami radar. Green will know we're coming and have us stopped somewhere on the way."

Ramón and Raúl eyed each other and laughed, though with his limited English it seemed Raúl didn't really know why he was laughing.

Ramón bathed in Travis's and Sonia's frown of confusion.

A glimmer of realization appeared in Sonia's eyes.

"Son of a bitch," she said. "You guys are gonna treat us like one of your shipments! Aren't you?"

"Well you are contraband, aren't you?" Ramón said, tilting his head and smirking.

This was too much for Travis. "What do you mean?" he said, turning to Sonia.

Sonia explained. "It's an old drug smuggling trick—he uses two planes—one's a legitimate flight with a flight plan and everything but then another plane, the plane with the drugs on board, flies right underneath the legitimate plane. As far as the air traffic controller can see, it's just one blip on his screen."

"That's brilliant!" Travis gushed.

Ramón laughed. "Very cute, lady, but also completely wrong!"

"What do you mean?" she said.

Ramón glanced back at Raúl and the other two men, none of whom understood the conversation this far. Ramón spoke to them in Spanish. "Ellos han estado viendo demasiada televisión! Creen que vamos a volar un avión debajo del otro!"

Travis only understood one word: television. He heard them all laugh. Raúl added to the laughter by saying something Travis couldn't understand—apart from a couple of words. "Ellos creen que es como *Miami Vice!* Nuestros pilotos no son tan buenos!" More laughter.

"So what then?" Sonia asked, gladly defeated.

"Big surprise. Right now we gotta get your asses moving. Raúl, quien va a pilotar este?" Ramón asked.

Both Travis and Sonia were thinking that they should've taken Spanish classes.

Raúl answered: "Todos nuestros pilotos estan en ruta—aunque tenemos uno listo para volar al Opa-Locka de Oeste."

Ramón wasn't impressed. "De que vale un avión sin piloto, tonto?!" he said, throwing his arms in the air.

"El único piloto que tenemos es Juan , y tu dijiste…" said Raúl. "Aw shit! Tráelo. Donde esta!?" hollered Ramón. Travis made out Ramón was pissed about something and was asking where someone was.

"Esta a Mano's," said Raúl.

"Aw shit. Tráelo y llévate estos dos para que te ayuden, necesitamos esos aqui."

"Everything okay?" Travis asked, hinting that a little translation would be nice.

"Kinda." Ramón suddenly had an air of regret about him.

"What's up?" asked Travis.

"We just thought we didn't have a pilot for a minute there—but we got one now."

"So everything's okay?"

"Yeah. My son Juan will be flying you."

"Thanks."

"Don't thank me yet. He's over at this dive across the intra-coastal and he's probably drunk as a son of a bitch. You and your girlfriend need to go help Raúl drag him outta there—I can't spare the men if we're gonna get your transport ready."

Travis tried to hide his concern. *A pilot with a hangover is better than no pilot right now.* "Okay. No problem. You mean you want us to help carry him?"

"No," Ramón said. "In case there's any trouble over there...it can get a little rough at Mano's."

"Oh," said Travis, his face dropping as fast as his Adam's apple. "But Sonia can come too, right?"

CHAPTER 81

WINCING FROM THE BITTER NIGHT AIR, First
Officer McClellan hurried up the jet stairs into the cockpit to
program the flight computer. But when he entered the cold,
darkened cabin, he realized he wasn't alone. The only smell
in here should have been the nauseating blend of jet fuel and
leftover food, but the customary odor was laced with something more pungent: freshly applied cologne.

McClellan heard movement. "Hello?"

More movement. Coming from the dark rear of the cabin.

He felt his heart kick his chest as a tall figure stepped from
the darkness with an eerie glow. He moved like a ghost.

"H-hello? Who is that?!" McClellan flinched back toward the stairs.

"Relax," said the stranger in a deep European accent.

"Who are you? What are you doing on board…"

"You're expecting me."

McClellan could make out the figure clearly now. He
was tall with brown hair and a hollow face. Olive skin, well
dressed in a suit. Then it dawned on McClellan.

Our extra passenger.

"You Green's passenger?"

"Yes." The voice was clinical.

"Let me know what I can…"

"Just do your job and follow your instructions. I'm not here. Make sure no one goes in the back compartment. Don't put the cabin lights on until boarding time."

"No problem." *Way too bizarre, even for this detail.*

"Good boy," came the slow, chilling voice. "Carry on."

McClellan just nodded and slid into the cockpit. The man disappeared back into the darkness at the rear of the cabin. As McClellan programmed in the flight plan to nowhere, he heard clunking and clicking noises from the rear compartment where the passenger hid. It sounded like firearms.

United is getting my resume tomorrow!

CHAPTER 82

THE STILLNESS OF THE TROPICAL NIGHT was broken by a Mercury engine surging to life, drowning out the rhythmic chirp of crickets. Raúl was waiting at the helm of one of a small flotilla parked outside the dilapidated warehouse. It was a white speedboat with a small bridge under a canopy and seats at the front and rear. Ramón stood on the dock shouting to Travis and Sonia, his voice competing against the throaty marine motor.

"Okay, if we're gonna make it to Dallas on time you gotta be back here with Juan no later than four. It'll take half an hour to get to the plane and about five hours to get to Dallas. Dallas is an hour behind, so you'll make it there by eight-thirty. Say half an hour to get downtown from the airfield so that makes it nine."

"Got it," Travis shouted. "Thanks, we really owe you."

"Forget it. You're Kramer's boy and Ramón owes him—so you're clear. Now if you wouldn't mind moving your ass…"

"We'll get Juan and be back in no time," Travis said, backing toward the boat.

"I wouldn't count on it, but good attitude!" Ramón laughed heartily, slapped Travis on the back and waddled back into the warehouse.

Raúl offered Sonia his hand to steady her embarkation, but she ignored it and jumped on. Travis stepped into the bow straight after and was nearly pushed backwards by Raúl thrusting the boat out into the Miami River.

Travis joined Sonia on the rear seat behind Raúl. He glanced at his dad's watch, and set the timer to countdown one hour.

"Why do we have to drive so slowly?!" he shouted to Raúl.

Raúl didn't reply.

"It's a no-wake zone," Sonia said, pointing to a sign on the riverside.

"I see. Where's this bar Mano's, anyway? They tell you?" Travis asked.

"It's over on Miami Beach Marina they said. Should only take about twenty minutes."

"Okay, so twenty minutes there and twenty back le—"

"Leaves us twenty minutes over there. What's Ramón so worried about? We just go in there, pick up this guy and bring him back."

"Who knows," Travis said. "But we really don't want to draw any attention to ourselves."

The slowly passing lights of Miami began to unnerve Travis. He watched the back of Raúl's fat, bald head as he carefully navigated the inland waterway snaking through the city. Travis stepped over.

"Raúl?"

He nodded.

"Faster? Rapido?" Travis said, pointing at the throttle lever to go forward.

"No," he replied, taking one hand off the wheel to wave a finger.

It seemed weird these drug runners wouldn't break a speed limit.

"Here!" Raúl said, pointing at two orange boats with

sirens, bobbing around menacingly as downtown loomed closer. Travis saw the U.S. Coastguard. He made a gesture of acknowledgment to Raúl and sat back down with Sonia.

"They'll be scattered up and down this river," Sonia said. "Count on it. This place is notorious—look over there." She pointed at a sign on a large brown concrete building which read: *Department of Homeland Security.* "When we get out of the river, he'll be able to speed up."

Once again, Sonia looked in control and her composure relaxed Travis. He felt the welcome breeze as the boat moved into wider water and Miami skyscrapers rose on either side of them. Despite all that had happened, and all that lay ahead, the urge to simply be with Sonia was ever present. He couldn't imagine a life without her now. Bizarre. He'd never known such a self-reliant woman and the way she made love was a testament to her nature: forceful and unrelenting. It was a refreshing change from the weak and needy girls he usually seemed to attract.

Her hair had freed itself of its disheveled state and the swelling on her cheek had gone down. Travis looked back at the wake the boat left behind, keeping her beautiful face in his periphery. Against the glowing tropical moonlight, her alabaster skin shone like an angel's, though she could hardly be described as such. What a paradox. His mouth formed a shallow crescent as he recalled how she'd put two of Ramón's men in the hospital earlier.

"So near, yet so far," she said.

"What do you mean?" he replied, snapped out of his indulgent distraction.

"We know Apollo's in Dallas, but here we are screwing around with some wino in Miami."

Back to business, Travis thought. *She's a pro first and foremost.* He couldn't have been further from her mind.

Travis put his hands behind his head and sat back. "Well, it's darkest right before dawn."

"Very poetic, but I can't see how Green doesn't know the location of the file—I mean, isn't it obvious? Being addressed to the sixth floor of the Texas School Book Depository?"

"It's not called the Texas School Book Depository anymore and I would have thought Leblanc would have known that. It's called the Sixth Floor Museum or maybe he just knew the street address. Even better: 411 Elm Street, Dallas."

"What if he didn't know and he sent it to the Texas School Book Depository?"

"It'd still get there—everyone knows where that is, but that's not what I'm wondering about really."

"What's bothering you then?" Sonia asked, meeting his eyes.

"Who's gonna receive that file? Who did Leblanc intend it for? I'm just hoping he knows someone reliable at the museum."

"Whatever. We just need to get there and get that file. My brother intended us to get it so he'd have thought of that. We just need to grab this Juan Martinez guy and get the hell out of dodge."

"Good point, you're ri—"

The deep gurgle of the outboard engine erupted into a high-pitched roar and the boat sped into open water, rendering Travis's voice inaudible. They were out of the Miami River and into the intra-coastal: the inlet separating Miami Beach from the mainland.

The speedboat raced over the foam. Dimly lit trawlers parked on docks fell back into a blur. The wind in his face drew Travis to the front of the boat. Holding the rails with trepidation, he eyed the fluorescence of Miami Beach. The airflow stifled him, but he didn't care. He felt alive. Adventure was coursing through his veins. A part of him wanted to suppress the feeling, but he ignored the impulse. He felt justified, and most of all, fulfilled regardless of the danger. His life suddenly had purpose. He felt grateful for simply *having* his life.

The bow bobbed down and the engine settled. Travis looked for the bar, but didn't so much see it as hear it. Loud, tuneless songs blared out, shouting, glasses chinking and wild screams came from a place on the water's edge as they entered the Miami Beach Marina. As they drew nearer, the neon sign flickered as if short-circuiting: *Mano's*.

The boat pulled alongside the dock next to Mano's. Sonia leapt off and helped Raúl moor the vessel and then helped the pudgy little Cuban off the boat. He dusted his black suit down, looking like the antithesis of a gangster and threw a hand forward at Sonia and Travis, as if he was about to lead troops into battle.

As they strode up the steps into the open bar, Travis's eyes scanned around nervously.

An oblong tiki bar sat in the middle of the room with a stage behind it. An aging Hispanic woman, who appeared stoned, was howling along with REM's "It's The End Of The World As We Know It (And I Feel Fine)" out of time and out of just about everything else as it played on the karaoke machine. She was completely ignored and drowned out by the people at the bar. The fashion was foot-long cigars for the men and tattoos for the girls. Fans under the thatched roof swirled the haze of smoke above the laughing and rowdy yammering. It was a modern-day pirate port of call. Travis admitted it wasn't the sort of establishment he'd frequent, but didn't see the threat. Ramón must have been pulling his leg again.

Raúl led Travis and Sonia through the crowds that had started to take an interest in the unfamiliar faces. Initial eye contact was just a little too long for Travis's comfort, so he decided to just focus on the back of Raúl's head as it bobbed through the smoke. Something clearly bothered Ramón about Juan flying them to Dallas and Travis felt it was something more than him just being drunk in this hellhole.

As they turned the corner, a staggering man lunged at Sonia's breasts. Before he even made contact, she had the hand he'd hoped to grope her with behind his back and pushed him into a table. Drinks spilled on the men sitting there. Raúl and Travis turned around. Travis pulled Sonia away into the crowd ignoring the disapproving stare she'd drawn from Raúl.

After passing the stage the second time, Raúl's head locked on to something. He made a beeline for it. A few paces further and Travis could see what it was. Lying face down on a corner table was a wet shock of black hair. Sitting next to that man was another Hispanic-looking man slamming his hands on the table and shouting: "Despierta degenerado! Me debes mis ganacias!"

Playing cards decorated with naked women lay strewn around the table next to empty glasses. The conflict seemed to be escalating.

"Juan!" Raúl shouted as he approached the table.

No answer.

Raúl hurried up to the table with Sonia and Travis trailing.

"Juan!" he repeated, pulling his head back to reveal the face. In that instant, Travis realized how well Ramón had aged. This guy—Ramón's son—was easily pushing fifty.

Raúl slapped him around the face but drew no response.

The man who'd been sitting with Juan lashed out at Raúl.

"Quien en diablo eres? Quiero mi dinero!" he said.

Dinero? Something to do with money? Travis thought.

"De todas maneras, cuanto te debo, idiota?" replied Raúl.

"Uh, I think Raúl just called him an idiot," Travis whispered to Sonia.

"El me debe dosciento cincuenta dólares!" said the man.

Raúl threw three hundred-dollar bills on the table. The man took them and walked away. *Obviously a row over a gambling debt.* Travis was relieved. Raúl, with the help of Travis and Sonia, pulled Juan to his feet. He might as well have been dead, as he wasn't helping at all.

This guy's going to fly us to Dallas?

The four of them shuffled conspicuously through the unsavory characters lining their exit route, drawing laughter as they went. *At least we blend in*, thought Travis.

With just a few yards to go, a large, sweaty hand clasped Travis's shoulder. A deep voice came from its direction.

"Hey you! Your fuckin' bitch girlfriend knocked my friend on his ass!" Travis turned slowly. The man was well over six feet and seemed just as broad.

"I–I'm really sor—"

"Sorry don't cut it, asshole," said the man, pushing Travis back a step.

Sonia stepped in front of Travis.

"Sonia, stay out of this…"

But it was too late. She'd already kneed him in the groin.

Raúl spun around with Juan draped over him like a rag doll. Two more men were coming at her now. Raúl threw Juan at Travis, who caught him only to be dragged down to the ground by the weight.

Regaining his balance and struggling to pull Juan to his feet once more, Travis looked up. He could no longer see Sonia with the bodies that surrounded her. Some were fighting each other and some—the unfortunate ones—were fighting her. They were dropping like flies around her in the center of the action.

Raúl blew past the perimeter. Like a bowling ball hitting a strike, his stocky little form smashed through the carnage.

The second Travis saw Raúl reach Sonia, he started to make his way down to the dock with Juan, who seemed to be waking up as he was out of the cigar smoke and into the sea air. Staggering along the water's edge, Travis kept looking back to see when Raúl and Sonia would appear.

Nothing. He decided to get Juan to the boat and then go back for them.

Travis propped Juan up against the mooring post, then turned to face the entrance to the bar. Raúl and Sonia burst out with a crowd of men in tow.

Raúl had picked up Sonia from behind and was backing out of the bar. Travis wasn't sure if Raúl was using her as a weapon or was trying to get her out of there before they both got shot. *Probably both*, he thought.

Travis jumped in the boat and heaved Juan in behind him, laying him down on the rear seat. "Come on!" he called out to Sonia and Raúl, who were running away from a pack of angry men hurling bottles, as well as abuse.

Raúl jumped into the boat, causing the whole vessel to rock violently. Sonia jumped in close behind and untied the mooring. She reached for the nearest object she could find—a billhook—and held it out like a spear at the pack of men chasing them.

The mob didn't seem to want to do more than drive Sonia and Raúl away. They'd slowed down, realizing they were chasing a lost cause.

As the speedboat tore away from the marina, Travis heard their faint cries die away.

Sonia eyed Juan then glared up at Travis, the bar fracas already forgotten. "For heaven's sake," she protested over the screaming engine. "*That's* our pilot?!"

"Relax. We'll sober him up—look he's already coming around," Travis countered, watching Juan lift his head up and throw up all over the floor of the boat.

Sonia stepped out of the way to avoid the vomit. "Are you kidding?" she said. "*Whose* side did you say Ramón is on?!"

CHAPTER 83

Ramon waited on the dock next to his warehouse with his hands on his hips, as Raúl drifted the boat into the inlet and cut the engine. Juan was on his feet now. Throwing up and the sea air had cleared his head.

Sonia moored the boat while Raúl helped Juan off. Travis looked at his watch—*we're on schedule but with no margin of safety*.

"Don't start with me," said Juan to his father, holding his head.

"What? I never said a goddamn word, but why do you do thi—"

"You see!" Juan said.

Ramón pushed two hands at him, but Juan continued, "Sorry I'm such a disappointment to you—why the hell am I here, anyway?"

Ramón took on a deliberate and neutral tone, like he was speaking to anyone of his gang. "You're going to Dallas—need you there by eight-thirty local so you take off at four-thirty."

"You crazy? I feel like shit!"

Ramón bit his lip. "It's an emergency, son. I need you." Ramón rocked back and forth uncomfortably. Something had changed in Ramón tonight.

Juan just stood in silence.

"You *need* me? Who are you and what've you done with

my father?"

"Shut up, just go on."

Juan's hostile veneer melted. "Alright, Pop, Opa-Locka West?"

"Yep."

"What's the cargo?"

"Them." Ramón pointed at Travis and Sonia walking on the other side of the dock with Raúl.

"Jesus, we're smuggling *people* now? They illegal aliens or something?"

"Friends, son. Just get 'em to Dallas as quick as you can."

"Okay, just let me ask though, have you been smoking the merchandise?"

Ramón gave Juan a brief hug and walked him to the vessel where Sonia and Travis were now boarding.

Travis watched Raúl rip a weatherproof canvas off of a boat. He called it a "cigarette boat." The craft was clearly designed for one purpose alone: speed. It had four large outboard engines. It was long, thin and pointed like a dagger. It would have looked like a competition racing boat had it sported red stripes and numbers, but the color scheme couldn't have been further removed; it was matte black.

Travis wondered if another thunderstorm was coming, but realized it was just Raúl starting the engines.

Sonia sprang into the now rumbling cigarette boat along with Juan. Ramón approached Travis. "Well, Danny, looks like this is it for us then."

"Thanks again for everything," Travis said, placing a hand on Ramón's shoulder.

"Don't thank me yet. This thing's nowhere near over. I said I'd help you, didn't say it'd be easy!"

"Still…"

"Okay, listen up," said Ramón. "Raúl's gonna take you

inland: up the river. Quickest way to the airfield is by this boat—the river becomes the Miami canal and it runs a straight line to the runway. Just do what Juan says. My Dallas connection will be waiting for you at the other end with a car to get you into town, okay?"

"Thanks for everything…"

"Get going!" Ramón slapped him on the back.

Travis stepped in and gave Ramón a nod and a look of grim determination.

No more than a second later, the rumbling increased and the dagger-like boat eased out into the river and stopped.

"What are we waiting for?" asked Sonia.

Raúl pointed back at the boat they'd gone to Mano's in. Ramón was getting in it and powering up.

"Cover," said Juan.

Travis had only heard the tail-end of the conversation. "What's going on?"

"I think I know," said Sonia with a smirk. "These guys are as slippery as hell. Relax. We're in good hands."

Travis, Juan and Sonia were thrown back into the rear seat as the might of the cigarette boat was brought online. With multiple roars and a rising bow, the black dagger was darting inland with Ramón keeping up as best he could.

The shoreline strafed past. The airflow was asphyxiating as it pushed hard against their faces. This was a rush. The matte black hull denied the moonlight glow and merged with the dark water. The camouflage was eerie but effective.

Juan eased himself into the small cabin. Probably to throw up again, Sonia speculated. Sonia's black hair trailed horizontally, the breeze making her pout.

"What about wake?" shouted Travis. "The Coast Guard will stop us."

"If they can catch us," Sonia said, looking back at the

pounding the water was taking at the hands of the four engines. "Plus, I've a feeling they've done this before."

The cigarette boat streaked further inland through Miami. The water narrowed. They passed Miami International Airport. Their speed made the thought of driving to this airfield seem ludicrous.

Travis glanced back. *Ramón is still keeping close. Even at this speed, our boat can't be using full power.* A cursory glance at the throttle lever confirmed the thought.

Travis saw a blue flashing light appear behind Ramón as he stormed past an inlet.

Coastguard.

Travis tugged Raúl's flowery shirt flapping in the breeze, but he only pointed in his rearview mirror to indicate he'd already seen it and slammed the throttle forward. Travis was thrown back into his seat. The bow rose up and the narrowing waterway flashed by faster than before.

Travis looked back at Ramón, who'd slowed down his boat to meet the Coastguard.

A decoy.

Sonia's head shot back with her laughter. "Told you," she said. "And anyway, I don't doubt Ramón's got half the Coastguard on his payroll!"

Juan emerged from below.

"Feeling better?" Travis asked.

"Yeah. Thanks," Juan said, looking decidedly less piquant. "We'll be there any minute."

"Great," said Sonia. "Are you okay to fly?"

"No problemo," answered Juan, waving a dismissive hand.

Two minutes later, the roar of the cigarette boat simmered down into its deep gargle as Raúl slowed and maneuvered it onto the bank of the Miami canal. It looked like the middle of nowhere—just darkness—the lights of Miami left far behind.

Travis saw headlights. Unsurprised, Raúl moored the black dagger.

He turned, shook Travis's and Sonia's hand and helped them onto land. He slapped Juan hard on the back and gave him a fat cigar, which Juan acknowledged with a salute.

"Let's go," Juan ordered, lighting his cigar. "It's only a mile to the hangar."

CHAPTER 84

"CAN I GET you anything, sir?"

Reese had briefed the pilot on their unusual mission this morning. "Follow that plane" seemed a lame command to give his pilot, but it's all he could do for now. Green was going to give the Bureau what they wanted on a plate, but only if Reese played it just right. He'd have to think on his toes, adapt and compromise. His flight crew would have to just deal with the vague orders.

"I'm good, thanks, Captain," he said, staring into an almost empty cup of coffee he was swilling around.

"Okay, let me know what you need and when."

"Sure thing," Reese said. "All I need right now is your assurance we won't be having any technical delays—I want to be airborne on schedule and with as much fuel as you can carry."

"Yes, sir. It's all good."

The captain left Reese to his thoughts. Reese wanted to be ready to go at short notice in case Green made any changes, but none had come through from Dulles Air Traffic as his plane sat on the tarmac.

Reese pulled out the file Jensen had given him and studied it for the eleventh time. There was no getting away from it: this mission was like none other he'd been on. And for now, anyway, he was on his own.

CHAPTER 85

THE CAR COASTED into Opa-Locka West Airport with its three passengers. Always upstaged by its bigger brother—Opa-Locka Airport in North Miami—it had been abandoned recently. Sitting on the edge of the Everglades in the Northwestern corner of Miami, it didn't look like much—a few hangars and small structures—but it had a runway and was right next to the Miami Canal. The perfect location for Ramón. Because it was an uncontrolled airport with no tower, it had served his purpose well before it was abandoned, but now that it was unused, it was even better.

The headlights had been switched off a half-mile before the car ground to a stop outside a small, corrugated iron hangar. Travis and Sonia trailed Juan Martinez out of the car. The driver didn't need to be told to wait until they were airborne.

Juan fumbled for a key to release the padlock from the thick chain on the hangar door. He unlocked it and cracked open the large metal door. He slid inside with his two passengers in tow and closed the door behind him. It was pitch black inside. Travis heard Juan shuffle across to the far wall. The hangar became illuminated and there before him, their transportation to Dallas was revealed.

It was the strangest looking aircraft Travis had ever seen. He frowned and watched for Sonia's reaction. Her mischievous look was good enough.

Juan began inspecting the plane. Travis ambled behind Juan doing his own inspection.

It was only a small plane: two seats in the front, two in the rear and some cargo space at the back. The typical size of light aircraft you'd see parked at smaller airports, but size was where the similarity ended.

Unsurprisingly, it was painted black. Its long, cylindrical fuselage had one engine on the nose and another one at the rear, each with *wooden* propellers. Its wings were placed at the back and looked like they doubled up as fins or rudders. There were also smaller wing-like structures out of each side, just ahead of the windshield. It looked like a black catfish. And just below those front airfoils was a word written in shiny italics: *Defiant*.

Juan was ducking and bending his way around his pre-flight inspection. Sonia was inside the cabin loading the rear seat with supplies she'd scavenged from Ramón's warehouse.

"This thing flies?" Travis said, joking to Juan.

"Like an angel, my friend," said Juan, checking the oil levels. "Plus, she's got extended range tanks, meaning we can fly direct to Dallas without a fuel stop. Pretty cool."

"Yeah, pretty cool," Travis said, feigning enthusiasm and trying to block out the nervous flutter erupting in his gut. *Nuts! I don't have my motion sickness pills with me. How different could a small plane be from the big ones anyway?*

"How does this plane avoid detection?"

Juan chuckled. "Any aircraft in busy airspace like this needs a transponder. It sends a signal to air traffic to let them know who you are. Obviously, we don't use one, but they'll still see a return on their radar screen—a little blip—only it won't have any identification attached to it."

Travis listened intently as Juan drained a sample of what he assumed was fuel from underneath the wings and gazed at the blue liquid, continuing his explanation.

"Air Traffic sends out a radar scan and anything metal that beam hits, it bounces back to them, right? That's how they get a blip on their screens."

"Yeah." Travis knew that much, at least.

"Well, this plane has no exposed metal," said Juan, smirking.

"What? How?"

"The body's made of light composite, not aluminum— look," he said pointing at the engine cowling. "The tail pipes are recessed into the body. They're not exposed either—"

"That's why the propellers are wooden!" concluded Travis.

"That's right. Metal props send the biggest return to radar, so they're dispensed with too."

"So did you build this thing yourself, then?" Travis asked.

"Shit no! It's an actual aircraft. Rutland makes it. It's a Rutland Defiant—they originally made it to get military contracts. Okay, love to talk aviation for longer, but we're ready to go now. Please." Juan waved Travis into the rear of the aircraft. Travis climbed over to meet Sonia on the back seat. Sonia handed him a headset. He put it over his head and put the microphone to his mouth. Travis watched Juan part the hangar doors, revealing the darkened airfield.

Stay calm. It's just another flight. Why didn't I bring my motion sickness pills!?

Juan bolted the doors in the open position and began pulling the aircraft forward out of its hiding place into the still night. The Defiant trundled over the runners of the hangar doors and came to a stop. Juan detached the tow bar and took his place on the front left seat. He turned to address Travis and Sonia as he buckled himself in.

"You guys okay?" Juan asked, pushing a thumb in the air. "All strapped in?"

"Yep," they said in unison, like a couple of kids.

"Shouldn't there be a safety briefing or something?" Travis asked Juan, flustered.

Juan obliged: "Yeah. Safety briefing's real simple. If you see me jump out of this thing and run, you follow my ass, okay?" His face was serious.

Travis felt his stomach sink and looked at Sonia.

"Makes sense," Sonia was serious too.

I'm flying with two lunatics.

"Oh, and don't touch nothing. You can speak to each other over your own intercom back there—all you have to do is talk, okay?"

"Thanks," said Sonia.

Then Juan started the front engine. The whole fuselage shook, vibrating with the noisy aero engine. Normal speech was already impractical and that was with just one of the two engines running.

Seconds later, the second engine—the one behind them—started. The noise and vibration grew to what Travis thought was a ludicrous level; he couldn't believe he had five hours ahead of him in these conditions.

The black Rutland Defiant taxied forward into the darkness with no lights on. Juan was clearly navigating from memory and appeared to know where he was going. Travis glanced out the window and noticed there were none of the usual lights you see; no red or green on the wingtips and no flashing strobes.

A plane built for a single purpose: stealth.

Juan parked the plane next to what could just be made out as a runway in the darkness. He increased power on the engines but left the brakes on. There was an unhealthy-sounding drop in revs. Travis broke out in a sweat. The Spartan cabin didn't have air-conditioning: the perfect conditions for Travis's vertigo to kick in.

Definitely out of control here.

Travis's stomach swam and his heart kicked against his rib cage. *Stay calm. Juan must know what he's doing.*

The engine revs dropped back to idle and Juan taxied forward, lining up with the pitch-black runway. It was an eerie sight.

The engine revs increased, much more than last time. Juan held the brakes on and the aircraft shook violently, like an angry racehorse locked into the starting gate.

As Juan released the brakes, Travis felt like he'd been hit across the back with a shovel. *We're taking off.* He breathed sharply, as he felt every little bump on the abandoned runway shudder through him.

With a lurch toward the sky, they were airborne.

He grabbed Sonia's hand.

"You okay?" came Sonia's tinny voice over the intercom.

"Feel sick… I get vertigo…"

"Oh Jesus," she said and began looking for something. Probably a barf bag. *Good luck on this plane.*

Travis pushed a hand at Sonia and put his hand over his mouth, breathing deeply. *Definitely* not *like a large plane.* He felt every little bump in the sky. So did the plane it seemed— swaying all over the place.

Thankfully, after a few gut-wrenching minutes, the air smoothed.

Travis settled himself. Out the window Travis could see the lights of Fort Lauderdale and beyond. He felt better looking out his side window rather than the windshield. More like sitting in an airline seat.

"Feel better?" Sonia asked.

"Yeah, thanks. Sorry about that." He still felt sick but hoped denial would quash it.

"No problem. Listen, we should try to get some sleep. We've got five hours to kill and we're gonna need our rest," Sonia said, offering him an oil-stained cushion.

Travis looked out of the window.

"Your choice," she said, and stuffed a blanket against the window, laying her head against it and closing her eyes.

Travis put his head back and closed his eyes too, though he failed to see how he could catch any rest in this environment.

Within minutes, he was asleep.

CHAPTER 86

As DAWN BROKE, Green's jet sliced through the gray morning overcast of Washington, D.C.

"Did you tell Green and that Nick guy about the rear compartment?" asked Captain Jakes.

"Yeah," replied McClellan. "Told them it was out of service and not to go back there—Green seemed to know I was just saying it for Nick's benefit. Man, that's the creepiest cargo I've ever carried."

"Don't worry yourself—like I said, let's just do this thing and go home."

In the cabin, Green sat across the table from Nick as they hammered out conclusions. Green produced a stack of paper and slammed it on the table.

"Somewhere in this stack is the address for Apollo. I want some answers about those bottom two lines on Leblanc's fax."

"I understand, but I…"

"Look. Relax. I know you don't want to commit to anything in case you're wrong and I bust your balls, but just lay some thoughts out for me, hmm?"

Nick took a deep breath and paused, reading sincerity in Green's eyes. "Okay. Let's forget the common link part for no, as that doesn't fit with anything. Now the 'address where cancer ended'—that really should tell us everything. We know the California Report banned Laetrile in November 1963, so we could assume Leblanc believes Laetrile is this so-called 'Cancer's Nemesis'?"

Green leaned forward, glaring into Nick's eyes. "Yes, that's correct."

"What? This whole thing's about cancer and Laetrile?"

"Go on with what you were saying."

"Alright. So then 'where cancer ended' should refer to something along those lines—something relating to Laetrile which was conclusive, or in favor of it."

"Go on."

"The Sloan Kettering incident would be one such reference, but it's not on the USPS list of recipients—and there are Laetrile clinics in Mexico. But it has to be somewhere in the States for USPS priority mail envelopes."

"So what else is there?"

Nick typed into his open laptop and stared at it, tapping a finger on the desk in hesitation.

"What?" awaited Green.

Nick spun the laptop around so Green could see.

"What's this?" Green said.

"The address where cancer ended *could* be talking about the Hoxsey Clinic—it was the first to start using Laetrile in the States before it was banned."

"Okay. And where is it?"

"It's not there anymore. It closed down."

"So where *was* it then?" Green persisted.

"Dallas."

Green frowned. "Could you get me all the names and addresses from the USPS list in Dallas?"

"Sure. No problem."

CHAPTER 87

AT PRECISELY 9,800 FEET, the Rutland Defiant tore through a clear sky over the Gulf of Mexico on a direct track to Dallas. The rising sun interrupted what little sleep Travis had stolen.

Rubbing his eyes, he glanced down at the morning light ricocheting off the deep blue waves and didn't feel too bad. The air had been smooth soon after take-off and, once he'd gotten used to the rhythmic hum of the two engines, he'd settled into a deep sleep. The unconditioned air in the cabin was now cool and fresh, a satisfying relief from the Miami stickiness.

After a rewarding stretch of his arms, Travis tapped the pilot—Juan—on the shoulder.

Juan jumped and shook his head.

Jesus. Juan was asleep too.

"Uh, Juan...everything okay?" Travis's sleepy eyes sprang open.

"Yeah, fine. Don't worry, the autopilot's on," came Juan's groggy voice over the intercom.

Travis adjusted his watch for Central Time. It was 6:51AM, Wednesday morning. *Dad's watch. We'll know about Mom today,* Travis thought, rubbing the bezel. Travis, on a collision course with this Apollo File, had realized that his mom and Apollo were linked. *A cure for cancer? I can save her!*

We have to get to the file.

"Hey, Juan. So we should be there in about an hour and forty minutes, right?" Travis said, willing the plane faster.

"Nah—these goddamn headwinds have been slowing us down—GPS reckons landing at 8:55AM now. Don't wanna push the engines any harder. It'll burn more fuel—we're already landing with just vapor in the tanks."

Too much detail.

Sonia stirred. Travis tapped his headset at her. She put her headset back on.

"Did you hear that?"

"No, what?" she said, with half-almond eyes, reaching for the bottle of water on the floor.

"We're landing at five minutes before nine. We won't make it to the museum in time for opening."

"Shit. Well, nothing we can do about it."

Juan's deep voice crackled over the intercom as he pointed downward out the windshield. "Look—New Orleans! I always like it when we make it back over land."

The mention of the city where Lee Harvey Oswald hung out in the summer of '63 thrust Travis into a train of thought he'd abandoned since the Andrew McNaughton revelation.

"You know," Travis began, "the crux of the JFK riddle comes down to the matter of Oswald being recruited at the Queen Bee Club in Tokyo. If he was *recruited* by the Soviets, it's case closed. Very few argue that he wasn't *at least connected* to the assassination and rightly so: too much evidence. So if he was recruited by the Soviets, that's perhaps what he was ultimately intended for—wet ops. His movements were classically Russian—confusion and deception—just like Igor Orlov's at the end of the war."

"Okay," Sonia said, pressing her palms against her cheeks.

"But something's been nagging me. Have you thought much about this whole McNaughton connection?"

"No, but you have," she said with a raised eyebrow.

Travis didn't notice her blatant disinterest. "Yeah, I have. And it's made me wonder if there was more to Kennedy's assassination than I first thought. Maybe it was more than just a coup d'etat. Maybe Oswald's mission was far more important."

"Like what?" Now he had Sonia's attention.

"Industrial espionage."

Sonia jumped up in her seat as if that had triggered her imagination in some way.

Travis continued. "Andrew McNaughton's escapades sound remarkably Russian too—supplying arms to one side and telling the other side where the shipment was. Confusion and deception spun everywhere just like Oswald and Orlov."

"Well, if he worked for Castro, he'd have had something to do with the Soviet-trained DGI, so that would figure... where are you going with this?"

"Maybe Kennedy's murder was economically motivated as well as political."

"I don't understand."

"Castro was desperate for money to fund his revolution. McNaughton pioneered Laetrile in America and was paid by Castro for his efforts. Indirectly or directly, Castro funded Laetrile in America through McNaughton. Did Castro see this as a way to both raise money and destabilize the economy of his enemy? The California Report put a stop to that though—and it was released the same month and year Kennedy was shot. Maybe the California Report was just one more reason to assassinate Kennedy."

Sonia gulped. "But this is all just speculation," she stammered.

"Yes, it is."

"Anyway, how would that destabilize the American economy?"

Travis spoke Dr. Rogers's words as if they were his own. "If there was a natural cure for cancer, the cancer industry, which employs more people than it has patients, would collapse. But not only that—the question then is what other drugs are unnecessary, and the whole house of cards tumbles down. Healthcare is a huge industry. The ripple effect would ultimately affect all business."

Sonia's eyes narrowed, listening intently.

Travis went on. "Many countries live in fear of upsetting America because of her power to impose economic sanctions. A large part of those sanctions are medical. Arms too. Weapons and medicine: the perfect combination from a business point of view—harm and heal. All markets cornered. If you weakened American medicine, not only would the American economy suffer badly, but one of America's most powerful bargaining chips would get taken off the table."

"I see your point," Sonia said in a hollow tone.

"I'm glad you do, but I think most Americans wouldn't like it." Travis folded his arms.

"Wouldn't like what?"

"The choice the Apollo File possibly gives them if we expose it to the world."

"What choice?"

"Do you want a cure for cancer or do you want to keep your job?"

Sonia huffed. "Yeah, I see. No surprise which choice the politicians would go for—voters need jobs to put a tick in the right box."

Travis continued, staring out the windshield. "I wonder... say it's front-page news tomorrow—that you and I revealed a conspiracy to suppress a cure for cancer. Then the newspaper went on to explain the impact on the economy. How would people feel?"

Sonia fell silent.

Travis turned his gaze to meet her eyes. "Let's say this was a book and people everywhere read our story, knowing they'd possibly lose their job if we got to the Apollo File first."

"People would never believe it."

"Probably not, but *which side* would the reader be rooting for?"

"Maybe you and I are the bad guys," Sonia said, feigning a spooky pose. "Maybe it's best the book ends with *Green* winning."

"If we're the bad guys in the book, then the reader's a conspirator."

"So which side would you choose?" asked Sonia.

"Well, economies can be resurrected. People can't."

"You're such an idealist," Sonia said with a chuckle. "You're a good guy stuck in a big, bad world—with a *wild* imagination. Now try and get some more rest!"

CHAPTER 88

BURNING AN OVAL into the sky six miles above Memphis, Green's jet had arrived at the holding point three minutes ahead of schedule.

Over an hour later, Green sat reading the shortlist of addresses—all Dallas names from the USPS list of priority envelopes sent from Washington.

There were only four names on the sheet of paper Green had positioned one inch from his side of the table:

John Jenkins, Aegis Industrial Systems Inc. 2800 N. Houston Ave.

Helen Vanderbilt, 411 Elm St, #120

Janet Hall, 4621 Ross Ave.

Dr. Arthur Burrows, 3278 Lancaster Road, #451

All names and addresses in Dallas, Texas but none of them the old address of the Hoxsey Clinic. *The address where cancer ended. Worth a guess. It was a very short shortlist, but who's to say it's the right list? That Dallas is the destination?*

Green's gut was nagging. He'd learned from long experience not to ignore that sensation.

Green knew his Dallas agents would get to these addresses anyway, but he wanted to be there first—he wanted to see the whites of the recipients' eyes and ensure Travis's little accomplice didn't get there and pull any tricks. *His companion is a major complication.*

Nick Maynard was asleep. Green gazed out the window at the cloud layer masking Tennessee below them. Not long to go now and this whole sorry episode would be over one way or the other; whether it was through him or his agents, the file would be found and destroyed.

Something nagged him.

Green scanned the Dallas list again.

Dr. Burrows is from the USPS list—his practice is plastic surgery: nothing to do with cancer. Besides, there are many doctors on the whole USPS list. Aegis Industrial Systems manufactures electronics. Janet Hall is a housewife. Helen Vanderbilt is a civil servant. And what the hell do the letters DGI from Leblanc's fax refer to?

The jet went into yet another right-hand bank. *Dallas... DGI...cancer...Laetrile...point where cancer ended...point where it ended...point? An unusual reference for an address.*

Green pulled out the fax and set it down on the table next to the Dallas shortlist (one inch apart). Then he ripped out the file on Leblanc.

Leblanc's father was in Dallas when Kennedy was shot— he was on protection detail that day.

The day we lost Lancer.

Lancer?

What did Hicks say when he raided Travis's house and found the fax: Something about the title on the page saying 'Lancer's Nemesis'?

Once Green had seen the fax himself, he realized Hicks had simply misread it. That much Green knew from Agent Meyer's account of the Bilderberg meeting.

Into another right-hand turn.

Wasn't Lancer shot on Elm Street?

Green looked at the file, the fax, and the shortlist. His eyes glossed over them. He looked up.

"Nick...wake up. The party's over."

Nick was jolted awake as soon as Green barked his name. "Sir? Any news?"

"Forget medical references. What *else* did the DGI refer to on that Internet search?"

"One second," Nick said, flipping his laptop open. "The Cuban Intelligence Service."

Green's frown intensified as he leaned forward over the table.

"This address here," Green said, tapping his finger at the entry of Helen Vanderbilt on the USPS list. "What's at that address?"

"One second," Nick said, tapping a few keys.

Green wrung his hands and stared, fixated on a speck of dandruff on Nick's sport jacket.

Nick's head bobbing up from behind the laptop almost caught Green by surprise. "That suite number at that address is the Sixth Floor Museum: used to be the Texas School Book Depository."

Green fell back in his chair, his eyes distant.

"Any new thoughts?" asked Nick. "We have to be certain—if we commit to one location and it's the wrong one, we could take ourselves far from the file's actual destina—"

No shit. Green waved a finger at Nick to silence his useless chatter.

Too much coincidence here.

Recap. Leblanc's father lost Lancer—in Dallas—at the hands of the DGI—and Oswald who shot from th...

Green looked at the fax once more.

His head lashed up, his eyes ablaze.

"Shit!" Green said, jumping up, leaping toward the cockpit.

Nick spun around in his seat.

The flight deck door swung open with a clatter.

McClellan froze. Jakes nearly choked on his coffee.

"Dallas!" Green screamed. "Get to Dallas right now!"

"Right away, sir," said Jakes, nodding at McClellan. "Which airport?" Jakes asked.

"What?" asked Green, his mind awash with possibilities. "How the hell should I...the one closest to downtown!"

"That'd be Love Field, sir."

"Love Field then—move this plane!"

Green barged out of the cockpit and slammed the door behind him, reaching for something to grasp as the plane banked suddenly for the change of course.

Green looked at Nick. "You idiot."

"Sir?"

"It doesn't say cancer it says *Lancer!*" Green snapped, reaching for his satellite phone. He could've happily bludgeoned the kid with it.

"Lancer?" said Nick, his face contorting.

"Shut up," snapped Green with an icy glare.

"Sir?" Norman's weary voice came on the line.

"Dallas—411 Elm Street, Dallas—that's where it is, Norm, I know it. Now listen, tell the Dallas detail not to approach, you understand? I said not to approach that address—they'll only fuck things up. They just need to be on standby."

"Very good, sir. Should I tell the other details around the country to stand down?"

"No...no, their assignment remains—those are the orders, Norm. Don't screw it up. And I want a car waiting for me at Love Field, Dallas, got it?"

"I'm on it right now, sir."

Green's thoughts brought a glow to his face: Travis was in Miami and couldn't possibly get to Dallas by car in time.

"And Norman?"

"Sir?"

"Get on the horn to Dallas Air Traffic Control—same deal as Miami."

Click.

Next item on the agenda: shoot Nick.

Nick was saved by First Officer McClellan emerging from the flight deck. "Sir, I have an ETA for you?"

"What is it?"

"We'll touch down at Love Field in Dallas at 8:32AM Central Time."

"Thanks. What time does the Sixth Floor Museum open?" Green barked at Nick.

McClellan walked back into the flight deck while Nick looked the information up on his laptop. "Nine o'clock, sir."

"Excellent. Ours for the taking."

Green's smile shone at maximum brightness, kind eyes meeting Nick's as he cowered in his seat. "Good job, kid!"

Special Agent Reese had just received a welcome phone call and was now in the cockpit of his jet, giving his flight crew new orders.

"Dallas Love Field. ASAP, Captain."

Reese lunged back into the cabin and snatched the satellite phone, breathing heavily. "Yeah, this is Reese. Get me the Dallas SAC. Now!"

CHAPTER 39

THE FINAL DESCENT of the Defiant into Lancaster Municipal Airport on the edge of Dallas was underway. Travis glanced at his watch, gripped it, willing time to reverse. *The museum will soon be open, and we aren't even on the ground,* he thought, staring at his tapping feet. Turbulence brought his head back up. It nearly brought his breakfast up too.

"Look," said Sonia, pointing ahead through the windshield. "Dallas."

Travis saw the downtown skyline looming ahead. "Yeah, I sure hope Ramón's people are ready with a car." He was pumped.

"They'll be there," Sonia said, nodding.

"Alright, strap in," said Juan. "Gonna be a bit bumpy!"

"It's going to get worse?" Travis said.

No reply from the pilot.

"Relax," said Sonia. "We'll be on the ground soon."

The runway loomed. Travis panned around the approaching airfield and saw it was in the middle of farmland and there wasn't even a control tower.

Juan fought the Defiant down toward the runway. Eventually, the plane leveled with the tarmac and squeaked its tires down. Travis breathed out with long-awaited relief while his innards untied themselves.

Taxiing across the tarmac, Travis made out a parking lot

among the collection of light aircraft and crop-dusters. He began scanning for someone who might be one of Ramón's men.

Nothing.

Juan brought the Defiant to a stop and cut the engines. Both propellers jerked to a halt and silence replaced the whining engines.

"Thanks, Juan, we really need to get moving. Is your guy there?"

"Okay, let's see."

Juan cranked open the flimsy door and hopped out, pulling his seat forward so Sonia and Travis could follow.

The flight from hell was over; never did asphalt look so kissable. Travis planted a wobbly foot on Texas ground and soaked in the dry warmth. It was a perfect day; the sun shining in a clear blue sky and a mellow breeze keeping the blaze amenable.

Juan broke into a jog. He entered the parking lot and looked around. Sonia and Travis caught up and joined the search.

They heard a car horn. There, sitting in a white Dodge Neon, was a Hispanic man waving at them. Juan waved back, sighed with relief and walked over. By the time Sonia and Travis had got to him the man was removing a miniature motorcycle from the trunk.

"Here's your car," said Juan. "When you're done, call Eduard here on this number and he'll take it back." Juan handed Travis a card with a number on and the keys. "Take it easy."

No time for long goodbyes. Eduard was now on his mini-motorcycle, scooting away.

"Thanks, Juan," said Travis, jogging round to the passenger seat to take his post as navigator.

"Yeah, thanks," said Sonia.

Juan sauntered back toward the Defiant.

As Sonia screeched out of the parking bay, Travis took a final look at the black catfish aircraft with unexpected gratitude. The car swung away and the Defiant was out of sight.

"Okay, eighteen miles to downtown," said Travis, studying the map he took from Ramón's office. "Take a right out of here and we should soon hit I-45. Go north and watch your speed—if we get stopped it's all over."

CHAPTER 90

GREEN WAS FIGHTING his way through morning traffic on the short journey from Love Field to Dealey Plaza, the very same journey Kennedy had made the day he was shot. Nick had been brought along even though his usefulness had expired—Green needed him off the aircraft and out of the way, so he sat there quietly. Another agent sat in the front seat next to the driver—Slater was his name. His wide form filled a crisp, black suit.

"Okay, Norm, what've you got for me?" Green said into the phone.

"Sir, none of the agents have reported anything and I'd say at least 80 percent of the destinations have been covered by them."

"Excellent—it's here, I know it is." Green rubbed his thigh furiously.

"Yes, sir. I had agents meet any aircraft that showed a primary radar return and flight plans were mandatory as in Miami. No sign of Travis. All general aviation aircraft at Dallas Fort Worth Airport and Love Field were met just to make sure."

"Good thinking, Norm. And keep any Dallas agents away from the Sixth Floor Museum for now. I'm handling it."

Green hung up. "How long before we're at Dealey Plaza?"

"Five minutes, sir."

Green settled back into his seat with the certain satisfaction born of closing a large business deal, then slapped Nick on the leg. Nick smiled nervously.

It's over. I've won. But of course I've won!

Green gazed out the window at the mirrored towers of downtown Dallas. He considered the Kennedy connection to the Apollo File. *Leblanc was one tricky bastard sending Travis that fax.*

But not tricky enough.

Green recalled that fateful day in 1963. He had been very young, but he remembered it like it was yesterday. Sure, everyone knew where they were and what they were doing the moment they heard Kennedy had been shot, but Green's knowledge of what happened was better than most. It should have been; his Agency had been heavily involved in the cover-up. His job was, in part, to ensure that the next generation of agents didn't realize any such thing. His mentor had told him the truth in confidence. Those words played back in Green's head as if from a dictaphone:

"Kennedy loved attention and contact with crowds... We told the stupid bastard to put the roof up on that motorcade. The roof wasn't bulletproof, but it would've given those shooters less of a chance, that's for goddamn sure... We cleaned the blood out of that motorcade before forensics could get there. Then we told those doctors at Parkland Memorial to go screw themselves and took the president's body out of there—couldn't give a crap if shooting a president wasn't against federal law back then. It was a race to keep the Agency alive and cover a whole bunch of screw-ups. And those FBI morons! They'd even received a note from Oswald before the assassination and didn't tell us this guy was in town. No wonder that note was destroyed after the assassination."

Green remembered watching Jackie Kennedy climb out on the trunk of the motorcade—Zapruder footage he'd seen a thousand times.

Most people thought she was trying to get away from the assault, but she was trying to retrieve a chunk of her husband's skull blown out the back of his head from the kill shot. Had the driver put his foot on the gas after the first shot, the grassy knoll shooter wouldn't have had the time he needed to finish Lancer off. Just 11.2 miles an hour. That's how slow the motorcade went to make the hairpin turn from Houston onto Elm. And Leblanc's father? He and a whole bunch of them on protection duty were out drinking the night before. No wonder they thought the first shot sounded like a firecracker. *Ridiculous*, Green thought, shaking his head. The average American thought his dreams had died that day. What a crock. He had no clue what was at stake in the weeks that followed the assassination.

"Almost there, sir," said the driver.

Green looked forward out of the windshield. They were off the freeway and making their way through the one-way system of downtown streets. Driving under the famous triple underpass and slope up on Elm Street into Dealey Plaza, Green glanced left at the grassy knoll and the white cross on the road where Kennedy took the bullet. It was the definitive crime scene.

A left turn onto Houston briefly, left again and they were outside the door of the Sixth Floor Museum.

Although the museum itself was on the sixth floor, built around the corner window Oswald allegedly shot from, the administration offices and entrance were on an extension to the ground floor.

Trailed by Slater—who had strict instructions to "keep his pie-hole shut"—Green jumped up the stairs to the entrance and burst through the glass door, making a beeline for the first staff person he could see. It was a young clerk at the ticket desk. Her nametag read: *Robin*. She was a young, dark-skinned girl in her early twenties. She quickly ended her personal call at the sight of Green.

"I'm here to see Helen Vanderbilt please, Robin?" Green said as if he was there for a job interview. "My name is Green. It'll only take a second." Green flashed his badge at her.

"Okay, can you hold on one second?"

"Of course. And thanks...Robin."

Robin edged over to another member of staff who picked up a phone.

Green studied his surroundings while he waited. A picture the size of a wall dominated the mostly brown brick lobby—it was Kennedy in the motorcade just before he was shot.

"Sir, would you follow me please?" said Robin.

Green gestured at Slater to stay put and followed Robin. "Helen Vanderbilt's office. That's where we're going, right?"

"Yes."

Robin escorted Green to a brown door behind the large picture of the motorcade marked *Authorized Personnel Only*. She swiped a card and took Green through to the curator's office. "Here you go." Robin pointed at the office door.

Green knocked politely, craning a sly smile around the door. "Helen Vanderbilt?"

"Yes. Mr. Green?"

"Yes. Thanks for seeing me."

Green simultaneously offered his hand and studied Helen. He tried to look into her eyes, but she was avoiding eye contact.

She knows why I'm here alright.

She was much older than he'd imagined. Probably in her

sixties, she had a gray bob and freckled skin behind a pair of green, oval-framed glasses attached by a chain around her neck. She had that librarian look about her: an air of authority. *Probably a lame-ass liberal*, he thought.

"How can I assist you, Mr. Green?"

Green struck, his bright veneer darkening. "Ma'am, I know that you received a priority mail envelope from Washington, D.C. this morning."

"No, I don't think I did. I could be wrong though…shall I check?"

"Please do," Green said. He fought the cloud of doubt that had suddenly appeared over his theory. *The file was here. I know it was. Or still is.*

Helen hit speakerphone and dialed. It picked up. "Hello?"

"Yes, Angela, did I receive any priority mail envelopes from Washington this morning?"

A pause on the line. "No. Postman's already been and nothing today, but…"

"Thank you, Angela." Helen cut off the call.

Green noticed.

"Sorry, Mr. Green, doesn't look like anything came."

Green just stared into her eyes, dead silent. She looked away.

She's not even asking why I'm here or what's in that envelope. She's as guilty as hell.

"You're not very good at this are you, Helen?"

"I beg your pardon?"

"What's your relationship to Clinton Leblanc?"

"Look, Mr. Green, I'm extremely busy and…"

"And I'll close this fucking morbid circus down and rip it apart if I have to." Green spoke calmly, but his dark eyes burned holes into Helen.

"How dare you!" Helen sprung up. "Please leave. I shall be making a complaint to…"

"Go ahead," Green countered, standing up, towering over her matronly form. "The complaint will end up on my desk. Now will you cooperate or not?"

"With what?!" she snapped.

"I know you were sent a data disc by Clinton Leblanc. It came by priority mail. You'll give it to me now or you'll be detained. You're either with me or against me."

"On what charge?" she demanded.

"Obstructing National Security makes you a direct threat. The Patriot Act, indefinite detention, no reasons needed and no goddamn phone call to your fucking lawyer!"

"This is outrageous! Now please leave."

Green calmly sat down again and pulled out his cell phone.

"Norm, send those agents round to the museum, we're closing it down and taking Vanderbilt into custody. Take her to the field office for questioning." He flipped his phone shut and opened his jacket, flashing his firearm. "You're coming with me. Where's your deputy?"

Helen backed down, frightened and unsure of her position. "Sh-she's in the next office."

"Call her in."

Helen dialed Angela again.

A woman emerged, dressed in the same conservative manner.

"Angela, is it?" said Green.

"Uh…yes."

"Good. Angela, Helen's being detained as a matter of National Security. The museum is now closed. All employees are to remain in the building until further notice or they'll be going with Helen. Is that understood?"

Angela put her fingers to her mouth and glanced at Helen.

"I said is that understood?!" Green shouted, standing up. Helen nodded meekly at Angela. "Yes…I understand."

Green led Helen Vanderbilt out of her office, out into the museum lobby with Angela following. "Slater, this place is closed and no one's to leave. More agents are coming. Angela here will lock the doors. Start checking the exits and secure them. And don't fucking touch anything! Wait until I return."

Slater nodded and pulled Angela away to the front desk, as a small crowd of employees gathered in the lobby, murmuring.

Outside, Green put Helen in the back of the black sedan. Helen needed to be taken off her home turf if her resistance was to be broken.

CHAPTER 91

SONIA MADE GOOD TIME in the little Dodge; nineteen minutes after leaving the airfield they were off the freeway, headed for the museum.

But it was 9:27 AM.

"There!" said Travis, pointing ahead at the red brick building on the corner of Elm and Houston. "The Texas School Book Depository."

"Okay. Where do we park?" said Sonia.

"Wait…there! There's a parking sign. Make a left just after Elm in front of the building."

The tires screeched as Sonia maneuvered the car through a tight turn. The car rocked to a halt in the parking lot behind the grassy knoll and they were out the doors and running to the entrance, up the stairs and…

…the door was locked.

"What time did you say this place opened?"

"Nine—nine o'clock—look it says right there on the door," Travis stepped back from the building looking for another entrance.

Sonia shook the other door, but neither one was opening. She peered inside through the glass and saw a middle-aged woman looking lost, pacing. She caught sight of Sonia.

As the woman approached Sonia could make out her name badge: Angela Postales. Angela waved her arms and mouthed, "We're closed." Sonia shook the door even harder than before. Travis joined in.

Angela looked around as if to check that someone wasn't looking, continuing to walk over. She unlocked the door and poked her head out through the gap. "We're closed, I'm afraid."

Travis spoke first, sensing Sonia probably wasn't best prepared to handle this situation. "Ma'am, we don't want to come in."

"What is it, then?" Angela shook her head at yet another strange occurrence that day.

"I believe something's here for us and we just need to pick it up. We're friends of the curator?"

"You're Helen's friends?"

"Yes, Helen's…" *Helen must be the curator.*

"Okay, what is it? You can't come in though, I'm afraid."

Sonia and Travis glanced at each other. *What's going on? This isn't right.*

"Why are you closed?" asked Sonia.

Angela peered back inside conspiratorially then whispered through the door. "Some government agents came and took her away for questioning—more agents are on their way."

Green! No.

Sonia's face sank. Travis stayed calm and thought on his feet. *If Green took her away they probably didn't get what they wanted from her. Nothing to lose except time.* He let it out: "Angela, my friend Clinton Leblanc sent something for me to pick up here…in the care of the curator, perhaps?"

Looking flustered, Angela replied, "Okay…what's your name?" Travis sensed this was the last window of opportunity. It was time to take out all stops.

What the hell. "Travis…Daniel Travis."

The name seemed to register with Angela. "Wait, I think I *do* have something for you. Helen put it on my desk yesterday morning. Hang on one second." Angela locked the door and marched off.

Travis and Sonia were emotionally spent: what Angela had just revealed was monumental. Was she about to hand over the Apollo File?! They stood against the wall by the door trying to remain out of sight.

Four minutes came and went. No sign of Angela.

Seven minutes came and went. *What's going on?*

Something's wrong. Time's running out.

"Something's happened to her," said Sonia.

"I know, I know. Any ideas?" Travis asked, panning around in all directions, feeling exposed. Like it was a trap.

"Let's move away for starters. We're sitting ducks here."

"Agreed."

With heads down, Travis and Sonia hurried away from the museum entrance, back toward the parking lot.

"Look for a place where we can see the entrance but still look inconspicuous," said Sonia.

Travis appeared skeptical. "Well, loitering around a parking lot probably isn't... Wait... Follow me!"

"Where are we going?" Sonia asked, quick-marching in Travis's footsteps.

"I know just the place... Actually, this is probably the only place in the world where you can loiter around a parking lot and *not* look suspicious."

They arrived at a fence bordering the parking lot from Elm Street and Dealey Plaza. There was graffiti on it in black spray paint: *The FBI did it*. Three other people were standing there.

"Here you go," said Travis. "We can see the entrance from here perfectly."

Sonia looked over the fence on to Elm Street and realized they were on the grassy knoll standing in the position of the second shooter. She couldn't help but pause for a second and take in whose footsteps she was standing in.

From this position you could have looked onto Elm Street and seen the cross on the road where Kennedy took the bullet. It seemed closer than you'd imagine. A much easier shot than the one from the Book Depository; a kid could have hit him from here.

Anyway, Travis was right. Loitering around the corner of a parking lot never felt so comforting.

They both scanned the entrance of the museum under the cover of foliage, but still there was nothing. The yammering of tourists coming and going was incessant, each group debating the number of shooters and which American agency masterminded it.

A black Chevy Suburban screeched up outside the entrance and four men ran out. They dashed up to the steps and one of them slapped his hand on the door.

"Green's men," Sonia said.

Travis stood and stared like a deer frozen in the headlights of an oncoming car.

Game over.

"Give me the museum's number. I'm gonna call her."

Travis rattled it off, wishing they'd called sooner. He put his ear next to Sonia's so he could hear everything.

"Sixth Floor Museum." The voice seemed strained. Not the welcoming tone you'd expect when calling a place like this. *Understandable*, Sonia thought.

"Angela Postales please."

"This is Angela." *She must have taken over the phones. Either that or all calls had now been routed to her office. Whatever. This was perfect.*

"I'm with Daniel Travis—you said you had…"

"Yes. Wait under the sniper's perch." Angela hung up.

"Come on," Travis said. Registering Angela's reply, he hurried Sonia away from the fence.

"Where's the sniper's perch?" Sonia asked, matching Travis's brisk march out of the parking lot.

Travis pointed up at the sixth floor of the museum as he marched off. "See that?" he said.

Sonia squinted, holding her arm up against the dazzle of the Texas sun.

Travis continued, "That corner window on the sixth floor—that's the sniper's perch—where Oswald shot from."

Inside the museum, the atmosphere was bustling chaos. Agents were covering exits, speaking into their sleeves. The staff were huddled in the lobby, some of them being questioned, all of them confused.

Angela slammed the receiver down and patted the envelope tucked in her pocket; it was sealed and addressed to *D. Travis.*

Helen Vanderbilt had given Angela the envelope yesterday saying, "Give this to D. Travis if I'm not around when he comes for it."

Angela knew that what she was about to do could get her arrested, but there was something imperative about the way Helen had spoken to her yesterday. Maybe this could get her dear friend off the hook. Hard to believe she'd done anything wrong.

Yes, this is the right thing to do.

Angela felt her stomach boil up with the rebellious spirit

of most JFK buffs and strutted out of her office, sticking her chest out.

She opened the door to the lobby and made a sharp right for the elevator.

An agent blocked her path.

"Where you going, ma'am?"

"Up to the museum."

"Why?"

"Maintenance on a couple of the exhibits—some things can't wait, I'm afraid. This is a historical landmark, you know."

The agent spoke into the microphone up his sleeve. "One coming up." He waved Angela through to the open doors.

Angela stepped in, realizing there would be another agent upstairs to get past. She pushed the button for "seven"—the "Call to Action" exhibit. She'd walk down the stairs to the sixth floor. Hoping it would look like she was up here already, she could sneak around the agent expecting her on six.

A few moments later, the doors opened with a ding and she stepped out into the dimly lit exhibit. Down a flight of stairs and she was in the sixth floor museum.

Only one window on the sixth floor could be opened. Surrounded by stacked boxes, the window was preserved in its original state. It was the window Oswald shot from.

Allegedly.

No sign of any agents. So far so good. Angela approached the plate glass protecting the infamous window and stifled a grin at the perfect cover already in place. The very same arrangement of boxes Oswald had used to hide himself would hide her too, though she doubted what she was about to do was quite so criminal.

She put the key in the small lock in the glass door and turned it, then gently pushed it open.

Easy. Now all we have to do…

"Stop!" boomed a voice behind her.

It was an agent.

Angela spun around. "What?" she said defiantly. Angela hated authority, especially in the place where she was the authority.

"What are you doing?" said the blond agent.

"I told your colleague downstairs. Routine checks of the exhibits. This is a National Historic Landmark. Look, if you think I'm just going to sit around and twiddle my thumbs while you…"

"Alright, ma'am," he said. "Calm down—go ahead."

Angela swung the door open and went in, closing it behind her. She felt the agent's eyes watching her, so she faked an inspection. She looked up and down, moved a couple of the boxes an inch or two and fiddled with a wall fitting before stepping toward the window.

She disappeared behind the boxes that covered Oswald.

No way can he see me now.

She opened the old window a couple of inches. Standing up, into view, she ran her fingers along the top of the frame to make it look like she was inspecting the window.

Then she disappeared behind the boxes again.

Now's my chance. She pulled the envelope from her pocket, crumpled it up into a ball and threw it out the open window, hoping Travis had understood her instructions.

She walked back out through the glass door and locked it behind her, realizing she was sweating.

"You okay?" said the agent with a glint of suspicion in his eyes. "You look a little flushed."

"Menopause," she whispered.

The agent's face went red. He nodded without looking at her.

Eight painful minutes passed.

Travis and Sonia stood on Elm Street staring up at the sniper's perch, pointing up at it each in turn, chatting: authentic tourists.

But nothing came.

"How much longer are we gonna have to keep this crap up?" said Sonia through gritted teeth, pointing upward with a forced smile.

"Jeez, so that's where Oswald shot from? Woah! Amazing," said Travis who'd noticed another pedestrian walking past them.

"I swear, if you say that one more time I'll k…"

"Sshh!" said Travis. "Look! The window opened."

Sonia looked up and in the same moment, they both watched a ball of paper tumble down to the ground. It landed a few feet from them.

Sonia grabbed it and plodded away toward the parking lot. Travis followed, staring straight ahead, silent.

It was all they could do not to run.

CHAPTER 92

THE DOORS SLAMMED on the white Dodge and Sonia handed the ball of paper to Travis. Sonia started the engine and pulled away. Travis felt rigid with tension and excitement. They stared ahead trying to look innocent, but deep down they felt like they'd just made off with the Tiffany Diamond. "Hard to believe this is Apollo," he said.

"Open it up," Sonia said, maneuvering through the parking lot.

Travis pulled open the scrunched up paper. It was an envelope marked to his attention.

Pushing his thumb under the seal, he felt like the mythical Pandora with her box. He hesitated, recalling his earlier thoughts: *Do people really want a natural cure for cancer? Do they mind the consequence of possibly losing their jobs?* In Greek mythology, Pandora released all the diseases and plagues from her box. Apollo would bring them back into the box and cure them. The Apollo File could bury the demons Pandora carried with her all these centuries.

Travis pulled out the piece of paper inside. He unfolded it.

The anticlimax hit him like a sledgehammer. It had just one line penned across it:

1107 Eyston Drive, Dallas, TX

"What does it say?" asked Sonia.

"It's an address."

"What?!" She stopped the car. "Let me see."

Travis handed it to her and reached for the map.

"I-I don't understand," Sonia said, staring at the address. "Is this what my brother sent? What's at that address?"

"I don't know but we're gonna find out," Travis said, studying the street index. "And before Green does too. Alright, here it is…take a right onto Elm…it's close on the edge of downtown."

Eyston Drive was one of those streets you wished you hadn't driven down: a street you could only arrive at by accident, unless you lived there. It was old and rundown. Abandoned cars sat in the street and old sofas decomposed on the porches of the dilapidated single-story wooden houses built along the unkept sidewalk.

"Okay, it should be on the right any sec…there it is!" exclaimed Travis.

Sonia kept driving past a couple of houses and parked the car. Travis knew the drill and didn't even think to question why—she didn't want to park directly outside the house.

They stepped out onto the sidewalk and edged their way back to number 1107. The streets were deserted. Upon closer inspection, these houses weren't low-class. They were probably almost as old as much of downtown Dallas itself.

The windows on 1107 had shutters, which were all closed. The porch was in disrepair and a rickety wooden garage sat in the backyard.

As they got closer, they could see a car in the drive that looked decidedly out of place: it was a new black Ford Mustang GT.

"Someone's here already."

"Go around the back way," said Sonia, making a beeline for the backyard. Travis followed Sonia's quickening step.

Travis and Sonia deftly trotted around the side of the faded blue wooden house and rounded the corner to the rear door. It was open behind a screen door.

"Does breaking and entering ring any bells? Maybe we should just knock?" Travis said with a strained whisper.

"We don't know who's in here—could be a trap for all we know," Sonia said. "Friend or foe, I'm not giving them any advantage—now you wait here for just one second until I give you the all clear, okay?"

"Alright."

Sonia disappeared inside.

Travis stood with his back against the wall and waited. Ghosts of happier times were everywhere. He studied the brown lawn. A rubber tire-swing hung from a tree by a tattered rope. A rusted tricycle sat next to the old, barn-like garage. A rotting, wooden picnic table lay in the corner next to an old-fashioned grill; the smoker type made out of an old oil drum.

Sonia had been gone too long. *What's she doing?*

Travis didn't hear any struggle inside. *Time to go in and see for myself.* He'd come too far and risked too much to just wait.

Travis pushed the screen door. It swung open with a creak. He found himself in a kitchen in need of renovation, though it was clearly still in use, if the dirty dishes in the sink were anything to go by.

No sight or sound of Sonia.

He crept in further.

Connected to the kitchen was a dining room full of pictures. Travis studied them. Some black and white, some color, all in dated frames.

Everything in this house was stuck in another time. There was a picture of two men, father and son, standing next to each other. On a shelf next to that, a football team. A trophy sat next to it. There was a picture of a tall, well-built man in his thirties with blond hair and dressed in a tailored black suit.

Still no sight or sound of Sonia, but he didn't want to call out.

Travis continued to study the photos. The next one was a picture of the older man—the father he supposed—standing next to President Kennedy looking like Secret Service.

This was Leblanc's parents' house.

Travis's head spun with possibilities as he frantically scanned more photos. His eyes stopped dead on one with an inscription below a picture of the son, in his suit again: *Clinton Leblanc, Secret Service 1999.*

Travis felt cold. His whole body erupted into goosebumps. *Leblanc must have sent the file here. But how and why did Angela have that note? Who sent the...*

Travis just got his answer.

Life went into slow motion as Travis stared at the sight before him. He could feel each breath swell his rib cage.

Oh-my-God.

Was he hallucinating? He glanced at the Secret Service photo once more.

A ghost was pointing a gun at Sonia as she walked toward him with her hands over her head.

No! No, it is him.

Clinton Leblanc.

Wearing a running suit, he was unshaven and had a bandage around his arm.

"Leblanc?" Travis said.

The blond man didn't move, he stayed focused on Sonia,

his target. She was uncharacteristically silent and didn't look at Travis.

Leblanc couldn't have seen her face and she's not saying anything to provoke him to fire, Travis speculated.

"Clinton Leblanc, I know who you are. Look, it's okay, I'm Dan Travis and that woman is your sister!"

The man didn't move or say a word. He just took closer aim at Sonia.

Travis confirmed the man in front of him was the same person in the photographs. *Yes, this definitely is Leblanc!*

A painfully slow two seconds later, Leblanc spoke: "I don't *have* a goddamn sister!"

CHAPTER 93

IT WAS LIKE A DREAM. Travis's vision was blurry around the edges.

There in front of him stood someone who'd come back from the dead claiming Sonia wasn't his sister after all.

In those brief seconds of silence, they each waited to see who would speak first. A haze of doubt set in as Travis recalled the events of the past few days. He didn't actually know for sure that Leblanc was dead. And Sonia had only assumed as much. And if this was Leblanc (*yes, it is Leblanc*) Travis couldn't understand why he was saying that Sonia wasn't his sister. Suddenly Travis realized there was one crucial detail missing from all of the photographs: Sonia.

And this address had meant nothing to Sonia!

Travis looked closer at Sonia. Her hands were cuffed on top of her head.

"Sonia?" Travis asked.

She said nothing.

"Dr. Travis," said Leblanc. "I know you've got a whole bunch of questions for me and I'll answer them, but right now I've got one for you: who the hell is she and where did you find her?"

"She said she was your sister," Travis said. "Sonia?" Still silence.

"Please come over here, Dr. Travis. I need your help securing her." Leblanc's tone of voice was calm. He seemed to know what Sonia was capable of; he was careful to keep her at a safe distance as he pointed the gun at her with both hands, relentlessly controlled.

Travis looked at Sonia again. He felt a headache from disparate bits of information he was trying to process. All they'd been through together— Sonia had helped him. *Why if she was the enemy? Who was the enemy? Did she help him because she wanted the file? Who did she really work for?*

I can't believe this is happening.

"Please, Doctor—step over very carefully and escort her into this closet." Leblanc was pointing to a white door on Sonia's right.

Only thing I can be sure of right now is Leblanc sent that file and he's standing right here. Travis decided to do as Leblanc asked.

Travis crept over and opened the door.

Sonia didn't resist and didn't look at Travis. Whatever threats Leblanc had made to apprehend her had worked.

"Now close it, please," said Leblanc, still keeping his distance and aiming the gun at the closing door. Travis obliged, though the thought of Sonia being an adversary disconcerted him. The door closed and locked automatically. It was a thick, metal fire door.

Leblanc lowered his weapon, exhaling deeply. "She's not going anywhere now." Then he held out a welcoming hand to Travis. "Sir, it's an honor to meet you."

Travis shook his hand, catatonic with shock.

Talk about surreal. Questions trounced Travis, but the first to come out was obvious: "I thought you were dead?"

"So did I," said Leblanc motioning toward a tattered paisley sofa in the living room.

Travis followed and took a seat. Leblanc was exactly how

Travis had imagined a Secret Service agent to be: proper and precise. In retrospect, Sonia didn't match that profile. *Isn't stinking hindsight always 20/20!?*

Travis had to slow his mind and keep it open. *Just listen to Leblanc.*

Leblanc took a seat opposite Travis. "Don't worry, the file's safe," he said with a wry smile. "And we're safe here. This house is off the grid. My parents owned it and left it to me when they passed. I still come down to maintain it every now and then. Can't bring myself to sell it. My old man used to protect Kennedy and the day JFK got shot in '63 was the end for my pop. He became obsessed with the whole thing— even moved us here to Dallas where it all happened. He just couldn't let go—got stuck in 1963 and never came back. He blamed himself for allowing the president to take a bullet like that. Ate him up so bad. He died of cancer soon after, then my mom followed him shortly." Tears were welling in Leblanc's eyes, but he fought them off by biting his bottom lip hard.

"Why didn't you just send the file here?" Travis asked, trying not to ask a hundred questions at once.

"Priority mail has to be signed for and no one was here— I knew they'd check my phone records and contacts file. I couldn't send it to anyone in those, so I sent it to Helen at the museum. She's an old friend of the family who I'd lost touch with some time back, but the address was easy enough to re-member. And I knew Helen could be trusted, not just because she's an old friend, but because she'd know what to do with the file if I didn't make it. God I'm so glad you came—my fax worked…"

"So you escaped from them. *Who are they?*" Travis asked.

"*They* is Green."

"Who's Green?" Travis snapped, desperate to know more

about the man who'd pursued him this week.

"Green's my boss—Director of the Secret Service—a real asshole. I realized they were onto me when I got home Monday and saw someone had been in my apartment, but I'm not sure—" Leblanc paused to look at the closet that held Sonia. "I saw they were coming and I had to think of a way to get the file out in case I was captured—I also wanted to contact you, so I tore the top sheet off of my research, wrote a note at the bottom of it and faxed it to you."

It all sounded so simple from where Leblanc was sitting—he was oblivious to the merry journey through hell Travis had suffered to be there. *Long story and too many questions to answer to put Leblanc on a guilt trip.*

"You sent the Apollo File to Helen at the museum—so is it still there? Because Green's already..."

"It arrived yesterday, not today. Priority mail takes one to two days and thankfully it was one. God bless the United States Postal Service is all I can say—Helen had it waiting for me yesterday. In case you showed up later, I gave her this address to give to you in an envelope with your name on it."

The obvious question came back to Travis. "So, how did you escape Green?"

"Went to my neighbor's, grabbed a priority envelope she'd paid for, ready to go just lying there. I took out her letter and put mine in—climbed out onto her balcony and ran to the nearest mailbox. I was being shot at by my own colleagues. Couldn't believe it! I fell in the river and they thought they'd killed me. I thought I was dead too—it was so dark and cold. Then I swore I saw my father—and light—swam toward the light and came up on the other side of the river." Leblanc was misty-eyed, distant.

"What happened then?"

Leblanc blinked back into the moment. "I was on protection duty that day so I was still wearing a bulletproof vest when I fell in the river. Tried calling you on your cell phone for days now, where were you?"

"Lost my phone. That's unbelievable," Travis said, referring to Leblanc's story. "So what made you break the code of silence?"

"Goddamn Agency's lost its way—we're more like secret police!" Leblanc calmed himself and answered the question. "A buddy of mine, Brewster, works on protection duty for the First Lady. Now, no one knows this, but she was recently diagnosed with cancer and found an alternative medicine clinic in Mexico, which cured her. Brewster told me all about it. Well, naturally I was interested because of my father's own death, so I began researching. Because of my pop I'd pretty much learned all there was to learn about the events surrounding Kennedy's assassination and I saw some weird coincidences between that and..."

"Laetrile?" said Travis. "McNaughton was the common link you referred to, wasn't he?"

"Yes, sir. Anyway, not even a week ago, an insider from the FDA contacts me out of the blue and gives me even more info! Was that great timing or what? Turns out the guy I protected—Vice President Cooke—was attending a Bilderberg Conference in Tampa to discuss nothing other than Laetrile."

Travis fell back into the old sofa with the belated comfort that his hunch had been right all along. Travis continued staring at Leblanc as the mystery that had tortured him since Monday unraveled before him.

"I got a micro-surveillance device from Intelligence Services and set it up in the conference room. My partner Meyer must have seen me though—son of a bitch. How am I supposed to turn a blind eye to something like that?! I may have taken an oath, but there's a line I won't cross—Secret Service is supposed to protect the president's life and the nation's currency—instead we've turned into some sort of goddamn Praetorian Guard!"

Sensing Leblanc was digressing, Travis interjected. "So where's the...the Apollo File, is it?"

"Apollo's safe—it's close by."

Travis felt his head lurch up in surprise. *Did he just say the Apollo File was close by?* He'd been chasing this moment for what seemed like an eternity, fighting adversaries, beating the odds to reach this point.

But Leblanc continued in a reserved manner.

"So who the hell is that girl Sonia and what's she doing here?" He appeared to want some reassurance before he'd reveal the location of the file.

Travis shrugged. "She approached me in New York and said she was your sister and a Secret Service agent—she knew everything about you and your father, the whole deal—I couldn't have made it this far without her." Travis hung his head. Everything Sonia had done and said started replaying through his mind like a black and white newsreel.

"Well, she's not who she says she is, that much is certain. This is worrisome," said Leblanc, rubbing the back of his neck.

"What is?"

"Obviously she came for the Apollo File and used you to get to it. The question is, who's she working for and how the hell did they find out about the file? Was there anything odd or suspicious about her or her actions?"

Travis thought hard. "Nothing springs to mind—just..."

"Just what?"

"She just didn't act how you do."

"Anyway," Leblanc began, "there's no shortage of people

who'd like to get their hands on the file. We've got the hard job of trying to find a loving home for it."

"Oh?" said Travis.

"Yeah, I mean no newspaper or TV network will run this—they're all owned by multi-nationals with a lot to lose. No government body will be interested of course and neither are the charities—"

"How do you know all that?" It seemed logical, but Leblanc seemed an unlikely person to know this.

"You'll know too when you see the file."

Leblanc was right of course. Travis had often argued that if the Watergate scandal happened today it would never be broadcast by the media; the notion of Woodwards and Bernsteins clawing for the big scoop was naïve these days.

Travis thought for a moment, and then it came to him. Something he'd already considered.

"That only leaves one thing—the last bastion of free speech," Travis said.

"What's that?" asked Leblanc.

"The Internet."

CHAPTER 94

AFTER FINALLY MAKING CONTACT with Jensen, Reese sat in his car outside the Dallas Secret Service field office. Jensen had been at the White House this morning and wasn't contactable until now.

"Dallas?"

"Yes, sir, Dallas. At around seven-thirty this morning he quit the holding pattern over Memphis and proceeded to Love Field. He then entered the Sixth Floor Museum, closed it down and took a Helen Vanderbilt, the curator, into custody. I'm outside his field office now awaiting further instructions."

There was a pause on the line. Reese could almost hear Jensen's circuits humming. "So have you got *our* Dallas field office involved yet?" Jensen asked.

"No, sir. Are we certain our target's going to lead us to the objective?"

"If anyone can get us there he can. We just have to be patient, Reese, and be careful. Remember, we need this."

"I'm gonna get airborne. Can you call the Dallas…"

"It's done."

"A chopper with a couple of agents is all it should take. All of them are on a need-to-know basis."

"Done."

Before Reese could reply, Jensen had hung up.

Two miles away, the man in a suit with the foreign accent—Phoenix—spoke in a phone booth.

"Green here."

"It's me."

His voice immediately required Green to find some privacy. "Stand by," he advised. "Where are you now?"

"Close."

"You have air transport arranged?"

"Yes—a chopper. Call sign is *Phoenix*."

"Okay good. Remain on the designated frequency. The target's location is still unknown, but be ready to execute."

"Roger." Phoenix hung up.

Dwight walked back into the small interrogation room where Helen Vanderbilt sat sobbing. "Now then, Helen, you were just explaining to me that Clinton Leblanc showed up yesterday?"

CHAPTER 95

"WE'RE NOT CONNECTED to the web here," said Leblanc.

"Okay, but that's the way to deliver Apollo to the public—*the world*! A website with streaming video that would come up in searches like *cancer* and so on."

Travis had a good relationship with the Internet. His earlier books quickly rose to the top of the bestseller lists through the same method: it was called 'viral marketing' and it spread organically like a disease. He knew what exposure the Internet was capable of.

"Okay," said Leblanc. "What's the first step?"

"First things first. We need to make a copy of the file—where is it? You can trust me," said Travis, squarely meeting Leblanc's eyes.

Leblanc nodded then produced a small jewel case with a tiny disc inside. "This is Apollo," he said, as if he was introducing Travis to the president.

Travis took the small case. He felt like he was holding an alien artifact. To be sure, this would have about the same impact on the world as evidence of life on another planet, he thought.

"Do you have a computer here?" Travis asked.

"I have a laptop over here. I didn't have time to get any copies on the way down—wanted to keep low profile and get to Dallas as fast as I could. But I made a copy of the file to the hard drive."

Leblanc ushered Travis back through to the kitchen where a laptop sat on a small table in the corner. "You won't need that now," Travis said, nervously pointing at the gun Leblanc still hadn't put down.

"Sorry." He placed it on the dresser in the living room.

"Alright," said Travis. "I want to take a look at what's on this disc, then we're going to get a website up."

Travis popped open the disc drive and placed the Apollo File in, slapping it shut. The computer whirred to life. Travis stared at the screen. He felt his stomach churn.

Seconds later, the Apollo File was playing.

It was the first chance Leblanc had had to see the file himself. The laptop screen went black before an image appeared. It was an empty room with a large conference table in the middle. Water, mints and writing pads were placed at each seat. It was a function room in the Grand Hyatt Tampa.

Leblanc and Travis pulled up stools and watched. The vantage point of the video camera gave a clear view of the entire table.

"They closed down a whole hotel just for this?" said Travis.

"Oh no—this was a little side meeting. There were many more guests. This was an off-agenda meeting with just a few select attendees," said Leblanc.

Soon, voices were heard entering the room, and then a procession of people, some of them Travis could identify, some he couldn't. Leblanc was the first to enter with a younger guy who also looked like Secret Service.

"That's my partner, Meyer."

Then the vice president—Richard Cooke—came in and walked toward the head of the table at the far side. Leblanc and his partner took their places standing either side of him. Close behind him were four men dressed in suits, none of them younger than fifty. Finally, a man with white hair and sporting the most expensive suit of all took a seat at the other end of the table in a position that obscured his face. He was first to speak. He commanded the room, as if he'd called the meeting. Moderating the meeting meant he was clearly the man in charge.

"Vice President Cooke, allow me to introduce you," the white-haired man said, gesturing to the other four men around the table.

Each nodded and smiled as their name was called out. "Dr. Joseph Richardson, Head of the American Medical Association, Peter Morwitz, Head of the American Cancer Society, Michael Maston, Head of the FDA, and Martin Crenshaw, Head of the National Cancer Institute."

The old guy was definitely calling the shots. The other five men waited for him to begin.

"Gentlemen," he began, "we have both a crisis and an opportunity. Mr. Vice President, your administration is currently slipping in the polls and you're hoping for re-election next year."

"Yes, indeed, and we thank you for your generous support…"

"And you'd like to be re-elected, I presume?" said the man facing Cooke.

He'd just interrupted the vice president of the United States. Who was this guy?

"We just want what every administration wants: a second term!" Cooke chuckled. No one else laughed as Cooke's face quickly regained seriousness.

The other four men sat silent.

"Then it's crucial we tackle this issue immediately," continued the man in charge. "Judging by the people I've summoned here today, you can guess what this is about: cancer. Vice President, your superior—the president—is about to make a monumental blunder by announcing his public support for Laetrile."

"But, he hasn't…"

"Not yet, but he will and this meeting is to ensure he doesn't. Reagan made the same mistake when he was president and we had to—well, take measures. I've called this meeting so that we don't have to go through that again."

Reagan was shot, Travis thought as he watched.

"But the First Lady…" Cooke stuttered.

"Yes, she's the problem. We know she went to Mexico because she'd developed breast cancer and has now become a rabid fan of Laetrile, but she has no idea what she's getting into. If she wants to enjoy a second term too, you need to make sure they understand."

"Understand what exactly?" asked Cooke, looking at the faceless man like a puppy would its master.

"America's economy would take a serious knock, the trade deficit would skyrocket. It's already unsustainable and you'd lose a major bargaining chip in international negotiations. Goodbye, second term."

"I understand, I'll…"

"I want to make sure you *do* understand. And you're not the only person in the room who needs to wise up either," said the white-haired moderator, eyeing the other four shuffling in their seats.

"Gentlemen, as I said, this is a crisis, but it's also an opportunity. Let's start with the opportunity. If the exponential rate increase of cancer in the market continues, it will soon replace heart attack as the number one killer in America. Currently, one in three people experience cancer, and looking ahead several decades, *100* percent of the market will suffer from it. That is assuming the current rate of yearly increase continues. Needless to say, this is a lucrative market which will only continue to get better as we look forward."

Travis balked with disgust. "This guy is giving a marketing presentation to promote cancer!" It was now obvious to Travis who the man in charge represented: the Cartel.

"The crisis, however, is emerging due to several factors, predominantly through an increasingly skeptical public looking to markets which cannot co-exist with our own—that's to say the competition blatantly contradicts our own products."

"Sorry...products?" interrupted Cooke.

"Chemotherapy: drugs and equipment, the revenues from which greatly contribute to those represented here today, including your own election campaign. Hospitals have billions invested in radiology equipment. It's a 110-billion-dollar-a-year industry and, if it disappeared, the ripple effect would, as I said, be disastrous. Consider how the exportation of drugs positively affects our out-of-control trade deficit. Even putting that aside, healthcare providers alone constitute 15 percent of the economy."

"Yes, I see," said Cooke. "And the competition is Laetrile?"

"Potentially yes, but we'll come back to that," said the man in charge, waving his scrawny hand. "Additionally, the Internet continues to undermine our message. The media are mostly under control, but the Internet needs to be regulated. Despite our manipulation of the media by compelling them to run stories on child pornography and terrorist recruitment in connection with the Internet, the government is still unable to regulate it, and of course, much of the media establishment is owned by our conglomerates, so there's no shortage of pressure."

"Yes, but this is a hard…" began Cooke.

"I know it's not easy, so we have to work hard to control the information the Internet provides and ensure Laetrile remains far down on peoples' web searches, but that's just one strategy. What we need to do now is stop the rot."

"So Laetrile actually works then?" interrupted Cooke.

A silence fell over the room as the attendees looked at each other, none of them wanting to answer such an inappropriate question. Cooke had just violated an unspoken protocol.

"I'll come back to that later. Now," continued the white-haired man, glaring at the director of the FDA. "Maston, your agency leaks like a sieve." Maston was silent.

Producing a piece of paper from his briefcase, "Your agency is paid hundreds of millions of dollars to get drug approvals and this here is the kind of treachery we can't afford: in 1970 former FDA commissioner Dr. Herbert Ley said, 'The thing that bugs me is that the people think the FDA is protecting them. It isn't. What the FDA is doing and what the public thinks it is doing are as different as night and day.' A historic example, I know, but with the Internet, this stuff lingers around indefinitely. There's more, as you know, Maston. In 1974, eleven FDA scientists actually testified to the Senate 'that they were harassed by agency officials…whenever they recommended against the approval of marketing some new drug.' Not good, now is it? We can't let this sort of thing leak out."

Maston folded his arms and remained silent.

The man continued, "And then there was the 1989 scandal where FDA reviewers were caught receiving bribes from some drug companies to speed their drug approvals through the system."

Maston finally spoke up. "I understand, but each year, thousands of people die from side effects…"

"Maston, side effects will always be present and what you probably don't grasp is that side effects are a good thing."

"A good thing?" interrupted Vice President Cooke.

"They're good in the business sense," said the white-haired moderator. "If a patient has one problem eased by a drug but then develops a different condition as a result of a side effect, that's repeat business—the patient will need another drug to cure the side effect and so on. Plus the fact that he'll have to stay on the initial drug to continue to reap the benefits that drug provided. Residual income." He spoke with an emotionless, matter-of-fact voice, but Cooke looked uncomfortable.

"Vice President, gentlemen, let's be realistic here. Pharmaceutics is a business, one that pays all your salaries, I might add, and business is about marketing, plain and simple. New markets emerge all the time, and with your help we will all prosper from them. Thanks to the medical establishment, we've re-branded certain ailments as diseases: heartburn is now acid reflux disease, for example, and being overweight has become a disease known as obesity. Everyone's a winner here. People are able to blame their condition on a disease and thus relinquish responsibility. It's worked well. Plus we've created brand new markets."

"Sorry," said Cooke. "What do you mean by creating new markets? Creating new diseases?"

Maston answered. "Diseases that aren't identifiable in tissue through a scan or sample. ADD or HIV are conditions which exist because we say they do."

The ringleader interjected. "All I'm saying is if we work

together, the status quo will stay in place and we'll all get what we want. Television advertising is another avenue, which is producing excellent results…"

The head of the AMA, Dr. Joseph Richardson, spoke up. "TV is one area causing problems. Dissention in the ranks, shall we say?"

"Oh?" the moderator asked. "All your doctors have to do is use their PDR. That's what we designed the thing for, that's how we trained them. They get paid a bonus each time they prescribe a drug, so what's the problem?"

"With respect, it's not as simple as that," said Richardson of the AMA. "Because of TV commercials, people are becoming convinced they have an illness when they don't and…"

"And with respect to you, Doctor, you're not a businessman. The more people ask their doctor if a drug is right for them the more the commercials are working and the more drug sales take place. It was an excellent strategy that worked with cold remedies and now we've simply extended it to other products. But, as you've entered the debate now, let's talk about the AMA. You have the ability to revoke the licenses that doctors worked so hard to attain and became so massively in debt for, and you're saying you can't control them?"

"Well, I…"

"Your track record isn't much better than the FDA's, is it?" The moderator produced another piece of paper from the stack he'd brought out of his briefcase. "In 1973, two former chairmen and one vice chairman testified before congress to say that the AMA was 'a captive of and beholden to the pharmaceutical industry' and in 1987 the AMA was found guilty of conspiring for the past twenty years to destroy the profession of chiropractics."

"Yes, I know all that, but membership is dropping and…"

"Keep your doctors in line! In a survey recently taken of seventy-nine doctors who were asked if they would use chemotherapy on themselves for cancer, 73 percent of them said they would never do so because of the highly toxic effects. For crying out loud, man, keep your doctors in line! Chemotherapy drug sales are over ten billion a year now. And drop in membership is no excuse. Private physicians are slowly being replaced by HMOs, group clinics and research centers, and we control or influence most of those directly."

"Faith is waning," Richardson protested. "The whole HIV thing is another time bomb waiting to go off after banning those home test kits. There is no damn virus."

Watching the screen, Travis was encouraged by Richardson's manner, it was like he wasn't happy about the heinous conspiracy. *Good for him. Finally, someone with a conscience.*

"Excuse me?' said Vice President Cooke.

Richardson explained. "There's no such thing as HIV. The guy who supposedly discovered it, Robert Gallo, was indicted for science fraud. Look, to identify a virus's existence you have to be able to take a picture of it so it can be catalogued for identification. To this day there's no scientific paper to prove any link between HIV and AIDS."

"But I've seen photos of the HIV vir…"

"Artists' impressions fed to the media," said Richardson. "The HIV test is simply a T-cell count. If your immune system's down, you could be HIV positive one day and then negative the next when you're feeling better. That's why the FDA had to withdraw those home test kits. Sure, people die of AIDS all the time but AIDS is just an umbrella name we've given to any affliction because of a low immune system. The reason it's so prevalent in the Third World is because of malnutrition. And AIDS doesn't satisfy two of medicine's most basic benchmarks for identifying viral pathogens:

Koch's Postulates or Farr's Law. The biggest cause of people dying from AIDS and HIV is the cocktail of drugs they're given to fight it."

Travis looked at Leblanc in disbelief. "Uh…yeah, I can see why this disc might cause a few people to have some sleepless nights," he said.

"Doesn't HIV cause AIDS then?" asked Cooke.

"If it does, how come thousands of people who have AIDS are HIV negative? Why are 87 percent of babies born HIV positive pronounced negative eighteen months later *without* therapeutic intervention?" countered Richardson.

"Gentlemen, please can we stay on the main issue here?" chimed in the white-haired man as he turned to his next victim: the head of the National Cancer Institute.

"Crenshaw, we have a problem at the NCI, don't we? You have a leaky ship too it seems, and with scandals like the Tamoxifen trials in 1994, you really don't need that."

"Tamoxifen trials?" asked Cooke.

"Yes," replied the white-haired man. "They really screwed the pooch on that one—even their director at the time was forced to resign. The NCI failed to control the British and Italian scientists who proved the drug had no benefit at all and that it was actually a carcinogen itself. But it's not all bad. The NCI gets taxpayer funding for drug research and then hands over the patents to the pharmaceutical companies. The Taxol joint venture was an excellent example of the sort of collaboration I'd like to see more of, but now one of your former directors—Dr. Dean Burk—is one of the most outspoken critics of the NCI and a sympathizer with the Laetrilists!"

"Yes, but there's nothing I can…"

There were no counter arguments allowed. The white-haired man rifled through more papers. "Your very own Dr.

Dean Burk is publicly quoted as saying, 'Laetrile appears to work against many forms of cancer including lung cancer. And it is absolutely non-toxic.' These things don't go away, you know, especially when that doctor is so eminently qualified. He's also said on record, 'In spite of the foregoing evidence...officials at the American Cancer Institute and even the National Cancer Institute, have continued to set forth to the public that about one in every four cancer cases is now "cured" or "controlled." Such a statement is highly misleading when systemic or metastatic cancers rate of control in terms of the conventional five-year survival is scarcely more than one in twenty.'" Which brings me to this point: why are you still using the five-year period to measure cures?"

"We could change that," said Crenshaw.

"The five-year period?" asked Cooke.

Crenshaw explained. "We say a cancer patient's been cured if it stays in remission for five years after treatment. If they get cancer six years later, we're allowed to say that was a new cancer for the purposes of our stats. We could reduce that to three years?"

"It would certainly help your figures, wouldn't it?" suggested the moderator forcibly, turning to the head of the American Cancer Society, Peter Morwitz.

"Mr. Morwitz, the ACS is a charity and therefore has to be run under certain guidelines—guidelines which you fall foul of, embarrassing us all. You're not supposed to be spending any money on political lobbying and yet you have spent tens of millions doing so. Leave that to us! You're transparent. This Dr. Dean Burk publicly accused you of 'lying like scoundrels,' which is hardly surprising when you make exaggerated statements like 'caught early enough, breast cancer has cure rates approaching 100 percent.' And then there's the funding issue: only 5 percent of the donations you receive go to cancer sufferers, the rest goes on salaries and overhead. Like I said, you're transparent and you need to find a way to be more creative with those numbers you release."

Morwitz nodded.

"Get your houses in order, gentlemen, first and foremost. Now we need to look at the growing threat from the competition. I'd like to invite suggestions. Anyone?"

"We're cracking down harder than ever on these goddamn Laetrile quacks," said Maston, head of the FDA. "People selling any nutritional supplements like apricot kernels can't directly say it cures, prevents, diagnoses or treats any disease, but they get around it. We need tougher legislation."

"Apricot kernels?" said Cooke.

"Yeah, they have Laetrile in them," said Maston.

"Oh, I see…"

"Yes," said the white-haired man. "And that's exactly why you have the cyanide scare. Use it!"

Maston nodded. "We do and on the whole it works— you only have to mention the fact that apricot kernels have cyanide in them and people conclude they're poisonous and don't go anywhere near them."

"Then make more of it! We should be seeing more press releases about cyanide poisonings from apricot kernels," said the moderator.

"There's one thing in our favor," said Maston. "It's easy to lump the Laetrilists in with all the other peddlers offering miracle cures. But going into a health shop with guns drawn to take apricot kernels off the shelf doesn't look good for the agency…"

"But if Laetrile doesn't work, why are we worried?" asked the vice president.

Silence filled the room. A long eight seconds later, the white-haired man spoke. "There is certain evidence to suggest

Laetrile does work." He waited to let it sink in. "But there's no money in it—"

"What about cyanide-releasing drugs?" asked the head of the AMA.

"Wait a second," interrupted the vice president. "Cyanide? Why would you want cyanide-releasing drugs?"

The white-haired man regained control of the conversation. "The cyanide in Laetrile is why it's had some success. We've been trying to manufacture a patentable drug that does the same thing but as yet have been unable to perfect the cyanide unlocking mechanism safely—the test mice almost always die in trials—but we remain hopeful. Research centers are sympathetic to our cause and generally deliver favorable results. They won't bite the hand that feeds them. Universities, too, are more than happy to comply: releasing sensational findings to secure grants is the norm."

"But people are getting more cynical," said Maston. "The Internet opens up a whole can of worms. Americans can readily see that tens of thousands of people are being treated in Laetrile clinics perfectly legally in a variety of countries around the world, many of them westernized countries like Switzerland, Germany and…"

"Don't be so sure," said the man in charge. "The American people are still very insular. The vast majority of them don't even hold passports and are loathe to consider anything existing outside their own borders. I would suggest a step-up in your campaign to warn the public about natural remedies and to carry out more raids on people marketing nutritional supplements incorrectly."

"We need a replacement for chemotherapy," said Maston, seeming to want to channel some blame toward the white-haired man. "It's antiquated and just isn't getting the results we'll need to compete with the Laetrilists. The truth is chemotherapy's an indiscriminate killer. It even kills the cells needed to fight the cancer. It was developed from mustard gas for Christ's sake…"

"Yes, and as I've said, we're working on cyanide-releasing drugs. And until that time…"

"They won't work," said AMA head Richardson. His rebellious tone was strengthened by Maston's complaint. "Laetrile's release mechanism can't be duplicated, and if our doctors try to offer a drug known to contain cyanide we'll undermine all our efforts to discredit cyanide as a cure for cancer. It would benefit the Laetrilists!"

"There's no cure for cancer," said the moderator. "Only survival rates. Cyanide-releasing drugs are just one thing we're experimenting with. Now, I have some content you should add to your information campaigns: it appears that most people who use the Laetrile clinics, do so as a last resort, when the cancer has gained too great a foothold. This lowers the Laetrile clinics survival rates to 15 percent because the cancer is in its more developed stage when Laetrile therapy is begun."

"But that's still more than one hundred times higher than chemo when it's used at that stage of cancer," replied Maston.

The white-haired man looked like he was losing control of the room and needed to reassert his authority. "Gentlemen, we're not solving any problems here. Now, I think we all agree at this stage it'll be far more productive to discredit Laetrile than it will to credit chemotherapy."

"As long as we don't draw too much attention to Laetrile in the process. There's no such thing as bad publicity," said Maston.

"Precisely. There's a balance," replied the white-haired man, now back in charge of the room. "Fear is the emotional hot button, gentlemen. Fear is what makes the world go around. It's what makes TV networks and newspapers run, it's what keeps the population in line and running to their government and other institutions for help. And of course, corporations like ours sell more products and we prosper. This is the very essence of how society operates—fear inducement. Going back to the FDA, Maston, this is something in your domain. You need to make examples of people. Please tell me the current status of the guidelines for marketing apricot kernels."

"It's the same as all nutritional supplements. You're not allowed to say it prevents, treats, diagnoses or cures any disease. However, they fight back saying that supplements help with the symptoms associated with disease."

"For example?"

"Well, cancer isn't the only disease that can be treated with a natural supplement. There are many. But to answer your question, if someone was marketing a nutritional supplement to help diabetes, they would advertise it as helping regulate blood sugar levels."

"Oh, that has to stop," said the white-haired man.

"I agree," said Maston, and they both looked at Vice President Cooke who dutifully made a note.

"And what would happen if a person didn't comply with those guidelines?" asked the moderator.

"Their assets would be frozen and we'd prosecute them. They may even face jail time," said Maston.

"Good. But what if there was scientific evidence to support those claims?"

"Doesn't matter. They still fell foul of the law."

"Excellent. These snake-oil salesmen need to know we mean business. I want to see more arrests, more business closures, more seizing of these nutritional contrabands and…"

"Trouble is, Laetrile's rightly classed as a *vitamin*. It's been designated vitamin B17," said Richardson.

"Yes, but is it actually a vitamin?" asked Crenshaw.

"Yes. It's essentially a nitriloside, a compound, which is found in a food, so it's not in itself a food. Nor can it be classified as a drug as it's non-toxic and water-soluble. It's a vitamin. This particular vitamin is found in the B-complex."

"Then we need to address vitamins too," said the man in charge. "I thought we were getting legislation through on that. You shouldn't be able to buy these vitamins over the counter. Doctors should have to prescribe them."

Vice President Cooke spoke up. "That one met with fierce resistance I'm afraid. The nutritional supplement industry has a lobby all to itself so I think it best we direct our attack another way. You said we were going to discuss how Laetrile works?"

"It's a theory but it's pretty sound," Richardson begun. "The hormone estrogen is in both sexes and appears in great concentration when a person's sick or has suffered some kind of trauma, perhaps serving as a stimulator or catalyst to create new cells to replace the damaged ones. What's known for sure is that when normal cells in the body come into contact with the hormone estrogen, they will reproduce, much like a fertilized egg in the womb. It's essentially a healing mechanism. If the healing mechanism carries on working after the healing is complete, cancer forms. If you think about why cancer forms—smoking, carcinogens or anything, which damages the tissue—this whole thing about the body's healing mechanism makes sense. Estrogen playing a part is clearly evident in the inherent risks associated with the contraceptive pill. A woman on the pill becomes three times more likely to contract cancer."

Richardson paused to take a sip of water and continued.

"Anyway, when the cancer forms, the body's natural reaction is to flood the affected area with even more new cells to seal it off, and so a lump forms: a tumor. If the body's successful, the lump will become benign, if not, cancer will result. This is why a tumor is only made up of a small number of cancer cells and why, in my opinion, one of our flaws is our fixation on reduction in tumor size as a measure of any success. We're not getting to the root cause. The tumor's just the symptom. And if you follow this whole theory, you understand why our immune systems have such little success fighting cancer. Cancer is a result of our own bodies so they won't see it as alien to the system. Ironically, cancer is a part of the healing process itself."

"It's only a theory though," Crenshaw of the NCI was quick to state.

"Truth be known," answered Richardson. "It's a theory that happens to dovetail with everything we know about cancer, like it or not."

"Please proceed," urged Vice President Cooke.

Richardson obliged. "Laetrile is essentially nothing more than purified B17 nitriloside. The B17 molecule consists of two parts glucose, one of benzaldehyde and one of cyanide all locked together. Only one substance can unlock this molecule: an enzyme called Beta-glucosidase. Beta-glucosidase isn't found anywhere else in the body but at the cancer cell itself, so the cyanide becomes unlocked from the B17 molecule only at the cancer cell. To counter the toxic effect of the cyanide, another enzyme called Rhodanese neutralizes it. Rhodanese is found in every part of the body except in cancer cells. The result is that the cancer cell is killed off."

"But if it's caused by an inadequate diet," said Crenshaw, "why are Third World countries practically devoid of cancer compared to their Western counterparts? Because they don't have the carcinogens, pollution and so on that we do."

Richardson replied. "You have a point, but if it's all about carcinogens how do you explain a person who contracts lung cancer but never smoked and lived outside of the polluted cities? Also, B17 is highly concentrated in apricot kernels but it's also concentrated in what one would consider a Third World diet: nuts and berries etc…"

"So gentlemen, that's the logic used by the Laetrilists, so that's what we have to undermine," said the white-haired moderator, unnerved by Richardson's defense of Laetrile. "Any suggestions?"

Crenshaw suggested. "We could end the debate once and for all with clinical tests. We'd supervise them of course."

"After the Sloan Kettering debacle?" said Richardson.

"From what I gather Laetrile's success is very dependent on the dosage—not too much, not too little. That's how Sloan Kettering was eventually able to discredit Sugiura's initial results," Crenshaw replied.

Suddenly, Travis's viewing of the Apollo File's sickening revelations was cut short by an equally sickening interruption.

CHAPTER 96

A FAMILIAR VOICE: "The only reason you're not dead…"

"What the—" said Travis, spinning around with Leblanc to meet the voice.

They froze.

Sonia.

She held Leblanc's gun at them. "The only reason you're not dead right now is because I was only to kill you if absolutely necessary. Close the laptop, leave the disc in it and put it on the counter."

"You used me," said Travis.

Sonia emphasized her instructions by letting off a round. A bullet zipped between Leblanc and Travis and embedded itself in the wall. Smoke twirled from the barrel. "And I'll take the handcuff keys too."

"Here." Leblanc complied. He unplugged the laptop and set it down on the counter along with the keys.

The gun poised for action, Sonia grabbed the keys and laptop from the counter. "The Dodge I came in has been disabled. I'm taking the other car, so following me isn't an option—just let it go, Dan." The cold expression on her face briefly thawed as she said Travis's name.

She removed the handcuffs and threw them at the two. "Put 'em on. One for each of you," she said.

They complied. "Now kneel down and face the wall." Awkwardly, they did as she commanded. Travis wondered how his life had suddenly become like something out of a movie.

The room fell silent for several seconds.

Had she gone?

An engine roared into life in the driveway. "She's gone!" Leblanc shouted, making Travis stand up with him. The cuff pinched Travis hard.

"Aghh! Yes, but…"

"Follow me!" said Leblanc, shuffling toward the back door and out in to the yard.

"What? Where are we going?"

"My pop's old car is in the garage, move!" They burst into the sunlight and Leblanc broke into a sprint yanking Travis with him. Both men tried to keep their cuffed arm straight so as not to pull the other man over.

Leblanc ripped open the wooden doors of the garage. They almost broke off their hinges with the force.

The car was old but looked fast.

Leblanc pulled Travis in through the passenger door and slid across to the driver's side of the red Stingray Z06 bucket seats.

Leblanc snapped down the sun-visor and the keys fell into his free hand. "It's a stick-shift. You'll have to rest your hand on mine so I can shift. Just keep it relaxed," Leblanc said, and turned the key.

The sound of it starting was like a sleeping giant who'd been rudely awakened. Travis felt his left hand jerk forward into first gear and the Stingray bolted out of its stable, through the yard and onto the street.

As it hit the pavement, Leblanc screeched to a halt, looking both ways. The race-tuned V8 engine gurgled impatiently.

No sign of the black Mustang.

"Downtown!" shouted Leblanc, and he accelerated into the street, in the only reasonable direction Sonia could have gone.

CHAPTER 97

THE DOOR OF THE DALLAS FIELD OFFICE interrogation room crashed open as Green ran out, "Get me a car!" Helen Vanderbilt sat weeping in his wake.

"Yes, sir," replied Slater. "Just us?"

"Just us! Move!"

Green and Slater flew out of the elevator running toward a black Chevy Suburban.

"1107 Eyston Drive. *Fast!*" Green swung into the back seat as Slater sped away, with squealing tires echoing through the underground parking lot.

The security gate lifted and Green's car burst out into the Dallas sun headed for Leblanc's off the grid residence.

Green ensured the black glass partition between him and his driver, Slater, was closed. He raised his left sleeve to his mouth.

"Phoenix, do you copy?"

The reply was hard to comprehend: the foreign accent competed with a noise that could only be that of a helicopter.

"Phoenix here."

"1107 Eyston Drive—I say again 1107 Eyston Drive!"

"Understood."

"There!" screamed Leblanc, ramming Travis's hand down into second gear with his. The engine's pitch rose and Travis followed Leblanc's stare. Over the rising red hood he made out the distinctive triple-taillights of a Mustang: a new black Mustang.

They were only seconds behind Sonia—the Stingray had closed the gap. But most of all, the sixth sense the Service honed within Leblanc had served them well.

"I see her!" Travis cried out.

They blew into downtown Dallas. Traffic was getting heavier and the shadows grew taller.

The gap was closing.

Closer, closer. Not too close.

Definitely Sonia. They could see the license plate.

"We don't want her to know we're behind her," said Leblanc.

But experience with Sonia told Travis it wasn't going to be as easy as that. He twisted his free hand, fumbling for his seat belt, and quickly buckled himself in.

Sonia took a right turn.

Then another. And another.

She was only making right turns.

"What's she doing? We're just going around in circles…"

"Oh, *shit*," said Leblanc, blinking as he realized his blunder.

"What?" asked Travis, but his question was answered.

The Mustang accelerated away in a chug of brown smoke from its tailpipe.

Leblanc gave chase, ramming Travis's hand down into second gear. The engine screamed and Leblanc shouted with it.

"She's onto us. Hold on, this is gonna be rough!"

Reese was perched next to the pilot of the FBI chopper as it tore across the Dallas sky, a pair of binoculars pressed against his Ray-Ban sunglasses. The agents he flew with knew only to follow his orders. Apart from his pilot, he had just two agents sitting in the back wearing their black combats, carrying a variety of munitions.

Until now, Reese's gaze had been trained on Green's black Suburban. But now something else had caught his eye: *another* chopper seemed to be on the same flight path.

"That chopper over there," Reese shouted over the intercom looking at the pilot. "Is that Secret Service?"

"Stand by," said the pilot. "No, sir. It's civilian—a civilian charter."

Reese raised his binoculars again to look ahead at the chopper. "Strange."

Then the civilian helicopter appeared to hover above a residential neighborhood near downtown Dallas.

"Which street is it waiting over?" asked Reese.

A pause while the pilot checked his GPS.

"Eyston Drive, sir—and it looks like that's where our target vehicle is headed too," he said, pointing to Green's Suburban.

"Alright, I don't wanna get spotted by these guys. Fly a random pattern keeping them in sight, though. Make it look like we're doing something else."

"Like what, sir?"

"I don't know, goddamn it—just fly casual. Like we're a TV network or something. Keep your distance."

The acrid odor of burning oil and rubber filled Travis's nostrils as his body lurched and his left hand jerked with Leblanc's shifting.

The Stingray stormed through downtown Dallas in pursuit of Sonia, closing the gap to within a hundred feet. Travis could see Sonia's face in her rearview mirror, they were that close.

"Our car's faster!" cried Leblanc, with a determined smile.

"Yeah," Travis said, his eyes locked wide in terror. They'd only had to gently swerve to avoid the light traffic on this road, but that was enough for Travis.

Throwing the emergency break, Sonia spun her Mustang into a violent 180-degree turn.

Leblanc could only speed past the smoke produced from her screeching tires.

The Stingray's rear wheels shuddered as Leblanc flung the car into a maneuver that mirrored Sonia's. Travis gasped and winced; it felt like the car was going to flip over. Travis saw smoke in the sideview mirror and looked at Leblanc. He was in control and the car stayed squat on the road. Travis was struck with horror as they faced oncoming traffic of this one-way road.

Travis felt his hand push into second gear as the engine snarled and fired the Stingray like a missile.

The gap was closing again.

Sonia maneuvered through the oncoming traffic. Cars swerved dramatically, flashed their lights and honked their horns, but they were just obstacles in her path. Cars swerved to avoid her only to find a red Stingray close behind.

Leblanc was anticipating the oncoming drivers well. He stepped on the gas harder, narrowly missing a motorist. Travis saw the expression of terror on the man's face. He had no idea.

Suddenly Sonia made a right turn onto a side street. The Mustang's rear-end spun out with the shock of the turn, but Sonia masterfully steered into the skid as the car accelerated away down the narrow road.

Sonia took another right turn, then a left.

Pedestrians pinned themselves back against parked cars, streetlights, signposts, anything they could find, screaming and shouting as they ran for cover.

"She knows we can outrun her in a straight line!" cried Leblanc. "She's trying to slow us down by making all these turns!" It was like Leblanc was thinking aloud. Just as well. All Travis could do was watch what unfolded before him and use his free arm to hold on.

There was a fork in the road. Sonia broke left. Leblanc broke right.

"This fork's shorter and the road meets again in a few hundred yards!" Leblanc said. Travis hoped he was right— they were thundering down a road with no sign of Sonia ahead.

They swerved to avoid a slower moving vehicle. Travis heard its horn as they blew past.

The road veered left. "This is it!" Leblanc shouted.

Travis braced himself.

Leblanc made a slight correction in their course and they were back on the street Sonia had gone down. Leblanc had hoped to close the gap, but she was nowhere to be seen.

"No sign of her! No! There was no way out…" Leblanc was interrupted by a dull thud at the rear as both their heads flew forward and the Stingray lost control. Leblanc fought to correct the swerving car with his lone hand as Travis spun round to look out the narrow rear window.

He saw a black Mustang: its angry headlights blazing right at him. They'd got ahead of her and now she was trying to drive them off the road.

The hunter became the hunted.

"Son of a bitch!" Leblanc shouted, still fighting the nose of Sonia's Mustang.

Leblanc slammed on the brakes, biting his bottom lip. He let the brakes go again. Sonia veered to the left and pulled out past them.

Down into second gear, the red missile went for the Mustang again.

Travis could hear an ascending wail of police sirens and saw flashing blue lights in the sideview mirror.

Green ran from Leblanc's empty house and leapt back into his Chevy. "Get a detail around that house right away—no one comes or goes until I get back!"

"Got it, sir," said Slater from the driver's seat.

Green shut the partition. As he was about to speak into his sleeve, his cell phone rang.

"Sir, it's Gomez from the Dallas office."

"What is it, Gomez?"

"The note for Travis at the museum: It's gone. Apparently Vanderbilt's assistant—an Angela Postales—got it to him. Our agents were just questioning her…"

"Travis? Are you sure?" *Un-fucking-believable.*

"Yes, sir. Also, you wanted updated reports on Dallas traffic and unusual…"

"Yes, yes. What is it?"

"Dallas P.D. are in pursuit of two vehicles downtown: a 2006 black Ford Mustang GT and a 1963 red Stingray Z6. Apparently they're tearing up the place, last seen going north on…"

"Registrations?"

"Stingray registered to a Clinton Leblanc and the Mustang's reported stolen."

Green hung up. He'd heard all he needed to. Down came the black glass partition.

"Patch into Dallas police radio and get me in that chase downtown. Move it!"

The Suburban screeched into action as Green put up the partition up and spoke into his sleeve.

"Phoenix?"

"Phoenix receiving."

"Police are chasing a red Stingray and a black Mustang downtown—red Stingray's our priority target!"

"Both the Suburban and the civilian chopper on the move, sir," said Reese's helicopter pilot.

"I can see," said Reese from behind his binoculars. "Follow them both."

"And if one breaks off from the other?"

"We'll worry about that if and when it comes to it," Reese said and gave a thumbs-up to the men in the back. They responded in kind. Reese checked his weapon.

The FBI chopper broke its orbit and buzzed downtown behind Green.

The standoff continued.

Sonia's attempts to shake off the Stingray had failed so far. The sirens Travis heard had faded but he knew Dallas police were involved.

Leblanc swerved out from behind a truck, but the truck began to turn at the same time.

"Shit!" Travis closed his eyes and leaned even though he knew it'd make no difference.

Leblanc turned the wheel and hit the gas, but it was too close. The Stingray collided with the side of the truck and scraped along its paintwork. Metal shrieked against metal and Travis watched the wing mirror on his side tear off.

The truck driver seemed to realize what was happening and stopped. Leblanc powered the Stingray from the scrape and back onto its path behind Sonia.

A Dallas police car pulled out from a side street and came side to side with Sonia, its blue lights flashing.

The encounter was brief. The black Mustang callously maneuvered the police vehicle off the road and it violently hit a parked car. Leblanc blew past the wreckage.

"Goddamn it! This isn't going anywhere. There's a gun in the glove compartment," said Leblanc. "Get it out."

"A gun? You're kidding right? What do you think this is? Some kind of…"

"Give it to me, but you'll have to take the wheel—relax—I'm gonna try to hit her tires, that's all."

Travis opened the glove compartment. Leblanc had even left his dad's gun in there. Travis placed it in the center console. "Here."

"Thanks. We just need a straight piece of road and you can steer with your right and I'll shoot with my left," said Leblanc, powering through another tight turn behind Sonia.

"Do you normally shoot with your left hand?"

"No."

"Phoenix here. I have the targets in my sights—and you."

"Stand by, Phoenix!" Green listened to Norman back in Washington over his cell phone.

"Sir, Dallas police have responded as we asked. Once the vehicles have been stopped they'll hold the suspects until your arrival, but right now it doesn't seem like they're having much luck stopping them."

Green hung up.

"Phoenix?" he said into his sleeve.

"Here."

"As and when the target comes to a stop, I want you to take position and let me know when you have a clear shot."

"Roger."

The partition came down as Green finished. "Sir, they should be just ahead," said Slater.

"Stay on it!"

Sonia powered ahead, approaching the triple underpass leading into Dealey Plaza. Just where the road narrowed, she cut in front of a couple of trucks that happened to be driving side by side in the path of the chase.

"Can't see her!" shouted Leblanc.

"This isn't going to work," yelled Travis.

"Can't get past—we're gonna lose her. Hang on!"

"What are you…"

Leblanc drove over the median to pass the trucks. The

unforgiving race car suspension bounced Travis's head against the roof as he felt his hand shift down a gear. They'd passed the trucks, which put them too close to the triple underpass—they had to choose a lane.

Too late. Shit!

There was smoke. And fire. They watched helplessly as the black Mustang, ahead of them, hit the concrete pillar of the triple underpass and burst into flames.

Thick black smoke engulfed the Stingray's cabin—blindness, choking fumes.

Leblanc lost control.

Travis felt something hit the Stingray hard under the floor and felt the car rise in the air on one side, spinning.

Travis couldn't see. Leblanc was quiet—too quiet.

It felt like they were on grass. Spinning on grass and he couldn't see...

Crack!

Travis's head hit the window frame and the car lurched as it came to a stop on the embankment next to white pillars and shrubs.

Everything was a blur.

Travis could smell gasoline. *Have to get out!*

He heaved the door open, but his escape was halted by a painful tug on his wrist reminding him that he was still chained to Leblanc.

"Leblanc!"

Nothing. Leblanc didn't even look like he was breathing. Travis saw the blond hair matted with blood.

He lunged over Leblanc to open the door and push Leblanc out. They tumbled onto the ground, blackened and bruised, Travis coughing violently, Leblanc still.

"That's them! Jesus, no one survived that," said Green, staring at the burning wreckage of Sonia's black Mustang. "Over there!" he ordered, pointing at the red Stingray on the grass in the middle of Dealey Plaza. "Phoenix, take position: the red car. That's the target," he whispered into his sleeve.

The black suburban drove onto the grass in front of the Stingray, lying there like a wounded animal. The police weren't there yet.

"Slater, come with me," ordered Green, ripping his gun from its holster as he leapt out of the suburban.

"Clear the area!" Green shouted to a small group of looky-loos. They saw his gun and badge and ran away.

Guns at the ready, Green and Slater approached the wreckage. Green heard sirens approaching. No matter. That's what Phoenix was here for.

"Travis! Leblanc!" Green called out, Slater cautiously following.

"Yes?" croaked Travis.

The voice came from behind a pillar of the underpass. Green and Slater spun around to face it. Travis was crouched down behind the pillar, using it for cover with Leblanc chained next to him, dead still. Travis was pointing Leblanc's gun at Green.

Slater took aim, but Green waved him to stand down.

"Put the guns down or you'll never get the file," Travis bluffed. His gun hand was trembling.

"Okay," Green said and nodded at Slater to do the same. They dropped their guns and placed their hands in the air.

But Green started moving closer. He beamed at Travis. "Is the file safe, Travis?"

A local news helicopter hovered overhead. The looky-loos had edged back to gawk. Sirens were getting closer.

"Close enough," said Travis, trying hard not to show his nerves.

"In position momentarily," said Phoenix in Green's ear-piece.

Green continued engaging Travis. "And what do you think you have there anyway, hmm?"

Travis remained silent. Out of options. Green looked like he was biding time. *What for?*

Green continued. Probing. "You think people actually wanna see that file? Look at those people over there watching. Look at those poor simple bastards! Shit, Travis, they go through life with their heads up their asses. All they want is stability, no…"

"What about truth? Freedom of choice?! People should make their own minds up," shouted Travis, spewing anger at the injustice Green wanted to impose.

"Truth? Freedom? People like you go on about freedom and question the manner in which people like me provide it for you. Freedom has a price!"

"Freedom isn't yours or any government's to give or take away. It's a birthright!"

"Is that so? You know, as well as I, they're a bunch of retards," gesturing at the crowd of bystanders. "They can't be trusted with something as complex as freedom of choice! Hell, they're lucky to even get a vote—even that scares the shit out of me!"

Green moved closer.

"Maybe, maybe not," said Travis. "But even if you're right and they are idiots, they should be cared for, not abused or systematically murd…"

"Travis, you know that people don't want to see what

you've got in your hand. Look up, Travis. You gonna shoot me on TV? *That's* front-page news—not that stupid file you've got. Shooting: that's what people really want to see!"

"In position and I have the shot," came the voice on Green's earpiece.

Green missed Travis's answer, not that it was relevant—the conversation was over. He was just playing for time. At that moment, Green's hired gun was in position with a high-powered rifle aimed at Travis. All it took was a single word uttered into Green's sleeve and Travis's head would spray-paint Dealey Plaza crimson. *Game over.*

Travis watched as Green lowered one of his hands to his mouth. *What's he doing?* "Stop! Don't move—"

Green continued.

"Shoot," Green said into his sleeve, and watched, waiting for the inevitable. Green's smile was large enough to burst his cheeks.

But nothing happened.

Green said it again only louder—at this range Travis still wouldn't be able to hear. "Shoot, shoot goddamn it!"

Nothing. *What the f...*

Travis heard a voice boom out behind him. "FBI! Don't move! Drop the weapon and put your hands in the air!"

Travis froze. It was over. *The FBI is in on this too?* He dropped the gun and turned around, doing his best to hold his cuffed hand as high as possible. There in front of him was a well-built man in a black suit with auburn hair and sunglasses supported on his broken nose, pointing a gun at Travis.

Green looked over, relieved, and held up his badge. "Green, Secret Service. FBI?"

"Yes, sir. Special Agent Reese," he said, holding a badge up without taking his sights off Travis. Reese walked over to

Travis and kicked the gun away.

Green continued, improvising, playing the next move. "Reese, you don't know how relieved I…"

Now Travis was unarmed, Reese pointed his weapon at Green.

"What the hell do you think you're doing, Reese?!"

"Dwight Green, you're under arrest."

Then a man in black combat fatigues materialized behind Green and took his hands, cuffing them together behind his back.

"Stay here," Reese said to Travis.

"I'm not going anywhere," Travis muttered, glancing down at Leblanc.

Sirens approached. Police vehicles and ambulances crowded Dealey Plaza. Travis watched as Reese walked with Green to the helicopter that had just landed on the grass. In the back of the helicopter was a tall, gaunt man, handcuffed next to another agent in black combat fatigues.

CHAPTER 98

"YOU'RE GOOD TO GO," said the paramedic, after dressing Travis's wounds. But Travis knew the biggest wound would never heal: the violation he'd suffered the last three days. He felt raped. Abused.

"Thanks," Travis said, staring down at his oil- and blood-stained shirt. He lowered his head staring at the ground: he'd begun to cry. The mixture of relief, elation, exhaustion and sadness was more than he could process.

Travis wiped his tears away and stared at the burnt-out wreck under the triple underpass. The firefighters were done and he realized both Sonia and Apollo were gone. Leblanc's Stingray had been towed away and Leblanc had been taken to Parkland Memorial Hospital.

Travis was still alive, but judging from the FBI agent standing in attendance, not free to go.

Travis watched Reese walk toward him from the police vehicle where he'd been standing.

"Dr. Travis, how are you?" Reese called out as he approached.

"I've been better." Travis still didn't know where Reese came from or why, but he wasn't going to mention anything about Apollo. Travis had learned to trust no one.

"I'm gonna need you to cooperate with a few questions," said Reese.

"I'd like to ask a few myself," Travis fired back.

"Like what?"

"Green. What was he arrested for? What's going on here?"

"That's classified and I really don't have t…"

"And I don't have to cooperate." Travis glared at Reese defiantly. *Enough.*

Reese frowned over his sunglasses and took Travis to one side, walking away from the army of people and emergency services now gathered. "Alright, but this is strictly off the record—if asked, I'll deny it— aw shit, most of it'll all come out anyway, but even so, you understand me?"

"Okay."

"Green's under arrest for abusing his authority, wrongful arrests, and using a mercenary for an unauthorized purpose— a mercenary who used to be an FBI agent. You saw him in the back of the chopper?"

Travis felt hopeful. "But how did you find out about all this?"

"We've had our suspicions for some time now, but Green's a big figure in Washington. Not your everyday arrest as you can imagine. We needed to build a strong case first and well, this provided it. Monday, Green started giving us all the screw-ups we needed. What exactly was he chasing you for?"

Good news and bad. Reese doesn't know about Apollo, but I've got explaining to do, or maybe not.

"How did you find us?" asked Travis.

Reese was far too experienced an interrogator to miss the fact that Travis was answering a question with a question, but he played along. "I believe you had a little skirmish with Green back in Washington?"

Travis didn't answer.

"You and *Sonia?* Well anyway, Green took Sonia's fingerprints to identify her. He already knew who you were, but not her. Anyway, Secret Service uses CIA databases for intel like that. As soon as her fingerprint came up at Langley, alarm bells went off and the CIA were obliged to inform the FBI. *Me.*"

"Why?"

Reese hung his head even closer to Travis's and looked behind over his shoulder before he spoke.

"The girl you know as Sonia Leblanc is Natasha Yuretsov. She's an SVR agent we've been after for a while. A sleeper." Reese watched for a reaction.

Travis looked down to mask his expression. *Oh my God! Sonia—Natasha—was a Russian spy who came for Apollo.*

He looked up once he'd composed himself. "And that's why the FBI was alerted?"

"Yep. Spies on American soil are FBI jurisdiction: Natasha's why I'm here. That's who I've been chasing. Green too, but she was the prize. It wasn't just the fingerprint though— the CIA had a tip-off from an old employee of theirs warning them about Green last Monday, that he had a suspicion there was possibly an SVR agent at large and that he could trace her location. It all happened Monday night."

"What was the informer's name?"

"I can't tell you, Doctor."

Travis smiled.

Kramer.

Reese looked back at the burnt-out Mustang. "Did you actually see Natasha, or *Sonia*, in the vehicle all the way to impact?"

"Yes—wait no—no, not exactly. What do you mean?"

Reese's face hardened. "I *mean*, were you chasing her right up to impact or did you lose sight of the vehicle just before impact?"

"We lost sight of it just before but only for a few seconds maybe. Why?"

"A few seconds is all it would have taken," said Reese, shaking his head, frowning. "Shit!"

"What do you mean?"

"There was no body in the wreckage," Reese said. Fortunately for Travis, he didn't need to feign surprise.

Sonia's alive. And that means Apollo's intact somewhere. Confusion and deception: classic Russian intelligence maneuvers.

"Look, Special Agent Reese, I really don't know how much help I'll be to you—I was clearly brought into someone else's fight here. I've got a thumping headache and just need some rest."

"No problem, but don't go anywhere. I still need to ask you some questions. My guys over there'll fix you up at a hotel. We'll talk tomorrow morning."

"I'm not going anywhere," said Travis, now caught up in the idea of a square meal, a hot shower and a soft, clean bed…

No. Mom. Today's the day. With this realization, all Travis wanted was a phone.

THURSDAY

CHAPTER 99

ALEX ADKA SAT in his office at the Embassy and read the file on his mahogany desk. His loyal agent had personally presented it to him. He needed to re-check the facts, as this time she had surpassed even her own expectations.

"Natasha, once again you've done your country a great service."

"Thank you," she said, sitting in the leather chair opposite his desk.

"Your injuries…are you feeling better?"

"Just some scrapes. It's nothing."

"It was most unfortunate the Secret Service raided Leblanc's apartment when they did. Anatoly should have had an easy task of retrieving…"

"So why did Anatoly fail? Why did I need to step in?"

Adka didn't care much to be interrupted, but he would make an exception. "Anatoly couldn't find the Bilderberg recording in Leblanc's apartment. It appears he got there too early. While he was waiting for Leblanc to return, he made a copy of some of Leblanc's notes containing references to the recording."

"And that was the notepaper Leblanc faxed to Travis?"

"Correct."

"Which is why the version of the fax I had was missing the note Leblanc wrote at the bottom of the page. Leblanc wrote that after Anatoly made the copy. And you identified Travis as a connection based on the fax?"

"Correct, Natasha. You did well to convince Travis you retrieved a copy of the fax from his house."

"People will buy anything. I knew Leblanc had sent a fax to Travis after he called the housekeeper from the bar." Natasha smirked. "Apologies for insisting on the face-to-face here in Washington. I just needed those IDs on Green and Kramer."

"I understand. By the way, Anatoly saw Leblanc shot with his own eyes, so you weren't misinformed there: bullet-proof vest." Adka pushed his papers to one side as a gesture that the meeting was over.

"One thing though," said Natasha. "Had you told me the contents of the Apollo File it *would* have been easier. I didn't know if it was about Kennedy or…"

"You would have been less convincing had I told you," snapped Adka.

"Yes, I understand of course."

"You will need a new identity and duty outside the United States for some time. Again, Natasha, your country thanks you. Suffice to say, the war against American imperialism will not be won militarily but economically, and you've played a large part in that battle. You should be proud. Dismissed. Get some rest."

Natasha left the room.

Adka placed Natasha's report in the folder and laid a copy of the disc on top. The disc was marked with the name Natasha had given it during her mission to retrieve it:

файл аполлона
(The Apollo File)

The Apollo File was safe in the hands of the people who'd engineered its production all along.

Leblanc was just a patsy as these Americans say, thought Adka, sitting at his desk. Leblanc had been manipulated into thinking he was doing it for himself when it was all for the SVR.

As news of the First Lady's use of Laetrile had made its way to Russian intelligence, they seized the opportunity. An SVR operative posed as an FDA insider and leaked information on Laetrile to the vice president's Secret Service agent, Clinton Leblanc, among other agents on protection detail in preparation for the operation. The SVR was unable to penetrate the very highest echelons of power, so they decided to use the minions entrusted by the powerful: Secret Service agents.

The internal stir caused by the First Lady's use of Laetrile had prompted Vice President Cooke to be invited for a crisis meeting, which the SVR learned of. Leblanc's position and the fact his father had died of cancer made him the perfect target to perform the production of the Apollo File for the SVR. The fake FDA insider tipped him off in advance that the VP would be attending this meeting in Tampa.

The hard part was manipulating Leblanc to do it. Provided Leblanc's conscience motivated him as expected and he recorded the meeting, it should have been as easy as sending Anatoly to steal it from Leblanc's apartment. But it seems the Secret Service found out about Leblanc and fought for their reputation with ferocity. And Leblanc was prepared to fight for the file too.

No matter, it was done now.

Finally, we have the tools to undermine mighty American pharmaceuticals and hence her economy. This time—in the time of technology and information—it will work. The same way the information age brought down Mother Russia's might, so too will it end America's, Adka thought to himself with the certain satisfaction only vengeance could bring.

But what became of the Apollo File now was out of Adka's hands. He placed the call he'd hoped someday to make: to his superiors in Moscow.

The Cold War never ended, the weapons merely changed.

FRIDAY

CHAPTER 100

TRAVIS STARED INTO the crackling fire in Kramer's front room. A somber, uncertain air lingered.

"Danno, I used to run CIA counter-intelligence for crying out loud. I knew you'd be alright. If she wanted you dead, she'd have killed you long before you turned up at my door, believe me. If I'd said anything, she'd have canned us both. Plus, she was your best bet to get out of that mess. You were just her means to an end."

"So you tipped off the CIA and reported Green too?"

"Yep. I called Rehnquist after you'd gone—your old uncle had to bail your ass out again. The FBI has backed down too, thanks to Rehnquist. No one but Green, you and I know about Apollo."

"I still don't see why Green was involved." Travis could still see the vivid image of Green's dark eyes over the barrel of a gun.

Kramer looked surprised. "Are you kidding? Up until '51 the Secret Service had to get its protection detail renewed annually by Congress—protection is *everything* to them. They're obsessed with it. The FBI has been trying to swallow the Service up for decades now. Ever since we lost Kennedy, they've been battling to keep the honor of protecting officials. If it got out that one of their agents had done what Leblanc did, the Service would have been finished. That's why Green tried to keep the other agencies out of all this. He couldn't give a crap about what's actually on the Apollo File or the consequences of its release on the pharmaceutical business. He was just trying to keep the Service's nose clean."

"Just like the JFK assassination cover-up?"

"Exactly like it. It's all about people saving their ass and avoiding embarrassment—just Washington power games and bull-crap."

Kramer made an attempt to steer the conversation away from Travis's recent ordeal. "Good news about your mom!"

Travis volunteered a half-smile but winced—his healing cuts and bruises still stung. "Thanks. She appreciated those flowers you sent. She loves tulips."

"I knew she'd be fine. Patti's a fighter, that's for sure. Ha!"

But Travis was reminded of those who were not so lucky as his mom. "It's a damn shame about Leblanc."

Travis hung his head and looked upon the abrasion marks on his left wrist where he'd been handcuffed to Leblanc. Though the encounter with the rogue agent was brief, Travis still felt his presence. He believed Leblanc was a ghost the first time he met him; now it seemed as though he really was one. The latent affinity between the two men had been shattered by Leblanc's demise from massive head injuries.

Kramer leaned forward with both hands on top of his cane. "Leblanc had already cheated death once. You only get one life in this game."

The wave of loss and betrayal hit Travis like a sledgehammer in the gut. He stared intently into the flames as Kramer kept trying to prop up his 'nephew's' mood.

"Danny, he knew the risks. He died. And that's it."

"But what did he die for?"

Kramer rubbed his fingers across his mouth, silent and uneasy.

Kramer usually had an answer for everything, but Travis glanced up to find him distracted, almost in a fugue. Kramer was gazing at a bottle of his arthritis medication on the side table.

"George?"

Kramer leaned over to his side table and adjusted the position of a glass case that boasted a medal. "He died fighting for what he believed in. It wasn't in vain."

"Are you so sure?"

"What do you mean?!" Kramer snapped at the uncustomary questioning of his viewpoint.

"Leblanc created the Apollo File. Now the Russians most likely have it. What will *they* do with it? Just use it as a bargaining tool? He died for nothing if the truth never gets out!"

Kramer leaned on his cane once more, a disturbed look in his eyes. "The Russians are back, Danno. They intend to use Apollo as a weapon or they wouldn't have gone to these lengths."

"Weapon? Since when was *truth* a weapon? What have we become if a foreign enemy can use truth as a weapon against us?"

"You have to understand there are bigger things at stake than—"

"George, you're from a different time. You were fighting an evil dictatorship. Who would you be fighting by suppressing Apollo? What would you be fighting for *now*?"

Kramer was silent.

With tensions high, Travis got up and wandered over to the window. Kramer scratched circles into the burgundy carpet with his cane.

Outside, a middle-aged man taking his poodle for a walk ambled by. Travis fixated on him.

The stranger outside stopped in front of Kramer's house while the dog sniffed a tree. Then he turned around and looked squarely at Travis through the window.

Travis locked eyes with the man for a brief moment. The man carried on with his walk, poodle in tow.

Travis speculated. "Anyway, maybe the Russians haven't taken into account how selfish and greedy we've become. Even if they released Apollo to the man on the street through the Internet or whatever, they need people to believe it and spread the word. Why would people do that if it meant losing their jobs?" Travis thrust an open hand in the direction of the dog-walker. "*Everyone's* a conspirator!"

Kramer spoke up defiantly, raising his cane. "No. The American people are better than that deep down and the Russians know it. Give the man in the street that Pandora's box and he'll open it."

Travis turned to eye Kramer. "You really think anyone who was given this information would believe it…and tell others about it?"

"Well, what would *you* do?"

Book Club
Discussion Questions

1. Father and son relationships are explored through several of the characters in *The Pandora Prescription*. Identify these relationships and describe how they differ from or are similar to your own experiences.

2. During Travis's attempt to get information from Ramón, a debate emerges about the legalities of contraband. Do you think this exposes a double standard in the law?

3. The mysterious, strong female character, Sonia, is at times in the novel both an ally and a suspect. Where do you believe her allegiances truly lie?

4. Where do you stand on the government conspiracy theories discussed in the novel?

5. The idea that the government could be wrong about something can be frightening, but nonetheless a proven reality of history. Can you think of any twentieth-century examples

where a ban against something has since been overturned?

6. The possible cure for cancer is discussed at length. With the current state of the pharmaceutical industry and its ties to the government, do you believe the events in the novel could happen in today's society?

7. Another core theme is karma; the belief that what goes around comes around. We see this reflected in the story, the characters and the historical events they discover. What examples from the novel can you identify?

8. How do your own experiences with healthcare relate to the events, themes and characters in the novel? Overall, which main character did you relate to the most?

9. The last line of the book is "What would you do?" Answer this question, as if you were in Leblanc's shoes.

10. Examine these two popular quotes:
   Ignorance is bliss. – Thomas Gray, English poet
   Knowledge is power. – Sir Francis Bacon, English philosopher

Which saying would you apply to the Apollo File and why?

11. Having read *The Pandora Prescription* what, if anything, do you intend to do?